YOUNGBLOOD

MATT GALLAGHER

SIMON &
SCHUSTER

London · New York · Sydney · Toronto · New Delhi

A CBS COMPANY

First published in the USA by Atria Books, an imprint of Simon & Schuster, Inc., 2016
First published in Great Britain by Simon & Schuster UK Ltd, 2016
A CBS COMPANY

1 3 5 7 9 10 8 6 4 2

Simon & Schuster UK Ltd
1st Floor
222 Gray's Inn Road
London WC1X 8HB

www.simonandschuster.co.uk

Simon & Schuster Australia, Sydney
Simon & Schuster India, New Delhi

A CIP catalogue record for this book
is available from the British Library

Paperback ISBN: 978-1-4711-5909-1
Trade Paperback ISBN: 978-1-4711-5908-4
eBook ISBN: 978-1-4711-5910-7

that is made from wood grown in sustainable forests and support the Forest
Stewardship Council, the leading international forest certification organisation.
Our books displaying the FSC logo are printed on FSC certified paper.

To Anne

In the desert
I saw a creature, naked, bestial,
Who, squatting upon the ground,
Held his heart in his hands,
And ate of it.
I said, "Is it good, friend?"
"It is bitter—bitter," he answered;

"But I like it
"Because it is bitter,
"And because it is my heart."

—STEPHEN CRANE

YOUNGBLOOD

PROLOGUE

I t's strange, trying to remember now. Not the war, though that's all tangled up, too. I mean the other parts. The way sand pebbles nipped at our faces in the wind. How the mothers glared when we raided houses looking for their sons. The smell of farm animal waste and car exhaust blending together during patrols through town, rambling, aimless hours lost to the desert.

How falafel bits got stuck between my teeth so much I started bringing floss on missions, along with extra ammo and water.

The sun, the goddamn heat. The days I couldn't sleep and the nights I wouldn't. How the power of being in charge got to me, how it got to all the officers and sergeants, giant, armed soldiers at our backs ready to carry out foreign policy through sheer fucking force.

How sometimes, many times, we were gentle.

The feeling of something—relief? gratitude? exhaustion?—when a patrol returned to the outpost and, for another day, we'd be able to ask ourselves just what the hell were we doing.

So little of Iraq had anything to do with guns or bombs or jihads. That's what people never understand. There was the desert. And the locals, and their lives. The way time could be vague and hazy one moment, yet hard as bone the next.

A lot of people ask, "What was it like?" and once, I even tried to answer. I was home, with old friends. They meant well, and while they didn't want a perfect story, they wanted a clean one. It's what everyone wants, and I knew that. But it came out wrong. I started off about imperial grunts walking over a past we didn't know anything about, but I could see their eyes glazing over, so I switched to the hajji kids playing in mud under bent utility poles, but that didn't work, either. An anecdote about finding a sheik's porn collection earned some laughs, but by then I'd lost them, so I stopped.

"What's an imperial grunt?" one asked later. "They help the SEALs get bin Laden?"

"Kind of," I said, even though we hadn't.

I miss it, which is a funny thing to think until I remember otherwise. Like the daily purpose—I miss that, as messy as it could be. I miss the clarity of trying to survive. Miss the soldiers. Even miss the *mukhtar* who was honest enough to hate us but still made us chai because we were guests.

And her, of course. She comes in fragments, slivers of jagged memory that cut and condemn. How she'd sigh before we talked about the past. How my mind ached after we considered the future. I failed Rana, failed her utterly, all because I tried to help.

What was it like? Hell if I know. But next time someone asks, I won't answer straight and clean. I'll answer crooked, and I'll answer long. And when they get confused or angry, I'll smile. Finally, I'll think. Someone who understands.

BOOK I

1

The alarm sounded through the still of the outpost. If I'd been dreaming, I'd already forgotten what about. I turned off the alarm and hopped down from the top bunk. It was another day. We'd been in-country five months, and hadn't even been shot at yet.

"Yo," I said. "The Suck awaits." The only response came from an industrial fan whirring in a dark corner. None of the bodies in the other beds bothered to move. As deceitful as time could be in a room without windows, my sergeants always seemed to know when they had another twenty minutes.

I shook out my boots to make sure a scorpion hadn't crept into them during the night. It hadn't happened to anyone yet, but still, there were stories. After knotting the laces and pulling on my fleece top, I walked through the dim and opened the door to the hallway. The platoon's interpreter was waiting there under a yellow ceiling panel, holding two cups of coffee. He was just a blurry shadow for a few seconds, until my vision adjusted.

"Hey, Snoop," I said.

"Lieutenant Jack," he said, handing me one of the cups. "We giving out moneys today? Sources been asking."

Wiry and excitable, even with sleep still on his face, Snoop had learned English from British missionaries and refined it with gangsta rap. His real name was Qasim, but no one called him that, not even the other terps.

"Maybe," I said. "Depends what the commander has planned."

Three long hallways shaped like a *U* formed the outpost's second floor. We walked down one of the *U*'s legs and turned right, passing rooms that stank of ball sweat and feet. The mansion had been built as a retirement gift for one of Saddam's generals, but nearly a decade after the Invasion, that felt like prehistory to us. Just something to bullshit about with locals. It was home to Bravo Company now.

Outside their room, a group of soldiers were cleaning rifles piecemeal. Oils and solvents cut through the sour air, and tiny metal parts glinted in their rags like diamonds. As Snoop and I neared, they stood, almost in unison.

"Shit, sir," a soldier said. "Didn't see you coming."

I unleashed a MacArthur impression, complete with a foppish salute. "You're making your country proud today, men," I said. It was important to carry on the junior officer tradition of disdain for ceremony. "Kill that grime. Kill it good."

They laughed, then returned to their seats and weapons.

We turned up the *U*'s other leg and walked into the command post. The night shift hadn't been relieved yet, and sat around the room in lawn chairs. Tracked-in sand covered everything, from the radios to the tabletops to the portable television in the corner roaring with musket fire from a Revolutionary War film.

"You all sacrifice a yak?" I asked. "Smells terrible in here."

"Least we're going to bed soon," a private said. "Enjoy the day, sir." He pointed to the whiteboard, where, under second platoon, ELECTRICITY RECON had been scrawled in loose, dreary letters. There was no mistaking the commander's handwriting.

"Christ," I said, already feeling the sweat-starched uniform and hefty body armor that awaited. "Not again."

"Electricity recon" was army language for walking around a neighborhood asking people how many hours a day they had power. Iraqis responded to the door-to-door interruptions the same way people back home dealt with Mormons with pamphlets. More than one local, usually an old woman, had told us to come back when we could provide power rather than ask about it.

I walked back to our room to get my grooming kit. My teeth needed brushing, my armpits needed deodorant, and after three days, my face finally needed a shave. Sergeant First Class Sipe sat upright in his bed picking eye goop from his lashes.

"Aloha," I said.

"Lieutenant Porter." He sounded cross. "I'm going to stay back today, draw up a plan for a sentry shack at the front gate. We're getting complacent."

"Would be good to come," I said. "For the new guys. Especially Chambers." The week before, a small group of augmentees had joined us. Chambers was a staff sergeant with combat experience, the rest cherries straight from basic. They'd all been quiet so far, watching and learning. "He seems squared away, but you could teach him how we roll."

"The rest of the platoon can handle that, sir," Sipe said.

More and more, our platoon sergeant had been finding reasons to stay inside the wire. Though it was hard for me to blame him—he was on his fourth tour to the desert, and only a year from retirement—it hadn't gone unnoticed by the others. And soldiers could be resentful souls.

Whatever, I thought. I've been picking up the slack.

• • •

A couple of hours later, thirty young men in body armor and helmets stood in the foyer of the first floor, an open, sunny octagon covered in red-and-white ceramic tiles. We all wore the lightning bolt patch of the Twenty-Fifth Infantry on our shoulders and had CamelBaks filled with clean, cold water strapped to us.

A fresco covered the wall leading down the stairway into the foyer, depicting ten smiling Iraqi children holding up their national flag. Behind the children stood an old man with a bushy black beard wearing a turban and a white *dishdasha* and a stoic-looking woman dressed in a dark gray burqa. The artist had given her a considerable chest. Both adults' hands rested on the shoulders of the children. The soldiers called the man Pedo bin Laden. She was the Mother Hajj.

After my patrol brief, I asked for questions. A stubby arm shot into the air from the rear of the group.

"Yes, Hog," I said, raising an eyebrow, my voice carrying a blunted inflection. The others laughed. We'd played this game before.

"Which hajji bodega we hittin' up?" he asked.

"We'll be in the market blocks," I said. I waved him up and handed over the town map. "You tell me."

"Hmm," he said. A native of Arkansas who'd enlisted at seventeen, Hog had a face that always looked like it was pressed against a window-pane, especially when he smiled. "Shi'a, mainly. Poor ones, too. Best bet is the old barber, his wives make crazy good dumplings. And might run into the Barbie Kid there—Boom Boom drinks."

"Drink one of those, you're begging for a piss test." I waited for the snickering to fade before continuing. "We'll be dismounted the whole mission—no reason to waste fuel on this. Should be back in five hours for *Call of Duty*." More snickering. "Anything else?"

"What if we find the enemy?" one of the new joes asked. Most of the platoon originals laughed contemptuously, causing him to blush. I felt bad for him. It'd taken some stones to ask the question.

"Cry havoc," I said. "And let slip the Hogs of war."

None of the men laughed. Too much, I thought, rubbing my bare chin under my helmet strap. Too much.

We stepped into the spring morning. The young day was already overcooked and smelled of sand and canal water. "Lock and load, Hotspur," I said, using our platoon nickname, swinging around the rifle slung over my shoulder. Technically, the M4 wasn't a rifle but a carbine, though only the country boys insisted on that detail. We each pulled out a magazine from the vests strapped to the front of our body armor. Every magazine was filled with thirty rounds of ammunition, weighing about a pound total. We slid the magazine into the rifle's well and smacked the bottom to make sure it stayed put. We pulled our rifle's charging handle, drawing the bolt back and then releasing it to grab the top round and push it into the barrel, the black magic of the gun slamming forward.

"Gets me hard every time," Sergeant Dominguez said, earning echoes of agreement. Five and a half feet of applied force, Dominguez had held sway in the platoon much longer than he'd held his rank. I'd learned early on to go to him when I needed something done that couldn't or shouldn't involve officers.

We moved toward the front gate, our staggered file stretching out like a slinky. Dominguez took the lead, as usual, while Snoop and I settled into the middle of the patrol, the terp carrying a black plastic rifle made to resemble the real thing. He claimed it made him less of a target, but we knew he carried it to try to impress any available Iraqi ladies. A pair of attack birds on their way to Baghdad flew over us, their rotors churning in mechanized refrain. We walked north on the sides of the road in silence.

A bronze fog hung over the town of Ashuriyah. It obscured our vision, though the occasional minaret crown emerged above the haze. I took off my clear lenses and wiped away the dust before deciding to hell with it and slipped them into a cargo pocket. While the fog shielded us from the sun's worst and kept the air relatively cool, I'd already sweated through my clothes by the time we reached the market blocks. My body ached in all the normal places from the medieval bulk of the armor: the blister spots on my heels, the knotted center of my back, the right collarbone that'd been turned sideways years before during intramurals. I pushed these bitchy suburban grievances away, tugged at my junk, and thanked Hog again for teaching me the importance of freeballing.

"No problem," he said. "But what do they teach at officer school if they don't teach that?"

We stopped short of the market and turned onto a dusty back street, walking by a lonely cypress tree. Small sandstone houses resembling honeycomb cells lined the sides of the road. A donkey cart filled with concrete blocks ambled by, the animal and boy driving it sunk in discomfort. On their heels came a rush of children clamoring for our attention and clawing at our pockets.

"Mistah, gimme chocolata!" they said. "Gimme football! Gimme, gimme!"

"You gimme chocolata!" Hog said, picking up one of the kids, twirling him around.

"Punks should be in school," Doc Cork said, reaching for a cigarette. For some reason, the other soldiers took great pride in the fact that our medic smoked. The only son of Filipino immigrants, he was a peddler of light, and pills, in a bleak world.

I turned to a child with doubting eyes, ruffled his hair, and pointed to him. "Ali baba," I said. The group of kids around him laughed and chanted, "Ali baba! Ali baba!" while the victim of my slander protested. No one liked being called a villain. I put my hands out and let the kids play with the hard plastic that cased the knuckles of my gloves.

Some of the guys were debating whether to provide the kids dipping tobacco and telling them it was chocolate, so I gave Dominguez the hand signal to keep the patrol moving.

"This is good, yo," Snoop said, waving around his dummy rifle like a flag. "Kids keep snipers away. They won't shoot with kids here, unless they are fuckups. People get angry about dead kids."

Near the hajji bodega, a group of teens were playing foosball in a plot of muddy weeds and poppies. The Barbie Kid was there, too, wheeling around a cooler and selling Boom Booms and cigarettes to occupiers and occupied alike. A gust of wind carried the faint scent of shit so pervasive in Ashuriyah. Sewer ditches and cesspools were still far more prevalent than indoor plumbing in this part of the Cradle of Civilization.

Snoop pointed to the table and asked if I wanted to play.

"Sure," I said. "Anyone got someplace to be?"

Most of the soldiers laughed, though I spotted the new staff sergeant, Chambers, glaring my way. He leaned against a telephone pole with wires hanging from it like spaghetti, his helmet tilted forward to cover his face in a deep shadow.

"Too nice to these little fuckers," he said, exposing a tobacco-stained overbite. There was a hard edge to his voice. This wasn't a joke—it was criticism.

Half the patrol started studying packed dirt, while the others turned to me. I needed to say something. I was the platoon leader. He was an interloper, a fucking new guy who wasn't supposed to be doing anything but watching and learning. So I shrugged and said, "It's not 2007 anymore. Things have changed. We're withdrawing soon."

"Right." He didn't sound convinced. "While you and the English-speaking hajj handle business, I'm going to show the guys how to pull security."

I nodded slightly and considered my options. Some noncoms couldn't help but test their leadership, and it seemed I now had one of those. My brother would say I needed to regulate. All in good time, I reasoned. There was no reason to crush a guy for having baggage from his last tour. I watched a pair of stray dogs along a ridgeline to the east. They were teasing a spotted goat with big pink balls that wanted nothing to do with them. I felt bad for the thing, but we hadn't been sent to Iraq to save goats.

Snoop tugged my sleeve to bring my attention back to foosball. Two teenagers built like cord had lined up across the table. The bar of our goalie proved sticky, but one of their strikers had been sawed in half somehow, so it evened out.

"They ask how old you are," Snoop translated. "They say you look too young to be a *molazim*."

It wasn't the first time I'd heard that. "Twenty-four," I said, trying to keep my voice flat. "Old enough."

Sweat rolled down my face and onto the table, dripping like dirty rain. It was too hot to be wearing anything other than a tee shirt. The teens suggested Snoop and I take off our gear. They thought American soldiers were crazy for wearing body armor outside. I grunted and took off my gloves to better grip the handles.

During the game, I listened to soldiers pelt Chambers with questions about firefights on his previous deployments, his Ranger tab, and what he meant by "exposed silhouettes." Hog's voice especially carried from across the dirt road, which bothered me.

"Sergeant?" he asked. "I heard, uh, you got tattoos for every enemy you've killed?"

Chambers pulled up the sleeve on his right arm, though I couldn't see what he was showing. The soldiers, now spread out in pairs and kneeling behind cars or peeking around building corners, all turned his way.

"Don't look at me, oxygen thieves," Chambers said, his voice stinging with authority. "Eyes out."

"Fuck this," I said, after giving up another goal that I blamed on the stuck goalie. I'd been to Ranger School, too. I had my tab. Why didn't they ever ask me about it? Because infantry officers have guaranteed slots, I thought. We don't have to fight to get in like the enlisted. "Snoop, call over the Barbie Kid. Let's get some work done."

I could tell the terp was annoyed by the way the game had ended, but he did as instructed. The Barbie Kid, all ninety pounds of him, moved to us with bare feet covered in dust, rolling a cooler of goods behind him. A dark unibrow raced across his forehead, and he stank like a polecat, wearing his usual pink sweats. The Barbie doll's face on the sweatshirt was smudged with mud and crust, forever spoiling her smile.

"Any ali babas around?" I asked.

The Barbie Kid looked up at me with his good eye, the lazy one staying fixed to the ground. "None the Americans would care about," he said through Snoop, his voice cracking but tart.

Fucking teenagers, I thought. They're all terrible. Even here.

I reached down and lifted the Barbie Kid's sweatshirt to reveal the handle of a long, dull *sai* dagger tucked into his waistband.

"Still carrying that around," I said. "You're going to hurt yourself."

The young Iraqi frowned, then argued. "He is a businessman and must protect his business," Snoop translated. "He asks why you care? There are boys younger than him who work for the Sahwa militias. They carry AK-47s."

"Good point," I said.

"Want any Boom Booms, LT? He offers a special deal, because Hotspur is his favorite platoon."

"I'm sure he tells that to all the girls. How much?"

"Two for five dollars."

As I rummaged through my pockets for money, a sound like wood planks slapping together broke the peace. Then again. My heart jumped up and my feet jumped back, unprepared for fired rounds. Chambers stood in the center of the road, back straight, rifle wedged tight into his shoulder. The bronzed dirt in the air had parted around him, giving off a strange, glassy sheen. A wisp of smoke curled out the end of his barrel and the goat with big pink balls lay collapsed on the far side of the street, near a pair of soldiers in a wadi. I exchanged a confused look with Snoop. Then the Barbie Kid unleashed the most primal sound I'd ever heard, a scream both high and low, as abrupt as it was lasting. He ran to the goat's body, and we followed, slowly.

"Goddamn it. What did I just say about keeping the enemy out of our perimeter?" Chambers yelled, lowering his rifle. "If that thing had been a suicide bomber, you'd be explaining to Saint Peter why the fuck you're so stupid."

The Barbie Kid fell to the ground next to the dead animal, cradling its body and petting it. He wept uncontrollably. The goat was lean to the point of emaciation, and its coat was splotched and stringy, like shredded paper. Its balls were even bigger and pinker up close. It'd been shot through the brain at the bridge of its nose, giving the look of a third eye. Fat, gray insects were hopping off its coat into the Barbie Kid's hair, so I kept my distance.

"Sergeant Chambers," I said. "We're not supposed to shoot animals. Higher's pretty strict about that."

"They're a menace," he said. "But okay."

I looked around the platoon. Most peered in at the scene, a strained quiet gripping them. There were no jokes, no sounds of spat tobacco, no jingling of gear. Dominguez shook his head and turned back out, instructing the joes nearby to do the same.

I pointed to the goat. "Pretty close to some of the men."

Chambers pounded his chest twice and hooted. "A perfect kill. Never a danger."

Snoop was on the ground with the Barbie Kid, placing a hand on his back. "LT Jack? This was his pet, his only *habibi*. He say his parents didn't let it in their house, but he fed it and played with it for many months. He's very sad."

"I can see that." I chewed on my lip. "For fuck's sake." I reached into my pockets and pulled out all the bills and change I could find: seventeen dollars and fifty cents, and eight hundred dinars.

"Tell him to take this," I told Snoop. "Condolence funds. And Sergeant? Throw some money in there."

Chambers sneered, but did as ordered, tossing a twenty-dollar bill to the ground.

The Barbie Kid wouldn't take the money, nor would he abandon the dead goat. Putting the bills and change into his cooler, we left him hugging and petting and snotting over the carcass.

The electricity recon took ten hours. I met with a half dozen Iraqi families over chai and flatbread, discussing the neighborhoods and the Sahwa militias and the problems with electricity and clean water. They had many questions, and I had few answers. Chambers ran security for the rest of the mission, staying out in the bronze fog the entire time. Throughout the day, both the Barbie Kid's scream and Chambers' hoot twisted in my mind like screws. Not even Doc Cork's headache pills could make them go away.

2

"Yo, LT Jack. Source called."

I looked up from the poker table. Snoop stood in the doorway, a swirl of dark skin and shadows. I could tell by his voice that the matter was urgent, but there was three hundred dollars in the pot. I'd spent a good hour sandbagging hands. Maybe some of the platoon originals saw what I was doing, but Chambers hadn't. He'd no clue, thinking I was just another dumb lieutenant who didn't know how to play cards.

"Duty calls." Dominguez's chipmunk cheeks widened into a grin as he rubbed his shaved head. He'd clean up quickly with me gone. "Insha'Allah. As God wills it."

"Something like that," I said. I stood and put on my uniform top, an amalgam of digital camo, tan and green and gray and ugly as puke. "I'll cash out when I get back." I followed Snoop out of the windowless room, the poker game resuming behind us.

In the two days since the goat incident, everyone had stayed silent about it. There wasn't much to say. I'd wondered how my brother would've handled things, since he was the perfect leader of men or something, but hadn't been able to land on anything specific. I could always call and ask, I thought, before rejecting the idea. He'd just lecture me for letting it happen in the first place.

On the other side of the outpost, Snoop and I angled by the command post, where Captain Vrettos hunched over the radio like a broken stork, updating battalion headquarters. He had a poncho liner wrapped around his shoulders and head as a shawl.

"Yes, sir, I understand the tenets of counterinsurgency," he was saying. His voice was brittle; he sometimes slept in there during the days, on a folding chair, so he could stay up and track our company's night operations. He must've been speaking with someone from battalion. "Clear and hold. Then build."

In a whisper, Snoop asked if I wanted to stop and check in with the commander. I shook my head wildly. When battalion got going on the tenets of counterinsurgency, there was no stopping them.

The interpreters' room lay on the far reaches of the hallway, across from a small gym. We walked into dank must. The other terps were playing a soccer video game in the dark. I flipped on the light switch and a ceiling panel flickered to life.

"Lieutenant," one of them said. "Surf's up."

"For the millionth time, I'm not from that part of California. I grew up in the foothills. By a lake."

The terps' faces remained blank. There was only one California on this side of the world, and nothing I could say would ever change that.

"Haitham called," Snoop said.

Haitham was the town drunk, a toy of a man with flitting eyes and rotting yellow teeth. He was also the Barbie Kid's estranged uncle. For being a Muslim on the bottle, we figured. We paid him twenty thousand dinars a month, and he still claimed he couldn't afford toothpaste.

"He drinks too much." Snoop liked him more than I did. "But he's no liar."

"True," I said.

"He say he watched us the other day. When the new sergeant shot the goat."

"He did? Why?"

"He remembers the new sergeant, from before. He say the new sergeant helped murder Iraqis during the al-Qaeda wars, when the Horse soldiers were here. Called him a white *shaytan*."

I leaned against a bunk with a wood frame and plush foam mattresses. It was a great mystery how the terps had ended up with better beds than us. "Horse soldiers?"

"First Cav," another terp said, eyes fixed on the video game. "The horse on their unit patch."

"Okay," I said. "They were here four, five years ago?"

Snoop shrugged. "I was a terp in the south then. And these Arab fuckclowns"—he pointed to the others—"were still schoolboys in Egypt."

Originally from Sudan, Snoop was an equal opportunity racist. The frantic mashing of buttons served as the only response.

"This makes no sense," I said, waving away Snoop's offer of sunflower seeds. He stuck a handful into his mouth. "Chambers is a big white dude with brown hair. Ninety percent of the army is big white dudes with brown hair."

"He saw him do this." Snoop let his right arm go slack and balled his hand into a fist repeatedly, causing the forearm to flex. "How he knew."

"Snoop—"

"He swears in Allah's name. Big thing to swear on. Even for fuckup Arabs."

I rubbed my eyes and fought off a yawn. The grind was getting to me. So was the heat, and it was only April.

"Some locals got killed a few years ago," I said. "I don't want to sound cruel, but this is a war."

"Ashuriyah used to be a bad place, LT. Before the moneys and the Surge and the counter-surgery. And check it, Haitham say a man the new sergeant helped kill? The only son of a powerful sheik."

"Counterinsurgency," I said, stressing the last four syllables of the word. "It's pronounced 'counter-in-sur-gen-cy.'"

"Yeah, that's what I say."

I didn't bother to correct him again. Maybe this is a big deal, I thought. But probably not. "Which sheik?"

"Didn't say. Just that he doesn't want to be a source anymore. Something about respecting the Shaba."

"What's that?"

"*Shaba* is 'ghost.'"

I gave him a puzzled look.

"Like respecting the dead," he added. I'd no idea what the hell that could mean.

"He knows we won't pay him anymore, right?"

Snoop nodded. "He's scared of something, for sure."

I walked downstairs to the cooks' pantry, grabbing a warm can of Rip It. It tasted like liquid crack should, flat fruit punch with a splash of electricity. I headed back to our room, hoping the poker game was still going, but instead found everyone napping or reading magazines. Rage Against the Machine blared from the speakers of an unseen laptop.

"Who won?" I asked.

Dominguez cursed under his breath in Spanish. I followed his stare to Chambers, who lay in bed, boots still on, hands wrapped behind his head. Straightening his arms, Chambers pointed to a black, hollow-eyed skull on his right forearm. Five other skull tattoos lined his arm from the bottom of his bicep to the top of his wrist. He balled his hand into a fist once, twice, three times.

"Nice try, Lieutenant," Chambers said, his eyes pale as slate. "But this ain't my first rodeo."

3
_____

Traffic checkpoints were the kind of missions we'd trained a lot for stateside, but didn't do much of anymore. The Iraqi army and police handled them. But on a late April morning in his airless office, Captain Vrettos said our platoon needed to complete one more joint mission to meet the month's quota.

"And," he said, "Bravo Company doesn't fudge quotas." He had the wide shine in the eyes that came with severe sleep deprivation, so I didn't fight it.

We went that afternoon. It was hot, but the sky was gray and cloudy. Chambers organized things while I conducted a radio check with the outpost.

"Dominguez! You got security from your twelve to your four o'clock. No son, your four.

"Fucking hell, Doc, have you ever unraveled razor wire before? Use your boots. Like this.

"Where your gloves at, Hog? Your pocket. Is that where they belong? Right is right, wrong is wrong, and you're a soup sandwich."

I had to admit, Chambers was instilling discipline in the guys. They'd need it when we got back to garrison life in Hawaii. He didn't like the way we parked our four armored Strykers, either, and reorganized them into a diamond position.

A rusty station wagon drove down the paved road and stopped at an orange cone fifteen feet short of the checkpoint. Chambers pulled the driver out of the car and showed one of the cherries how to pat down a local, twisting the man's clothes into bunches while searching. Wearing a gray *dishdasha* and a turban, the driver—an old man with a large lip sore and a salt-and-pepper beard—looked bored, moving only when a *jundi* from the Iraqi army asked him to open the trunk. The old man waved at me like we knew one another. He was on his way a few minutes later, the silence of the desert replacing the sound of his car's motor.

I pictured myself calling Hog a soup sandwich. Even in my head it sounded contrived.

I walked over to the stone guard shack on the roadside. It was the only piece of shade for miles on the bleak stretch between Ashuriyah and Camp Independence, the base to our east that served as a northern border for Baghdad proper and as a logistical hub. Chambers joined me a couple of minutes later.

Our new squad leader looked out at the road, still critiquing our positioning. Low and broad, he swung his shoulders side to side, stretching his back. Deep lines slit his face, creases that gave him a rugged sort of dignity.

"How old are you, Sergeant?" I asked.

Chambers spat out a wad of dip. "Thirty last month. Don't tell the youngbloods, though. Don't want them thinking their papa bear is too old to whip their ass."

I'd thought him older. A pocket of acne scars on his temples somehow aged him too, as did stained teeth and his gray, pallid eyes.

"Got a wife or girlfriend back home? Kids?"

"Two ex-wives, four kids that I claim." He waited for me to laugh. "Two in Texas, the others, not sure. Last I heard, they were moving back to Rochester."

"Huh." Though it was common enough, I hated hearing about young children having to deal with divorce. My mom and dad had managed to stay friends, but that tended not to be the norm. "Lady back home?"

He snorted. "Learned that lesson. Hope you're smarter than that, Lieutenant. Jody is a dishonorable son of a bitch, and he got your woman months ago. When they say there's no one else, just know there always is. Part of a soldier's life."

Good thing Marissa and I broke things off before we left, I thought. Though she had stressed that there was no one else. A lot.

"Jody can't get a girl that don't exist."

I had no idea why I'd said "don't" instead of "doesn't."

"Been banging a new piece of ass at Independence, when we're there," he continued. "Intel sergeant from battalion. A choker."

There was only one intel sergeant from battalion he could be talking about, a quiet woman with milk chocolate skin who somehow filled out the shape-repressing uniform with curves and angles. I'd talked to Sergeant Griffin a few times. She was kind. Every enlisted man in Hawaii had been trying to get with her for years. None had been successful, as far as I knew.

I whistled. "How'd you do that?"

"Power of persuasion," he said, his voice slurring past the tobacco nestled deep in his cheeks.

I fumbled about for a change of topic. Talking about women I didn't know was one thing, but Sergeant Griffin was a fellow soldier.

"Rumor has it you've walked this strip of paradise before," I eventually said.

"Fuck, Lieutenant." He considered his answer, longer than seemed natural. "I've spent more time in the desert than I can remember."

"Oh yeah? With who?"

"Once to the 'Stan with Tenth Mountain. Two times here, with Fourth Infantry right after the Invasion, the other with First Cav. Now back with the Electric Strawberry."

I bristled at his use of the derisive nickname for the Twenty-Fifth Infantry, though I wasn't sure why—I myself had used it often enough. I leaned against the shack and stuck my hands in my pockets, looking far into the brown sands. Lasik-sharpened eyes might've spotted a lone mud hut, but besides the large berm to the north that hid the canal, there was nothing. This was our no-man's-land.

I heard laughing and looked over at the checkpoint. Doc Cork and three other soldiers were watching something on a cell phone. Two *jundi*s with them began air humping, one with his rifle, the other with a metal detector. Dominguez, up in the Stryker's gun turret, flung a water bottle at one of the gyrating Iraqis, hitting him in the back.

"Savages," I said, trying to impress Chambers, belatedly realizing he might have thought I meant our own soldiers. He didn't appear to care either way.

"So," he said. "It true our commander's a fag?"

"I guess." I'd met Captain Vrettos' purported boyfriend many times before we left. A CrossFit coach, he'd come in and led physical training once, and could bench more than anyone, even Sipe. That'd stopped most of the gay jokes.

Chambers shook his head. "What the fuck has happened to my army."

"He's a really good leader," I said. "Everyone's a little gay, right?"

There was no response. A minute or so passed. A gust rose up, spraying our faces with sand pebbles. I shielded my eyes with an arm. Then it was over, and the stillness returned.

"What you all call this place again?" Chambers asked.

"Checkpoint Thirty-Eight."

"That's right." He paused. "Used to be Sayonara Station."

"Why's that?"

He looked at me in a way that made me understand. "Oh," I said.

His blistered lips thinned into a smile. "You know why we have the checkpoint here, Lieutenant Porter?"

I sucked down some warm water from my CamelBak tube. Petty alpha male games with the sheiks were one thing, but playing them with our own noncoms irritated me.

"I don't."

He pointed north to south, perpendicular to the road. "A big smugglers' trail back in the day. The ravines give cover all the way to Baghdad. Totally drivable, even in shitty third world cars. Checkpoint Thirty-Eight"—his voice rang with disgust—"wasn't established to search vehicles on the road. It was to dismantle a Shi'a insurgent logistical route."

I looked north and then south. "Interesting. Shi'a?"

"Yeah. Mainly Jaish al-Mahdi. Back when the Mahdi Army had balls."

"Oh." Whenever a guy had deployed before, it always had been rougher and tougher, more of a crucible than his current deployment. "I've read about that." That it was the clear truth in this case only irritated me further. "The Sadr uprisings."

"Yes, sir. Real combat. None of this counterinsurgency handholding bullshit. Just kill or be killed." He paused again and spat out another wad of dip. "It made sense."

I didn't know what to say to that, so I said something else. "I'm going to make sure the joes are drinking water. Hog almost had heatstroke last month." I started walking toward the checkpoint, but turned around after a few steps. "Hey. The name Shaba mean anything to you?"

Still leaning against the shack, Chambers took off his right glove and wiped away thick beads of sweat that had gathered under his sunglasses at the bridge of his nose.

"Ahh-shu-riyah," he said, sounding out the syllables. "Still coughing up sand from the last time."

Something about his voice, both flippant and mocking, triggered a switch. I tilted my head and smirked. "What about any civilian killings around here?" I asked. "Local gossip."

We stared at one another, cloudy green meeting pale slate. I stopped smirking and held my breath and my pulse thumped and thumped. He put his sunglasses back on.

"Been in the army for almost ten years now," he said. "First squad leader taught me it's better to be tried by twelve than carried by six. He's dead now. Turned to pink mist trying to save a hajji kid. But he was right. I don't question any soldier's decisions in combat. We all made judgment calls, and made them in split seconds. It wasn't right, it wasn't wrong. Just part of the job description."

"And Shaba?"

"No disrespect. But don't go asking questions about things you don't want answers to, Jackie. That's my advice as a professional military man."

I was too shocked to react. I'd been challenged before, but not like this. Not this direct. I didn't know what to do. Worse, he knew that.

I turned back around and walked to the checkpoint. The heat loomed over us for the rest of the afternoon like holy venom, pushing into triple digits despite the overcast. Two more cars drove through while we were there. Nothing of interest was found.

4

The desert was empty and brown on the ride back to the outpost. From the Ashuriyah back roads, it seemed boundless, stretching every which way in a sea of chapped earth. I'd avoided Chambers the rest of the time at the checkpoint, keeping near the radio. But doing that hadn't gotten rid of a strange prickling in the back of my mind.

Standing out of a rear hatch, between gulps of baked air, I considered Haitham's phone call to Snoop. Then I asked the soldiers for their thoughts on the Iraqi.

"Never trust an alkie, sir," Hog said from the driver's hole, causing me to turn down the volume dial of my headset. "All they care about is booze. That's how it works in Pine Bluff, at least."

I looked to my right, where another one of the joes stood, a sulky kid from Ohio named Specialist Kucharczyk. His wide shoulders barely cleared the hatch.

"Agree with that, Alphabet?" I asked.

He shook his head, readjusted his goggles, and went back to watching the roadside.

"That's our Alphabet," Hog said. "Man of few words."

The sky had cleared somewhat. The sun slid across it, leaving crayon streaks of orange and red. Sand berms gave way to shacks made of tin. At a stone arch bearing the image of a bespectacled, snow-bearded cleric, our Stryker turned left. An eight-wheeled armored fighting vehicle the shade of caterpillar green and shaped like a parallelogram, the Stryker was called "the Cadillac of Mesopotamia" by the men. General Dynamics had designed it for urban assaults, meaning it could go eighty miles per hour with an infantry squad in the back or be retrofitted with a 105-millimeter tank gun, depending on the mission. I preferred the more luxurious features of the vehicle, like the iPod dock.

Once the turn was complete, Dominguez spoke through his headset from the machine gun turret.

"Hog."

"Sergeant?"

"You could learn something from Alphabet. It's good for a soldier to be quiet."

With the sun in slow retreat, Ashuriyah had begun to stir. My platoon's four vehicles were lined up in a row like ducklings and staggered to minimize the effects of an IED blast. The smell of hot trash filled the air. We crept through the town marketplace, pretending to scan for suicide bombers, hoping instead to spot a pretty teenage girl.

Young men in jeans glared at our armored vehicles and kicked at the newly laid asphalt under them. Women dressed in black burqas shuffled from shop to shop, keeping their heads bowed. Middle-aged men hawked fake cans of Pepsi and real blocks of ice, waving at us with one hand and stroking their mustaches with the other. Children threw rocks off the Strykers' tires and yelled phrases of random, broken English. Old men played dominoes on the side of the road, so used to foreign soldiers they didn't bother to acknowledge the war machines rolling by.

Some of us waved back, some of us didn't. Some of us smiled, most of us didn't. Someone in the trailing Stryker tossed candy to the children. We weren't supposed to do that anymore, not after a unit across the canal ran over a kid and turned him to flesh pudding.

That's Chambers' vehicle, I thought. I kept picturing the look on his face when I'd asked about Shaba. What had that been about?

"You should talk to Alia," Dominguez said. "She grew up here. I bet she could give you the lowdown."

"That's my girl!" Hog said. "For an Iraqi, she sure can slob the knob." A few seconds passed. "That's what someone said, anyway."

"I didn't hear that," I said. "Play the damn game." It was an open secret the outpost's cleaning lady doubled as a hooker for the enlisted guys, and if whispers counted for anything, business was booming for the forty-something. The other platoon leaders and I had adopted an informal Don't Ask, Don't Tell policy on the matter. We were well aware there were worse pastimes to pursue for soldiers at a far edge of the world.

We turned right, the outpost rising above the slums like a desert acropolis. With the afternoon siesta over, the area teemed with activity, from the sheiks at the front gate dressed in fine white *dishdasha*s to the snipers prowling the roof behind drooping camo nets.

"Why the man-dresses here?" Alphabet asked, pointing to the sheiks.

"Sahwa contracts, probably," I said. I had deep misgivings about our alliance with the local militias, but tried to keep them to myself. "Always a negotiation."

"Fucking Sahwa," Alphabet said, spitting into the wind. "They killed Americans before we paid them off. I know they did. It's just, I don't know. Dishonorable."

"Yeah, they got paid," I said. "And maybe it was dishonorable." Our Stryker stopped in front of the main entrance, and its back ramp lowered. Inside the vehicle, sitting on long cushioned benches, Snoop and Doc Cork woke up. The terp hopped out. "It was also smart."

I took off my headset and followed Snoop's gangly steps through the entrance and into the outpost, clearing my rifle and stripping off my body armor. I felt another headache coming on and couldn't stop thinking about Chambers calling me Jackie. In the air-conditioned office upstairs, I filed the patrol report while the platoon refueled before heading in themselves. Outside, the heat endured.

5

Though the outpost didn't have internet—something the joes bitched about constantly; how else were they going to meet women?—we did have access to satellite phones in a first-floor storage room. After mulling over my exchange with Chambers for a couple of days, my pride finally caved and I called my brother. He'd know what to do.

Four makeshift phone stalls had been jammed into the room. Alphabet was using one, hunched over with his back toward the door. He didn't realize I'd come in. I sat down in an empty stall and started dialing, breathing in more stale bleach than air. Will picked up on the third ring.

"Yo," I said.

"Jack!" he said. "You okay?"

"Yeah, yeah. Just calling to catch up."

A deep sigh blew over the connection. "You know calls are usually bad news." He sighed again, though this one was less pronounced. "So. My little brother a war hero yet?"

"Hah. Not quite." Captain William Porter, Commanding, West Point graduate class of 2002, had pulled two of his soldiers from a burning Humvee during the Battle of Baqubah in 2007, earning a Silver Star. "Just lots of meetings about a water filtration project. Things have settled down a bunch since you were over here."

"That's what the news says. Keep alert, though. Don't drop your guard."

"Yeah."

"Chin up, man," he said. "Who better to deal with guerrillas rising against empire than a descendant of Irish rebels? We were bred for this shit."

"Yeah." I bit down on my lip, not ready to prostrate myself in front of him and reveal weakness. "How's Stanford?" I asked. He was in his second semester of business school. "Enjoying it?"

He laughed. "Glad you asked. Got our goon on the other night."

Will started bragging about his latest conquest, something I wouldn't have cared about even in person. He hadn't been like this growing up, but time and war had changed him. The principles of his youth had walked off with the former friends and exes whose names we couldn't mention anymore because they'd incurred his Old Testament wrath, and returned in the form of army values like LOYALTY and HONOR.

I'd once asked about this potential inconsistency in his worldview, after a Thanksgiving meal that'd brought us home to Granite Bay. He'd quoted Walt Whitman: "'Do I contradict myself? Very well, then I contradict myself, I am large, I contain multitudes.'" Then he'd switched over to Dr. Dre: "'I just want to fuck bad ladies, for all the nights I never had ladies.'"

"Ladies?" I'd laughed. The badass terrorist-killer was still an awkward romantic at heart. He'd been unable to bring himself to say "bitches" in our mom's living room. I'd kept laughing until he punched me in the chest.

Back in Iraq, hot whispers and quiet sobbing were coming from the other side of the plywood wall separating the phone stalls, and my attention drifted that way. I listened for snippets of Alphabet's conversation while my brother's voice continued blitzing the receiver, their words slowly intertwining.

"Met this group of undergrads," Will said.

"How could you?" Alphabet said.

"A senior, I swear. Naughty little thing."

"We were supposed to get married."

"Short, brunette, curvy."

"Drunk. What kind of excuse is that? Why were you even out with other guys?"

"She said we needed to find someone for her friend."

"Tell me everything. What you did. How you did it."

"All about it."

"Why?"

"Barely remember what happened."

"Tell me why."

"Needed an ice pack for my bottom lip the next day."

"Why!"

"Wild one."

Alphabet slammed his phone down and left the room, white as a root. I made a mental note to check on him. Dear Johns always meant suicide watch.

"So that was my weekend," my brother said. "Speaking of, how are things with Marissa?"

Marissa was the last thing I wanted to talk about, and not just because I didn't know how things were with her. So instead I explained my walking, talking leadership challenge, focusing especially on how Chambers felt about counterinsurgency.

Will was unimpressed. "You need to get rid of him," he said. "I had noncoms like him. They're cancers. Cut him out, it's that simple. Talk with your company commander yet?"

"Captain Vrettos is overwhelmed by all the Sahwa stuff. He'd just tell me to 'drive on' or something."

"What about your platoon sergeant? Sipe. He's the senior enlisted on the ground. He should be all over this."

A green fly had made its way into the phone room, hovering near the ceiling. I slid off a flip-flop and put it on the table. We'd been keeping a running tally, companywide, and I was tied for third place with twenty-four confirmed kills.

"Nice guy, but he's checked out," I said.

"So this Chambers guy is essentially the senior noncom in the platoon?"

"Pretty much. And the guys really respond to him."

I braced for a lecture about establishing authority, but surprisingly,

Will held back. He seemed too concerned for reproach. "Any soldiers have your back?" he asked.

"My vehicle crew. But they're all joes. And the Doc. There's Sergeant Dominguez, but he just got his stripes a couple months ago."

"That's fine. You have eyes and ears in the ranks. Use them."

"Okay."

"Listen, Jack, this kind of thing could prove problematic. 'War is war' assholes were great for the army when I deployed, but they're only trouble now. We're not going to kill our way out of Iraq, you know that. If you don't rein him in, something could happen that sticks. Like, professionally."

"That's why I called. What should—what would you do?"

I took a swipe at the fly, midair. I missed. It buzzed furiously in response.

"Go to higher. You on good terms with the battalion commander?"

"The Big Man? Think so. He's always slapping my shoulder and telling me to keep it up."

"Good," he said. "If you could find some piece of hard evidence about this old murder, a witness or something. Someone reliable, not the drunk. Then go to the battalion commander, explain that you aren't accusing anyone of anything, but you think it's best he be moved to another unit until the issue is resolved."

The fly circled the plywood wall and landed. I let it crawl for a few seconds until it stopped moving. I needed to be quick. And firm.

"It's not a matter of whether he actually did it. It's a matter of finding someone reputable who says he did."

"Got it," I said.

"Good. Keep me updated. And call Mom and Dad, or at least e-mail them once in a while. They're worried. Won't leave me alone because of it."

"How they doing?" I looked under my sandal and found number twenty-five. "I know I should call more, but when I do, it's always—I don't know. Like, I tried to tell Mom about the poverty over here. She kept telling me to fight to stay compassionate, which, no offense, isn't a concern right now." I swallowed. "You know?"

My brother loosed a sharp laugh. "Think about it. They're children of World War Two vets. They met at a hippie protest. Now they're two-time military parents. It's complicated for us? It's complicated for them."

"Hell of an American story," I said.

"Something like that," he said. "Just stick all the bullshit into a compartment in the head. Lock it away. You'll have time for it once you get back."

"Cool." I didn't feel like talking anymore, and I needed to think about things. "Hey, I gotta go. Talk soon?"

"Sure, Jack. Be safe. Be strong."

I hung up and shook fly guts off my flip-flop. Crossing the first-floor foyer, I stepped outside onto the smoking patio. Translucent camo nets were draped from the overhang, forming olive walls of faint light, like we were shrouded in a castle of seaweed. The walls swayed with the wind. I remembered why I didn't come out here often: the rectangular patio always smelled of wet cigarette. A pair of sergeants from third platoon sat in lawn chairs with cigars in hand and rifles in their laps, talking about midnight raids from previous deployments. Beyond the concrete blast walls ringing the outpost came the sound of a scooter backfiring, causing both sergeants' heads to snap up. Then they each laughed and accused the other of being a fucking pussy.

I chewed over Will's counsel. It seemed a little cold. But some situations call for pragmatism, I thought. The sergeants went back inside with playful salutes, and the streets went mute. Droning prayers from the large mosque to the north proved my only company. For once, I didn't mind them. I took in a deep breath of wet cigarette and watched the green camo nets ripple slowly with the wind, marking time.

6

M an oh man, LT, is first squad pissed at you," Hog said.
I laughed from the back hatch, watching our headlights
strike through the countryside dark. The road air was brisk, and I tried
not to swallow any kicked-up gravel.

"Because they're pulling outpost security tonight instead of third
squad?" I asked. "Seems silly."

"Don't mess with a man's schedule over here, sir. It's bad juju."

Dominguez was right about that. But I wanted to talk to Fat Mukhtar
without Chambers there, so I'd switched things around. Given his hos-
tility to meetings with locals, he hadn't fought me on it. He'd just said,
"Enjoy the chai, sir," through a mouthful of dip, snuff bits covering
his teeth. Then he'd gone back to reviewing Sipe's plans for the sentry
shack at the front gate.

Our Strykers pulled up to Fat Mukhtar's. Two of his guards, wearing
khaki button-downs, pulled aside razor wire so we could pass. Palm
trees lined the entrance to the compound, part of a small Sunni hamlet
west of Ashuriyah, one of many in the area we referred to collectively
as the Villages.

Fat Mukhtar had owned two villas before he became a Sahwa militia leader, and built two more since. In the daylight, we would've seen
buildings painted eggshell white with gold trim, staggered in pairs,
forming a square. Now we saw them as dim gray outlines, winding and
weaving formlessly like dotted lines on a map.

"Always reminds me of a drug palace. Like *Scarface*," Hog said.

"Shut up," Dominguez responded.

"I'll shut up when I finally get out of this hole. I pin on corporal next
month and get my own fireteam. Your wetback ass is gonna miss me!"

"You are my favorite redneck."

I'd considered confiding in these two about my struggles with, and plans for, Chambers, but decided against it. They were too junior. I'd use them as sensors, like Will had suggested. We parked at the end of a flagstone driveway, behind a herd of black Land Rovers and Mercedeses with tinted windows.

Fat Mukhtar waited at the foot of the Stryker's lowered ramp, his white *dishdasha* not long or loose enough to hide his stomach rolls. His goatee was freshly trimmed, and a thatch of black curls topped his head. I kicked Snoop awake and hopped to the ground. Alphabet followed.

"Salaam Aleichem," I said, raising my right hand to my heart and cupping it.

"Hah-loo." Fat Mukhtar raised two fingers into a peace sign and peered into the dark bowels of the Stryker. "Vrettos?"

"No," I said. "Just me. Just a *molazim*." The Iraqis always wanted the commander to show up to meetings, even the ones that didn't deserve his time or attention.

"Surf's up," the *mukhtar* said. I sighed.

A fireteam followed us to the main house, while Hog, Dominguez, and the other crews stayed with the vehicles. We walked into the front room and took off our helmets. Mauve curtains swathed the long shoebox of a room in an effort to cover the cement walls. Watercolors of rivers and forests from the old American Midwest hung from the far wall. We sat down on a garish red rug, some knockoff from Beirut, and the servants brought out chai and flatbread. Both tasted like warm sweat.

After a few minutes of hollow pleasantries, Fat Mukhtar brought up business. "My Sahwa need payment," he said through Snoop. "My men get nervous without payment. Brave, yes, loyal, yes, but they aren't warriors. They are farmers with guns. And farmers with guns make mistakes."

"What did Captain Vrettos say about the payment plan?" I asked.

"He say next month. But it's always next month."

I was glad he remembered what the commander had said, because I hadn't.

"Then it's next month. But—if you're interested, I could get your group to the head of the line on payday."

The *mukhtar*'s eyeballs lit up like an illum round, and he stroked his goatee. All the tribal leaders viewed getting paid first as a signifier of clout.

"Who is Shaba?" I asked.

The *mukhtar* cleared his throat and grinned faintly. "Shaba was an American soldier," Snoop relayed. "He say, 'You didn't know him? You're an American soldier, too, right?'"

Fat Mukhtar laughed once Snoop finished translating, his jowl wobbling, which caused the terp to join him. I stared through both men until Fat Mukhtar raised his fingers into peace signs. Then he continued, his Arabic slushy in the damp room.

"He say Shaba was famous here, with the Horse soldiers," Snoop said. "A man with much *wasta*."

"*Wasta?*"

"Like power, but with people. Very important to Arabs."

"What made him famous?"

"He was the moneyman; that was the big thing. Gave out moneys to sheiks and to businesses. He was also very good at finding the terror men. He talked Arabic, but would pretend not to, and listen to the people. Iraqis talk about things in front of Americans, believing they don't understand. Shaba could. And—wait, I must tell Fat Mukhtar to slow down."

I waited.

"The *mukhtar* say Shaba could change faces when he wanted to? He say it's a special American army trick only the greatest soldiers can do. I don't know, LT Jack. Crazy Arab talk."

"Ask what Shaba's real name was."

"That was some time ago. The *mukhtar* doesn't remember. He wants to know how you learned of Shaba?"

"A source. Can't say more than that."

Fat Mukhtar erupted at Snoop's words. "A source? That's what you call Haitham? The little man is the only one who would still speak of Shaba." Snoop translated while Fat Mukhtar wheezed with delight. "I didn't know he was back in town. Do Americans really have enough drink for him? He is where whiskey goes to die!"

My face turned red, and I tried to hide my shame in a large bite of flatbread.

Fat Mukhtar stopped laughing, eventually, then spoke again. "He asks if you would like to see a photograph of Shaba," Snoop translated.

"Please."

Fat Mukhtar clapped his hands and yelled to his servants. A scrawny teenage guard soon stumbled into the room holding a toucan on one arm and a photo album in his other.

Fat Mukhtar reached for the bird first, placing his forearm out so it could perch there. The bird hopped down with a croak, its yellow-and-green bill nipping at the Iraqi's open, empty palm. Electric yellow splashed across its face, its body and tail deep black. Fat Mukhtar had often spoken of his preference for his exotic birds over his children.

"This one is Sinbad," he said.

"Sounds like a pig." Snoop looked disturbed. "Maybe a donkey."

Fat Mukhtar reached into the folds of his *dishdasha* and produced pellets shaped like berries that the toucan went at with zeal, the Iraqi laughing as it ate, stroking its tail with his free hand. The bird's blue eyes were surrounded by a ringlet of green, a pair of bright monocles that never left the corners of the room.

I pointed to the photo album still in the guard's arm. "May I?"

The teenage guard didn't say anything, but I grabbed the album anyhow.

It was like a flipbook of the entire fucking war, a dust storm of long-departed tanks, uniforms, and faces. I recognized the coffee stain camo pattern of the Invasion-era army and the doorless Humvees of pre-insurgency Iraq. Then came the sectarian wars and the Surge, signified by the louder digital camouflage and the larger up-armored vehicles. The soldiers and marines looked familiar and alien at the same time, like they were from a yearbook of a school I dreamed about, ebbing and flowing in a grim light. Fat and skinny, tall and short, smiling and sneering, their eyes were all the same. Where are these men now? I wondered. How do they remember this place? Do they think about it anymore? Do they hate it the way we hate it, or is their hate more profound and authentic, free of boredom but soaked in blood and memories? About halfway through, a large thumb pressed down on a photograph.

"Shaba," Fat Mukhtar said. The guard now held the toucan.

The photo had been taken in the same room we were sitting in. Same cement walls, same curtains, even the same red rug. A noticeably younger, less round Fat Mukhtar stood in the middle of the picture in a *dishdasha*, arms around a pair of stout black Americans. All smiled. In the foreground, off to the side, a slight, brown-skinned man crouched, plain-faced. Sporting sharp black hair and sideburns that defied regulation length, he wore a staff sergeant's rank on a plate carrier, and his uniform didn't fit quite right. He gaped at the camera rather than smiling at it, revealing a chipped bottom tooth.

"Looks Arab," Snoop said. "The *mukhtar* say many believed he was Iraqi, because he was brown and small."

"He does," I said. "I see it."

"Some even thought he was a son of a rich family who bought their way out to escape Saddam's secret police. But the *mukhtar*, he doesn't believe that. Thinks it was a story put out by the Americans. For *wasta*."

I zeroed in on Shaba's nametape. Though the shot was blurry, a couple of seconds of study produced an answer: Rios. I quietly verified it with Alphabet.

"Ever hear of this guy before?" I asked Snoop.

He shook his head. "I'll keep my ears open."

Sinbad began croaking again, loud and distressed, as if it were alerting the flock to a predator. It flapped its wings, clipped in the center, and the smell of bird shit filled the room. The teenage guard looked at his arm and groaned, then left with speed. Fat Mukhtar laughed and laughed, jowl wobbling, offering a peace sign to his departing guard.

Shaking my head, I tried to regain control of the meeting, snapping to get Snoop's attention. Then I pointed back to the photograph.

"What happened? To Rios, I mean."

A beat passed, then another. Someone's stomach grumbled. Fat Mukhtar spoke in a monotone, allowing Snoop to translate his words sentence by sentence.

"*Molazim*. For that? For that, you'll need a lot more payments. That was Ashuriyah's problem. Not ours." Then he leaned against the wall and called for his hookah.

7

I took off my boots and crawled up the side of the black metal frame and into the top bunk. Wrapping myself in a poncho liner that still smelled of tropical Hawaii, I pushed my temples together, but they pulsed back against my palms like a metronome. I wished our room had windows so that it didn't always reek of balls and heat and sand. Closing my eyes to hide from the dull, pounding light I'd forgotten to turn off, I thought about other, better smells, like perfume and sex.

We'd spent most of the late morning and afternoon rehearsing dismounted battle drills with the *jundi* in the gravel courtyard behind the outpost. It hadn't gone well. It'd been hot. And confusing. And really fucking hot.

Their platoon leader was on leave, so I'd been stuck explaining officer tasks to *jundi* sergeants, which wouldn't have been so bad had their noncoms understood that they were more than glorified privates. The concept of empowered and professional enlisted leaders was new to the Iraqis, something that became plain when they talked during instruction and asked questions about lunch. It wasn't until I took out my M9 that some of them decided to feign caring.

"They hate pistols," Snoop said at the time, telling me nothing I didn't already know. "The weapon of Saddam's secret police. For executions!"

I smelled my own stink. It wasn't pleasant. So I thought of someone who was. I thought of Marissa. I thought of how she always smelled like mango, even after a long run through Granite Bay. I thought of the slight crook in her smile and the small gap between her front teeth. I thought of the way she would sleepily scold me for not cuddling enough, for never cuddling enough. I thought of how she'd read on her front porch for entire summer afternoons, gossip mags, thick historical biographies, old newspapers, anything she could find, legs tucked under her into cushions, eyes slapping across the pages like sneakers on pavement. She'd look up every forty minutes or so, just to make sure I was still there, and wink in mock seduction. I loved her most in those hours, before the suburban sun became suburban stars, when our plans became communal property with friends who didn't matter the ways we mattered. When we were all our own.

The *jundi*s were all their own, too. They were okay at entering and clearing buildings—they'd had plenty of practice with that. But here we were, still trying to convey the concept of reacting to contact by splitting into support and maneuver elements. On the fifth attempt to answer the question "Why?" I'd snapped and said, "Because we win wars and you don't, that's why."

Snoop had said he didn't want to translate that, and Dominguez intervened and asked if he could try. He did a better job even though he was a sergeant and I was a lieutenant.

The headache came like fire the third hour of the battle drills. I hadn't been drinking enough water. We had the rest of the afternoon off, and I'd wanted to spend it calling my parents and maybe even Marissa, but now I couldn't, or at least wouldn't.

I thumbed the thin bracelet on my wrist. Sometimes I told people it was a good-luck charm. Maybe it was. The beads were red, green, and yellow, the colors of Hawaiian sovereignty. Marissa and I had bought matching ones from a shrimp truck on the north shore as a joke, two mainland *haole*s as representative of the Hawaiian occupation as the Union Jack on the state flag.

"I'm no imperial pawn!" she'd laughed at my accusation, long, delicate arms dancing through the wind of the ocean drive, crystal blue to our front, green, jagged cliffs at our backs. "I'm going to be an environmental lawyer. I'm going to change things."

"I'm going to change things, too," I'd said. "Just in a different way." Then I'd held up my braceleted wrist and pointed to hers and asked if we were making a mistake.

"Oh, Jack," she'd said. "Just appreciate the moment. Things are already too complex."

I didn't want to think about complex anymore, so I thought about something else.

The first time Marissa and I had slept together, we'd been on the slide of a neighborhood park, underneath a row of cedars and a black well of sky. We'd called it a midnight brunch, a bottle of cheap red wine and grilled cheese sandwiches wrapped in tinfoil. I'd collected together a few blades of grass, two dandelions and a three-leaf clover, and handed her the bouquet with ironic flourish. Not bad for a high school senior. "Mister Romance," she'd said, pulling me down with resolve, her soft lips filling my mouth.

She hadn't responded to my e-mails in a few weeks. Maybe I'd come across as too needy. Facebook said she was "In a relationship." Or maybe not needy enough. Back when I had civilian hair, shaggy brown like a Beatle, she'd made me use coconut-scented shampoo because she said it smelled nice. As long as she wasn't back together with that lurp she dated before me, I was cool with it. He was a real estate agent now, for Christ's sake.

Or that orangutan of a dental student. He had bad gums.

Or that tennis player with spiky hair. He smiled too much. What a fucking clown. Anyone but that guy.

I tried thinking about some of the others, like the Danish tourist I'd met in Honolulu the year before, who'd called me Mark the next morning. Sometimes she was the answer, but not this time. I kept my eyes closed and breathed in a cloud of mango and Marissa's body went up and down that slide and up and down and my pants went up and my hand went down and—

"Sir?"

I poked my head out from under the poncho liner and opened my eyes, finding a burly, confused Slav.

"Alphabet?"

"Doc Cork gave me these. To give to you."

I grabbed the pair of white pills from his palm with the grace of a startled dog. "Thanks, man." There was a long pause. "Sleeping pills." There was another long pause. "Things better at home?"

"Yes, sir, sure are." The skin on his face so used to frowning flipped upright. "Thanks for checking on me so much. Meant a lot."

I sat up and leaned against the wall, arms draped over my knees. I'd always been all angles and elbows, there wasn't a joke about it I hadn't heard. Sitting like that also hid the proud little grunt standing at attention in my lap.

"Course," I said. "What are lieutenants for?"

"Yeah."

"We're halfway done. Remember that. Like a run to Kolekole Pass— we're on the downslope, back at the barracks before you know it. Just need to keep moving."

"Good call, sir." He pursed his thick lips, blood draining from his face. "It's okay for people to make mistakes, right?"

I chewed my bottom lip. He and his fiancée couldn't be more than twenty. Young love meant young heartache, something I knew all about. He had an unmolded roundness about him, the type of Rust Belt clay that had been switching out high school football jerseys for the uniform of a soldier for generations.

Then I remembered that Alphabet hadn't played high school football. He'd been on the debate team.

"Sure is, Alphabet," I lied. "All relationships go through rough patches. What matters more than anything is honesty. All that other stuff? Just static."

"Roger that. Want some water to wash those down?"

"Gracias."

I popped the pills and drank the entirety of Alphabet's canteen because he said it was okay. It tasted lukewarm like bathwater and had sand bits in it that slid down my throat and into my stomach. I was waiting for Alphabet to leave the room, but he lingered at the bunk. I wasn't sure if he wanted to talk more about his fiancée.

"Something else on your mind?"

"Was just wondering," he said. "Why'd you join the army?"

"Huh." It was a strange question from a soldier. Civilians back home asked it all the time, and I'd learned the stock set of responses to keep them and their fixed notions at bay. College money. Participate in history. Because someone had to. All were true, but none answered the actual question. "Lots of reasons, I guess. What about you?"

"To be part of something." Alphabet looked ready for the front of a cereal box, he seemed so damn serious. While I was touched by my soldier's earnestness, alarms began ringing in my head. Purists broken by the realities of life were capable of crazy things—especially ones with access to guns and bullets and fucking grenades. When he grinned to himself and shook his head, betraying some perspective, I praised God and then the other two parts of the Trinity for good measure.

"Kid stuff, you know?" he continued.

"That's good," I said, "You should be proud you were like that. Most people go through life never serving anything but themselves."

"Yeah."

I didn't know what else to say, so I said "Yeah" too. We'd had our moment and it'd passed. Alphabet left the room with his canteen, and I lay back down. I realized I'd never answered him about joining up, but that could wait. So could the calls home, and Marissa, and the goddamn war. It could all wait.

8

I visited other tribal leaders, but none would talk about Shaba or acknowledge they knew of him. I asked if any of their sons had been killed in the war, but they all said no. Haitham wouldn't pick up his phone, and we found his hut abandoned and empty. And the tension between Chambers and me simmered like a mortar round left in the sun too long. He resisted counterinsurgency-related missions and instructions, spending free time planning raids and training the joes accordingly. I responded by relaying orders through Sipe or the other squad leaders.

The morning of May Day, we passed under the stone arch and the image of the cleric. The sky was blue and clear. In the lead, my vehicle kicked up drapes of sand until we reached Route Madison and its pavement, paid for by the American taxpayer through a contract awarded to the local power tribe, the al-Badris. At least they finished this one, I thought. The water filtration project was still nothing but a collection of pipes and cement blocks on the banks of the canal. Local gossip claimed the Tamimi tribe was to be awarded that job, until they withdrew their offer after last-minute negotiations with the al-Badris.

Corruption, I thought, warm desert wind enveloping my face. Bribery. Gross waste of government funds. Perhaps Iraq understands democracy after all.

My heels ached after a week of foot patrols, two blisters filled with rich, cloudy pus. I'd pop them with a knife at Camp Independence, where twenty-four hours of hot showers, uninterrupted sleep, and non–Porta John shitting awaited.

We passed small groups of Iraqis walking the other way on the roadsides, toward Ashuriyah. Most seemed to be older men and women, though there were some children and teenagers in their ranks. The men all wore black *dishdasha*s and the women black burqas, while the kids dressed in an array of Western-style clothing, glowing bright like sequins against the pious robes of their elders.

I thought they were pilgrims going to the large Shi'a mosque in the north of town. It was Friday, the Muslim holy day.

"Not quite, sir," Hog said from the driver's hole. "The terps said it's to celebrate a battle Ali won back in the day. Shi'as love that dude."

"Yeah?" Dominguez's voice dripped with amusement. "Who'd he defeat?"

"Glad you asked," Hog said. I didn't need to see the wide smile on his face to know it was there. "She was important." He went on to tell us about Aisha, the Prophet's widow, and how her forces fought Ali at the Battle of the Camel, because of course it'd be called the Battle of the Camel.

"A woman went crazy after her man died, and started a war over it," Dominguez said. "She wasn't a chicana?"

A female voice filled our ears. "Emergency," it said, the words soft as fog but demanding. "Exit the vehicle immediately, exit the vehicle immediately."

Everyone laughed. Hog had pressed the emergency button on the control panel. Many of the joes swore that they'd track down the body that belonged to the voice, to marry her, no matter what she looked like, no matter how old. I wondered how much money and research had gone into determining that young soldiers responded to feminine persuasion.

A short, staccato cough of machine gun fire ripped across the desert. I felt my stomach clench up.

"That's straight ahead," I said.

"Roger," Dominguez said. "First platoon's at Checkpoint Thirty-Eight."

The radio raged hot. Officers as far north as the canal and as far east as the highway demanded to know what sort of battle had interrupted the war, and why. I turned off the radio and ordered the platoon to stop at the checkpoint.

We arrived two minutes later. The ramp dropped. A white car down the road lay like a squashed slug, strangely two-dimensional under the sun. Doc Cork and others jogged ahead to where a crowd of locals was gathering, but I stayed put to look at the car straight. A thin plume of smoke floated up from its engine. The car was between two orange cones used as checkpoint markers. Four other cars and a minibus had pulled off to the side of the road behind it, none having pushed past the first orange cone. Windshield shards glinted under the sunlight like daggers.

I walked past the other platoon's vehicles to the white car. At the driver's door, I leaned in through the open window and smelled iron. A heavyset man in a *dishdasha* sat back in his seat with a frozen glare. I'd seen the look before, on my mom, when we'd almost hit a deer on a mountain drive. Both his feet seemed to still be searching for the brake. Machine gun rounds had chewed through his body, leaving slabs of ill-cut flesh and human sludge. As I peered closer, I saw that the right side of his chest had been separated from the rest of him, held together by licorice sticks of entrails.

I wanted to think he hadn't suffered, but that wasn't really possible. I figured him to be about Chambers' age, in his early thirties, which wasn't old but probably older in Iraq than it was in America. On the other side of the car, sprawled across the passenger seat and the center console, was a smaller man of similar age and dress. He had jug ears and a furry soul patch, and a cluster of large, red polka dots perforated the right side of his body. He must've turned to his side at the last second in an effort to shield himself.

A group of first platoon soldiers arrived, pulling out the passenger's body by the core. A stream of blood began pouring out over the center console. The soldiers groaned. I left them to their task, walking back down the road.

The gunner of the lead Stryker was still in the turret, shoulders slumped, hands tucked into his ballistic vest. I called up at him, but he either couldn't hear me or didn't care to. I couldn't make out his face. Rather than continue to bother him—for what? I thought—I walked to the back of the vehicle, where I found their platoon leader standing on the downed ramp, finishing a radio call.

"Porter," he said. He took off his helmet with shaking hands. Small pockmarks covered his temples and cheeks. He took a swig of bottled water. "We are so fucked."

"*Shaku maku*, bro," I said, hoping the native greeting would both relax and ground him. "What happened?"

He told me they'd been at the checkpoint for seven hours, since before dawn. There hadn't been much traffic all morning, either foot or vehicle, just the steady drip to which we'd all been subjected. They'd been set to rotate back to the outpost an hour earlier, until higher had ordered them to stay indefinitely because battalion intelligence had determined that "military-age males might use the religious pilgrimage as cover to run guns into Ashuriyah in a white sedan."

"I asked if one of the targets was named Mohammed," he said. "They said to stop being a smartass and report back when we found something."

His platoon's dismount team had been finishing the search of another car when the white one appeared, moving quickly and traveling west. It hadn't slowed at the first orange cone.

"We're well into this," he said, his voice turning barbed. "They know the rules."

He'd been in the stone guard shack when he heard the gunner and the dismounts yelling for the car to stop. It'd all happened so fast. When the car neared the second orange cone, the gunner opened up with the machine gun, aiming for the engine. Those were the rules of engagement. The gunner had followed the rules of engagement. The platoon leader pulled out a laminated index card from his breast pocket to reinforce this point; all soldiers were supposed to carry one, as it came printed with the updated rules for when it was okay to shoot and when it wasn't, albeit in nebulous lawyer jargon that confused more than clarified. I patted my own breast pocket and found it empty. I must've left my card in the laundry again.

Except now it didn't matter that those had been the rules of engagement. It didn't matter that the car matched the description given to them by battalion intelligence. It only mattered that there hadn't been any guns or IED-making materials or even a switchblade in the car. It only mattered that there were now two dead hajji civilians and three injured hajji civilians and the company commander was furious because the battalion commander was furious because the brigade commander was furious and he was so fucked, they were all so fucked. One of the dead men's mothers was on the side of the road, and he couldn't bring himself to go over there.

He sat down on the ramp and bowed his head against balled fists.

"Sayonara Station," I muttered. "He was right."

"Huh?"

"Never mind. Don't worry about the crowd, man, I'll handle that. And don't worry about higher. I mean, these things happen. It'll be okay."

The void in his white, watery eyes told me he didn't believe me. As I walked toward the gathering crowd, I realized that I didn't believe myself, either.

About twenty Iraqis stood on the gravel, some of them pilgrims, others bystanders. Facing them was a group of first platoon soldiers tending to the wounded or the grieving. My men were helping. Doc Cork had his medical kit out; he was dressing the head wound of a gored Iraqi woman, telling her through Snoop to go to the hospital and yelling at Alphabet to find her bottled water. A *jundi* consoled a frightened boy squatting in the dirt. Chambers held back a pair of angry young men, skinny as thatch, who wanted to get to the white car on the road. Chambers told them to wait, and when they kept pressing forward, he squared his rifle like a pugil stick and pushed them back.

The mother was there, too, dressed in a cotton striped dress and a red head scarf, surrounded by consolers. She wailed in hot Arabic, thumping her chest and lifting her head skyward, as if wresting fault from above. She was short with wide shoulders, what my college friends would've called a Soviet plow, not that any of us had ever worked a farm. Trench-deep cracks in her face rose and fell through her skin. I got as close to her as the protective circle would allow—five feet or so—when an older man with a salt-and-pepper beard grabbed my forearm.

"*Fasil!*" he said, citrus on his breath and a large lip sore on his mouth. "*Fasil!*"

I looked at him with confusion and shook my arm free. He stared back with the hard, unblinking eye of poverty.

I took a step back. I'm no great Satan, I thought. He reached for my forearm again. I took another step back. He kept repeating the same word, so I turned to the soldiers and asked if anyone knew what he wanted.

"*Fasil*," Snoop called out. He and Sipe were dealing with other enraged locals farther down the roadside. "Blood moneys America owes their family. To make things good."

I pulled out my notepad and a pen, wrote down the outpost's phone number, and handed it to the man. Then I pantomimed calling a telephone. He nodded slow, as if trapped in a fever dream.

The crowd gradually dispersed. Alphabet ran up to say that the commander wanted us at Camp Independence, "Time now." The checkpoint was going to be crawling with field-grade officers soon. I patted Doc Cork on the shoulder as he packed up his medical kit and walked over to my platoon sergeant and terp.

"The driver was addicted to khat, according to one of his neighbors," Sipe said, lighting a cigarette. "Might explain why he kept driving."

"Khat is nothing," Snoop said. "Children chew it. He just made a stupid mistake. Arabs, yo."

I felt the distant pangs of a headache bearing down with the heat. The inside of my mouth was dry. I licked my chapped lips, shrugged, and began walking back to our vehicles.

"Another thing," Sipe said. I turned around. "Your man, Haitham. He was here, in the minibus. Got hit with shrapnel in the neck from a ricochet. He bounced, though, before we got on scene. Something spooked him. Other than the dead guys, it's all the Iraqis wanted to talk about."

I didn't know what to make of that, so I said nothing.

As we drove by the still-smoking white car, soldiers from first platoon were trying to pack the driver into a nylon body bag. Nearby, his two angry friends and the old man held the mother, still thumping her chest and wailing for answers. The soldiers zipped up the bag and carried it over to her.

So, I thought. That's what a dead civilian means.

9

We had a few hours free at Camp Independence while the maintenance team checked the Strykers. The platoon scattered, most of the joes heading to the chow hall to gawk at female support soldiers. Chambers said he was off "to dip my pen in company ink," which I presumed to be a reference to Sergeant Griffin.

I stopped at the shower trailer first. In a narrow fiberglass stall, behind a blue curtain covered with penguins, I washed away two weeks' worth of grime. The other stalls were occupied, too, so the hot water faded quickly as I popped the blisters on my feet. The forever glare of the dead driver had lingered, but I shook free of it, along with paranoid thoughts of the soldiers in Karbala who were electrocuted to death in a KBR shower trailer like this one. Then I shampooed my hair. It didn't take long, since Hog had given the entire platoon a buzz cut that morning. A few loose dark brown strands whirled around the shower's drain before disappearing into the underbelly of the trailer. So long and farewell, I thought. Thank you for your service.

After toweling off, I brushed my teeth and shaved. The body in the mirror looked strange. Dark circles ringed his eyes like a raccoon's. I called him Hotspur Six, and he called me the same. He looked younger than I remembered—something about the way his face collapsed in at the cheekbones and the way his chest concaved where finely tuned gym muscle used to be. I'd always thought experience was supposed to age people. He smiled toothily when I told him to, but I didn't think he meant it.

I changed back into my uniform and walked to the cybercafé, a sandblasted bungalow covered in satellite dishes. I took a seat at one of the desks, woke up the computer, and googled "Staff Sergeant Rios U.S. Army Ashuriyah Iraq."

Why did I care? Because getting rid of Chambers mattered. In only a couple of weeks, his presence was transforming my platoon. My brother was right: men like him were time bombs. Also, I was bored with paying off sheiks and teaching *jundi*s rifle discipline over and over again. I was intrigued by the idea of war, a real war, occurring in the same streets and mud huts I now called my own.

The death pitch in the Iraqi mother's cries probably had something to do with it, too.

The search led to an entry on iCasualties: "Staff Sergeant Elijah Rios—KIA, nonhostile event, near Baghdad, Iraq, April 4, 2006." An obituary from a small-town newspaper in Texas said that Rios had dropped out of community college after 9/11 and enlisted in the army, and was survived by a mother, Ninel, and a sister, Sarah. A variety of links led back to the same 2009 Associated Press story that outlined his family's struggle with the military bureaucracy to recover his full remains—"a small amount of tissue found on army equipment was positively identified through DNA testing as belonging to Rios, enough to classify him as Killed in Action," the story read.

It went on to quote Rios' mother: "My son is partially in the ground here, one or two inches maybe. But most of him is still over there. Just 'cause the Pentagon lists him as 'accounted for' doesn't make it true."

When I returned to the bay, the maintenance team had a message: the Big Man wanted to see me. "How wonderful," I said. The warrants just grunted and went back to the engines. They'd seen plenty of sarcastic lieutenants come and go. I turned around and walked up the long asphalt snake that led to battalion headquarters.

The walk was flat and drab. I poured canteen water onto the pavement, and it hissed in reply through the fierce triple-digit heat. I picked up some discarded flyers calling for participants in the Camp Independence softball league and stuffed them in my cargo pocket. Hog would appreciate this latest artifact of fobbit life.

Proof of the might of the military-industrial complex lay everywhere. Trailers lined the road with pickups in front of them, most marked with Halliburton decals. Other trailers advertised deals for new cars or cash advances for deployed soldiers. Beige tents and warehouses dotted the horizon like mole hills, every single one a KBR structure. The chow hall gleamed in the distance on the northern fringe of the camp, a sprawling ivory planet unto itself, ringed by Burger King, Taco Bell, and Pizza Hut stands. I wondered if I had time for a Whopper with cheese, but decided I didn't. Each step the other way deepened the craving, and soon all I wanted was a patty of cooked cow stuck between sloppy, gooey pieces of cheese and bun, but I was a military man, and military men put duty first and stomach second.

I walked by a group of soldiers roasting in the sun as they filled sandbags for a bunker. They were part of the base's work detail, a receptacle for malcontents and PTSD head cases. I asked some of them about their work. We were at least a mile away from the living quarters.

"For the contractors," they said. "In case of a mortar attack." They forgot to salute me, but I didn't care enough to correct them.

The air-conditioning in the operations center roared, and it took my eyes a couple of seconds to adjust to the dim green glare of laptops. I smelled warm cheeseburger coming from one of the workstations. My belly growled in resentment. An admin soldier grabbed my rifle, placed it in the weapons stand, and hurried me into the Big Man's waiting room. I knocked twice and entered.

The Big Man sat in a metal folding chair parallel to, rather than behind, his desk. The battalion flag hung over him limply, and the room smelled like burnt matches. Ever the linebacker, he motioned with his fist to sit across from him.

"I understand your platoon was the first to reach Checkpoint Thirty-Eight this morning."

"Yes, sir," I said, pulling up a chair. "Quite a scene."

"That's what happens when small-unit leaders lose focus," he said. The Big Man exhaled slowly through his nostrils, his lips pursed as if choking off an inner rage. My mom had grown up an admiral's daughter and said that senior officers functioned so that no truth could betray the myths, of either the past or the mind. It came with the rank, she believed, and it wasn't something they were able to leave at work. I wondered if some of that was going on with the Big Man now. How could more focus have slowed that white car or made the machine gun a precision weapon?

He directed a fist my way. "I'll be relieving both the platoon leader and the platoon sergeant, and that gunner—well, I'm not sure yet."

I sat up straight, clearing my throat. "From what I understand, sir, he followed the rules of engagement."

A pulsing neck artery and deep scowl suggested the Big Man felt otherwise.

"I understand you've been having some issues explaining the nuances of our mission to your platoon," he said.

"I have?"

"Sir."

"I have, sir?"

"Lieutenant, counterinsurgency is a complicated task. A thinking man's war. Requires care, restraint. An appreciation for the gray."

"Sir, I'm all about the gray," I said, grasping for a foothold on which to hoist myself back into his good graces.

The Big Man wasn't having it. His eyebrows rose like crucifixes until I stopped talking.

"We're the army, Lieutenant. We like blowing things up. For years, we've been trained that we're the hammer and every problem is a nail. That's not going to do it here. This is a guerrilla war. Where were you during the Invasion? I was in-country. You know what we learned?"

Another "Clear-Hold-Build" speech was coming. I'd memorized it long ago: Clear an area of insurgents. Hold that area to keep it clear, so the bad guys can't move back in. Build up the area with civil affairs projects and money and shit. So while the Big Man went on about battles I'd never heard of and soldiers I didn't know, I stared at a speck of dirt on his pink, bald head and thought about how unfair it was that Will, of all people, was free and blithe while I was stuck in this hellhole. He'd been so awkward in high school—all honors classes, cross-country races, and student newspapers. He actually came home his prom night, like an idiot. I'd been twelve at the time and stayed up playing *The Legend of Zelda*, telling our mom to lay off the cigarettes and go to bed. After he closed the front door quietly at midnight like a good boy, I met him in the kitchen and asked if he'd finally done it. When he told me to shut up because he didn't want to talk about it, I promised myself I'd never be like him.

The crimson flush in the Big Man's cheeks brought me back.

"You hearing me? We're replacing your platoon sergeant."

"Yes, sir. I mean, no, sir. I mean . . . wait, what, sir?"

"I'm a patient man, son, but you're testing it. I've received reports that your platoon needs a jolt. To refocus on the fight. I talked with Captain Vrettos, and in addition to replacing first platoon's leadership, we decided Sergeant First Class Sipe is burned out. He's been reassigned to operations staff. Which means you get a chance to start over with a new battle buddy and prove yourself more capable of the responsibility with which you've been charged."

"Who's my new platoon sergeant?"

"Staff Sergeant Chambers."

An anchor dropped through me.

"Sir, Staff Sergeant Chambers is not—"

"This isn't a democracy, Lieutenant Porter." He smiled and came over to my side, patting me on the back. "You'll learn a lot from him. He's a perfect match for you, and for Ashuriyah. Been over here before, you know. Very same place. The green machine loves itself some irony. Isn't irony something your generation appreciates?"

I stood up and mumbled a "Yes, sir."

"Surf's up, Lieutenant Porter."

I saluted and left the room to retrieve my rifle. Already at head-quarters, I made a quick detour to the civil affairs office. The cavern-ous trailer stunk of stale potato chips and freshly ripped ass. A dumpy, haggard-looking major was alone there, playing *StarCraft* online. It took five minutes to sign out twenty-five thousand dollars in stacks of hundreds, our company's Sahwa payment for the next month. I held my breath as I waited. The money fit into a black canvas backpack that the major had me sign out.

"We're responsible for those," he said. "Return it next time you're here, and I'll give back your hand receipt."

I thought about the Big Man's words, and the major's, too. In college, I'd learned about tragic irony and dramatic irony. But on the long walk back to the maintenance bay, I couldn't remember the difference.

10

The Big Man had asked where I'd been during the Invasion, though he hadn't waited for a response. I was glad for that. I'd been protesting it.

It was the month of my seventeenth birthday. Marissa and I weren't dating yet, but I'd asked her to prom ten weeks in advance to make sure no one beat me to it. After two years of riding the junior varsity bench, I hadn't made varsity basketball, so I went to games with friends and made fun of the guys who had. I was smart, but not as smart as I thought, and lazy, but not as lazy as I pretended to be.

I tried not to deal with the Global War on Terror, but it couldn't be helped, both at my mom's house and my dad's. Will had completed his officer training and joined his unit. He was going either to a war in the mountains or to a war in the desert, and neither parent could stop talking about how "real" it suddenly felt. Try as I might, I never felt the same.

My mom had always insisted we eat dinner at the table, but now angry television debates about weapons of mass destruction and yellowcake filled that time. I had to remind her to eat her whole meal, usually after she talked about how another pasty, overweight middle-aged man from the office had told her how much he respected her eldest son.

"Three or four?" I'd ask. My mom and I liked playing the Vietnam deferment game.

I hid out in my room and took the dog to the park a lot. Nothing about anything made sense, especially not my goofy older brother going to combat. He'd never shot a gun growing up. He'd never even liked G.I. Joe. His bedroom was as he'd left it, spartan clean with comics and baseball cards in the closet, but now there were framed diplomas from West Point and Ranger School on the wall.

I didn't go in there much. It reminded me of a tomb.

School proved a welcome refuge from world events, at least until a Friday government class in late winter. I walked in at the bell and took my seat, finding the whiteboard too late.

IRAQ: FOR OR AGAINST? it read. Usually I didn't mind class discussions, but this one felt different, like a threat.

People had opinions about Iraq, strong opinions. As discussion turned to argument, eyeballs began sneaking my way. Trapped in the back corner, I couldn't escape them, no matter how far into my seat I slid, no matter tightly I crossed my arms. A usually quiet baseball player said we had a responsibility to spread freedom. An always-loud student government rep said we had a responsibility to listen to the United Nations. That made the baseball player and his allies laugh. "Back-to-Back World War Champs!" someone shouted.

"What about the people who have to fight?" the student government rep said, her voice cutting through the laughter. While I didn't know her well, I knew she came from the other side of Granite Bay, the not-as-nice part. "Easy for us to joke, no one from here joins the military. No one from here will get hurt. Or . . ."

Now everyone in the class was looking at me, open-faced. Stupid Will, I thought. Why did he always need to be different? I didn't say anything, though. I just straightened my back and kept my arms crossed. Fuck these people, I thought. They deserve shit.

The teacher, a pasty middle-aged man old enough to not have three or four Vietnam deferments, called on me.

"Your brother," he said. "This must feel very real for you."

I stared blankly and thought about what to say, trying to figure out what the rising feeling in my chest was. I decided to be brave and say nothing at all.

The baseball player talked again. "Porter's brother is going to kill terrorists. How awesome is that? A freaking hero. Anyone who thinks different doesn't love this country. Protestors? Pussies, that's what my dad says."

"Jesus Christ." The words spat from my mouth like little arrowheads. "So dumb," I said. I'd always hated being told what to do, how to think, being pushed around for other people's means. It was probably why Chambers bothered me so much years later, and definitely why this guy did. No simpleton jock would use my brother's life to win a class debate. In those mad, dizzy seconds, I thought of my mom, I thought of my dad. They weren't pussies. They were the opposite, something I'd always known but only then understood.

"So dumb," I continued. "Being against war makes you un-American? Okay, Joe McCarthy. I'm proud of my brother. But he's glad people are protesting, even if he disagrees with them. 'Cause at least they're thinking."

That got me thrown against the lockers a week later by a group of outfielders, though no one threw a punch, because they didn't want to get suspended.

After class, the student government rep walked over as I packed up my things. "That was great, what you said."

"Thanks," I said.

"A group of us are going to Sacramento tomorrow morning," she said. "You should come."

"For what?" People didn't just go to Sacramento.

"For the largest protest in human history."

"Sounds dramatic."

"If you count everyone across the globe," she continued. "Kind of cheating."

When I told my mom I was going to Sacramento, she didn't say much, just asked if I had money for lunch and reminded me to layer.

There weren't as many people there as the newspapers would claim, but there were still a lot. It was more carnival than rally: there were bongo drums and cowbells, chants and synchronized dances. A group of college-age girls were naked except for yellow warning tape wrapped

around their bodies. We marched down 10th Street, past the state capi-
tol, to Cesar Chavez Plaza. There were a lot of peace signs made out of
Hula-hoops, chalk outlines of dead bodies, and at least four different
guys dressed as Jesus. It'd rained the night before, so it was cloudy and
damp, and some of the others bought overpriced sweatshirts that read
NO BLOOD FOR OIL because their moms hadn't reminded them to
layer. Street vendors sold puppets of the president and vice president,
and I thought about buying one for Marissa but I didn't know what her
politics were, or if she had any. We ate the Peace Rally Special for lunch,
a seven-dollar chicken club.

Eight of us had come from Granite Bay, making the thirty-minute
trip in someone's parents' Yukon. I knew everyone there, but not well;
they were older or more involved at school or both. I'd slept on the way
there, but couldn't do that while walking, so I made small talk with the
student government rep and her friend, the theater club vice president
who'd once filibustered a pep rally over the Cuban embargo. I asked
why she'd done that.

"You know," she said. "Do my part."

I nodded solemnly.

Once we got to the park, we crunched together like tinfoil to fit
everyone. A state senator gave a speech, followed by the star of a
mildly popular 1990s sitcom. They weren't the A-list protestors that
San Francisco got, but they were both good. It was hard to hear them
over a man in a Guy Fawkes mask who kept shouting "Liar!" anytime
a politician's name was mentioned, regardless of their stance on Iraq.
He even called Desmond Tutu a liar. To tune him out, I watched a
demonstration in the far distance, near the fountain, a group of men
lifting a coffin draped with flags: they'd carry it a few feet, set it down,
and do it again.

Those are vets, I realized, tipped off by their olive jackets and navy
mesh caps. Some were even pasty and overweight, though most were
angular and ragged. They weren't yelling about liars. They didn't seem
to be saying anything at all.

I watched the vets and their coffins for the rest of the rally. They slowed over the ensuing two hours but never stopped, cutting through the crowd like a piece of large driftwood. I was transfixed by the ceremony of their movements, by their commitment to one purpose. I romanticized each man's life story as I found his face: the ne'er-do-well from Oakland who was a medic in the Delta, the country kid from Auburn who learned to fly helicopters in the army, the rich boy from Napa who moved like a fucking jungle cat.

They're not here because things are simple, I thought, like everyone else is. They're here because things are complex.

Then the speeches ended, and the vets went one way and we went the other.

Back in the Yukon, people were excited, raw energy passing from person to person in a current. Sitting a row ahead of me, the student government rep asked what I thought. I said the Vietnam vets had impressed me greatly.

"Baby killers," her friend said, the filibustering one. "Guilt is why they do that. Guilt for the war crimes they were never punished for."

I waited for her to smile, to show she was joking. It never came. That bothered me. My uncle had served in Vietnam. So had a middle school history teacher. They were kind men. They hadn't been at My Lai. They weren't baby killers, and neither had my grandfathers been, in their war.

"Urban legends are funny things," I said. "You hear about the crazy girl who hijacked a pep rally? To rant about a country she's never been to?"

That earned some snickers from the group, but it also ended any hope for peace in the Yukon.

"At least they have an excuse," my adversary said, shifting in her seat to look at me properly. "They were drafted. They didn't volunteer to murder innocents."

Distantly, beyond the loud anger, I heard someone say that most Vietnam vets had volunteered, but the time for thoughtful discussion had passed. What mattered now weren't good points, or accurate points. What mattered now was victory.

We turned onto the highway, heading northeast. Back to suburbia, back to Granite Bay, back to lakeside summers and fireplace winters. I took a deep breath and rested my chin on a fist. Then I asked if she liked the song "Imagine."

"Of course," she said. "It's so powerful."

"Imagine no countries," I said.

"Yes," she said.

"Nothing to kill or die for," I said.

"Yes," she said.

"All the people living life in peace."

"Yes."

"Now," I said. "Imagine a worldview more nuanced than a three-minute pop song written by a stoned degenerate."

I knew next to nothing of Lennon's personal life, but damn if it didn't sound good coming off the tongue.

Things escalated from there. She called me glib. I called her shrill. She called me a warmonger. I called her a poser. She called me an asshole. I called her a bitch. She said that my brother had volunteered to kill babies, which made him a baby killer, which made me a baby-killer apologist.

In later years, I'd imagine myself responding with something smart, like "In a representative democracy, we're all complicit." Or "Your parents pay their taxes? They're as guilty as anyone." Or "Soldiers volunteer to serve their country. It's their country that decides where to send them." Instead I just said I wasn't going to listen to a goddamn moron who couldn't get into Chico State. Which was a silly thing to say, and not just because she'd matriculate at Reed in a few months.

We were both yelling, and the driver pulled over and said we needed to stop or get out. I did so without a word, though it was still surprising when the Yukon pulled away, leaving me with a mouthful of highway dust. I walked to the nearest exit and into a McDonald's for a milk shake. I was trying not to cry but couldn't help it, and the Hispanic kid behind the register gave me a large shake for free. I sat alone at a corner table until I calmed down, then I called my dad. He always made jokes about his protesting days, so it seemed better to call him.

When he arrived, we sat in quiet for a few minutes. The tears were gone, but I knew my eyes were still red.

"Tough day?" he eventually asked.

"Just dumb," I said. "All of it."

"Yeah," he said. "That can happen." Then he took me home and made his specialty, toasted peanut butter and banana sandwiches soaked in honey, and we watched an Eastwood movie.

11

The afternoon bloomed desert reds and desert golds. We waited at the front gate of the outpost for the two brothers to collect their blood money. They were late.

"Arabs," Snoop said, spitting out sunflower seed shells onto the dirt path, his voice filling the sticky May air. "Not like the Sudanese, Lieutenant Jack. We are a timely people. And consider-ate. Arabs make jokes about clocks not following time. Not even funny jokes."

The soldiers tasked to wait with us agreed with our young terp; it was my crew, two on the ground, one in the Humvee's turret behind a limp machine gun. They all looked as hot and bored as I felt, our body armor and helmets like shackles fixing us to the ground. We need to build that sentry shack, I thought, if not for safety, then for some goddamn shade. Without it, we had no choice but to wait in the open, blast walls behind us, fat sun above, the little town of Ashuriyah to our front.

"Chill, guys," I said, beads of dirty sweat running under my helmet and down my face. "Their cousin got shot for driving down the road. Funeral probably ran long, that's all."

"We didn't kill him," Alphabet said from the turret. He took a swig of bottled water before continuing. "First platoon did, trigger-happy cowboys. Who do they think they are, the SEALs?" Then he burped, loud and proud, wronged as only a young soldier pulling someone else's duty can be.

I agreed with him, but couldn't let him know that. So I told him to make himself useful and scan the two-story apartment buildings across the dirt road to our south. He grabbed the binos and stood on his tiptoes, his wide, blocky frame limiting his mobility.

"Empty and abandoned, sir," he said. "Like always. Staff Sergeant Chambers says the guards on the roof should scan those buildings, not us. He says we couldn't do anything from here even if we needed to."

I seethed. Escaping Chambers was impossible, like his shadow had been stapled to my heels. "I don't care what Sergeant Chambers told you," I eventually said. "I'm the platoon leader. Not him."

Another forty minutes passed in slow drips of sun. We killed time with great precision, skipping rocks and telling stories of home. Stories of girls, stories of late nights and foggy mornings, stories exaggerated and stories seared into outright lies. The desert heat bleached everything, including the minds and memories of its occupiers. Alphabet once drank a fifth of whiskey in an hour. Dominguez lost his virginity to a friend's aunt. Hog had cliff-dived into the Arkansas River from fifty feet up. Snoop knew a girl in Baghdad's Little Sudan neighborhood who said he had the biggest dick in all of Mesopotamia, and who was he to question her?

"Got any good stories, sir?" Hog asked.

"Hmm." I stroked my bare chin and considered. The frat boy in me wanted to participate. But the officer in me demanded I tread carefully. "Didn't party much in high school," I said. "But in college, I went to class in a SpongeBob bathrobe for a semester."

I patted my slung rifle for effect. The soldiers laughed. The younger guys liked hearing stories about college. It gave them something to look forward to after this, even the ones who knew they would never use their GI Bill funds.

The soldiers started talking about the platoon roast slated for that evening, before our night patrol—a rare scheduling blip, with no one on guard duty or out of the wire. One of the cooks had traded with a local storekeeper for a goat. I reminded them that I'd been invited, so any General Order No. 1 violations would have to be furtive. I laughed to let them know they could, too.

The sound of a car motor droned through the still, coming closer and echoing off the blast walls. My chest seized up, and my muscles went taut. I wasn't the only one: like figures in a diorama, we took our places, poised and alert.

We were what we pretended to be.

As the ranking enlisted man, Dominguez took the lead, walking through a maze of razor wire set across the dirt to impede car bombs. Hog followed, moving with more self-consciousness but less care. Alphabet rotated his turret from side to side, like a swivel, to remind the approaching car he was up there and so was the machine gun. I assumed my place behind the last strand of wire, shoulders cocked, back straight, head rigid, visualizing how the imperial officers of the past had stood when they bought peace for their country in strange lands far from home.

The car pulled up to the checkpoint, its driver idling the engine. Dominguez instructed both the driver and the passenger to get out. It was a blue sedan, similar in make to the one shot up by first platoon. The Iraqi brothers stood to the side, where Hog patted them down and then searched in and under the car. After the driver opened the trunk, Dominguez shouted a strident "All clear!" The soldiers and Iraqis began walking around the wire strands, and I went to the back of the Humvee for a black canvas backpack filled with stacks of hundred-dollar American bills, twenty-five hundred in total.

We called it condolence funds. They called it *fasil*. Blood money seemed most apt, though Captain Vrettos had freaked when I'd called it that the previous night. "That's cynical," he'd said. "We can't afford to be cynical right now." I'd wanted to argue that the army's distortion of language was far more cynical—"military-age male," for example, militarized any Iraqi with a penis between the ages twelve and sixty, whether a harmless shepherd or a zombie Zarqawi—but one look at the commander had suggested he wasn't interested in philosophical debate. For such a slender man, he could be quite intimidating; there was something feral about his unkempt hair and ever-thinning eyebrows. So I'd just said "Yes, sir" and left it alone.

We converged in front of the Humvee. I'd expected the brothers to arrive in traditional man-dresses because of the funeral, but both wore the uniform of the urban young man on the prowl: tight dress shirts open at the collar, pressed slacks, narrow pointed leather shoes that shined like sunspots. Both wore long, tidy mustaches and smelled of ginger; the one I presumed to be older had rolled up his sleeves to display a heavy gold watch, while the younger one kept thumbing prayer beads in the palm of his hand.

"Salaam Aleichem," I said, raising my right hand to my heart and cupping it.

The older Iraqi stared at me with hard, angry eyes, two black stones rolling across a flat berm of a face. Snoop chewed his lip while Dominguez waved the soldiers back to their positions at the gate. I looked past the brothers and up at the sun and reminded myself that I was the one with the gun.

It was the younger Iraqi who ended the standoff. "Salaam," he said, curtly.

I turned to him and spoke. "Snoop, tell these guys the money is all here. They can count it out on the hood of the Humvee. One will need to sign a contract stating receipt." Snoop nodded and started translating before I interrupted him. "They can't keep the backpack. Battalion needs it."

Snoop nodded again, pursing his lips and tapping his foot in the manner of a professional athlete feigning deference to a referee. I waited out their conversation, watching a large roach the color of sand shimmy across the ground. Then I remembered that Iraq didn't have roaches, and even if it did, they didn't have two claws and a raised trident for a tail. I took a step back while Snoop tried to smash the scorpion with his boot. It escaped under the tire of the Humvee.

"Fuck," Snoop said. "A *shaytan*."

I shivered in the heat. Getting blown into gut soup by a roadside bomb? I'd reconciled myself to that possibility. An unseen sniper's bullet eating my little eternity like a goat eats a can? I'd never know the difference. But the chance of a silent assassin in hard-shelled bug form lying in wait under my pillow or in one of my boots had proven a recurring panic. The things didn't even bleed. I looked back up at the Iraqis. The older brother was glowering, all flat-topped aggression, while the younger brother fiddled with a dead tooth in his mouth, eyes still hunting for the scorpion. Then the older one grabbed the contract from Snoop and signed it on his brother's back. While he did this, I noticed his signing hand had the pinky nail grown out. It gleamed in the light. He shoved the sheet of paper at me and barked at Snoop.

"He say . . . well, I not tell you. But their cousin was no ali baba, he say. He worked the date groves by the canal."

"And the part you didn't translate?"

Snoop sighed. "'To the eyes of Hell.' An Iraqi slur."

I nodded and stuck my hands in my pockets. My feet ached. So did my right collarbone, that old bane of a wound. An exoskeleton of sweat had formed under my body armor and uniform. No amount of water would end the drought in my throat. My men had already been out here for too many hours and wouldn't be relieved until this was over. In theory, I wanted to empathize with these men who'd lost a loved one to an ignorant, violent occupation they called the Collapse. In theory, I found the exchange of blood money by any name, in any culture, to be abhorrent. In theory, my memories of their dead cousin's sundered intestines and his wailing mother meant something more than just still-shot photographs soaked in gore. In theory, in an air-conditioned classroom I'd once sat in with great clarity and wrath, I would grasp and grapple for a solution that bridged this vast divide, because it was the right thing to do, because right things to do were worth grasping and grappling for, and not just in air-conditioned classrooms.

In practice, though, things were different. They just were.

"Insha'Allah," I said, back straight, shoulders cocked. I folded up the contract and stuck it into a cargo pocket. Then I walked to the outpost, leaving any regrets at the gate, discarded waste for strangers to take away in the dead of night.

At the entrance, I cleared my rifle and stuck my muzzle into the tin barrel, jerking the trigger with a quick squeeze. Click. No negligent discharge for me. The heat stayed at the door, a loyal ghoul that would await my return.

The foyer was cool and bracing. The air was tinted orange and filled with dust—no door could keep out the desert sand. Trudging up the stairs to the living quarters, I looked up at the fresco covering the wall. I blew a kiss at the Mother Hajj and told Pedo bin Laden to leave the children alone. Both stared back, unsmiling.

• • •

I needed to nap before our night patrol. The soldiers wanted to raid a house, but battalion intel had no houses to raid. Instead we were to escort the engineers as they filled potholes along the highway to the east. The field-grade officers referred to counterinsurgency as "a thinking man's war," which appealed to the left coast elitist in me, but deep down, I wondered how thoughtful using money as a weapon really was. It could get complicated, certainly, and messy, like downstairs at the gate. But thoughtful?

At a metal rack upstairs, in the hallway, I stripped away the apparatuses of war and hung them on hooks one at a time. There was a ritual to donning armor, deliberate and purposeful, like the warriors of old dressing for battle, but taking it off always seemed an exercise in frenzy. The helmet came off first, my scalp gasping for air; then the slung rifle; the knee pads that were really extra-large elbow pads because my matchstick legs couldn't hold real knee pads; the elbow pads that were in fact elbow pads; then the vest that held our extra rifle magazines and Jolly Ranchers. I ripped apart a set of Velcro straps at my sternum and lifted the body armor up and over my shoulders, a turtle escaping its shell, and set it on the tile floor. I'd shed sixty pounds of gear in ten or so seconds. Once I bent over and loosened the laces of my boots, I felt human again.

Our boxy, windowless room smelled of dirty mop water. Along the near wall, at the foot of the bunk I'd once shared with our old platoon sergeant, our new platoon sergeant was rifling through a cardboard box of books.

"The hell, Sergeant Chambers," I said. "Those are my things."

There was no response, so I repeated myself.

This time he looked over with slate-gray eyes and smiled. Bits of dark brown snuff covered his teeth. His tan, sweat-stained undershirt was tucked in, and flip-flops peeked out from the bottom of his uniform pants. He usually napped through the late afternoon.

"Lawrence of Arabia, sir?" he said, lifting a faded, dog-eared copy of *The Seven Pillars of Wisdom* I'd ordered online months earlier. "Self-aggrandizing bullshit. You should've gotten the abridged version. Saved yourself some time."

We were alone. He always managed to fill a room with his presence, each slight movement a little tremor of possibility. I'd never noticed it before, but his hands, large and ragged, shot out of his forearms rather than tapering in from them, like he didn't have wrists. I walked over to the box and pulled out another book, squaring my shoulders. Built like a piano, he had more than a few pounds on me, but I held a sizable height and reach advantage, if things came to that.

A puncher's chance, my brother would've said. *A fool's hope*, my mom would've replied.

"What about Che?" I asked, holding up a copy of *Guerrilla Warfare*. Its thinness flapped in the fan's wind. "*Viva la Revolución*?"

He snorted. "We offed that fuckstick in the Bolivian jungle. *La Revolución no viva*," he said.

These books were the only possessions in Iraq that I cared about. I wanted to tell him to stop challenging my authority all the damn time, not to mention stay out of my personal effects. But the moment necessitated restraint. He was the new platoon sergeant. I needed to work with him, at least until I could figure out a way to link him to the alleged kill team. A thinking man's war, indeed. I exhaled through gritted teeth, slow and sure, and smiled.

"It wasn't technically 'us,'" I said. "But true enough."

He set down the Lawrence book and walked across to his own bunk, six hollow-eyed skulls on the underside of his right arm swaying like voodoo on a string. After putting a large wad of dip into his mouth, he kneeled on the ground and pulled an olive-green trunk out from under his bed. After unlocking it, he reached in and grabbed a thick paperback.

"Want to read about insurgencies?" he said, tossing it to me. "Don't read their own mythologies. It's all propaganda. Read that," he said, pointing to the book I'd caught. "That's how an empire deals with the barbarians."

"Huh." It was Caesar's *Conquest of Gaul*. "Didn't know you were such a reader. But Caesar didn't write propaganda? 'Course he did."

He snorted again and slurred through the dip nestled in his cheeks. "Try this one, too," he said, throwing *The Confessions of Saint Augustine* in my direction. "If you're into that sort of thing."

He locked the trunk and slammed it back underneath his bunk. I pretended to study the back cover of his second book recommendation. I'd read it before. Parts of it, anyhow.

"Tell me, Lieutenant." I put down the book to find Chambers a foot away from me, looking up with those damn gray eyes. His chest rose and fell in slow breaths like hills, and he smelled of wet tobacco. "What do you think we're doing here?"

I studied a crack in the Sheetrock of the rear wall. "Making a fucked-up situation less fucked-up, I guess," I said. "You were over here when civil war seemed inevitable. The Surge pushed everyone back from the brink. We need to maintain that." Out of the corner of my eye, I saw his head tilting, wanting more—of what, I didn't know. "What about you?"

He forced a choked laugh. Then he blinked, finally. "I'm a simple cog in the machine. Just a door kicker lucky to have his high school diploma. Don't get paid to think."

"Well."

He started walking back to his bunk, but then turned around. "One more thing. We got to change the platoon name. Hotspur? That shit is amateur hour. We need something hard."

"I like Hotspur," I said. "It's got panache."

"Panache."

"Yep." I realized I'd been leaning back into my bunk's frame, arms crossed, copping the posture of a street hustler. I decided to be firm. "The name stays as long as I'm the platoon leader."

Chambers shrugged. "No worries. I'll be here for years after you leave. For three, four platoon leaders. It's all about the endgame. Don't they teach that at officer school?"

I grunted and told him I'd see him at the roast later. Unable to find sanctuary in my own room, I spent the next hour in a part of the outpost I was rather unfamiliar with: the small gym across from the terps' room. Dumbbells didn't provide answers, but they did provide purpose.

• • •

I walked outside to the back patio. Night was near, the mating call of beetles just shrill enough to rise above the nearby generators that powered the outpost. Four wood picnic tables sat on a concrete slab, each squad assigned a table, forty men in sweat-starched uniforms ready to eat. I saw Chambers at one of the far tables, so I took a seat at the nearest one, next to Doc Cork.

"Welcome to family dinner, sir," Hog said, across from us. "Smell that meat? I heard it's 'cause one of the cooks is old friends with Sergeant Chambers. Celebrating his promotion."

I turned to watch the goat rotate over the burn pit. It was plump, moving in slow revolutions, like a clock without a minute hand. Two joes stood at each end of the goat, turning it with a steel rod held up by stakes. Burn pits were used for all sorts of refuse, from classified documents to used batteries, but it seemed suitable for roasting local cuisine, too. Cotton candy smoke billowed from the pit, drifting west.

After waiting for the soldiers to cycle through the food line, I grabbed a plastic tray and heaped mashed potatoes, macaroni and cheese, and deviled eggs onto it, skipping the salad bowl. One of the cooks put chunks of tender, pink goat meat on my plate. It smelled of heavy pepper. In theory, I detested the military-industrial complex that made things like fresh deviled eggs in the desert possible. It was wasteful. It was excessive. It further separated us from the townspeople we'd been charged with protecting. That was all true. In practice, though, indulgence filled stomachs, and included ice cream for dessert.

The goat proved too chewy. Most of the soldiers around me ate with abandon, though, like some unseen, angry parent would emerge to punish them if they didn't clean their plates. I ate slower, stopping when I got full, pushing around what remained on the plate so it looked like I'd eaten more than I had. My stomach had always been a bit of a princess. I washed the meal down with a cold can of Rip It, flat fruit punch with a special jolt that'd keep me awake for the night patrol.

As I ate, I listened to the soldiers argue about whom they'd rather have sex with, Jessica Alba circa 2006 or Shakira circa 2008. I declared myself team Alba. Doc Cork said both of them were too skinny, he needed a woman with some meat on her, a thick ass, too, which sent the table into hysterics. Each of the tables hummed with similar banter; we rarely got together as an entire platoon anymore, and never at the outpost. Once dinner ended, I stood up on the bench and clapped my hands.

"Hotspur!" I said. "Settle down. Want to say it's great to be together in the same place since . . . well, Kuwait. Two more things: third and fourth squad, we still have that engineer escort tonight. Also, join me in recognizing our new platoon sergeant. Congratulations, Staff Sergeant Chambers. We're all looking forward to working with you in your new position."

After the applause faded out, the men began chanting, "Speech! Speech!" Chambers grinned, tucking his overbite behind his lower teeth, and waited them out. A dim sky now hung over us, with only red lens flashlights and the blaze from the pit illuminating the area. Someone tended to the fire with lighter fluid, swelling the flames wide and red. Chambers moved in front of the pit to speak. Because of the slight incline of the hill, and the way the flames danced shadows up and down his silhouette, he seemed a pastor delivering a dark sermon. The pealing cadence in his voice reinforced it. Wayward souls, these soldiers were, but not beyond his redemption. Not yet.

"I want to tell you all a story. A war story," he said. "Listen to it. Learn from it. The best soldier—the best man—I ever knew was a noncom named Elijah Rios. We deployed here together, a couple years ago. He was bona fide, a real warrior. I owe everything to him. He saved my life."

His eyes moved from man to man in slow consideration.

"Before we left, we thought we were steel. But even those of us who'd deployed before didn't know what hard was. Not yet. Our platoon sergeant, he had an idea. Kept saying it wouldn't be like the Invasion, or Afghanistan. That the war had changed, evolved. Kept calling us youngbloods, to try and get us focused. We thought it was a big joke. Ha fucking ha.

"He was right, though. Things were raw. Got hit every day. Daisy-chain IEDs. Snipers. Even a female suicide bomber once. This was before the generals bought off the insurgency. Before the sheiks turned on al-Qaeda. It was everyone against everyone, and everyone against us.

"Got intel one night that an al-Qaeda group had moved into a Shi'a neighborhood, going around and executing people. Trying to get everyone to vacate so Sunnis could move in. Didn't think much of it, was happening all over Iraq, on both sides. Just another mission, we thought.

"Didn't know the exact house they were in, just the block. So we sent the whole company. Set an inner cordon, outer cordon, whole nine yards. But anyone worth a fuck wanted to be kicking down doors, going house to house. That's where I was. That's where Elijah was.

"First eight or nine houses were all dry holes. Tenth house, everything went to shit. First room, we found a guy loading an RPG behind a couch. We shot him in the face, but then all his buddies knew we were there.

"That fatal funnel in doorways you hear about when you learn how to clear rooms? No fucking joke. Took three squads for that one house. Eight enemy spread across five rooms. Eight.

"Killed them all.

"Three wounded, one dead on our side.

"Should've just blown the house up with a tank round, but higher wouldn't clear it. Collateral damage, they said. So it was up to us. The grunts. The trigger pullers. The goddamn infantrymen. That's why we're here, gentlemen. To do what no one else can. What no one else will.

"Somehow, some way, we pushed our way upstairs. Couldn't make sense of anything, everything was too dark or too bright in the night vision. A grenade went off, couldn't hear, neither.

"Three of us stacked outside one of the last rooms and reloaded. There was no door, and we could hear a voice on the other side, fucking with us. Say what you will about al-Qaeda, but they weren't cowards. Not the real ones.

"I went in first and saw a flash of light, of movement, in a corner. So I turned that way. I shot twice, and glass exploded everywhere, falling to the ground. Shots came from behind at the same time. All I could think was, Fuck. I'd been had.

"The bastard had set up a mirror so I'd go that way, chasing his reflection. He had a clean shot at the back of my skull. If the guy behind me hadn't recognized that, I'd be dead. If the guy behind me hadn't pulled his trigger faster than hajj pulled his, I'd be dead.

"That guy was Elijah.

"I didn't know what to say. I think I sputtered out thanks or some shit. He just looked at me and nodded. 'I got you, youngblood,' he said. 'I got you.'"

I no longer heard the beetles or the generators, and neither did anyone else. My right leg twitched and twitched and I swallowed loud, looking around to see if anyone had heard me. Chambers continued.

"Elijah had a philosophy he lived by. *De Oppresso Liber*. Anyone hear that before?"

Even if someone had, no one spoke.

"Means 'Liberate the Oppressed.' It's the motto of the Green Berets. Elijah planned on joining them after our tour. He didn't just say it, either. Had it tattooed on his chest. He fucking meant it. He fucking lived it."

Someone in the shadows shouted, "Preach," which was echoed a few times. Chambers pressed on.

"Some of the squad leaders and team leaders here know what I'm talking about. They saw it, too. Humvees swallowed in fire, bodies liquefied by metal and heat, all because of a wrong turn or a gunner not spotting a wire fast enough."

The sound of helicopters, attack birds, moving from Camp Independence sliced through the night. Rather than let them interrupt his benediction, Chambers raised his hands, palms up, and absorbed them into it, the rotors his very own monk chants. It all seemed quite natural, somehow. It really did.

"Hear that?" he shouted over the WHOOSH WHOOSH WHOOSH of the blades. "Savage. That's what this is all about. Staying alert. Staying ready. Staying vigilant. They're gonna get some before they get got." He took a deep breath and closed his eyes as the birds flew south, toward Baghdad. His head drooped down. Seconds passed in a shrouded hush. Then one of the joes up front quietly asked what'd happened to Rios.

Chambers opened his eyes and smiled. His voice lowered, and I couldn't tell if he was betraying the quiet sort of rage that lingers within men after something vital, something matchless, breaks inside, or just faking the same.

"Dead," Chambers said. "Because he didn't stay vigilant. Even he— I'm telling this story to show it can happen to anyone if you let down your guard, even for a moment. Don't think that because the war seems over that it is. Right now, out there, men are plotting to kill you. To kill your friends. And like those birds, the only way we make sure that don't happen is to get some before they do. You hear me, Hotspur?"

"Hooah!" the platoon grunted in unison.

"I said, 'You fucking hear me?'"

"Hooah!" They were louder this time. Fiercer, too. I wasn't sure if he was done. Part of me hoped so.

Part of me didn't.

Something blossomed out of the dark near the pit. It crawled under the firelight, then down the hill, capturing Chambers' attention. He raised his boot and then thought otherwise.

"Get a cup," he said. "One of the large ones."

It was a camel spider. I'd seen them before—at a distance, though, not like this. Yellow with brown fur, it was thick like a cigarette pack. It kept poking its front pincers and gaping angry jaws at us as we passed around the cup. Some sort of insect blood, probably beetle, was splattered across its mouth like a child's art project.

"Men," Chambers said from the other side of the fire. "Heard some of you caught a scorpion at the front gate. True?"

I was about to answer that we'd just missed it when a voice beside me spoke. "Roger, Sergeant. Mean little fucker." It was Alphabet.

"He upstairs?"

Alphabet nodded.

"Bring him down," Chambers continued. "What better way to end the night than a prizefight?"

As Alphabet went inside, I sought out the gate guards from earlier. I found Hog first. He explained that after I'd left, the scorpion had reappeared from under the Humvee.

"One of the Iraqi brothers grabbed it," Hog said. "By the tail. Then we put it in a jar."

They set up a ring next to the bonfire, a cardboard box with its bottom pushed open. They dumped the camel spider in first, and it poked the walls of its new prison, all four corners and two square feet of it. Testosterone bogged the air, and red flashlights flitted over the ring like police sirens. I looked around and didn't see jaded boredom anymore but something else.

I wondered if I should stop the fight. I decided not to. I wondered if I should leave the fight. I didn't.

"No need to be queasy." Chambers spoke to me from across the ring. A red light shined up from a wristless fist onto his face. "Your man Lawrence did this. It's a proud tradition."

"All good." I grinned. "Who you got?"

"Scorpion," he said. He must've smelled the stink of easy money on me. "You thinking spider?"

"Everyone knows the scorpion always wins. I'm not that green."

He winked. "Guess not. How long you think the spider will last, then? I'm in a betting mood."

The soldiers crowded around us, shouting suggestions, picking sides. I studied the two combatants. The camel spider was at least twice as big as the scorpion. Besides, I reasoned, it'd take time for the scorpion's venom to seep into the spider's bloodstream, or whatever circulatory system spiders have.

"Two minutes," I said.

"I'll take the under," Chambers replied. "How's a hundred bones sound?"

I nodded. I had faith in the big ugly.

Most of the soldiers did not. I looked around and, intentional or not, nearly all of them had slid over to Chambers' side of the ring—and the scorpion's. Through the firelight, I spotted a friendly face.

"*Et tu*, medicine man?" I said.

"Sorry," Doc Cork said. "Like you said. Everyone knows the scorpion wins."

I nodded again and felt a hand on my shoulder. "We're with you, sir." I turned around and found Alphabet standing behind me, heavy Slavic gaze holding steady, with Hog next to him. "What's two minutes?"

Then he burped loud and proud, reeking of digested goat. I'd never loved another man more.

Dropped from its jar, the scorpion landed on its feet, and the camel spider went straight at it, jaws wide, fangs bared. Under a spotlight of red incandescence, the camel spider trying to pierce the scorpion's exoskeleton with its pincers, the scorpion bobbing and weaving to keep clear of the spider's bloody furnace of a mouth. The smaller creature was soon boxed into a corner, maintaining leverage due to a jagged pebble. I needed the spider to stop being so aggressive, but asking an arachnid to go guerrilla and outlast its opponent rather than murder it as soon as possible seemed pointless, so I just shook my fist and howled. Similar sounds emanated from around the ring. The camel spider sank its front pincers into the top of the scorpion's shell and began pulling it into its jaws, a long, slow death march. I howled again, something resembling the word "yes" rising from the wilds of my chest. The camel spider began gnawing on the scorpion's head. The arthropod held off ingestion by ramming its claws against the bulk of the spider and shoving, a sort of dark arts horizontal push-up. Then it raised its trident. My eyes snapped wide as the tail moved back and forth, to and fro. The spider stopped chewing, hypnotized. Like a black lightning bolt, the scorpion plunged its stinger down into the camel spider, straight through a bulbous eye. A horrifying rattle followed, something like a leaking balloon, and the camel spider collapsed on its belly, pincers out.

"Time?" someone asked.

"Eighty seconds," Doc Cork said, reading from the digital green of his wristwatch. "Team Scorpion wins."

I bellowed bitterly as Chambers and most of the platoon cheered and crowed.

"See, men," Chambers said. "That's what happens when you hesitate. A motherfucking stinger comes for your brain. Don't be that camel spider. Be the scorpion."

The scorpion freed itself from the dead spider's jaws and took a victory lap around the dirt ring, claws raised. I accepted Alphabet's offer of a cigarette, even though I didn't smoke. Chambers asked if I could pay him next time we made a run to Camp Independence, and I said yes. Then he used two cups to collect the scorpion and started walking to the perimeter gate. The soldiers protested, saying they wanted their prizefighter for future bouts.

"Keep a scorpion as a pet?" Chambers yelled behind him. "Do I look crazy?"

He tossed the scorpion, cup and all, over the gate and into the desert. Some of the men kept grumbling, but it'd been done. There was nothing left to do but search for a new contender, if they cared to.

I lingered at the burn pit for an hour. Soldiers drifted into the outpost two or three at a time, calling each other youngbloods, telling one another to "be the scorpion." Only Alphabet remained. Perhaps sensing my mood, he stayed quiet. I coughed my way through the first cigarette and then asked for another. As I watched the fire smolder into loose petals of ash, I couldn't shake the feeling that I'd just lost something important, something that mattered, even if it was just a pretense of that something.

I pulled an assault glove from a cargo pocket and picked up the spider from the ring, holding it in front of me. A thick, green jelly oozed from the hole in its eye.

"It thought it was tougher than it was," Alphabet said, walking close to study the carcass himself. "Tricked us into thinking that, too."

I tossed the camel spider into the burn pit.

The desert seemed still, placid. I spat onto the ground and tried to sound ironic.

"Insha'Allah," I said.

"Yeah," Alphabet said. "Something like that."

12

Snoop, I want to meet with Alia. How much for thirty minutes?"

"I thought you didn't do that." He looked at me like I'd disappointed him in some profound way.

I dismissed him with a wave of the hand. "Don't worry about that. How much?"

He tapped at his knee, seemingly hesitant to upset the delicate laws of the outpost's ecosystem. He was right, of course. Officers weren't supposed to ask for the cleaning woman.

"Just this once," I said. "No one will know."

"Forty dollars. No dinars."

"Set it up. And Snoop? I'm going to need you there."

He tilted his head to the side, then shrugged. "If you want. That costs double. But no gay freaky-freaky, okay?"

Two hours later, after explaining to Snoop exactly why he was needed there, we stood face-to-face with Alia in a town council office downstairs. Everything was taupe-colored, the carpet marred by a deep stain the shape of Wisconsin, the walls adorned by a small portrait of a long-dead mayor. Three electric lamps in need of dusting hung from the ceiling, giving the room a bright golden glow.

Alia didn't present herself as an exotic jezebel selling her body for profit; short, chubby, and dressed in a black *abaya* and head scarf, she just looked like someone trying to get by. She removed her veil, and I recognized the bags and wrinkles of a hard life. There was a coldness to her face. She was wearing perfume that smelled like a mixture of honeysuckle and kerosene. I gestured for her to join us at the rickety conference table, and, after some coaxing by Snoop, she did.

"Snoop, explain to her that she's not here for . . . sex." I took a deep breath and looked at the locked door. I'd never spoken to a prostitute before. "Tell her we need to discuss something."

"She wants to know if you still pay for time."

"Of course." I slid across two American twenties I'd gotten from a Camp Independence ATM. "Tell her she'll get more if she answers thoroughly."

Snoop crinkled his eyebrows in confusion.

"Good. She gets more money if she answers good."

"Ah."

Snooped conveyed the message and then signaled to me that she understood.

"I want to know about an American soldier named Rios," I said. "The Shaba."

She raised her chin, curious chestnut eyes meeting mine. I dropped my gaze to the concrete floor, my cheeks flushing from the intensity of her stare. When I looked back up, she wore a sad smile.

"He was a wonderful man," Snoop translated, matching the soft tone of her voice. "The best American to come to Ashuriyah."

"Why? What was so great about him?"

Snoop gave me her answer. "He was a true *habibi* to Iraqis. He wanted to help and gave all good people moneys, like teachers and storekeepers. Other Americans cared about certain Iraqis, but he cared for all of them. She say it's because he wanted to be one of them."

"How's that?"

"She say this is a dangerous topic, LT. She say she needs more to talk about Shaba."

I slid a ten across the table. It stayed there for a few seconds before she grabbed it with long, elegant fingers that seemed to belong to another body. Her eyes remained on the table.

"He wanted to be one of who?" I asked. "The Sunnis? Shi'as?"

While Snoop questioned Alia, I studied her face. She wasn't beautiful by any stretch of the imagination, but under the worn skin was a round, intelligent face made up with dabs of green eye shadow and a subtle blush. You could also tell she plucked her eyebrows—not a common practice for women in Ashuriyah. Also, she had pouty, bulging lips that could certainly do what Hog had said they did.

A whiff of perfume filled my nose, and to my dismay, the humblest beginnings of an erection stirred in my groin. My eyes opened wide and my cheeks flushed again and I scrunched my legs together, which made things worse. I looked at my boots and thought about cold water and basketball statistics and medical reports of soldiers coming down with the clap and—

"LT Jack? You hear me?"

"Sorry, man. Say that again."

"She say if Shaba didn't die, he would've desert-ed the American army and moved to Iraq. Is that possible? Or just crazy bitch talk?"

I wasn't yet sure, but it was something.

I continued, and began thumbing the beads on my bracelet. "I understand that Shaba was a great soldier, that he spoke Arabic and caught bad guys and brought peace here," I said. "But what can you tell me about the murder of a local when he was here? By American soldiers."

Snoop translated. She spoke. Snoop groaned. "Any talk of murder costs more, LT. She is running a swindle! I do not think you should give her more."

I slapped a five on the table. She didn't respond. I slapped a second five on the table. Snoop cursed under his breath. Alia nodded this time and slid the two bills off the table and into her chest. Something about her just then, the combination of an arched eyebrow and the faintest trace of a smile, suggested a guile I hadn't recognized before. A second later, it was gone, and she was just a cleaning woman with a sordid side business again.

"Who was murdered?" I asked.

She answered, but Snoop shot back in Arabic, his voice assuming a sharper edge than usual. She replied in turn, her voice measured. Then he barked a laugh and shook his head in disgust. "Lots of people, she say. This was a bad place a couple years ago. She needs more details from you, then maybe she can remember." Snoop faced me, lowering his voice. "LT, I don't know if she knows what you want, but it will take too much moneys to find out. Just my opine-ion."

We turned back to Alia, who watched us with her forehead slanted down, eyes straight and hawk-like. I decided I agreed with Snoop.

I cupped a palm and whispered to him: "Think she understands English?"

"Maybe," he whispered back. "She's smarter than I think before."

I took a swig of Rip It, and my right leg began to twitch. I tried to hold it in place with my hand, which only resulted in it slowing its tempo. What a world, I thought, turning the beads of my bracelet again. So much for the hooker with a heart of gold.

"Want to know why Shaba wished to move here?" Snoop asked. "That sounded important, maybe."

"Ask away." Perhaps I just need to get fired, I thought. Or quit. Let Chambers win. The staff lieutenants had a pretty nice life on Camp Independence. Hot showers. Steady meals. Air force females at the swimming pool. That was one of the good things about the military: they kept paying you whether you worked hard for it or not.

And leave my men in the charge of a fucking psychopath? I thought. Or leave Iraq without my Combat Infantryman Badge? Fuck that.

"LT? She say Shaba wished to stay for a beautiful woman. Rana, the only daughter of a powerful Sunni sheik. Shaba was supposed to marry her."

"How *Romeo and Juliet* of them," I said. "How does Alia know that?"

"She won't say. Which means more moneys. She did say that Shaba and Rana was a big Ashuriyah secret, even after he died." He sighed deeply. "That's how Arabs are. All feelings."

"How *did* Shaba die?" I asked. "And did it have anything to do with that murder I mentioned?"

Before Snoop could translate back to me, Alia raised her hands up and pantomimed a rifle, squeezing the trigger with her back fingers.

"Like anyone else in Iraq," Snoop said. "By the gun."

"You are one cunning lady," I said. She stared back vacantly. "She remember Chambers?"

"No. All American army men look the same to her, except the black ones. For more moneys, she will tell the whole story of Shaba and Rana. She thinks you would like to hear it. But it's a long one."

"I'm sure it is." A twitch in my temple started up, complementing the one in my leg. I had only five dollars left, and I remembered what Will had taught me about gambling once: know when to walk away. I slid over the last bill and told her to stay quiet about our meeting.

"Al-ways," she said in strained English, clasping her hands and bowing her head.

I was already in the doorway when Snoop called after me.

"LT? She wishes to know why you kept playing with your bracelet during the meeting. She asks if it's special."

I spun around quickly, like a dancer. The two of them had risen from the table, and while Snoop's face was lit with interest, Alia's remained fixed on the ground.

"Nothing like that," I said. "Just something to do."

It took a lot of resolve not to slam the door behind me.

13

Captain Vrettos went to Camp Independence that evening for a meeting. His patrol left a little after dusk. I forced myself to wait ten minutes and then walked across the outpost to dig through the files in his room.

I looked in at the command post first. The TV was on, a ragtag, rebellious police squad discussing how to bring down a mighty drug ring. The pulse in my neck felt like a giant's steps, but none of the guys on duty seemed to notice. All they cared about was the television screen. I backed across the empty hallway to the commander's room, trying to look natural.

A Master Lock held the door fast. Captain Vrettos was a bit of a paranoiac, always demanding the corner seat, asking if his name had been mentioned in gatherings he missed. I figured it had something to do with the brutality of his first deployment to Samarra, or the whispers about his "alternative lifestyle" back home. Regardless, he'd shared the number combo with the company officers in case of emergency.

I doubted this met his definition, but it met mine.

Dank and cluttered, the room resembled an opium den as much as it did the headquarters of a military commander. Maps of Iraq and Ashuriyah covered part of the gray Sheetrock walls; the rest was swathed in dirty uniforms, undershirts, and two woodland camo ponchos on hooks. A Rod Stewart poster from a 1992 concert in Berlin hung over the corner bed, a green cot with an orthopedic pillow and a poncho liner bunched together. The sandbagged window let nothing in; the only light came from a desk lamp that made Rod's feathered yellow mullet gleam.

"Christ, sir," I said. "No wonder you're grumpy all the time."

I turned to the steel desk at the foot of Captain Vrettos' cot. During planning sessions, he'd pointed to the filing cabinets and complained about the backlog. Our outpost had been established in 2004 and every unit rotating home left junk for its replacement to sift through: intel reports, promotion and award packets, vehicle manifests, et cetera. After seven years, that junk had piled up. Some of us had suggested destroying it all, but Captain Vrettos had said no, for fear of throwing away something higher might request. So the backlog remained, our own company adding to its annals daily.

In one of the cabinets, somewhere in the paper mines, I hoped to find a nugget about Rios or the dead local or something—anything— that would rid me of Chambers. His sermon after the goat roast had stuck with me, and though I didn't understand the dark thoughts it'd filled me with, I knew I didn't like them.

It was slow going, especially when I got to the spreadsheets. I'd never been mistaken for a patient man, and avoiding file cabinets was one of the reasons I'd joined the army to begin with. My pulse eased, but the nerves stayed. What if the commander came back early? What if one of the soldiers noticed the open lock? What if Chambers went looking for me?

Two and a half hours after breaking in, I checked my watch. The commander's patrol would be back in an hour or so. My eyes ached and my head swam slowly, like a goldfish. Hundreds of folders and papers surrounded me in haphazard piles I'd failed to keep organized. Other than a 2008 investigation into a lieutenant pocketing funds intended for local business grants, I'd found nothing of note.

I fought off quitting one more time and reached into the back of a new cabinet pocket, pulling out a stack of manila folders. Most were filled with equipment inventories stamped with First Cav unit designators. Near the bottom of the stack was a thin, cream-colored folder labeled "Fumble Recovery." Three typed sworn statements slid out, all from the spring of 2006. Two were xeroxed copies, while the third was smudged with dirt and had been folded in half. Rios' name was sprinkled throughout each.

"Here we go," I said.

"Hotspur Six." My body went rigid. I hadn't expected a response.

I was fucked. Done for. Caught red-handed snooping through my commander's room. How hadn't I heard Captain Vrettos come in? I put my hands up like I'd seen meth addicts do on television, stood up, and turned around to face my fate.

"Hotspur Six, do you copy?"

There was no one else in the room.

My mental bearings snapped into place. I was still alone. Captain Vrettos was still at Camp Independence. The voice was coming from the walkie-talkie clipped to my belt loop.

"Hotspur Six, this is Hotspur Six-Golf. You copy?" It was Dominguez.

I took a deep breath before answering. "This is Hotspur Six."

"There you are. You're needed at the front gate. Got a local here requesting to speak to an officer. I think."

With Captain Vrettos at Camp Independence, and the other platoon leaders on patrol, that left me. I folded the manila file in half and jammed it in a pocket.

"There in five. You copy, CP?"

"We copy, Hotspur Six."

"Send a runner to wake Snoop."

"Roger."

I cleaned my mess hastily, throwing piles of folders and papers into the desk. I uttered a silent prayer to whichever deity protected office interlopers, slung my rifle, and poked my head into the hallway. It was empty. I secured the lock and walked downstairs, ignoring the urge to turn around and put faces to the watchers I felt behind me, real or imagined.

• • •

The Arabian night was cool and blue. I circled our sandstone citadel, navigating the razor wire and blast walls that surrounded it in layers. Pale blinking lights in the distance helped guide me to the front gate, beacons courtesy of the few locals wealthy enough to purchase generators. The squat two-story buildings across the dirt road were about a hundred feet and a world away; the entire block was dark and abandoned, and had been since America made this place an edge of empire.

"It's the sir! Ain't it past your bedtime?"

"What's up, Hog." It was my crew on shift again, mostly: Hog, Dominguez, Alphabet, and a husky private from third platoon named Batule. They stood in front of a Humvee, machine gun barrel pointing up at the muddy stars.

"Tool, why aren't you out with your platoon?" I asked.

"Part of your platoon now," Batule said. "Swapped bunks this afternoon."

"Who authorized that?"

"The platoon sergeants, I guess."

Dominguez spoke, all monotony and undertone. "Platoon daddies talking trades. I'd expect more to come."

Another power play by Chambers, I thought. Even though senior enlisted managed personnel, they were supposed to run these things by their officers. It was a matter of decorum. I sized up Batule. Thick, dense, and prone to smashing things. Chambers' ideal, no doubt.

"Where's this hajj?" I said, more harshly than intended. "And where is Snoop? I don't have all night."

As if on cue, Haitham stumbled out of the black and into sight. The little man held a glass bottle and reeked of whiskey and filth. He wore an oversized soccer jersey, the green one of the Iraqi national team, and moved with a limp.

"The fuck you been?" I asked. "And what happened to your leg?"

"Molazim!"

He dropped his bottle, which met packed dirt with a thud, and grabbed my shoulders with both hands.

"Molazim!" he said. "Karim! Ali baba! *Okht!* Karim . . . keeel! *Shaytan* keeel Karim! Karim okht! Ali baba! *Okht!"*

His rotting teeth and hell breath were too much, so I pushed him off. Haitham's eyes bulged, and he collapsed to the ground, rocking himself back and forth, his head between his knees. I couldn't tell if he was talking to himself or crying.

"Mad sorry, yo!" Snoop ran out of the shadows wearing a do-rag and a fleece jacket, pulling up his basketball shorts as he made his way over. "They didn't tell me which gate."

"Talk to him," I said, pointing at Haitham. "Figure out what he wants. And say we're sorry we shot his nephew's goat."

As Snoop kneeled down next to a still-rocking Haitham, I walked over to Dominguez, who was leaning against the near side of the Humvee.

"This place never ceases to amaze me," I said, shaking my head.

Dominguez spat out a wad of dip. "Sir, can I tell you something?"

"Of course."

"You didn't hear it from me."

"*Está bien.* What is it?"

He scanned my face in the dark, and lowered his voice. "Staff Sergeant Chambers been pulling in the squad leaders, tweaking the rules of engagement."

"'Tweaking'?"

"You know what I mean."

"He can't do that. Captain Vrettos can't even do that. Those are set by the battalion commander."

"Lots of gray in those rules."

"Mmm." I paused and hoped it made me sound thoughtful. "Why you telling me this, Sergeant?"

The dip in his mouth slurred his words and puffed out his chipmunk cheeks. He spoke with memory rather than from it. "In Afghanistan, we got hit bad. Forty percent casualty rate. So we got trigger-happy. One day, during a firefight in the mountains, a little girl got killed. Shot through the forehead, brains everywhere. Worst thing I ever seen. Screaming mama, raging papa, a total shitshow. She was still holding a fucking dinosaur coloring book we'd handed out a couple of days before. No one knew who had done it, but we all blamed ourselves.

Could've been a Taliban round, but we were sure it was us. That day destroyed the unit in a way no enemy could." He spat out another wad of dip and started cleaning the remnants of snuff from his teeth. "Thought you should know."

This, I thought, this is why I need to get rid of Chambers.

I cleared my throat. "Maybe it's time to bring the guys together, do a refresher course on what we can and can't do. Wouldn't hurt anyone."

"Good idea, sir."

"Thanks. And, well. Thanks."

Rather than respond, Dominguez nodded to Snoop and Haitham, who were still behind us. I turned around.

"Haitham drank too much whiskey," Snoop said. "Talking like a crazy man. About ghosts and phantoms, the bad days in Ashuriyah."

"Before you came down, he was ranting about ali baba," I said. "And he mentioned *karim*. What's a *karim*?"

Haitham still had his face between his knees. The terp had to lean in to hear what the drunk said, but a few seconds later he had it.

"Karim is a person." Snoop's voice dropped to a strong whisper. "Karim was al-Qaeda. Dead now."

I felt an anger rising in my chest, red and hot like a fire poker. The looks of confusion on Alphabet's and Batule's faces didn't help. "Just find out why he's here, Snoop. Tell him if he doesn't get to the point, we're going to drop him off in the Shi'a part of town."

After a minute or so of rapid-fire Arabic, this: "Haitham wishes to go to Camp Bucca. He say jail is safer than Ashuriyah now."

"Snoop—"

The little man cut me off and pointed north, toward the ancient mosque.

"He say he will tell you everything, he swears by the shrine. But you must promise him Camp Bucca."

I'd heard enough. I wanted to read the sworn statements in my pocket and get to bed. "Tell him to come back tomorrow, sober. We'll sit down and talk then."

I started walking toward the outpost. Then came a low, singing pop, howling with consequence.

I dropped to the ground and waited for more fire. None came. I counted to three with my eyes shut tight. Some combination of angel and instinct induced me toward the Humvee for cover.

"Contact to the front!" Dominguez shouted. He'd dropped to one knee and held his rifle at the low ready. He swung his night vision goggles down from his helmet. "Anyone get eyes on?"

"Negative, Sergeant!" Hog said. He'd somehow made it up the Humvee's turret to the machine gun.

"Scan the rooftops and windows across the road, Hog—fucking sniper."

"Roger, Sergeant."

"Tool, report."

"Got nothing." He was somewhere in front of the vehicle, in the vicinity of the gate.

I was racking my brain for what the manuals said the platoon leader needed to do in situations like this. I drew a blank. "Snoop?" I asked into the air. "You okay?"

"Yeah, LT," he said from somewhere on the other side of the vehicle. "Haitham, too—he's with me."

That was when Alphabet started gurgling. He sounded like a broken sprinkler back home. But it wasn't anything that technical or complex. Just blood spilling out of a throat.

Dominguez shined a white light onto Alphabet. He'd been shot three feet in front of me and his legs were bucking, one at a time. Left, right. Left, right. Left, right.

"CP!" I shouted into my walkie-talkie. "This is Hotspur Six. Casualty at the front gate, a friendly! Request medevac immediately!"

The voice that came back was incredulous. "A casualty?"

"Yes, did I fucking stutter?"

A blur of barking orders rushed past me.

"Tool. Third platoon is on their way down. Take point and clear the buildings across the road. Fire at anything that fucking moves."

"Roger, Sergeant."

It was Chambers. He slung his rifle and grabbed Alphabet by a body armor strap, dragging him toward the blast walls.

"Hog, stay up there and provide cover. Fire at anything that fucking moves."

"Roger, Sergeant!"

"Dominguez. You and the terp help me with this. Sir, get a medic down here. Lieutenant Porter, that means you."

I still held the walkie-talkie in my hand, but my mind was stew, so it took me a second to process what I needed to do. Then I did it.

Chambers got Alphabet's body behind the barriers before anyone could catch up to them. A group of twenty hustling bodies and jangling gear emerged from the outpost. Third platoon. They followed Batule, bounding and covering into the black night. The mechanical swerving of Hog in the turret sounded like a garbage truck eating trash, and it reminded me that there was still a sniper out there. I ran behind the blast walls to check on my soldier.

Doc Cork was there. He'd managed to stop the bleeding with some gauze pads and adhesive tape. Both Snoop and Dominguez were on their knees, holding Alphabet's shoulders with one hand and his palms with the other. I asked Doc Cork if I could help, but he shook me off and stuck an IV into Alphabet's arm. I wasn't sure what to do with my hands, so I leaned down and stroked Alphabet's left calf.

You joined to be a part of something, I thought. I joined to believe in something. Not that different. Not the same, but not that different. I wish I'd told you that.

Then I told him that.

His body armor had been stripped and his breathing was low and labored and his legs weren't bucking anymore. Chambers ran up holding a litter, and he and Dominguez prepped Alphabet for movement to the landing zone while Doc Cork held the IV bag high.

I grabbed a litter handle to help carry it. It was lighter than I'd expected. The bird had a hard time landing in the field behind the outpost; it was whipping up too much dust. Chambers produced a pair of ChemLights from a cargo pocket and guided the pilot down. After the helicopter landed, collected Alphabet, and took off for Camp Independence, Chambers remained in the field. I walked over to him, kicked-up dust falling down on us in a dry rain. He was in his undershirt, tapping his arm tattoos with the ChemLights as if he wanted to inject neon into his bloodstream. The black skulls on his arm throbbed in the dark, little halos of fluorescent green.

"Smart thinking," I said, pointing to the sticks. "You might've saved him."

He looked back and smiled, his eyes dilating in the neon light.

"No," he said. "But I'm not going to lose another one like this. You know what the best way out of something is, Lieutenant?"

"What's that?"

"Through. The best way out is always through."

I shivered in the desert, alone.

14

SWORN STATEMENT

File number: 4z08

Place: CAMP INDEPENDENCE, IRAQ

Date: April 30, 2006

I, First Lieutenant Tyler L. Grant, make the following free and voluntary sworn statement to Major Edward P. Price, whom I know to be the Investigating Officer for the Command Investigation into the circumstances of the death of Saladin Jalal al-Badri on April 12, 2006. I make this statement of my own free will and without any threats made to me or promises extended.

I am currently assigned as the platoon leader to 2nd Platoon, Charlie Company, 2-48 Infantry Battalion, 1st Cavalry Division. I have been the platoon leader since September 7, 2005.

Our unit deployed to Iraq on July 1, 2005.

On the morning of April 12, my platoon was given the "kill or capture" mission of Saladin Jalal al-Badri, aka the "9 of Clubs" of our unit's target deck. Saladin was an alleged member of al-Qaeda in Iraq in the town of Ashuriyah. This mission was part of Operation Fumble Recovery, the search for my platoon's missing squad leader, Staff Sergeant Elijah Rios.

On April 12, at approximately 0100, our command post in Ashuriyah received a tip on Saladin's bed-down location. Captain Tisdale, the commander, assigned the mission to my platoon. We didn't have time for a full rehearsal, so as the soldiers prepped the Humvees, my squad leaders and I planned to have second squad raid the house while first and third squads formed an outside perimeter in case of runners.

I don't remember exactly when the platoon arrived at the target house, but I believe it to be around 0135. I ordered the platoon to have all weapons on "Red" status, aka locked and loaded, since battalion intel considered Saladin "armed and dangerous."

First and third squads formed the perimeter and second squad stacked against the house. No lights were on and there was only one door, in the front. I gave the order to raid the house.

There were two shots, and then a pause, followed by two more shots. I found out later that Corporal Daniel Chambers, a fireteam leader in second squad, fired both sets of "controlled pairs."

I don't know what the standard practice is for placement of fireteam leaders in room-clearing stacks. I don't micromanage, and leave decisions like that to my noncoms.

By the time I entered the house, all the rooms had been cleared. One military-age male lay in the center room, two shots in his chest and two in his forehead. The platoon medic declared him dead, and using the photo we had from our target deck, I identified him as Saladin, aka the "9 of Clubs." A loaded AK-47 rifle lay next to his body. I was informed that he raised it as my men entered the house, prompting Corporal Chambers to fire.

I don't remember which side of the body the AK-47 was on. I updated the outpost and oversaw intel collection. I had the soldiers take photos of the body and rifle, for evidence.

No other persons were found on the premises, and papers and computer equipment were collected for analysis.

I am not aware of the use of "drop weapons" and would have stopped their use immediately had such a thing been occurring in my platoon. Nor have I seen any convincing evidence of their use in my platoon, during the Saladin mission or before. I cannot explain why the AK-47 was first photographed without a clip and then photographed with a clip inserted into it, though it seems likely one of the men felt it important to clear the weapon for safety. I regularly brief my platoon on the rules of engagement and believe every soldier in my platoon understands and abides by them.

I never saw any of my soldiers with an AK-47 in their possession before or during this mission. The AK-47 recovered during the raid was turned over to battalion, along with the other evidence.

I never heard of any drop weapon allegation until the CID interview.

I have an open door policy. I don't think my soldiers are afraid to tell me what's going on in the platoon at their level. I don't think they would hesitate to come to me if things were going wrong. I visit their rooms at least once a day, sometimes twice. We have a good relationship.

NOTHING FOLLOWS

_____

_____

_____

_____

_____

INITIALS OF PERSON MAKING STATEMENT: TG

15

SWORN STATEMENT

File number: 7t45

Place: CAMP INDEPENDENCE, IRAQ

Date: April 30, 2006

I, Corporal Daniel R. Chambers, make the following free and voluntary sworn statement to <u>Major Edward P. Price</u>, whom I know to be
the Investigating Officer for the Command Investigation into the
circumstances of the death of Saladin Jalal al-Badri on April 12,
2006. I make this statement of my own free will and without any
threats made to me or promises extended.

I am currently assigned as alpha fireteam leader in 2nd Squad, 2nd
Platoon, Charlie Company, 2-48 Infantry Battalion, 1st Cavalry Division.

My platoon conducted a raid on a house of a known al-Qaeda
operative the morning of April 12. I served as point man for the
room-clearing team tasked with entering the target house. I always
serve as point on raids. I lead from the front.

Upon entering the target house and through my night vision, I saw a
shape in the main room. The shape looked like a man and it raised a
rifle toward me. I did not have time to yell to put the weapon down.
I fired two sets of controlled pairs on the shape's center mass. The
shape was the al-Qaeda operative.

I am aware of the practice of "drop weapons," though only as an example of something not to do. I have never witnessed their use, nor have I ever participated in such a practice.

I do not recall whether the AK-47 raised at me had a magazine in it. It was a judgment call made in the matter of seconds, and it followed the rules of engagement.

I do not recall if the AK-47 was wedged in the operative's left or right shoulder. I do not recall what side of the body the AK-47 was recovered from.

Before the raid, I was not aware of any connection between the targets Saladin al-Badri and Karim the Prince. I have learned since that they were cousins. From what I understand, Karim the Prince is suspected of kidnapping my squad leader, Staff Sergeant Rios, while the al-Qaeda operative this is about was uninvolved.

NOTHING FOLLOWS

_____

_____

_____

_____

_____

INITIALS OF PERSON MAKING STATEMENT <u>DC</u>

16

SWORN STATEMENT

File number: 5z30

Place: CAMP INDEPENDENCE, IRAQ

Date: May 2, 2006

I, Captain Kenneth D. Tisdale, make the following free and voluntary sworn statement to <u>Major Edward P. Price</u>, whom I know to be the Investigating Officer for the Command Investigation into the circumstances of the deaths of Saladin Jalal al-Badri on April 12, 2006, and Karim al-Badri on May 1, 2006. I make this statement of my own free will and without any threats made to me or promises extended.

I am currently assigned as the commander of Charlie Company, 2-48 Infantry Battalion, 1st Cavalry Division. I have been the commander since May 15, 2005.

Our unit deployed to Iraq on July 1, 2005.

On the morning of April 12, my company's second platoon was tasked with a "kill or capture" mission of Saladin al-Badri, aka the "9 of Clubs." They accomplished this and I have nominated the shooter, Corporal Daniel Chambers, for an Army Commendation Medal with Valor.

On the morning of May 1, my company's second platoon was tasked with a "kill or capture" mission of Karim al-Badri, aka the "Jack of Hearts," aka "Karim, Prince of al-Qaeda." They accomplished this and I have nominated the shooter, Lieutenant Ty Grant, for a Bronze Star Medal with Valor.

I chose second platoon for these missions because they are my best platoon at kinetic operations.

I do not know the name of the source that informed us about the bed-down location of Saladin al-Badri. I try not to micromanage my intel team.

The source who led us to the bed-down location of Karim al-Badri, known as "Haitham," works for Karim the Prince's father as a Sahwa militia shift leader.

Both Saladin al-Badri and Karim al-Badri were shot in accordance with "kill or capture" guidance from higher. Both men were armed and intended to fire upon friendlies. My soldiers followed all current rules of engagement.

The similarity between the outcomes of the two missions does not raise any concerns for me. Both men were known operatives of al-Qaeda. It's unsurprising that they would use similar tactics in dealing with US forces. Al-Qaeda routinely tries to take advantage of our rules of engagement, which they know almost as well as we do.

I am aware of, and took part in, the debate over whether the man shot on May 1 was indeed Karim the Prince. After investigation, we determined conclusively that it was him. Though no identification was found on the body, and brain matter obscured his face, a hooked nose and wire rim glasses matched the target's description. Further, the body measured 5 feet 6 inches tall and approximately 145 pounds in weight, also a match.

Two other men were detained on site and captured without incident.

They are presumed to be Karim's bodyguards, also affiliated with al-Qaeda, and were turned over to interrogators at Camp Bucca.

I'm not aware of the use of drop weapons, and have never had reason to suspect that such a practice was used by my company. The allegation was made three times, once for Saladin al-Badri, once for Karim al-Badri and once before, in January—each time anonymously. I took these allegations seriously, despite the lack of evidence. After careful review, I concluded that the utter lack of evidence suggested the allegations must have come from a disgruntled junior soldier. They have no bearing in reality.

I also want the record to show my company's successes since Staff Sergeant Rios went missing. Charlie Company has been the main element for all of Operation Fumble Recovery, a division mandate. We've detained 34 Sunni locals and 9 Shi'a locals during the operation and killed four enemy insurgents.

The fifth man who died was an elderly local. He died of a heart attack, not through the actions of my soldiers, who tried to resuscitate him. As per battalion policy, the family was offered condolence funds, which they accepted.

Though Staff Sergeant Rios' body has yet to be found, he is now classified as killed in action due to a tissue sample found on his recovered plate carrier. We will continue our search for his full remains so they may be sent home to his family. Though our relationship with Karim the Prince's father, Sheik Ahmed, and the Sunni Coalition of Ashuriyah have been negatively affected by these events, I consider the matter closed.

I also believe the matter of the drop weapons should be closed, as my understanding is that there's zero evidence. Unless the battalion commander recommends otherwise, I will keep second platoon's leadership in place. With only two months of our deployment left, it makes little sense to change things up in my most capable platoon. I won't punish them for doing their jobs.

NOTHING FOLLOWS

_____

_____

_____

_____

_____

INITIALS OF PERSON MAKING STATEMENT <u>KT</u>

BOOK II

17

The days of rage returned to Ashuriyah underneath a strawberry cream sky. Gunfire rolled across the town in a torrent, block by block, street by street, house by house. Shi'a gangs began calling themselves Jaish al-Mahdi again and fought among themselves for power, while Sunnis segmented into al-Qaeda, 1920 Revolution Brigade, and Jaish al-Rashideen and fought over control.

A generation of angry young men who knew nothing but strife, they all wanted establishment blood on their hands, like their dead fathers and missing brothers. That meant Sahwa blood. And *jundi* blood. And American blood. In between, they killed one another's families; we found the heads of three storekeepers in a ravine on one patrol alone. Their skin had been charred beyond recognition and their jaws hung open in everlong shock and their neck stems were roots to nowhere, smelling of smoke and maggots.

The Salah prayers echoed every dawn and dusk, carried in the desert wind. Civil service missions became movements to contact, presence patrols became raids. We shot bad guys dressed in black who multiplied into more bad guys dressed in black. Everything smelled like shit and hot trash, from the huts we raided to the sewer wadis we stepped into to the indolent blue streams where we found rockets in the banks. The locals huddled in kitchens and bedrooms during midnight raids, mere outlines of people in night vision green.

Late one morning, an artillery round hidden in the carcass of a camel exploded next to our vehicle. Our Stryker flipped onto its side and everyone lived, though Doc Cork and I got concussions and Dominguez spent hours getting camel guts off his face and vest. He didn't like talking about it.

Ortiz of second squad wasn't as lucky. The night of the D-Day anniversary, he looked up at a crescent moon and stepped on a dismounted IED buried in the dirt, which sent hundreds of metal ball bearings screaming through his ballistic vest and his doll body twisting through the air. Missing both legs and one arm, he suffocated to death in the sand because the metal balls had punched holes through his lungs. We had to pull Doc Cork off the corpse. He didn't cry, though some of us thought it would be good for him to.

Losing another soldier did something to me, too. Two things mattered now and only two things: honor and survival. Sometimes in that order, sometimes not.

"There's a beast in the heart of every fighting man," Chambers said to us under hooded eyes. "And it's time to embrace it."

"Embrace what?" I asked.

"Embrace it before it embraces you."

And like every fighting man before us, that's what we did, as the red coal sun turned the world to flames.

18

A *na Amreeki. Ayna taskun?"*

"Good, Lieutenant! And if the Iraqi you encounter is female?"

"Ayna . . . ayna taskuneen?"

"Jaeed!"

"Thanks, Snoop. *Shukran*, I mean."

He grinned. "Iraqis will be impressed. Americans that speak Arabic are . . . seal-a-brated?"

"Celebrated. Ce-le-brated."

"Yeah, that's what I say."

We sat in the terps' room by ourselves, he on a top bunk chewing on sunflower seeds, me on a plastic chair next to the television, an Arabic dictionary in my lap. The rotating fan in the corner blasted out hot breath. I checked my watch: we'd been at it for an hour.

In addition to improving my Arabic, these sessions with Snoop allowed me to avoid the unfinished paperwork in my room. Somewhere between the sniper and the IED attacks, everyone in the platoon had earned the Combat Infantryman Badge, which meant we'd "actively engaged the enemy in ground combat," which wasn't supposed to matter, but it did. It mattered a lot. It meant we'd finally been to war. I just needed to finish typing out the reports to prove it. And I would, as soon as I stopped associating the award we'd wanted so desperately with the two dead soldiers it had cost.

Snoop leaned over the top bunk. "Hey, LT? Can I ask a favor?"

"Shoot."

"I need a letter from an American officer saying I am a good interpreter, and an honest person." Snoop looked embarrassed, as if pushing himself to continue. "After the war, I hope to move to America. Letters from officers help get the right papers for this."

So the terp had dreams. "I'd be happy to," I said. "But I'm just a lieutenant. You should ask someone higher ranking, like the colonel."

Snoop smiled. "He already said yes. He said I should ask you, too, since we work together."

I remembered a news article I'd seen online about the arduous visa process for interpreters. "What happens if the papers don't go through right away? Back to the Sudan?"

"No." His frown enveloped the room. "War is there, too. It followed us here."

I hadn't known that about his homeland, and suddenly felt very small.

There was a quick knock at the door. A couple of inches too long, it opened with the sound of a popping jaw. It was Dominguez. Or his head, at least, freshly cut and shaved. Fuck, I thought. I knew I'd forgotten to do something.

"Sir? The service kicks off in fifteen. First Sergeant wants everyone there ten minutes early."

"We'll be right down."

Dominguez left, the door still ajar.

"Well," I said to Snoop, slapping my thighs as I rose, "let's do this."

He nodded, mumbling to himself in Arabic. It sounded like a prayer.

• • •

Ortiz's memorial service began with a company roll call. Four platoons abreast in the gravel courtyard behind the outpost, called to attention by First Sergeant's booming, brassy voice. The crushed pebbles under our boots simmered after another day of unrelenting heat. The sunset wore a thin ribbon of clouds like a garter, and a pale wind carried the flavor of sewer into my mouth.

"Batule!"

"Here, First Sergeant!"

"Butler!"

"Here, First Sergeant!"

I stood behind the platoon, Chambers in front of it, chest out and back straight as a date tree along the canal. I snuck a glance behind me at Captain Vrettos, rocking back and forth on the balls of his feet, anxious and exhausted as ever, his skeletal frame threatening to tip over. Behind him, in a formation of their own, were the terps. A couple tried to imitate the position of attention, but only Snoop had it right, shoulders square and heels together, toes pointed out at a forty-five-degree angle.

"Demo!"

"Here, First Sergeant!"

"Dominguez!"

"Here, First Sergeant!"

It'd been three weeks since I'd broken into the commander's room and Alphabet had been killed. This was our fourth service since that night. The first for Alphabet, whose fiancée found out about his death on Facebook hours before a military chaplain came to her door. The second for Mackay of headquarters platoon, after he turned himself into pink mist in a Porta John. The third for Reed and Dela Cruz of first platoon, whose Stryker rolled over a mine packed with a charge of eight hundred pounds of high explosive. The vehicle had gone poof into the stonewashed sky, and someone's small intestine knotted around a telephone wire. The wire was cut down to retrieve the intestine, much to the locals' displeasure, but it had been impossible to figure out whom the organ had belonged to. Reed? Dela Cruz? One of the survivors, sent home to a half life of amputated limbs and never-ending VA appointments? We'd guessed Reed, and included it in his pile.

"Lieutenant Fields!"

"Here, First Sergeant!"

"Gilotti!"

"Here, First Sergeant!"

No one else at the outpost knew about the sworn statements. I'd considered sharing them with Captain Vrettos, but he'd never get over the breaking and entering. Confronting Chambers about them seemed reckless. I'd toyed with the idea of confiding in Dominguez or Snoop, but knew neither could do much. I'd folded up the statements in my Lawrence of Arabia book, figuring that'd be the last place anyone would look, especially Chambers. Then I hid the book inside the trunk under my bed, which now had a metal lock of its own, because I now had secrets of my own.

Only Will knew. He was in the process of tracking down the two officers from First Cav, Grant and Tisdale. "It's a small army," my brother had said over the phone. "And a smaller officer corps. I'll find them. Then we'll make sure Mister Kill Team becomes someone else's problem."

He'd also repeated his suggestion about finding an Iraqi willing to write a statement about Chambers' actions in 2006. Alia had played dumb again, Haitham had disappeared again, and Fat Mukhtar had demanded to speak to the Big Man before writing anything about an American soldier. I'd backtracked immediately, telling Snoop to blame it on a translation error, something he'd sulked about for a couple of days.

In the meantime, Ashuriyah burned.

"Ibrahim!"

"Here, First Sergeant!"

"Janis!"

"Here, First Sergeant!"

It wasn't just Ashuriyah, either. All of greater Baghdad seemed trapped in the amber of violence. Sadr was threatening to lift the Mahdi Army cease-fire while the media aired reports about when the rest of Iraq would return to chaos, its inevitability not even a question. Rumors swirled that the generals at division believed our town was the catalyst for the resurgence of attacks, something that hung over Captain Vrettos like a gallows rope. PowerPoint slides and briefings now included terms like "containment" and "body counts," and not ironically. We weren't even supposed to call the outpost an outpost anymore, because of the Status of Forces Agreement with the Iraqi government; it'd been declared a "joint security station" to stay open.

"Ortiz!"

A balmy hush filled the courtyard. I resisted the urge to scratch my shoulder blade. A finch sang in the day but was not answered.

"Private Diego Ortiz!"

Someone in the ranks whimpered. The finch called again, still with no answer. Into the dusk dripped the smell of yesterday's blood.

"Private Diego Santiago Ortiz!"

The pale wind gasped. "He is no longer with us, First Sergeant," Chambers said. A three-volley salute of fire followed.

Crack.

Crack.

Crack.

There were no more birdcalls.

Time melted. A bugle sounded taps. The Big Man gave a speech about sacrifice and duty. My throat was dry and scratchy for want of water. We lined up one at a time to say our good-byes. A portrait of Ortiz leaned against a stack of sandbags, in front of a pair of his spare tan boots. His rifle was black and shiny, wiped cleaned of blood and sand, and mounted into the ground, muzzle down, with the bayonet fixed. A helmet sat on top of the rifle's buttstock and a set of stainless-steel dog tags was wrapped around the vertical grip. The tags read:

ORTIZ

DIEGO, S.

240-83-6230

O+

ROMAN CATHOLIC

I was last in line. For some reason, for no reason, for all reason. Hog finished ahead of me, whispering the words of the Lord's Prayer before walking away. The words "kingdom," "glory," and "power" cut through the air with Protestant severity. I wondered if Ortiz's family would appreciate a Cotton Belt Baptist's supplication for their son. It probably didn't matter.

I stared at the portrait. He looked older in the framed photograph than he had in person, his eyebrows more prominent, his chin fuller. The "Welcome to Iraq" speech I'd given him was the only meaningful conversation we'd had. He'd been a good soldier. That was what Dominguez said, anyhow. The burden of the moment felt like a boulder bearing down, and I wasn't sure if I was supposed to feel more or less guilty than I did. I stroked the corners of his dog tags and wondered why there were still rubber sound silencers on them.

"I'm sorry," I said. I tugged at the bracelet on my wrist, studying the pattern of the beads, red, green, yellow, red, green, yellow.

I started a Hail Mary, but stopped a few words in. I couldn't remember all of it. I saluted and took a few steps toward the outpost.

"You all right, sir?"

I turned around. First Sergeant had been behind me the entire time, his hulking frame a silhouette against the swelling purple sky.

"I'm good. Thanks, Top." I paused and tried to think of something worth saying. "We have a couple angels looking over us now, you know?"

First Sergeant's face remained stiff. "Yes, sir."

He grabbed Ortiz's rifle by the rail guards and asked if anyone in my platoon needed it. I shook my head and said we were good. He told me to take it anyhow.

19

That summer, I learned the fate of a college friend named Randy Chiu. He'd been a few years ahead of me in ROTC, a fraternity brother, and, having grown up in Irvine, he was another suburbanite exiled to rural Oregon. He'd deployed to Afghanistan, but it was all the same war because the same people were fighting it—on our side, at least.

Most of the cadet class of 2005 had signed contracts in the days and weeks after 9/11. Some claimed they did it for honor or patriotism, while others kept hidden dreams of battlefield glory. Not Chiu. No, Chiu signed his ROTC papers on September 10, 2001, after his parents told him they'd lost everything in a poor investment and couldn't afford a private liberal arts education anymore. The army could, though, and the recruiting officer was all too happy to bring in a cadet of Chiu's academic merit.

Whenever the timing of his ROTC contract signing came up, Chiu talked like his immigrant grandmother. "Wahhndy," he said, "you have wuck of wingless bird." Then, back in his own voice, he'd add, "Growing up, when she said that, I always just thought Grandma was a mean, cranky B-word. Turned out, she was right."

Of Taiwanese descent, Chiu was one of four minorities in our ROTC program, and the only Asian. Vietcong jokes were relentless. Chiu went along with them, often volunteering for the role of the enemy—the nefarious bad guys from our operations orders were always nationless and colorless—during field exercises in the woods behind the ROTC department.

"It's awesome being the bad guy." Chiu liked to brag about being a forest jihadi. "The cadre shows us where to attack, but never stays with us. Guaranteed nap, every time. Plus, one time I watched a soccer girl and a Sigma Chi hook up on a bench by the lake. They didn't think anyone could see them."

As fellow cadets, we learned to tolerate Chiu and his idiosyncrasies. Most of the cadre, though, as professional military men and women, didn't know what to do with him—he couldn't march, he couldn't shoot, and he couldn't help but turn every aspect of training into a circus. But Chiu could make people laugh, even adults, and that can take someone a long way. The only person Chiu could never crack was Sergeant First Class Miller. Sergeant Miller seemed to hate Chiu, which made sense, because Sergeant Miller hated everyone. A combat veteran of the famed Ranger Regiment, none of us could figure out how or why the Vein (a nickname we whispered behind his back, due to a huge blood vessel that bulged from his forehead) had been assigned to an ROTC unit in wartime.

The other cadre members were approachable and friendly, over-weight and nearing retirement. The Vein was rarely approachable, never friendly, and as far from being fat as he was from retiring. A fist of a man, he led our 6:00 a.m. physical training sessions on weekday mornings, loudly conducting exercise drills outside the dorm windows of oversleeping cadets until they joined us. No one dared defy Sergeant Miller, not unless one counted Chiu's detached perplexity as defiance.

We were more concerned about Chiu's relationship with the Vein than Chiu was. He simply attributed it to some sort of existential dif-ference. "We're just oil and water. Fire and ice. Military service and Young Republicans!"

Leadership labs occurred every other Thursday afternoon for three hours. The first twenty minutes were spent drawing dummy rifles, made of a hard synthetic rubber, from the arms room. Then we marched to the woods and executed various drills under the guidance of Sergeant Miller. One bright spring day, at the beginning of training, the Vein asked for volunteers to serve as the enemy ambushers. Chiu's hand shot into the air.

"Not today, Chiu," the Vein said. "Today you're going to learn some actual infantry tactics, whether you like it or not."

"A simple no would've worked," Chiu muttered. Three other cadets were selected.

Once the chosen enemy disappeared over a hill and into the forest to plot in secret, the Vein announced he'd be conducting a uniform inspection. Groans bounced from cadet to cadet like a pinball; uniform inspections meant uniform deficiencies, which in turn meant mass punishment.

Chiu, a frequent offender of uniform inspections, was third in line. We all held our breath as Chiu's canteens were tapped, but miraculously, both were filled with water. We all winced as the Vein pulled at the straps on Chiu's outdated flak vest and load-bearing equipment, but they held in place. The Vein straightened Chiu's patrol cap, then gave him a toothy sneer—the closest thing to a smile he ever offered any of us—while slapping him on the back. Chiu almost fell over, rocking forward on his tiptoes to catch his balance. But just as Sergeant Miller seemed ready to move to the next cadet, he lifted the bottom of Chiu's camo top to reveal a royal blue belt and shiny silver buckle. The groans returned. Army dress regulation called for a black fabric belt and a black buckle with field uniforms. Chiu instead wore a belt from a trendy surfwear company, and while we understood it was the only belt Chiu owned small enough for his narrow waist, Sergeant Miller did not.

"Titty fucking Christ, Chiu. Who do you think you are, a parade marine?"

"No, Sergeant," Chiu said, deadpan. "I'm Randy Chiu. ROTC cadet?"

The undertone in Chiu's response did not go unnoticed. "That's it, Iron Mikes for everyone. To the water tower and back, all thanks to Randy Chiu, eternal soup sandwich!" We did as told, some laughing, others cursing Chiu for his inability to right himself.

When we returned from the water tower, our young quadriceps burning like brush, the Vein gathered us together.

"Listen up, heroes," he said. "I know all this seems strange now. Like a game. But this is going to keep you alive in a couple years. Going to keep your platoons together. You'll be in charge of soldiers' lives. I can't impress the seriousness of that upon you enough. You will be in charge of people like me." He paused, wrapping his hands behind his back. "How's that make you feel?"

I didn't know about anyone else, but it made me feel lacking. I'd no idea how I'd ever lead men like Sergeant Miller to a meal, let alone in combat. They seemed born to another time, when practical skills like knowing which way north was and how to tie a hundred knots were something more than party tricks. Good thing the wars are almost over, I thought. Only the older cadets need to worry.

When no one answered him, the Vein called on the only hand raised.

"It makes me feel good," Chiu said. "Because if my sergeants in the real army are like you, they'll usually be right. Which means I'll make good decisions."

We tried not to laugh. The Vein held back for a few seconds, but couldn't help himself. " 'Usually'? " he asked.

Chiu just shrugged.

Two hours later, our squad lay motionless in a small depression in the woods, watching ants crawl over us. Bladders ached. Throats throbbed. Backs itched. But we couldn't move for fear of crunching sticks or pinecones that would give away the advancing squad, which had gone on assault while we stayed back as reinforcements. A discerning eye would've noticed the semicircle of rubber muzzles sticking out into the great beyond, but discerning eyes had better places to be.

"Don't. Move." A nasal voice whispered from the center of the depression. Nervous glances over our shoulders confirmed what our ears had told us: Sergeant Miller had walked into the middle of our defensive position.

"The other squad has been captured," he said, taking a knee. "Chiu is now your commander." Forgetting our security responsibilities, we turned to Chiu, whose face had turned to ash. "What now, Cadet Chiu?"

"We . . . we need to get our guys back?"

"Correct. And the enemy doesn't know you're here. They'll let their guard down. Believe it or not, you have the advantage."

With prodding, the Vein got Chiu to order us out of the depression and through the woods, in the direction of the lost squad. To Chiu's credit, he maintained control over our movements. By splitting us into two fireteams, one moving at a time, a sort of leapfrog motion developed. Minutes later, those of us in the front heard muffled voices.

Chiu crawled up to us, Sergeant Miller following. The voices got louder and louder, and between tree trunks and foliage we saw a short line of faux prisoners about a hundred feet away, the faded inside-out uniform of the enemy interlaced among them.

"Now's your chance," the Vein said. A man of action, he treasured opportunity above all else. His eyes were dancing with anticipation. "Initiate an assault, Chiu!"

The correct way to initiate an assault in modern war, or even pretend modern war, is to open fire with the primary weapons system, in this case, the rubber M249 light machine gun. The element of surprise maintained absolute precedence, as battles could begin and end in seconds. All the Vein wanted was for Chiu to give that order, so the cadet carrying the machine gun could yell, "RAT-TAT-TAT!" and then the rest of us would begin firing our rubber rifles in "BANG BANG BANG!" succession. Questions that tours in Iraq and Afghanistan taught us—like "Couldn't you potentially hit the prisoners?" and "Why didn't you radio higher for support?"—didn't exist in ROTC, nor did they cross our minds then. Nonetheless, what followed couldn't ever have been right, even in the pretend wilds behind the ROTC department.

Desperate to initiate the assault, Chiu picked up a large stick at his side and stood up, rifle in his other hand. Before the Vein could snatch him back down, Chiu pointed the stick in the direction of the prisoners' march and unleashed a raw scream, not a semblance of hesitation in his voice:

"CHAARRRGGGGGGGGGGGGGGGGGEEEEE!"

Chiu ran north, fireteams following, unsure of what else to do. Some began yelling themselves, and a bizarre mix of Rebel yells and howling filled the woods. First dismayed, then frightened by the voices and bodies coming their way, enemy and prisoner alike fled, eager to return to a world of power naps and stale beer. We followed, running with a child's delight we believed long ago shed, only to find that the advances of puberty and irony hadn't killed it off after all.

Chiu's Charge, though never again attempted and often derided, went down in the annals of university history. Sergeant Miller made no mention of it at physical training the next day. In the years after, though, Chiu swore the Vein flashed him another toothy sneer that morning. "Even he," Chiu told us, "recognized my tactical genius."

A week after his unit arrived to Afghanistan, Chiu was nearly killed in a mortar attack south of Kandahar. A round crashed through the roof of a housing trailer, carving a master sergeant in half. Shrapnel from the explosion cut through Chiu's upper leg, almost severing a major artery. Medics stabilized him, but not quickly enough to save the leg. A smaller piece of shrapnel cut off a chunk of his left ear, leaving him partially deaf.

In my stead, my brother visited Chiu at the hospital. A general had already come by and awarded Chiu his Purple Heart, something he'd taken to using as a bookmark for his robot romance novels. He seemed in good spirits, given the circumstances, and Will asked about old college stories to keep the mood light. One of the first tales my brother heard was Chiu's Charge.

"I never figured out what the right answer to that situation was," Chiu said after finishing the story, shaking his head. "Guess it doesn't matter now, does it?"

20

The joint part of the joint security station arrived the morning after Ortiz's service: twenty *jundis*, all wearing the baked chocolate chip uniform of the Iraqi Army. The change had to be done to maintain a permanent armed presence in Ashuriyah, something the town council had requested from Captain Vrettos, who had to clear it with the Big Man, who had to clear it with the brigade commander, who had to clear it with the division commander, who had to clear it with the Multi-National Force–Iraq commander, who had said yes.

They moved into the stale, dusty rooms of the first floor, to the fury of nearly everyone.

"Everyone in my fireteam is sleeping with one eye fucking open," Dominguez said.

"I'm gonna smell like camel jockey now," Batule said.

"I can't believe they're making us live with sand niggers," Snoop said.

"My men are as bothered as yours," Saif, their platoon leader, said. "As officers, we must lead by example."

I patted Dominguez on the back and told Batule to keep his mouth shut and had some of the black soldiers explain to Snoop the irony of his slur, but I hadn't known how to respond to the Iraqi platoon leader. During previous interactions, Saif hadn't revealed any hint of his fluency in English, the result of twelve years of tutoring with an uncle who'd once lived in Toronto.

"Before, I watched and learned," he said. He was nearly as tall as me and twice as wide. Though he was only in his late twenties, the stresses of war, combat helmets, and a young daughter had left his hair a black horseshoe. He maintained a trim mustache and couldn't understand why American infantry officers weren't supposed to grow one, since every culture but ours knew that mustaches and masculinity were intrinsically linked. "I've seen many Americans come and go. Your units all work differently from each other."

I asked what else he'd learned.

"For one, there is a difference between allies and partners. Allies do their own thing. Partners work together. For two, Americans have good hearts, but get impatient when they don't sleep enough." An eddy of cigarette smoke and yellow molars whirled up at me. "Especially young *molazims* far from home for the first time."

I laughed and accepted his invitation for a planning session over chai the following evening.

The two people whom I'd believed would be most distressed by the *jundi*s in the outpost didn't react the way I thought they would. Alia refused to answer Snoop's questions about how it affected her side business. And Chambers stressed to our soldiers that it meant progress in the greater mission.

"Appreciate you pretending for the guys," I said, after walking into his lecture in the joes' room. "Them bitching about it isn't going to change anything."

"I meant it, Lieutenant," he said. "Every word. I don't plan on coming back here. Anything that brings that closer to reality is fucking worth it."

Just because he said he meant it didn't mean I believed him. We donned our body armor together in silence, me groaning as the armor pressed down on my shoulder blades, him grunting as he velcroed his torso straps. He caught me staring at his strange, wristless hands, though he probably thought I'd been looking at the skull tattoos.

Downstairs, we passed Alia mopping the red-and-white tiles of the foyer. She kept her head bowed, serene as a church bell.

• • •

The June heat was grave. First and second squad stood near the clearing barrels, as did three of Saif's men. Snoop played Game Boy to the side, a black ski mask pulled over his face and bunched under his helmet. The brigade had mandated that terps weren't allowed to wear masks on patrols, but Captain Vrettos had turned a blind eye to it, leaving it up to the translators themselves. Since the sniper attack, Snoop hadn't gone outside without the mask. He said Jaish al-Mahdi was hunting him, in both Ashuriyah and the Sudanese neighborhood in Baghdad where his family lived. Without Captain Vrettos' relaxed policy, he swore he would already have quit.

I studied the crater-eyed faces in American uniforms. A few wore unauthorized patches of a dark scorpion where the Twenty-Fifth's lightning bolt should've been. Everyone called us the scorpion platoon now, even the commander, though I'd insisted on keeping the Hotspur call sign. Many of the soldiers were familiar, but some were not, a result of Chambers' platoon trades.

We had . . . six new soldiers? I wondered. Maybe seven. I needed to ask for an updated platoon roster. I thought of Ortiz and Alphabet and tried to form their faces out of the scattered shards of memory but could put together only parts of their portraits, which were different and wrong somehow.

"Gather 'round, killers. Snoop, turn off the game and translate for the *jundis*."

"Okay, LT."

"Today we're collecting info on Azhar, better known as Dead Tooth." I looked for a familiar face and found Washington, fresh from explaining sand niggers to Snoop. "Corporal W, what can you tell us about Dead Tooth?"

"He's got a dead tooth," Washington said, earning a few laughs. Satisfied, he continued. "Youngblood punk using his daddy's rifle."

Chambers' pet phrase coming out of my soldier's mouth irritated me, but I kept it to myself. I asked who Dead Tooth was aligned with.

"Al-Qaeda," Washington said. "At least he says that. Probably just a pretender."

As soon as battalion had sent a photograph of the new insurgent leader, I'd recognized the younger cousin who'd picked up his family's *fasil* payment in the spring. Same long face, same thin mustache, same brown, crooked teeth filling his mouth. Captain Vrettos had sighed deeply when I'd mentioned the history, then charged our platoon with capturing him because of my "superb diplomatic skills."

"Reports say he's been hiding around the Sunni Strip, in the northwest. Write this down, guys." I stopped for a beat before continuing. "That's where we're going. The mosque blocks."

"Fobbits got nothing else?" Chambers asked from the back. His voice had acid in it. "Why have an intel shop if they're only gonna tell us what we already know?"

"Above my pay grade," I said. "Let's focus on what we can control." I finished the patrol brief, reminding them that Dead Tooth was wanted in connection with the increase in IED attacks. After asking if there were any questions, I paused. I hated this part of the combat ritual. "Hotspur, you know the deal. Be the scorpion," I said.

"Be the scorpion!" they echoed.

We locked and loaded and filed to the front gate, Dominguez walking point yet again, zip cuffs dangling from his vest like a necklace of plastic ears. Another platoon's soldiers occupied the Humvee and sentry shack, a wigwam of ammo crates and sandbags. Some of the guys had wanted to name the shack after Alphabet, but it hadn't taken.

American soldiers pushed into the unknown once more. We moved with edge, adrenaline juicing our blood, a hyperconsciousness the civilized world could never replicate. If hajj was going to get any of us, he'd have to earn it. There would be no more shots in the dark on the unsuspecting. Over the past few weeks I'd grown proud of what we'd once considered routine. A platoon of infantrymen, young, silly, fierce men from the country and the ghettos, marching into the outposts of hell because no one else would. And I went with them. They'd proven themselves now that things mattered. More than anything, I needed to prove myself worthy of being their lieutenant. Their LT.

A storm brewed as we pushed west. The trash-strewn streets were empty save for dust cyclones spinning at corners like little orange pinwheels. Most Iraqis stayed in the shade during the cruel afternoons, but the storekeepers and porch denizens usually remained firm. Even they had fled the elements today. As we walked, Ashuriyah turned into a biblical van Gogh, the wind painting everything it touched in dizzy strokes of churning earth.

"Simoom season," Snoop said.

"What's that?" I asked, wiping dirt from my lenses.

"The poison wind."

As difficult a time as I was having staying vertical, our interpreter found it impossible. He had one of those angular, bony bodies that only looked natural leaning on something. Wobbling around with his crooked mask and a plastic rifle tucked under an elbow, he resembled a hungover bank robber. Batule, now the radioman, shook his head at our terp and laughed. I smiled and tapped Snoop lightly on the helmet.

We shifted north into the mosque blocks. A small high school building made of granite lay at the intersection. Closed for the summer, chains wrapped around its gate like a metal python, rust gnawing away at the padlock. Big blocks of spray paint covered the gate and parallel walls.

"Jaish al-Mahdi graffiti," Snoop said. "Telling young Shi'as to defend their homes and families."

We crossed through a long thistle meadow. The houses to the east were dilapidated clay mounds, but the ones to our west, nearer to the great mosque, were made of sun-dried brick and sported tall, spiked gates. Dark bullet scars marked the walls of both neighborhoods.

Halfway through the meadow, I stepped into a puddle of mud hidden by weeds, turning my tan boots the color of ground coffee.

"Watch your step," I told the soldier behind me. It was Ibrahim, one of the new guys Chambers had traded for. He had a reputation as a kiss-ass, but he'd been quiet and dependable with us, if not entirely self-motivated.

"How are things?" I asked. "Must be weird switching."

"Good, sir." He pushed a pair of army-issued glasses up the bridge of his nose, the type of chunky, plastic-rimmed lenses worn by hipsters in Brooklyn. "I'm enjoying the new start."

He walked tall but with the type of shiftlessness large men had when they'd never gotten used to their size. He seemed soft but considerate, and asked about my feet. I said they didn't blister anymore, they'd finally hardened, though I left out my daily moleskin and baby powder treatment. I remembered a conversation from months before, in a leadership meeting, and asked if he'd had trouble with his old platoon because of his religion.

"Kind of. But it wasn't because I'm Muslim. Some of the guys were always trying to get me to translate, but I don't speak Arabic. I mean, I'm from Buffalo."

There went my next question. It would've been nice to have another fluent speaker to practice with. I asked how he felt about Hotspur. He said things were fine. His team leader was Dominguez, so I trusted they were. Then he said he was thankful Staff Sergeant Chambers had intervened on his behalf. I wasn't so sure about that part. I told him to come see me if anything came up, and pushed forward in the formation.

We emerged from the meadow onto a yellow wedged avenue known as the Sunni Strip, running east–west and connecting two larger roads. Even the Iraqis didn't know how a pocket of Sunnis had come to settle in this part of Ashuriyah, so near the Shi'a mosque, so far from their larger enclaves in the south of town and the villages out west. During the sectarian wars, the area had been ground zero for local terror, complete with kidnappings, gang rapes, and a torture house where a medieval rack was recovered. Somehow, some way, the Sunni Strip had held. To the northwest, a mile away, the minaret tower loomed through the orange haze, spirals of stone crested by an Ottoman dome older than the flag on my shoulder. To the northeast, I could just make out the stone arch that served as both entry and exit to Ashuriyah.

Cypress trees scattered around the courtyards swayed to nature's will. All three dozen adobe homes on the Sunni Strip were new, a gift from the powerful Tamimi tribe and supposedly subsidized by the Iraqi parliament. Sahwa checkpoints marked both sides of the Strip, and I walked to the nearer one, where a black Land Rover with tinted windows was parked. My soldiers and the *jundi*s found security positions, taking knees next to cars and lying down in small depressions. Batule loped behind me, a radio strapped to his back like a green bullseye. Before I reached the checkpoint, a rear door of the Land Rover opened and there was Fat Mukhtar, arms wide, hands formed into plump peace signs.

"*Habibi!* Surf's up!"

Pressed against the Iraqi's mass in a hug, I felt his man boobs pushed against my chest plate. He pecked both cheeks, and I air-mouthed reciprocation. He wore a loud powder-blue tracksuit instead of a mandress, and his thatch of curls was stuffed under a checkered headdress of red and white. Aviator sunglasses and white sneakers completed the outfit.

"The hell?" I whispered to Snoop, who was getting the same treatment. "We're *habibi*s now?"

"He's showing off, yo," Snoop said, now released from the tribal leader's embrace. "Wants people to know he's close with an American officer."

"*Wasta*." I winked.

"*Wasta*."

Fat Mukhtar then tried to shadowbox with me, but stopped when I stood there and rubbed my helmet rather than play along. He was checking on his men, he said, as the Sunni leaders rotated responsibility for posting Sahwa on the Strip. What luck it was to bump into each other like this!

It was the first time we'd seen each other since the deaths of Alphabet and Ortiz. He expressed his condolences and assured me that his men were looking for the sniper. In a dark tone, he whispered something to Snoop, who asked him to repeat it with an air of disbelief.

"He say the sniper is a new terror man called 'the Cleric.'"

"Huh? The guy from the arch?"

"Not him. That cleric has been dead many years. The *mukhtar* is not sure if the Cleric is a real holy man, but that's the name he goes by."

The topic of conversation reminded me I should move around while in the open; between the trailing radioman and lengthy discussion, I was prime sniper bait. Now pacing, I thanked the *mukhtar* for the information and, in broken Arabic, explained that we wanted to know about Dead Tooth. He answered so furiously I was unable to understand, turning to Snoop for help.

It was true, he told us, Dead Tooth had been hanging around the Sunni Strip. But his own family had chased him away because he refused to recognize the authority of the *fasil*.

"Law is everything," Fat Mukhtar said. "And *fasil* is the ground of our law."

He advised us to look for Dead Tooth in the south of Ashuriyah, where the poorer Sunnis lived. "Or among the Rejectionists," he said. "Shi'as will hide anyone for moneys."

"Speaking of," Snoop said, "he asks about the next Sahwa payment."

Two teenage Sahwa guards in khaki on the far side of the vehicle began chanting *"Fuluus! Fuluus!"* until Fat Mukhtar yelled at them to turn back around. It was rather terrible theater, though I appreciated the effort.

"We'll call soon," I said. "Only a couple weeks more."

Fat Mukhtar tucked his neck into his chest, jowl pushing out, a sinkhole of excess skin. An odd way to express displeasure, I thought. He knew that Sahwa paydays were scheduled by the commander, at least until the Iraqi government took them over.

Something occurred to me. "You still want to be paid first, right?" I asked him. I let Snoop translate but didn't wait for an answer. "Azhar's family lives on the Strip? Take us there."

We walked a quarter of a mile to a two-story house with white trim and a balcony. Fat Mukhtar banged on the courtyard door while I waved over a fireteam. The storm had weakened, though the wind still proved too much for Snoop, who was now using his plastic rifle as a cane. A Sahwa guard who'd followed us pointed to the plastic rifle and laughed. Snoop barked back in Arabic. The guard pounded his chest twice before returning to the checkpoint. Snoop mumbled to himself and spat on the ground where the guard had stood.

Chambers emerged from the cloud of orange dust with Dominguez, Hog, and Ibrahim in tow. Though I wanted nothing more than to be rid of our platoon sergeant, I'd learned that including him in decisions minimized blowback. Chambers took in the balcony and sneered. "Comes from money. Interesting."

"Think we'll find anything?" Ibrahim asked.

"Nope," Chambers said. "But he's been here. Hard for rich kids to get away from Momma's tit."

We all laughed, even Dominguez.

"Almost forgot." I pointed to the *jundi*s, who'd huddled together under a nearby cypress tree. "Bring them, too."

Without a word, Dominguez walked over to the Iraqi soldiers, shaking the nearest one by the collar, and gestured for them to follow him. They did, though the one whose collar had been violated spoke with ire to Dominguez's back.

While Dominguez took the soldiers and *jundi*s into the house to search cabinets and upturn mattresses, Chambers, Snoop, and I met with the family and Fat Mukhtar in the courtyard. It made for a crowded space, and I kept having to push a fern out of my face to make eye contact with anyone. A man with cracked skin and a gray worm for a mustache glared at me while his wife, covered in an *abaya*, yelled at Snoop and wagged a finger in his face. Chambers stepped to the side to play with two girls and their Barbies, which were Arab in appearance and had various face veils as accessories. Then the woman turned her finger toward me. Even though the top of her head barely cleared my sternum, I took a step back and used the fern as a shield.

"We're being gentle!" I told Snoop, rifle slung, hands raised. A sniper on the Strip was hypothetical. This lady was not. I took off my lenses, helmet, and gloves and tried to look as boyish as possible. "Tell her that."

My charms had little effect. She kept yelling, and her husband kept glaring. Fat Mukhtar tried yelling back, which just angered her more.

"Azhar!" I said, trying another approach. "Azzzz-harrrr."

That flipped a switch. She bowed her head and spoke to Snoop. I strained to understand, but quickly gave up.

"What news do you bring of their son?" he translated.

Neither of us had much to share. The husband confirmed what Fat Mukhtar had said about their disowning Dead Tooth, though that decision seemed to be a source of marital tension. I asked about the older brother, and he said he was at his Sahwa post. He asked if Azhar was to be killed. I said capturing their son alive was our goal, so if they knew anything at all, it'd be wise to tell us. They said nothing. I asked how their dead cousin's mother was doing, remembering her wails and pleas. They said she was grieving, but Insha'Allah, she would find peace soon. The husband asked if we'd stay for chai after the search. Ibrahim appeared in the doorway, ducking under the frame. He asked me to follow him inside.

"Wait until you see this," he said.

We walked through a living room covered in sleeping mats and blankets; during the summer, Iraqis sleep in large, airy rooms or on the roof. A ceiling fan spun creakily from above. Over a kitchen of stainless steel, a staircase rose, angling into wooden beams that held the balcony. Upstairs, there was a small bureau in the hallway. Next to it hung a religious streamer, green with a yellow rim. On the bureau was a picture frame. I picked it up. Two Iraqi boys smiled for the camera, dirt field and palm trees behind them. They both had long faces and mop-tops, their resemblance to one another uncanny, arms draped around each other's shoulders to show they were good brothers. They wore matching jerseys, and the elder held a soccer ball. The younger stuck out his bottom row of teeth like a mule to show off a recently displaced tooth: Dead Tooth when he'd been Baby Tooth. I set down the photo and followed Ibrahim into a corner room that smelled of ammonia.

One step in, a smirking Dominguez handed me a placard. A crease ran down its center like a fault line. "A *jundi* found it," he said. "Folded up in the family Koran."

Opening it, I was greeted by an oversized face of an imam frothing orders. The artist had even added the spit coming from his mouth, which was a nice touch. The imam wore a white *dishdasha* and a black headband, and his chin fell off the image in a cascade of beard. Behind him, toy men in masks held rockets and guns, facing an unseen, encroaching enemy. A hollow sun marked the top of the placard, jagged Arabic slicing through it.

Back downstairs, Snoop explained that the face belonged to a Wahhabi, the most radical of Sunnis, who called on true Muslims to destroy Shi'a and American dogs alike.

"It doesn't say al-Qaeda on this," Snoop said, holding it up. "But it's theirs."

The family swore they'd no idea where the placard had come from. One of the little girls started crying when she saw it, and the husband insisted it must've been Azhar's. Without any way to disprove that, I left them the outpost's phone number, saying to call if they heard from their son and wanted him to live.

I put my helmet back on, then my gloves, then my lenses. As we turned to leave the courtyard, Dead Tooth's mother spoke, to no one and everyone at once. After a long silence, Snoop translated. "She say this is our fault," he said. "Azhar was a good boy before the Collapse."

•　•　•

We walked back into the simoom. I watched a dust cyclone of plastic bags whip around a pair of soldiers, who poked at it with their rifles. As we moved west down the Strip, I asked Fat Mukhtar why the family had been so hostile.

He shrugged and adjusted his headdress in the wind, a world-weary blueberry in a tracksuit.

"It's not easy seeing your country occupied by foreigners," Snoop translated. "The *mukhtar* has a good point."

I wanted to ask Fat Mukhtar about Shaba again, or if he knew anything about civilian murders in the past, but Chambers was only steps behind. The two men hadn't seemed to recognize each other, or have any interest in each other, for that matter. One had seen plenty of brawny American sergeants before, while the other had met plenty of outlandish Arab chieftains.

"Tell me how this ends," I muttered.

No one else knew, either.

Fat Mukhtar stopped at a tin shack. It bore the message YOUSEF'S: BEST FALAFEL IN ALL IRAK! in English on a doorway sign, a gift from some previous American unit. At Fat Mukhtar's suggestion, we ordered a late lunch. A young shop boy ran into the shack to deliver our order. While we waited, the *mukhtar* told us he was getting a bear from Syria for his zoo.

I laughed. "A bear in the Middle East? Sure."

"He say it's true, LT. The Syrian brown bear. A cousin of your grizzly."

I pulled out my pad and made a note to google this later, to prove Fat Mukhtar wrong. Bears didn't come from Syria. They needed trees.

The sense of being observed returned. I looked around. Inside the falafel shop, behind a thick screen door, stood an old man with crossed arms. I recognized him, but couldn't place from where, and that bothered me. I didn't forget people. I waved, long and wide. He waved back.

"Yousef," Fat Mukhtar said through Snoop. "Just a falafel man, but a good falafel man. Many morals."

A group of children delivered the falafels to our patrol. Soldiers and *jundi*s strewn across the Sunni Strip greeted the children with pats on the head and shiny coins as tips. My falafel was handed over by a girl in a purple head scarf who had black gemstones for eyes and a gaping red void for a nose. I looked closer and realized it was actually two red voids, one for each missing nostril. Burns covered much of her upper body. The skin on her arms was like paper, and when she cupped her hands to ask for a tip, I could see the bones in her fingers flexing. I pulled out a twenty-dollar bill and folded it into her tiny palms. Her smile burned through us all.

I swallowed away the lump in my throat while Fat Mukhtar bit his bottom lip. Only Snoop found words. "Allah protect her," he said. "If you're up there, fuckclown, You protect her."

I wasn't really hungry anymore, but forced myself to eat. The falafel tasted like desert—dry dough, chickpea, and tangy yogurt, all soaked in cucumber juice and olive oil. Fat Mukhtar said we should try Yousef's lamb, too, but through chewed food I said we needed to go.

"One more thing, LT," Snoop said, listening to Fat Mukhtar. "He asks about Haitham. He say they are old friends, and the *mukhtar* has a gift for him."

Before I could respond, another voice spoke behind us.

"Why do you talk to that guy so much? He's just a damn drunk. Always has been." It was Chambers. I didn't know how to answer either of them, so I did the most outrageous thing possible. I told the truth.

"We don't know," I said. "We don't know where Haitham is."

• • •

The patrol pushed south into Shi'a territory. The muezzin escorted us there, the afternoon prayer chanting gloomily at our backs. I had too much to think about, so I didn't think about any of it. The simoom found renewed life, blowing us kisses of hot sand and flying trash. I grabbed the hand mic from Batule's back and told the outpost we were heading in. As I hooked the mic back to the radio, the day ruptured in gunfire.

"Contact to the rear!"

I ran that way with Batule and Snoop on my heels, passing bodies in the prone behind whatever cover they could find, eyes and rifles out. At the tail of our staggered column, in front of an appliance store, I found Chambers standing over a body, bent slightly at the waist, legs on each side of the torso, a cage fighter about to finish off a dazed opponent. His rifle was slung.

"What happened?" I asked, trying to limit my panting. Washington and two *jundis* were there, too, all on one knee. Washington took a long, slow drink from his CamelBak tube. Hog stood to the side, his squished face bewildered, holding his rifle like it had soiled itself.

"Barbie Kid," Washington said, pointing to the mass underneath Chambers.

"Sergeant," I said. He didn't respond, and I noticed the dull shine of a *sai* dagger in his right hand. "Sergeant Chambers."

"Fucker just tried to stab me," he said. His voice was hard and flexing. He tossed away the dagger and straightened his back, moving his boot to the Barbie Kid's chest. He pushed down with his foot, evoking a sharp cry from his captive.

"Easy now," I said, walking next to the pair. "Talk me through this. Who was firing?"

"Hog," he said. He kept his face down, lensed eyes staring through the ground. "Shot out a window."

I looked across the street. Glass shards decorated the ground below an empty window frame.

"Negligent discharge," Washington said. "No good."

I looked at Hog, who shook his head and gripped his rifle tight. "I—I don't know what happened, sir. I heard shouting and I turned around, thinking it was Dead Tooth, and it just—it just happened."

"No one was hurt," I said. "Let's be thankful for that."

Underneath Chambers' boot, the Barbie Kid's unibrow bent up and down, his good eye darting wildly. His arms shook like twigs on a branch, and he gasped for air, still recovering from the boot stomp.

"How the hell did he get so close?" I asked.

"Ran up from behind," Chambers said. "I heard his steps and tossed him to the ground before he could take a swipe."

"Must still be mad about his goat," Washington offered.

While we pulled the Barbie Kid to his feet and zip-cuffed him, Chambers straightened his arms and balled his hands into fists over and over again. I looked up at the floaty orange dust. Back when I'd longed for excitement, sulky teenagers with self-designated nicknames and confusion over gender identity hadn't been what I'd imagined. Our grandfathers had pushed back the onslaught of fascism. Just what the fuck were we doing?

21

July 1 9:05 PM

Jack–

Grant is dead. Killed himself a couple years back. He tried to testify at Winter Soldier a few days before, but the organizers deemed him too unreliable. Who blows their brains out in their childhood home for their parents to find? Jesus.

A few of my classmates knew him from Fort Hood, said he was a good dude who never pulled it together post-deployment. Happens to a lot of guys, unfortunately. (We'll talk about that when you get back–being a leader doesn't end when the bullets stop flying.)

Enough preaching from me.

Found Tisdale–we have some mutual Facebook friends, but none are close enough for me to inquire about him. Got his email if you want to write him or something–KenDTisdale75@gmail.com.

Any luck finding a local to write a statement? I'm telling you, that's your ace in the hole.

Nothing really new here. In San Fran for that summer internship. So many hot women in this city, it's ridiculous. And my apartment is above a gourmet barbecue joint. I don't even know what that means, but it smells delicious.

Be safe, Jack. And be strong. Only a couple months left.

Will

P.S. CALL MOM AND DAD

P.P.S. Grant was born and raised in Twain country. Hannibal, Missouri. Thought you'd appreciate.

I stared at the screen in a trance. Grant was dead. By his own hand. I hadn't known the guy beyond a name on some papers, but still.

Maybe it was because his mud huts were now my mud huts. Maybe it was because he'd once been a junior officer overwhelmed by the ambiguities of the desert and I was now a junior officer overwhelmed by the ambiguities of the desert. Maybe it was the shared relationship with Chambers, or the vision of him trying to right his wrongs at Winter Soldier, seeking absolution.

Maybe it was just the day, the moment, the headache.

I promised myself I'd track down his family when I got home, the same way I would Alphabet's and Ortiz's. New Concord, Ohio. Hannibal, Missouri. Tucson, Arizona. I'd make a road trip of it.

We had internet at the outpost now, in a third-floor guest room formerly for embedded reporters. Journalists didn't come to Ashuriyah anymore. First Sergeant said they were all in Afghanistan. A green fly buzzed around my head. I waved it away, and it landed on the computer. Walls of plywood formed small cubbies, each soldier tucked into a station like a lunch box.

My watch said I was late. I refreshed my e-mail one last time, hoping for a note from Marissa. Still nothing, despite my last e-mail to her being titled S.O.S.! (JUST KIDDING). I'd wanted to know if she'd come visit Hawaii again when we redeployed. I resisted the urge to rip the bracelet from my wrist, and logged off. To calm down, I thought about partying with my brother in a city saturated with young women. It helped, a little bit.

The hallways were filled with the dissonant sounds of men at war. From the ancient, guttural cadence of bullshitting to the iron poetry of machine gun bolts slamming into place, I breathed it in and told myself to value it, to cherish it, that someday it would be moments like this I'd miss, even if the moment itself wasn't worth missing.

On the second floor, pockets of huddled soldiers mumbled greetings as I passed. I smiled back, cracking jokes and slapping backs, presenting the image of the blithe lieutenant because I thought they needed that. Free until the next morning, most of my sergeants were playing poker in our room. I'd been invited, but said I couldn't make it. I didn't like gambling with my men much anymore. It wasn't how I felt when I lost, either. It was how I felt when I won.

I turned down the stairwell and found Captain Vrettos coming up it, a poncho liner wrapped around his shoulders and head.

"Jack!" he said, grabbing my forearm with both his hands. "Was looking for you. About to start a movie. The new Civil War one."

His eyes were cracked and bloodshot. My eyes had been red like that before, back in high school when I'd smoked too much and needed Visine before I went home to face my mom's inquisition. Captain Vrettos looked like he could use some weed.

"Sir? You need to sleep. The runners will wake you if anything pops."

He shook his head, telling me he was fine, he could sleep when he was dead. After explaining that I had a meeting with Saif scheduled, I pressed once more, asking what the point of delegation was if not for sleep. He straightened the hunch in his back and said to remember my rank. I nodded and said I'd left Caesar's memoirs on his desk like he'd asked, in case he got bored with the movie. The Mother Hajj and Pedo bin Laden escorted me down the stairs. She was looking more despondent than I remembered; he, more manic.

The foyer was warm, and the evening air was wet. As I moved into the Iraqi Army quarters, I stroked my slung rifle. I had three full magazines in my cargo pockets. There had been a rash of green-on-blue attacks in the past month, all out of our sector, sudden moments when *jundi*s or Iraqi policemen turned their weapons on their Coalition allies. I wondered if I should have brought Tool or Dominguez with me, but figured it was too late.

A wine-red curtain spread across the entry of the first room in the hallway. I heard hip-hop blaring, so I knocked on the open door and poked my head inside.

"*Molazim* Saif?"

Four *jundi*s were watching MTV Middle East on the couch. I smelled dirty laundry and sour body odor. On the screen, an Egyptian clone of Notorious B.I.G. rapped in hoarse Arabic, pointing at the gold chains around his neck and to the luxury sedans behind him. The room was dingy, splashed with bright colors from the television. None of the Iraqis turned around, but one pointed silently to the room across the hall.

"*Shukran*," I said, and removed myself.

Saif was in the next room, a narrow nook he occupied alone. He wore a dull black undershirt shoved into cargo pants. Under the yellow ceiling light, the folds in his forehead were more pronounced, the clipped hair on the sides of his head highlighting the baldness on top. Built like a pear, he was somewhere between stocky and fat—Hog would've called him "country strong." His skin, darker than that of most of the local Iraqis, was the color of an old penny.

His quarters were sparse, the Sheetrock walls bare. Three pressed uniforms hung in his dresser, the Iraqi flag shoulder patches facing out, green Arabic scrawl darting and cold. Taped to the side of the dresser was a picture of his daughter, a bucktoothed girl with a sunflower in her ponytail. Below that was a hand-colored engraving of the Hanging Gardens of Babylon. A plastic trunk sat in a corner, locked, a rifle-cleaning kit on top of it. A pullout couch was in the adjacent corner. I accepted his invitation to sit across from him on the floor, my back against the near wall and legs out, his legs tucked under him and his back straight.

He began by chiding me for my tardiness. I told him I didn't think

Arabs cared about time. He laughed, shaking his head. I complimented his digs and asked if he ever got lonely.

"We are different, Loo-tenant Porter." I asked him how so. "We keep separate from the soldiers. Better for discipline." I waited for more. He pointed to my rifle. "A soldier's weapon, not an officer's weapon." He patted the semiautomatic pistol in its holster on his leg, the Glock's metal rattling.

"My M-Nine is upstairs." I didn't carry my pistol much, but felt it necessary to point out that I had one. "But yeah, we're big on equality. All for one, one for all sort of thing. Goes back to George Washington, I think."

"George Washington?" Saif raised an eyebrow. "One of your slave-owner presidents, yes?"

He stood to go brew the tea in his makeshift kitchen, a wooden counter mounted between his couch and dresser. He seemed embarrassed to be using an electric kettle, and spoke of how seriously his father took chai.

"Begin with springwater," he said, twisting the cap off a plastic water bottle. "Not tap, never distilled. The more oxygen your water has, the better the chai." He poured the contents of the bottle into the kettle and pressed a green button. The kettle rumbled to life as he sat down again.

We discussed how we'd become army officers. He'd originally become an Iraqi policeman to escape his family's rice farm south of Baghdad, near the banks of the Euphrates. He'd been at the police academy when the Invasion occurred.

Saif wanted to know about my childhood in California, refusing to believe I didn't surf. He scoffed when I suggested the suburban dream was decaying, telling me that American-style villages were all the rage in the affluent parts of northern Iraq. When I said I'd spent a college semester in Ireland, he asked how the Irish had dealt with their diaspora.

"We have the same problem now," he said. "All the minds have fled—the doctors, the politicians, the businessmen."

The kettle beeped to indicate the water had boiled. The *jundi* platoon leader kept talking as he rose to his feet again nimbly, a physics problem in action. He scooped Earl Grey tea leaves into a small teapot and cracked open two cardamom pods into the pot.

Though he'd been raised Shi'a, his grandfather on his mother's side was a Sunni, something that proved useful during the Surge, when the Iraqi government, desperate for diversity in the Shi'a-heavy army, offered bonuses and promotions to souls brave and stupid enough to make the jump.

"The ministries didn't actually want us to switch," he said, pouring the boiled water into the pot, shielding my view of the procedure as if it were some secret recipe. "They were under pressure from the American generals. The Shi'as controlled the national government for the first time, and wanted to keep control of the army and police. The Sunnis countered by creating the Sahwa gangs. So I used my grandfather's name as my own, and was sent to officer school and got more pay. My trainers didn't run me off, once they realized I was Shi'a like them."

"Higher didn't catch on?"

He loosed a cavalier smile. "I blamed the paperwork. It was one of my family names, so it wasn't hard."

Setting the teapot on top of the kettle, Saif resumed his seat across from me. "The leaves soak for ten minutes," he said. "Proper chai must be dark, with lots of sugar. Nothing like the Iranians make. That's not tea. It's water."

Pretending to understand what this brewing preference signified about Persian culture, I thought about how the only food or drink I could make was an orange cappuccino for my mom. I couldn't even cook, unless instant ramen counted. This seemed like hard evidence for our earlier discussion about the decay of suburbia, but I wasn't about to embarrass myself like that in front of a colleague.

"You've been quiet, Loo-tenant Porter." His head tilted in consideration.

I sighed. For weeks—months, really—I'd needed nothing more than a sounding board to salvage my sanity. Will could do only so much from across the sea, and Marissa was still unresponsive. But I barely knew Saif. I wanted to trust him. I really did.

"Tough day. My platoon sergeant almost got stabbed over a dead goat? I don't know. Maybe the heat's getting to me. And I just found out that a friend killed himself back in the States."

"Was he a soldier?"

"An officer. A young officer. Like us."

Saif leaned over and put his hands on my shoulders. "I mourn with you. The martyrs who fall after are still warriors. You will see him again."

I didn't know how to explain that I'd never met Grant, so I just said thank you.

We swapped information on Dead Tooth. He hadn't known about the shooting death of Azhar's cousin, but said it didn't surprise him. Excuses for stupidity were an insurgent's calling card, he said. He seemed skeptical of Fat Mukhtar's claim that Dead Tooth wasn't welcome on the Sunni Strip, saying that one of their sources had seen him there the night before. He called the Sahwa leaders ali babas, arguing that they were just armed thugs who'd filled the power vacuum created after the Invasion. That may be true, I said, but they're still our allies.

"Allies or partners?" he asked. "Big difference."

"Insha'Allah?" I was growing fond of the many meanings this one Arabic phrase provided.

The sweat underneath his pits had gathered into pools, and he plucked small hairs from his mustache, hiding the freed hairs in his palm. Dark, puffy circles hung under his eyes like speed bags. Everyone touched by war seemed aged or corroded in some way. Saif wasn't even thirty yet, but he had the calloused look of a man nearly twice as old.

"You hear anything about a new insurgent named the Cleric?" I asked. "Got a tip he was involved in the attack on my soldier last month."

"The Cleric?" he said. Seconds passed in warm, heavy silence. I realized belatedly there was no fan in the room. "A bad joke. The Cleric is dead."

Saif stood again and took four long steps to the chai. He placed two cubes of sugar in white teacups, pouring the tea from the pot over the sugar. He then stuck a small spoon in each cup and set a biscuit on each of the saucers.

"It's hot," he said. The chai was golden-brown, like wheat husk. I took a sip and bit my lip while my tongue simmered.

I was about to explain the tip, but Saif spoke first. "The Cleric was a powerful sheik in Ashuriyah some years ago, after the Collapse and al-Qaeda wars. He was a tribal leader, not a real cleric, but the towns-people called him that out of respect."

"The guy on the arch?" I asked. "With the beard?"

Saif nodded. "Yes. Sheik Ahmed."

"Ahmed." I closed my eyes and bowed my head, remembering the name from a First Cav statement. *Though our relationship with Karim the Prince's father, Sheik Ahmed, and the Sunni Coalition of Ashuriyah have been negatively affected* . . . "I've heard of him."

"He died of tuberculosis before I came to town as a police cadet. We did security for the funeral procession because his family wouldn't allow the Americans to come. He'd worked with them for many years, but it was his dying wish."

"Because they killed his son." The words tumbled out of my mouth like dominoes, and I took another sip of chai to mask my enthusiasm. Now cool enough to taste, it reminded me of warm Kool-Aid. "That's what I heard," I added. "An American kill team. Supposedly."

Saif waved off the rumors of past civilian murders, claiming every Iraqi town and village had them. "Propaganda from the militias," he called them. He said he'd heard of the sheik's al-Qaeda son, though he didn't recognize Karim's name. Nor did he seem to recognize Chambers, laughing off the notion that he was the same man who'd frightened locals in 2006.

"Just as all Iraqis look the same to your eyes," he said, "all Americans look the same to ours."

"You never heard anything about a kill team?" I asked again. I hadn't revealed that Chambers had admitted to being in Ashuriyah before, but something about Saif's dismissive laughs made me think he knew more than he was letting on. "What about a guy called Shaba?"

Saif raised a bushy eyebrow. "Shaba."

He set down his saucer and pushed himself up once more, his knees cracking. He went to the trunk in the corner, looking over his shoulder as he unlocked it, as if to ensure that I wasn't memorizing the combination.

Everyone's so goddamn paranoid around here, I thought.

He sifted through his trunk, stacking folders of passports and driver's licenses in the corner. Confiscated from detainees, he said. He pulled out an envelope of photographs, flipping through them before raising one into the air.

He handed the photo over. An American soldier's plate carrier, a thinner, lighter version of our body armor, was covered in blood and dirt and set against a house wall. Much of the photo was a void of black, and the time stamp read, APRIL 5, 2006, 4:25 A.M. The nametape was missing, but the rank was not: the barbed chevrons of a staff sergeant pierced through the dark.

"My police mentor gave me that, when the army assigned me back here," Saif said. "Said I needed to remember what Ashuriyah really was."

"The hell?" I asked, shaking the photograph as if an answer would fall out of it.

"Let me remember." He sighed, returning the piles of evidence to his trunk. "The older I get, the more my mind turns into that of a Marsh Arab."

Yes, of course he'd heard the legend of Shaba. Shaba was the man who could travel by shadows at night to kill terrorists but handed out money in the day to the townspeople. His mentor had been on duty the night Shaba disappeared and had taken the photograph I now held. After a long firefight near the stone arch, they'd rushed to the scene, finding only the bloody plate carrier and shell casings. Hundreds and hundreds of shell casings, Saif said, his mentor had always stressed that. They looked for Shaba for many months but never found him.

He'd first learned of Shaba at the sheik's funeral. The townspeople couldn't shut up about him. No one knew what had happened, not exactly, but there were theories.

"Like what?" I asked.

"Just crazy gossip," Saif said. "Some said Jaish al-Mahdi killed him because he'd joined al-Qaeda. Others said the opposite. He was out there by himself that night, that's certain. No one knew why, not even the Americans. So strange."

As for the sheik, he'd had many relatives, but his wife had been dead for years, and there was only one living child, a daughter. And no one had seen her for some time. Not until the funeral.

A jewel, Saif said. Even from afar, even covered in her mourning burqa. She'd caused a minor scandal by refusing to wear a face cover, opting instead for a translucent veil. But she didn't seem bothered by the reactions it provoked. She walked, Saif said, like royalty, snubbing everyone she passed on the street, looking down on everyone else even when they were on level ground. She'd come to Ashuriyah with her husband and two little boys. The townspeople said the youngest looked so much like his father, but the eldest had a different appearance, Iraqi coloring with no Iraqi features.

Some of the townspeople said an American soldier had raped the shiek's daughter during the sectarian wars. Others said the dead sheik had promised her to an Anbar doctor. Still others said she'd been taken as a wife by al-Qaeda, and when her husband was killed by the Americans, she'd gone to prison and given birth there.

But most people, Saif said, simply didn't want to talk about it. They hushed the others and told them to respect the memory of the sheik. It was funny, he said, even though he'd returned to Ashuriyah many months before, he hadn't thought about these names and people for years.

"They are the past," Saif said. "It is the future I'm interested in."

"The daughter?" I asked, trying to contain my interest behind a swig of chai. "She alive?"

He shrugged. "Ask the cleaning woman. She used to be one of Sheik Ahmed's servants."

My mind reeled. Had Alia meant to mislead me? Had I asked the wrong questions? Had she been conspiring with Chambers this entire time? She'd said that Shaba had "died like anyone else in Iraq. By the gun." What exactly had that meant? It seemed like the more I learned, the less I understood.

"What troubles you, Loo-tenant Porter?" Saif asked.

There was no more chai in my glass to drink, so I sucked on what remained of the sugar cube. I wanted to tell him everything, how everything was troubling me, the past, the present, and the future. But I kept down my half-drawn story of love, war, and consequence. I looked back at Saif. He'd resumed sitting on his knees. He was a thick, sweaty, balding man with brown skin from here. I was a thin, sweaty baby face with white skin from there. He was still a them. I was still an us. No amount of chai could change that.

"Nothing," I said. "Think I could hang on to this for a while?"

His eyes followed the photograph in my hand. He seemed to be in deliberation with himself, though I couldn't tell why.

"A gift," he said with a tight smile. "We are partners now."

I nodded and handed him my glass and saucer. After a handshake and arm clasp, I left the room, stealing a glimpse of him locking his trunk behind me. Later I pulled out my own trunk and stuck the photograph into the Lawrence of Arabia book with the sworn statements. It seemed the thing to do with a bloody vest.

22

D awn found me on the back patio listening to the call of the muezzin, waiting for Alia.

Rise, rise and offer the Fajr prayer to Allah, the muezzin called. I
pulled out a cigarette and lit up, holding smoke in my chest as long as
I could, exhaling slowly.

I hadn't slept. Because of Saif. Or Alia. Or Marissa, who'd finally
written back with three paragraphs about a life I no longer understood.
Or because Alphabet was less clear in my memory with every new day.
Or because of Grant. Or Dead Tooth. Or Chambers, who, other than
detesting me and possibly being a bloodthirsty murderer of innocents,
had kept the platoon together during the previous month like a goddamn professional. Or because I'd returned from my chat with Saif to
find Ibrahim waiting to tell me that the Muslim jokes had started in
our platoon, and could I make the soldiers stop? Or because of Rios'
bloody vest. Or because I still needed to call my mom, who wanted to
hear my voice so much she was pretending to be fine. Or because of
the clerics, both the one who'd killed Alphabet and the one whose spirit
watched over Ashuriyah from the stone arch.

A burning oil refinery far in the west licked the horizon, its orange
flame hovering like a torch. Slightly nearer, a sea-green minaret lac-
quered in grime shot up out of Sumerian dust. It was mounted with
speakers that carried the call to prayer throughout the Shi'a slums.
There were rumors that during the sectarian wars it carried calls to
battle instead. Calls to battle the heretic Sunnis. Calls to battle the foreign infidels. Calls to kill and calls to die and calls to martyr.

When Will and I were kids, we'd hated going to church. We'd preferred
talking to God on our own terms. And as children of a half-Catholic,

half-Presbyterian divorce, we were able to. Catholicism provided pomp and ceremony, which had its place, but the Presbyterians promised access, and who didn't have something to yell into the ear of God?

Will always had plenty to say. He didn't think I could hear him at night, when he cried and prayed underneath his pillow, but I could. The wall between our rooms wasn't that thick. He'd burned with righteousness his entire life, something that didn't go over too well in high school, not with teachers, coaches, or girls. He'd had it tougher than I did growing up, something I never gave him credit for, because acknowledging it would only have made it worse. I'd always managed to fit in, even when I wanted to be different.

He went to West Point because that's what people like him did. I went to regular college because that's what people like me did.

We both went to war because that's what people like us did for countries like ours.

I considered the minaret and thought about our grandma. The spring before she'd been diagnosed with Alzheimer's, she attended my middle school's poetry recital. She'd come to California some six decades earlier as a young girl, part of the great Okie migration. She never left, valuing home and family over everything but the Presbyterian Church, pocketing sugar packets and clean napkins at every restaurant we went to.

Will had just gotten into West Point, and even though 9/11 was still three years away, she held on to him in the audience as if it were December 1941 all over again. He sat there like a raw-headed figurine while our grandpa made sure everyone in a ten-row radius knew that they were sitting near the future chairman of the Joint Chiefs.

I stumbled through the four stanzas of "The Road Not Taken," which somehow made it more endearing to the audience.

"I'm very proud of you both," our grandma said after the recital. After she passed away, I learned her first fiancé had been mowed down by Japanese machine guns on a tiny island called Guadalcanal. "But, William, Jackson, too much introspection is bad for the soul. All things in moderation. Pray, then poet, then pray again. You come from devout stock. Never forget that."

I tried to remember, but some days were harder than others.

Back in Iraq, I held up my cigarette and blotted out the minaret. A curl of smoke drifted from it, and I narrowed my eyes until the minaret fell out of focus and looked like a burning Twin Tower on a television screen. That day was a long time ago, now.

Alia would be in at eight, I remembered. As I checked my watch, a small rock skipped by my feet.

"*Molazim!*" I heard a voice trying to whisper and shout at once. My eyes scanned the patio, but no one was one there. "*Molazim* Ja-ak!"

It was coming from the other side of the perimeter gate, to the north. I charged my rifle and walked that way, to where Chambers had dumped the prizefighting scorpion a couple of months before. The chain-link fence was covered with a semitransparent camo screen. Squinting through the zig hooks and the screen, I saw an outline of a frail man with a hunch in his back.

"Haitham," I said, letting my rifle sling go slack. "How's life on the lam?"

His response was irritated and incomprehensible. I'd no idea how he'd gotten through the outer perimeter of blast walls or avoided the American eyes on the roof—so much for our improved security, I thought. His soccer jersey was caked in dirt. Grabbing the walkie-talkie clipped to my belt, I considered my options.

"Snooooop," Haitham sounded out. He pointed at me. "*Molazim.*" He pointed at the outpost. "Snooooop." Then he crossed his forearms into an X, something I took to mean he'd only speak to us.

"CP," I said into the walkie-talkie. This is Hotspur Six. Wake Snoop and send him to the back patio. Got some paperwork for him to look over."

We waited in silence, the early morning slashing our faces with light. I didn't mind being alone, but hated sharing quiet with other people, something about the way it made my brain roll around. I began whistling a jingle from a Disney musical about a group of 1890s newsboys on strike, something Haitham mimicked. Is he making fun of me, I thought, or have I found a fellow fanboy? As a kid I'd memorized the matching dance steps, but before I could test the Iraqi on the routine, the metal door of the outpost clanged open. I whistled again, shrill and without melody, to get Snoop's attention.

The terp proved too groggy to be confused or bothered. When I explained we had a visitor, he just shrugged and stuck a clump of sunflower seeds into his mouth.

"Arabs," he said.

I asked if they'd speak slowly so I could pick out words and phrases; I was getting better at understanding Arabic, though getting people to understand mine was something else altogether. Snoop obliged, but Haitham was in no mood to play tutor.

"He asks about Ismail," Snoop said. "The townspeople say the Iraqi Police are hitting him."

"Who?" I didn't know an Ismail.

"His nephew," Snoop said. "The Barbie Kid."

"Of course." I'd heard the same rumor, and had been meaning to check on the teen, though I didn't have the same pull with the Iraqi Police that I did with the *jundis*. I promised Haitham I'd look into it and make sure his nephew was being treated well, though it might be a while until he was released. Through the fence screen, the little man nodded.

I turned to Snoop. "Tell Haitham the *mukhtar* asked about him," I said. "Has a gift or something."

At Snoop's translation, Haitham's voice became even faster and rose in pitch. The terp said to slow down, and then just cut him off.

"He say the gift the *mukhtar* has is a bullet. Then he speaks of the bad days in Ashuriyah again," Snoop said. "He will tell us important things. But only if you promise him Camp Bucca. He wants jail, LT. Still."

"For the love of Allah," I muttered. None of the insurgents we wanted in jail could ever be found, while this guy, one of our sources, was begging to be locked up. "I'll do what I can," I said. "But he'll probably have to cop to plotting against Coalition forces, or something."

The little man nodded again, cleared his throat, and tried to straighten out the hunch in his back. Then he spoke, slow and deliberate, stopping occasionally so Snoop could translate.

"He's stayed away from us because he must hide from everyone. The sheiks of Ashuriyah hunt him because of the mistakes of the past, which must be explained. Some years ago, he served a sheik named Ahmed. He served the sheik and his family loyally.

"He brings up Shaba again. He say Shaba and Sheik Ahmed were very close. He say—he say Ahmed promised his only daughter to him. They were to be father and son."

Snoop turned to me with an arched eyebrow and spat out a few shells. "This is bullshit. No Iraqi father would marry his daughter to an American soldier. No offenses."

I laughed. "Remember what Alia said about that woman Shaba wanted to marry? Maybe it's not bullshit. Let's hear him out."

Snoop shrugged and kept translating through a mouthful of seeds, his voice soaked in doubt.

"The sheik's true son was al-Qaeda. Karim. He hated Americans and swore to kill his father for working with them, and Shaba for violating his sister. So Karim recruited al-Qaeda in Ashuriyah. Every Sunni boy who could hold a gun heard his speech. 'No foreign invaders!' he said. 'No Shi'a scum on our land!' he said. 'We will make a government of Islam!' he said. Many ali babas joined him. They sneak-attacked Shaba at night, dogs with no honor.

"The sheik suffered over the betrayal for many nights. His blood son had killed his oath son. It was the saddest of houses during those days."

I realized I was gripping the holes in the chain-link fence as I listened, getting as close to Haitham's words as I could. I wanted to hear more about Rana, and about Shaba and Rana. Snoop had his face in one of his hands and yawned widely as he waited.

"The sheik still loved Karim, but he'd loved Shaba, too. And he loved Iraq. Not this place, the country he knew, but the dream. Iraq the idea. So, after many nights, he decided to help the Americans capture his son. His spies knew where Karim's hideout was. Then the sheik told Haitham to lead the Americans there.

"Haitham wants us to know he is no traitor. He told the Horse soldier lieutenant that Karim was to be captured, not killed. Sheik Ahmed knew a life in Camp Bucca was still a life. But the kill team *shaytan* did not care. He only cared about making Iraqis dead." Snoop paused in his translation, then grunted. "That's not true, LT Jack. Sergeant Chambers is a good sergeant. I know this."

I was tired of Snoop's interjections. "Let. Him. Finish," I said.

Snoop sighed, but continued. "Haitham say he always trusted Americans. Allah charges Muslims with protecting all People of the Book. But then he saw the Horse soldier lieutenant shoot Karim, and saw Sergeant Chambers put a rifle next to his body to make it look like a battle. He say he saw black skulls on his arm that night and knew he is a *shaytan*. He knew they all were.

"Haitham ran from the hideout. He wouldn't return to the sheik's, because he thought he'd be blamed for what happened. He went south, to the Euphrates, where he heard Sheik Ahmed had put a death fatwa on him. He believed Haitham told the Americans to murder his son. So Haitham stayed away from Ashuriyah for many years, only returning to help his family, he say. He hoped people had forgotten. But they hadn't. The other tribal leaders keep the death fatwa on him, to honor Sheik Ahmed.

"This is why he hides and the only job he could find was as a source for us. This is why he wants Camp Bucca now. But he will only turn himself in to you."

Haitham kept speaking, his silhouette trembling through the screen. I may not have been able to understand him, but I could still hear the terror in his words. Snoop shook his head and ran his fingers through his gums to get rid of any remaining shells. "Now he kisses your ass," the terp said. "You are his friend, a good American who cares about Iraqis blah blah blah. Which, yeah, is true. But he say it because he needs you."

I patted Snoop on the shoulder. "A wise man once said that Haitham drinks too much but he's not a liar." Snoop grimaced at the reference to his own advice. "I know you're tired, man. But bullshit or not, Haitham risked his life getting here, and—" Before I finished my sentence, something ferocious flipped my stomach. "Wait," I said. "He's the one the sniper was after that night. Not us. Not Alphabet. Him."

I didn't need to wait for Snoop. I could tell by the hesitation before Haitham's reply. I pictured myself climbing the fence and choking the Iraqi to death, but all I could do was stand there, dumbstruck and feeling ill.

"He's very sorry, LT," Snoop said. "He didn't know for sure until that night. As a show of trust—whoa. He will tell us where Shaba's bones are."

I took a deep breath, the importance of recovering an American soldier's full remains only beginning to seep through the cracks of my mind. Alphabet was dead, yes. But at least we'd been able to send him home.

"Go on," I said.

That was when a popping like a champagne cork echoed through Ashuriyah. We watched scattered fireballs tumble over the market blocks. Thud. Thud. Thud. The muezzin's chants had ended and the sky was gray and smoked.

"Mortars!" my walkie-talkie said. "Mortar fire in town!"

Rifle in hand, I pushed away from the fence and ran into the outpost, a thought still dangling from above, a thought that had nothing to do with ghosts or bones or mortars.

When we were children? When my brother and I had talked to God on our own terms? Maybe we hadn't been right to do that, yelling into His ear. But we hadn't exactly been wrong to do it, either.

23

We rode to the sound of the guns.

Four Strykers screamed east, bowels packed full of grunts ready for a fucking fight. The champagne popping of mortars had been replaced by the cracking of rifles. "Just go," Captain Vrettos had said, so we went.

"Dismount to your right and take cover behind the vehicles," I said over the platoon net. "The contact is to the south. Don't engage unless you positively identify a target."

"That means they're holding a weapon," Chambers said from his vehicle. "Slow is smooth, smooth is fast. Nobody be a fucking hero. Heroes get people killed."

The Stryker came to a stop. The ramp dropped like an anvil and angry air rushed in. Bodies piled out in front of me. I felt Snoop's hot sunflower-seed breath on my neck, and as my first boot hit packed dirt, Dominguez's voice shot over the radio speakers: "Contact to the north! To the north!"

I stopped moving and watched the vehicle behind us launch a smoke grenade, masking us in a wispy cloud.

What did he mean, the north?

I heard a whistle. Then another whistle. Then a snap. Bullets ripped at my head, pinging off the Stryker cage behind me.

Close. Close. Very close.

I swung around to the other side of the vehicle for cover, grabbing Snoop from the ramp.

So, I thought. That's what he meant by north.

A tank rolled by, machine gun blazing away atop its blocky beige frame. Rounds ricocheted off it steadily. A long, arched barrel pointed out its turret, the apocalypse's very own compass marking the way north. The flag on its side identified it as Iraqi Army, and I recognized one of Saif's sergeants standing out of the hatch. The streets were empty aside from war machines and hunched silhouettes of soldiers, forsaken by all who called the neighborhood home.

"Lieutenant Porter! Over here!"

Through thick, powdery dust, I saw uniforms and hand waves and I moved north again, head and back down. Snoop followed. We joined Washington and his fireteam behind a square building made of clay, huddling low behind it.

More IA tanks drove into the Shi'a neighborhood on both sides of us, rattling with automatic fire. A bald white soccer ball sat at my feet, an artifact of a game that would never pick up again. I grabbed the hand mic on Batule's back.

"Anyone see what the IAs are shooting at?"

"Negative!"

A squad of *jundi*s ran between buildings to join us, bunched together like a spring. A spray of rounds tore into them. One fell, but found his way back to his knees and kept moving. Another fell forward and didn't get back up, a lake of crimson staining the yellow dirt underneath his chest. The remaining IAs responded by shooting their rifles from their hips and bounding to our position. Washington ran out and grabbed the fallen Iraqi by the armpits, dragging him to cover. His gloves ran red with blood and he took them off and tossed them to the ground with a look of disgust.

Doc Cork turned the *jundi* over and said, "Already gone," before going to the other *jundi* and applying a pressure dressing to a hemorrhaging shoulder.

"Sir, what are we doing?"

"Lieutenant Porter, we need to move. Now."

"Sir!"

Voices swirled and my thoughts boiled and I heard myself breathing too loud. I took a sip of water from my CamelBak, but all I tasted was dust. The air was dry and coiling. Searching my mind, I couldn't remember anything tactical from the manuals, so I concentrated on a soft ache on the top of my ribs where our body armor was held together by a thick Velcro strap. Then I remembered something else.

"Washington," I said. "Ever see *Band of Brothers*? When they advance on the Nazis from behind a tank?"

He grinned, and I reached for the radio to order Hog to maneuver the Stryker between buildings. Life imitating art imitating life, I thought. I'm a fucking postmodern boss.

Behind the creeping vehicle, we moved forward like a needle into a vein. Chambers and a fireteam from fourth squad ran to join our staggered column. Twelve rifles wedged tightly into shoulders swept over every window and every corner in quick, anxious scans. Chambers said "Nice" about using the Stryker as a moving shield, and I nodded, proud. The radio squawked. Batule said Captain Vrettos needed to talk to me, but I said to relay that we were busy getting shot at. A neighborhood of rectangular wheat-colored houses surrounded us. Packed dirt turned into runny black sludge, and I stroked the safety trigger on my rifle and noticed a couple of the men had already flipped theirs to semiautomatic or burst. I didn't correct them but instead looked up at the sun and realized it was now morning. Fat beads of sweat ran from the padding underneath my helmet down my face and into my mouth. We came upon a small depression with ruined concrete blocks stacked like a midget Stonehenge, and I exhaled.

"Quick halt here, guys. Need to update the commander."

I went to grab the hand mic on Batule's back, and when I got there, the world turned to mud.

•   •   •

I couldn't see anything or hear anything, but I knew I was still alive because my mouth tasted like sewer. I lifted my head, heavy with helmet and sludge, and wiped my eyes clean, and then my ears, which filled with the staccato humming of machine gun fire. It was Dominguez, unloading the machine gun into the second floor of a sandstone house fifty meters west. I pulled myself to my knees.

"Sir! You okay!" It was Batule, leaning on one knee, firing into the same house as Dominguez. Over cloth, I grabbed my dick, my balls, my face, and my calves.

"I—I—th-think so!" I spat out runny mud. "The fuck happened?" The words came back in fragments.

"Sniper!"—RAT-A-TAT-TAT. "Sergeant Chambers"—RAT-A-TAT-TAT. "Tackled you"—RAT-A-TAT-TAT.

I followed Batule's finger to the square hole where a dark round had lodged into a concrete block—head level, right behind where I'd been standing.

I exposed myself, I thought. Made myself a target.

"Cease fire! Cease fire!" The voice came from the front side of the Stryker. It was assured and singed, like the desert itself.

"Washington, take the two fireteams and clear that building. I doubt anything's alive in there, but make fucking sure," Chambers continued.

The gunfire had tapered off to scattered shots in the far distance, and two tanks rolled back south like a pair of cantering steeds. One of their gunners stood out of his hatch and waved at us. I moved around the back side of the Stryker and stood next to Chambers. His breaths were deep, but nothing else suggested unease. His back was straight, his shoulders cocked, his bearing pleased. He tapped my helmet.

"All right, Lieutenant? Gotta be smarter about grabbing the radio. Marks you as an officer. They know our procedures better than we do."

"Sergeant, I . . ." I took off my right glove and put out my hand. "Thank you."

I thought for sure he was going to say, *I got you, youngblood.* But he didn't, and I was thankful for that. He just smiled, all tobacco-stained overbite, and took my hand. Then he winked.

After the guys cleared the building, I walked upstairs to look at the enemy. There were four of them, teenage scarecrows made of dirt, all torn to bloody straw. The one we decided was my sniper had brain matter spilling out of his skull, a white, slick jelly. Another cradled an AK-47 in his arms.

Hog came up, too, and vomited in a corner. Leaders have to deal with things like this later, I told myself. So I put those thoughts into a compartment of the mind and shut it tight and tapped at the floor and asked how long it would take the owners to mop up the jelly. Not long, came the reply. It's not very sticky.

The next hour was spent piecing together why and how. The Iraqi Army said a group of Sahwa started firing at them while they were responding to the mortars. A tribal dispute, they claimed. The Sahwa said the Iraqi Army started firing at them while they were responding to the same mortars. A Shi'a-Sunni dispute, they claimed. Both groups said men dressed in black who appeared in the middle of the firefight were the ones who shot at us. "Jaish al-Rashideen," the IA said. "Jaish al-Mahdi," the Sahwa said.

"You know how they are."

"You know how they are."

I knew how they were. But still, I thought. None of the dead boys had been wearing black.

24

Washington got a medal for valor under enemy fire. Dominguez got a medal for valor under enemy fire. I got a medal for valor under enemy fire that was really for being an officer under enemy fire. Chambers got a medal for saving the life of an officer under enemy fire.

We drove to Camp Independence for the ceremony. It was held in a quad of yellow grass behind headquarters. Old Glory and the battalion flag hung from a pole in the quad center, flapping indolently under light clouds. Battalion staff walked through the ranks, shaking the men's hands. The soldiers saluted their faces and laughed at their backs, calling them fobbits and rear-echelon motherfuckers, holding the ethical high ground of the grunt because it was all they had.

Meanwhile, I watched Sergeant Chambers and his intel girlfriend, Sergeant Griffin, talk in excited whispers. They'd snuck behind a storage trailer where they thought no one could see them. She smiled and squeezed his hand, and while he didn't smile, he did squeeze her hand back.

The ceremony was short and mundane. The Big Man called us to attention and told us we'd lived up to the scorpion name. "This is what Clear-Hold-Build is all about," he said. Then he gave a speech about honor and freedom and wished us a happy Fourth of July. He concluded by reading a passage from the Bible, Numbers 31:

> Every thing that may abide the fire, ye shall make it go through the fire, and it shall be clean: nevertheless it shall be purified with the water of separation: and all that abideth not the fire ye shall make go through the water.
>
> And ye shall wash your clothes on the seventh day, and ye shall be clean, and afterward ye shall come into the camp.

Being a Gospels man, I wasn't sure what to make of that. The Yahweh of the Old Testament always seemed like a petulant maniac to me, though the selected passage didn't sound so bad. It sure fired up the Big Man, who finished the reading by pounding a fist into his palm and saying, "Now you're in camp! And you're staying here, for the night at least."

He expected the soldiers to cheer, and when they didn't, he stopped talking and started pinning on medals. He should've known the last thing my men wanted was to stay at Camp Independence. We'd gone feral. It was no place for us.

When the Big Man got to me, he said he'd always known I had it in me and that I'd lived up to my brother's name. He thanked me for my service to country, and I saluted. I'd never hated another man more.

Afterward, soldiers milled around in groups. I spotted Sergeant Griffin standing underneath a building ledge, and walked over to her. "We're all really excited for you guys," she said, beads of clear sweat rolling down her face. "Everyone thinks you're one of the best platoon leaders in the whole battalion, even the brigade now. You did great out there."

"Thanks," I said. "Couldn't have done it without my platoon sergeant. Wouldn't even be here without him."

She nodded knowingly. We spent the next five minutes talking about her son, who'd just graduated kindergarten back in Hawaii. She was very proud of him.

In the middle of the yellow grass, the Big Man yelled at Captain Vrettos for not making the violence go away in Ashuriyah. It was fucking things up all over, from Baghdad to DC. It was awkward, considering everyone in the quad could hear, so I dismissed the platoon and told them to behave themselves and not get used to the luxuries of base life.

The confusion on their faces said I didn't need to worry about that.

We'd been assigned to the temporary living quarters on the other side of the base, a large tent with cots. I began walking that way, not sure what I wanted to do with my freedom, but certain I wanted to be somewhere else while doing it.

Ibrahim caught me at the edge of the yellow grass and said the intel officer wanted to see me. I asked what he had planned for the day.

"They got Skype here, so I'll call my parents," he said. "And tonight is Salsa Night at the club—all the fobbits go, it's supposed to be crazy. Me and the guys are gonna give the females some scorpion dick!"

I wasn't sure what that meant exactly, but wished him luck.

• • •

I walked across the quad to the intelligence office, a long, low-roofed building made of concrete. It was topped with a row of satellite dishes and barricaded with wire mesh. Like all the headquarters buildings, chipping paint of crossed rifles and infantry blue trim adorned its walls. A dull American flag sticker marked the doorway like a heliograph, though the stripes had been blanched pink and gray in the sun. A corner of the blue peeled out, and I ripped at it, taking a handful of stars inside with me.

The din of keyboards and laser printers came from every direction, multicolored PowerPoint slides and diagrams of insurgent cells covering the walls. Despite the yellow sunshine coming through the windows, every light in the room blasted bright. I posted myself in front of a corner air conditioner, lifting my uniform top to bathe in air. I heard voices complaining, but didn't move.

The battalion's wanted list lay on a corkboard above, ten insurgents who operated as far south as the Baghdad gate, as far east as the Tigris, as far north as the canal, and as far west as Anbar. Most of the names and faces were unfamiliar, other companies' banes, but the gaping face of Dead Tooth had been pinned on the top row with the words WHERE-ABOUTS: UNKNOWN written underneath. Scanning the rest of the list, I double-taked near the bottom. A black-and-white mug shot of Haitham, his straw hair pushed back and sticking up like an electrocuted cartoon, sat above an index card with the word CLERIC written on it. Stupid fobbits, I thought. How could they mistake a source for the sniper?

"Happy America Day, Lieutenant Porter." I looked across the office. The intelligence officer, a captain, stood at his cubicle, arms crossed and lips pursed.

"Sir. You wanted to see me?"

He pointed to his cubicle. I took a seat on a metal foldout perpendicular to it. Wayward stacks of PowerPoint slides and maps covered his desk. A framed Duke degree hung on a cubicle wall.

So it's true, I thought. He'd brought his diploma to war.

"Thanks for coming to my office, Jack." I'd thought offices required doors, so I waited for him to smile, but one never came. "Wanted to talk to you about the targets you can't find."

Something sour laced his words. I didn't like it and I didn't like how he looked down from his padded spinny chair and I especially didn't like the way he'd inflected the words "you" and "can't."

I pointed to the chair's wheels. "Cool lifts."

"Why the hell can't you find one teenage kid?" he asked, leaning toward me. He'd kept his words measured and low, but flaring nostrils betrayed him. "Brigade is busting my balls while your platoon is gallivanting around like a bunch of amateurs."

"'Gallivanting.'" I arched my eyebrows and smirked my smirkiest smirk. "Didn't hear that word in the quad today. Sir."

The captain didn't respond for many seconds. I concentrated on not blinking and listened to the shuffling papers and typing from surrounding cubicles. I thought of Sergeant Griffin in one of those cubicles, working so she could get home and walk her son to school. They were soldiers, too, I remembered. They'd volunteered, the same as us.

"Look, you have your job to do," he eventually said, leaning back in his chair. "I have mine."

"I apologize, sir," I said. "We have the same goals. Which is why you should know that photo for the Cleric is wrong." I pointed toward the corkboard. "That's a source named Haitham."

It was his turn to smirk. "That's why I called you in here, Lieutenant. I don't know how you gather intel, but it's not being done correctly. Haitham *is* the Cleric. Verified it with spec ops yesterday."

I fidgeted, causing my slung rifle to strike the metal legs of my chair. It gonged through the office.

"That doesn't make any sense. He was there when Alphabet got shot. Right there. Even if he was in on it, someone else pulled the trigger."

The captain rolled his eyes and crossed his arms. He'd regained whatever cerebral authority sustained him. "Doesn't matter who pulled the trigger. We're after big fish, because we're almost done here. Let me repeat that: America. Is. Almost. Done. Here. Spec ops says Haitham is the big fish. You know better than them?"

"Spec ops isn't stationed there. *I'm* stationed there. *I'm* the landowner. And Haitham is not the Cleric. Hell, he wants to go to Camp Bucca."

"Then bring him in. He's not a ghost. Go kick down some doors." He shrugged. "Wish I could join you."

I was too confused to respond. There's no way Haitham is the Cleric, I thought. Then I thought about his ghoulish tendency to arrive just before tragedy, and his gift for disappearing just after tragedy, and decided maybe there *was* a way. Maybe this was why he'd shown up the other morning, filling my brain with a crazy Shakespearean tale from the past.

I thanked the intel captain and rose, turning a half step and considering. Since the firefight, I hadn't thought much about the kill team or First Cav. And despite his throbbing, insatiable douchebaggery, he was probably the right man to ask about that.

"Something on your mind?" he asked.

I closed my eyes. Shaba and Rana seemed like fragments from a morning dream floating away. I thumbed the Hawaiian bracelet on my wrist. The past doesn't matter the way the present does, I decided. Not right now, at least.

"Nope," I said. "All good." Then I walked out, flipping off the black-and-white photograph of Haitham, a man who'd lied about the kill team, and lied about Chambers, and helped kill one of my soldiers.

I decided to shower, stopping first at the base exchange for shampoo and a bar of soap. It was a hot walk, the afternoon sun banking low, miles of military might spread across rolling dust lands. At a water station in front of a graveyard of Saddam-era tanks, I stopped and watched a pair of air force females run by in shorts and tees. They looked up as they passed. My eyes dropped to the ground like loose change.

I drank a bottled water and kept moving. The tank graveyard simmered behind me, the skeletons and bones of vehicles long ago destroyed, long ago scavenged for parts, serving no purpose now but to sit in the sun and melt.

The base's shopping center was located in the core of Camp Independence, in a dry gulch. Big-screen televisions blared from shops' front windows. Signs displayed pictures of new trucks, and instructions on how to ship vehicles home, tax-free. Vendors hawked local antiques and pirated DVDs with fervor. If I hadn't been concentrating so much on the people bumping my back and scanning the crowd for suicide vests, I'd have appreciated the surreality of it all.

HAPPY INDEPENDENCE DAY! The base exchange greeted me with a scrolling digital sign, above automatic doors that ushered me into chilled aisles of surplus goods. I found soap and shampoo quickly, but lingered in the refrigerated section, grabbing a Coke and sticking my head between two bags of frozen green peas.

The peas kept an emerging headache at bay, so I stood like that for ten minutes, shopping items at my feet, rifle slung, leg twitching from the crowd outside. I put the bags back only when the stares of strangers mattered more than the relief. Then I added a bottle of painkillers to my haul, paid, and left.

After a long, hot shower, I massaged my feet and collarbone and put the uniform back on. I'd thought about things in the stall and knew what I needed to do next. In one part of my life, at least, I wanted clarity.

• • •

I got lucky. She was online and responded quickly to the Skype invitation. I set up my webcam and headset and waited for her to come to life on the screen. I'd chosen a corner stall, away from prying ears and curious eyes. I sat up tall, shoulders back, and took a deep breath, smiling for the camera.

The feed was grainy. She wore a pair of thin, rimless glasses and had her hair up in a ponytail, though a few loose brown strands swept across her forehead. She wore a long-sleeved shirt I recognized and a pair of conch earrings shaped like moons that I didn't. I studied the apartment wall behind her, looking for clues, but it was blank and empty.

"*Shaku maku*, Marissa," I said. "How goes it?"

"Jackson," she said. "What time is it there?"

"Almost dinnertime. Pretty early there?"

"Yeah," she said, somewhere between sass and insolence. I'd always adored her temper, except when it was directed my way. "Got up for a run."

"It's nice to look at you," I said, because it was. I wanted her to smile, but instead she blinked twice and frowned.

"You look thin," she said. Her voice was raspier than usual. I wondered if she was smoking again. "Your face, especially. You eating? You and your bird belly."

"If I wanted to be mothered . . ." I began, trailing off. That last word reminded me of the shot-up civilians, and the dead driver's mom on the side of the road, but I didn't know how to begin to tell Marissa about that. I wanted to tell her about the firefight, too, and the medal, but that all felt foul suddenly, as I realized I was just hoping to impress her. So instead I said, "I'll be eating as soon as we're done. Thought I'd take this rare break from war to talk to my girlfriend. That okay?"

She groaned and put her head in her hands. I watched her fingers tap her temples like little drum sticks. She'd always had such soft skin. Sometimes, on those lazy California afternoons on her front patio, I'd stroke her arms until she asked me to leave her alone so she could read. Her voice didn't have the playful lilt to it that it had then.

"Don't call me that, Jackson. Do not call me that. You're the one trying to push me away. This was your idea, too, remember? To avoid becoming a cliché?"

"Push you away?" I felt red coursing through my veins and knew I should stop, but wouldn't. "Are you retarded? You're the one who barely answers my e-mails."

"I just did!"

"With pointless bullshit. You're the one pushing away. Even now, when I need you more than I've ever needed anyone."

That made her cry. Even though that'd probably been my intent, something about the tears sneaking down her face filled me with regret and self-disgust. I apologized for calling the things that made up her days pointless, but that just made it worse.

"What am I supposed to say?" she asked, daggers in her voice now. She wiped her eyes and held my gaze through the screen. She'd always been tougher than me, always been able to cut through my reckless parrying to get to what mattered. "I don't say anything because everything I say is wrong. I don't reply because I don't know how to."

"Well, try. *I'm* trying."

"Bull," she said. "You never communicate with anyone until you explode. I can't read your mind. I won't let you blame me for that. You know your mom had to tell me what happened to your soldiers? I'm so sorry for that, Jack. I'm so, so sorry."

"Don't bring them up," I said. "You've no right." I shook my head and leaned back, sneering at the camera. "This was a mistake. To hell with it." After a few moments of silence, I pointed to my bracelet. "Remember this?"

She smiled sadly, the gap in her teeth finally showing. She tugged at one of the moons in her ears. "Of course," she said. "That week meant a lot."

"Where's yours?"

"It's here. Somewhere. I wear it, just not running."

"Sure," I said. "Sure."

Her eyes filled with tears again but she blinked them away. The feed was so bad I couldn't make out the deep blue of her eyes. I wished I could reach through the connection and seize those irises and keep them as stones in my pockets, to hold anytime I wanted.

"Why did you order my boyfriend a box of elephant dung, Jack? How do you even find something like that? It was gross. And so immature."

I asked her to repeat herself so I could think of something.

"No idea what you're talking about." I sat on my hands to keep them from moving. "I didn't even know you had a boyfriend." I clenched my molars together, and my heart pounded against its cage. "But if it's who I think, he's a fucking tool. Thought you were better than that."

Marissa closed her eyes and rubbed at her forehead. I shouldn't have snapped at her for mentioning Alphabet and Ortiz, I thought. She'd been trying, just as I'd asked. When she opened her eyes she leaned in and kissed the screen. There it is, I thought. Two stubborn souls raised on too much reality television, our fights always ending as quickly as they began. And even though we were arguing, we were talking now. That seemed important.

I was about to return the kiss when she said, "I'm sorry, Jack. I love you. But I can't do this. Please don't write, don't call. Not until you get back and become you again. I'm sorry I'm not strong enough. But I didn't volunteer for this."

The connection winked out and went dead. She'd logged off. As I sat there staring at a black hole of a screen, the creeping sense that something irreplaceable, something matchless, had just broken within. I realized she hadn't asked how I was.

I hadn't asked her, either.

Stumbling out of the cybercafé, I passed a joe Skyping with a kohl-eyed goth lady holding a toddler. The two adults were laughing together at the child's burps. I paid the Kuwaiti employee in the front, walked outside, and found a Porta John to dry-heave into.

• • •

It was twilight when I came out. My hands were shaking and everything seemed fuzzy and distant, and I decided I needed something to do, like eat. I walked through the gray dusk to the chow hall, passing tents and warehouses and clusters of soldiers in workout clothes talking softly. A dark melody had filled the desert, a blend of finches, seething air, and helos slicing through the sky.

The chow hall was a big white magnet north of the shopping gulch, a massive canopy that seemed to hover over the pale sands. Part circus tent, part martial pretense, it was ringed by blast walls and protected by counterbattery radar. It could serve over a thousand soldiers at a time and up to fifteen thousand a day, not including the ones who gorged at the nearby fast-food shacks.

As I replayed my conversation with Marissa over and over again, the shock and hurt wore off. My steps turned to strides. I pushed up my patrol cap high so the back was on the crown of my head and the brim pointed to dull stars. It was more comfortable this way, and it identified me as a field officer who didn't give a fuck. I held my rifle from the rails, not bothering with the sling. In the land of fobbits, I was king. No one approached or even gave me a sideways look, which made me angrier. More than anything, I wanted a fight. I *needed* a fight.

I found one at the chow hall entrance.

To the side of the snaking line stood three of my soldiers, Washington, Batule, and Doc Cork. Washington was arguing with a soldier whose back was to me, his face contorted. He took a step back and started to raise his fist before Doc Cork grabbed it with both hands and held it down. In response, the unknown soldier shot a wagging finger into Washington's face, cursing. I moved between the bodies like mercury.

"Corporal Washington! Chill." Doc Cork squeezed Washington's forearm and whispered "The LT" in his ear. Washington exhaled slowly and his shoulders drooped.

"Sir," he said. "Me and the chief here was just discussing what he meant by 'you people.' As in 'You people never know who's boss.'"

Everyone separated, and we stood in a tight circle. The chief warrant officer was built for a parade, every corner crisp, his boots unsoiled. His face exuded the pink shine of a daily high-and-tight.

"We're supposed to be postracial now, Chief," I said. "I'm sure you were just about to explain that."

"It has nothing to do with him being black!" The chief shook his finger again. "I meant young soldiers who have been promoted too quickly and have no discipline. He in your platoon, Lieutenant?"

"Yes."

"Then you can tell me what the hell that scorpion is." He pointed to Washington's patch, but his eyes were all over my lopsided cap. "I don't care what medal he got today, he's still a soldier. Their uniforms are un-sat. Yours, too. This isn't the bush."

I smiled goofily. "You a regs man, then? Regulations are important." Out of the corner of my eye, I saw uncertainty cross my soldiers' faces. "Wouldn't you agree?"

"Yes, Lieutenant." So certain. So smug. "That's why I stopped him."

"Then why the *fuck* aren't you at attention when addressing a commissioned officer of the United States Army?"

It was like I'd backhanded him. He snapped to attention, unleashing a sarcastic salute and yelling, "Sir, yes, sir!" Every eyeball in the chow line was now on us. I had two options: escalate the spectacle or end it.

"Your service to country tonight is noted, Chief." I leaned down into the man's face, our noses touching, his stunted seafood breath tickling my chin. "You're dismissed."

"Lieutenant." He spoke low now so only I could hear him. "Do that again, you'll spend the rest of your life drinking through a straw." I was going to call his bluff, but he continued. "You think you know me? You know shit. Just 'cause I don't wear it, don't mean I don't have it—I've been blown up more times than years you've been alive. Your boys are out of control. So are you. Rein it in. Be a leader. Respect the uniform. Respect yourself." With a salute, he was gone into the dirty night, just another shape drifting through the camouflage sea.

"Show's over!" I shouted to the line, where heads ogled and voices jeered. The madness had passed. Now I was just embarrassed. "Enjoy your meal, vote Republican."

"Holy shit, sir." I turned to the soldiers. It was Doc Cork. "That was awesome."

"Thanks, LT," Washington said as we exchanged knuckles. "Owe you one."

The three soldiers moved away while I got in line. Then something gloomy pricked at me and I called them back. I asked Washington and Batule to remove their scorpions until we returned to the outpost. They balked.

"That guy was a racist," Washington said. "Why you taking his side?"

"I don't doubt that. But he's right about the patches. Tell the same to anyone rocking the scorpion at Salsa Night. We'll be back soon."

"But, sir—"

"Did I stutter? Move out."

Whatever goodwill I'd earned was lost. They walked off grumbling about power-tripping officers, but replacing one another's patches. I envied them for their solidarity.

"Lonely," I sang to myself, not ironically, not cheerfully, watching the three soldiers fade away. "I'm Mister Lonely. I have nobody . . . for my own."

They served surf and turf for the holiday. The cooks wished me a happy Fourth, and a thickset female with a dreary smile told me she'd been up twenty hours preparing food, and I felt bad for every mean, nasty thought I'd ever had about fobbits, because the truth was we needed them more than they needed us.

I ate in a back corner. On a nearby television, I watched Cleveland sports fans burn the jersey of some basketball player, a self-proclaimed messiah who'd left because winning was hard there and it'd be easier in Florida. After a tenth jersey burned, the howling of proletarian pride and pain broadcast across the globe, I went outside and bummed a cigarette from a contractor. We tried small talk, but his English proved rudimentary and my Korean nonexistent, so we smoked next to each other in quiet, observing the night.

Watching soldiers come and go through shadows, I longed for the other side of the wire. It didn't always make sense out there, but sometimes it did. And it offered purpose. I forced myself to contemplate the sniper shot that'd almost turned me to pink mist, and I fantasized about what that would've done to Marissa. A sick pleasure took hold; I saw her weep and regret. Her life would've never been the same. It would've destroyed her. Then I saw what it would've done to my parents, to Will, and I remembered it would've destroyed me, too, in the most literal of ways. Chambers, I thought. Chambers saved me. He'd said to embrace the beast within, and now I knew he'd been right. He'd been right about everything.

I'd see Haitham and Azhar dead before we left, I promised myself, not because I hated them, but because that was what I was supposed to do. That was why we were here. I walked to Salsa Night, my patrol cap tilted up only slightly.

An empty warehouse on the southern rim of the base, the club lay at the end of a gravel path, next to the airfield, in a deep mire of Halliburton trailers. The generals intermittently tried to shut down the club, but like an obstinate weed, it kept returning. Higher had relented in order to maintain the perception of control. Officers weren't supposed to go, but we weren't banned from it, either.

I just needed something to do.

The walk was dark and quiet. At the airfield, I watched a group unload a cargo jet with neon ChemLights, little dancing birds of hallucinogen. The crates alongside the fence line were filled with machine gun ammunition and milk shake powder mix. There was no other activity on the tarmac. Cresting a small ridge, I heard the club rumbling well before I saw it, a shining boom box of a building. Blue and yellow lights flashed through partially boarded windows, and I asked myself if watching bored joes grind up on each other was really how I wanted to spend my evening.

A slobbering whistle filled the darkness, followed by the sounds of exploding air. I looked up for fireworks but instead saw mortars running down the cheeks of night. To the north, the noise of earth being punched from above echoed. The base alarm system shot to life. I ran forward for a bunker without knowing where one was.

At the intersection of the gravel path and a back gate of the airfield, I found a sandbag mound. I jumped into it headfirst, landing with my rifle under me. I groaned, having knocked the wind out of myself, failing to notice the large shape on the other end of the bunker.

"You okay, sir?" it asked.

"Sure," I took a deep breath and spoke through gasps. "Forgot to tuck and roll." I peered through the tunnel and rose to my knees, the brim of my cap brushing the ceiling of the bunker. "Ibrahim?"

"Yeah." My eyes adjusted to the dim. He looked like a sad panda at the zoo, gnawing on a jerky stick like bamboo. His plastic-rimmed glasses kept slipping down the bridge of his nose as he chewed. "What's going on?"

"Mortar attack. Shouldn't last long."

"Oh."

I sighed and asked what was wrong. He said nothing. I said that was an obvious lie, and since we were going to be spending the foreseeable future together stuck in a bunker, he might as well tell the truth.

It wasn't just one thing, he explained. It was everything. He'd Skyped his parents earlier, only to learn his sister was talking about dropping out of college. Even though Dominguez had said he was a good soldier and getting better every day, he didn't think that was true. And ever since we'd made the other joes stop teasing him, they just ignored him, which was worse. That'd been what happened at the club that night. He'd heard them and some fobbit females laughing at his back as he left, minutes before the mortar strike, and he'd taken refuge in here to be alone.

"Good times," he said, forcing a smile. "But how are you, sir? Enjoy your day off?"

"Oh yes," I said. "Was swell."

The attack passed and, soon after, the strident "All clear" sound rang out. I told Ibrahim to get a good night's rest and then tried to follow my own advice. I left him in the bunker with his jerky wrappers, knowing I should talk to him some more, but unable to summon the energy. We all had our personal tragedies to bitch about.

We left for Ashuriyah at dawn. I snapped my bracelet and dropped broken beads onto the desert road one at a time, like breadcrumbs. What had once led home now led nowhere.

25

The mortar attack's origin point came from eastern Ashuriyah, leaving Burger King a pile of ash, with two Bengali contractors and one soldier dead. We needed to end the war, and end it immediately. During a meeting in his room, Captain Vrettos asked for ideas.

"Split the platoons," Chambers said. "Platoon leaders take half the guys for the day, platoon sergeants take the rest at night. Doubles our patrols. They focus on counterinsurgency, we focus on the killers."

"We'd be stretched real thin," First Sergeant said.

"Done," Captain Vrettos said. "I'll try anything at this point."

I didn't have any better ideas, so I kept my mouth shut.

Afterward, Captain Vrettos found me in the hallway. Hollow-eyed, he asked me to cover for him that afternoon at the wake of a Sunni tribal leader. He hadn't slept since the firefight three days before. I said of course. I couldn't tell if it was exhaustion or gratitude that caused his eyes to water.

Outside, the sun was a hammer. Midday, high July, we piled into our Strykers once again. The soldiers napped on one another's shoulders, rifles between their legs. I stood out of the hatch and watched sandstone buildings drift by, then hills. Even though we drove south and then east, away from the stone arch, I could still feel the wire-rim glasses of the Cleric on us, watching.

Billowing chimney smoke marked the house of the dead sheik, a black funeral flag draped from a balcony. A lone cypress stood idle at the edge of the yard. The hand-me-down Humvees of the Iraqi Army and the black Mercedeses of the tribal leaders lined the side of the dirt road.

"We late, sir?" Hog asked, parking behind the other vehicles.

"Thought we'd be early," I said. "So of course."

I'd never met Abu Mohammed. He'd been ill since our arrival. But he'd long been a patriarch in the al-Badri tribe, and his sons claimed he was an early supporter of the Sahwa movement. He'd been buried the day before, at a Sunni graveyard, today marking the beginning of the three-day mourning ceremony.

A large cylindrical tarp had been erected in front of the house, under which twenty or so visitors had gathered. Leaving my helmet and rifle, I told Batule and Snoop to join me. I asked Snoop to leave his plastic rifle. I considered telling him to do the same with his ski mask, but didn't, thinking about what Saif said about the difference between allies and partners.

Rolls of green Astroturf had been spread across the yard. One of Abu Mohammed's sons welcomed me as I stepped from dirt to turf, and I handed him a bouquet of desert poppies I'd picked that morning in the meadow behind the outpost. In dense Arabic, he asked where Captain Vrettos was.

"Emergency at Camp Independence," I managed. "He sends his condolences."

Under the tarp, I greeted groups of Iraqi men, most of whom I didn't recognize, raising my right hand to my heart and cupping it. The old men returned the gesture, but most of the younger men insisted on shaking hands. A carload of women in burqas arrived, and I watched them enter the house, taking off their shoes at the entrance. I asked Snoop where they were going.

"Women and men can't mourn together," he said. "They go into the house to drink coffee and tell stories of the dead sheik. And make the food, yo."

The atmosphere was solemn, and I quickly ran out of ways to say, "He was a good man." As servants brought out the first platters of food, Saif found me and explained that fried eggplant served cold on pita bread was a traditional dish. It was a wild garden of dough and oils, and we ate with our hands, sharing the platters. Following Saif's lead,

I dipped the bread into a side of hummus. We washed the food down with spiced chai, which somehow cooled me in the heat.

"Did you hear?" Saif asked through mouthfuls. "The police released Ismail this morning. Saw him leave his cell. Sullen young man. Didn't look too beaten, likely because you intervened. That was a good thing you did."

I was surprised they'd released the Barbie Kid already, but the brigade JAG officer had determined an attempted *sai* poking didn't qualify as a murder attempt. I decided to let Chambers hear about the teen's release from someone else; he'd just rage about how much the army and Iraq had changed for the worse.

The second group of platters consisted of dried apricots and some sort of chopped salad I had no interest in. Fat Mukhtar arrived, too, his three wives and many children hustling inside with bowed heads, armed guards and the toucan Sinbad staying outside with us. One of the guards held the bird on his forearm, though it nibbled from Fat Mukhtar's hand with its keel bill as he fed it bread from the communal platter. Saif grunted at the scene, but said nothing. Neither did anyone else.

"There's a strange feeling in the air now," Snoop whispered in my ear.

The bird regurgitated into his feeder's hand, a yellow and deficient slop. Fat Mukhtar rolled his eyes and wiped his hand clean on his guard's black muscle shirt. He shouted something in Arabic, which brought laughs from throughout the tarp.

"He say the Reconciliation means he must square with Shi'as," Snoop translated. "But he doesn't have to square with toucans."

I smiled at the *mukhtar*. His greeting under the tarp proved far more tepid than the hug I'd received on the Sunni Strip, just a limp peace sign under glazed eyes. Around the collection of frail old men, he seemed even larger than usual. His goatee was freshly trimmed, as usual, but his thatch of curls had been slicked back with grease for the occasion. As we made our way through the third course, a mix of goat meat and brown rice, he walked to our side of the circle, speaking low to Snoop.

"He say it is wrong to talk business today, but wishes to know if you've learned Haitham is the Cleric. This true, LT? It doesn't make sense to me."

"Yeah." Through his mask, I could sense Snoop's skepticism. "Battalion told me yesterday. Crazy, but true."

"Surf's up," Fat Mukhtar said.

Then he asked for us to turn off the machine in the Strykers that made cell phones stop working, as the sheik's sons were expecting calls from loved ones.

"No idea what you're talking about. We don't have that kind of technology," I said, plain-faced. "Excuse me, I have a completely unrelated matter to attend to."

I walked past the cypress tree to our vehicles and gave Dominguez the "kill the jammer" hand-and-arm signal; remote-detonated IEDs weren't a concern at the moment. Returning to the tarp, I noticed something odd on the shoulder of one of Fat Mukhtar's guards, standing off by himself and holding a silver AK-47. I called over Snoop.

"The fuck?" I pointed to the Ranger scroll he'd sewn onto his khaki Sahwa top. "Where'd you get that?"

From a Ranger, of course. It was a gift. They'd worked together on a recent mission he couldn't tell us about; it was "top secret." I thought about how battalion had learned of the Cleric's identity—the still-alive one—and looked past the guard to the waddling *mukhtar*. He held his toucan in front of a sad, wizened old man, laughing while the bird croaked.

So many secrets here, I thought, trapped in a glint of the afternoon sun. So many veils, too.

After I rejoined the mourners, a group of old women in black *abaya*s were exiting the house, moving with slow steps to the tarp. They chanted dirges, low and ominous. The old men passed around a collection plate, which Saif quietly explained was for the women, professional mourners hired to sing of the dead's accomplishments and the world's loss. They'd go for hours, if necessary, and would return each afternoon of the three-day ceremony. I tossed in a ten-dollar bill.

I hadn't seen Snoop sneak away, but as the lamenters performed, he waved me to the back of the tarp. He held his phone tight in his hand.

"Haitham," he said. "He asked if we were at the wake for Abu Mohammed."

"Shit."

"I didn't tell him. But he say if we were here, we should dig near the cypress tree. He say—he say we will find the body of Shaba there. Then he hung up."

I turned around to look out into the desert. Nothing but yellow badlands until Baghdad, I thought. Who knew how many bodies lay in the barren earth beneath us.

"I am just a terp, but we should dig at that tree," Snoop said. "I believe him."

I strode to the cypress, all gnarled branches and leaves like asparagus. The dirt around its trunk was cracked and sun-scorched. None of it looked disturbed. Then I looked up and saw the Iraqis looking over their shoulders at me, pretending to listen to the dirge.

"Get Saif over here," I said to Snoop. "We need to be delicate about this."

The Iraqi lieutenant's eyes flashed like pinwheels when we told him, and he stroked his pistol holster. I argued we should wait to dig until after the mourning ceremony, but Saif pointed out they knew that we knew now. Unless we wanted to post guards for three days, we needed to dig right away.

"It'll be better if my men do it," Saif said. "And your Muslim soldier."

I sent Snoop to the sons to explain that we weren't trying to be disrespectful, just following a tip. The laments ended as Ibrahim and the *jundi*s put shovels into dirt. Two and three at a time, the mourners fell away to their cars and homes, Fat Mukhtar leaving with his guards in a Mercedes. Only the dead sheik's family remained for the excavation.

It took ten minutes for one of the *jundi*s to find a piece of plastic. It stuck out of the ground like a candlewick, crusted in dirt and barely discernible. Thirty minutes after that, we stood around a shallow hole with a bag of human remains in it. The body had been stripped and burned, giving the carcass a smoky, charcoal shine. Maggots had long ago chewed through the clear plastic to feast on the insides. The skull wasn't attached to the body but had remained intact, falling to the bottom of the bag. I stepped into the hole to look it in the eye. A chipped bottom tooth was fixed prominently in its mouth, death reckoning life with the stupidest of grins.

"Not right," Saif said, looking up at the branches of the rigid cypress. "Even to an enemy. Such things are against Allah's will."

I heard the joes whispering from above, around the tree. "Think it still has the Green Beret tat on it?" one asked. The others told him to stop being stupid.

"Who is it, sir?" Ibrahim asked, his face and words drained of color. "Or was it, I mean."

"Not sure." I set the skull and bag back in its hole. "But he may have been one of us, once upon a time."

Then I got on the radio with Captain Vrettos, apologizing for waking him, telling him he wouldn't believe what we'd found.

We detained the sheiks' sons, though battalion let them go the next day, since none of them lived with their father and they all claimed ignorance of the body. The remains were sent to Baghdad and then to Germany for identity confirmation. Per higher's instructions, we spent the rest of the afternoon digging up the entire yard, looking for more bodies. We didn't find any.

We returned to the outpost in the early evening, just as the desert beetles began trilling. Chambers met me at the top of the stairs, under the watchful stares of the Iraqi wall mural. He'd donned his body armor for a night patrol while I was preparing to shed mine.

"You found him," he said.

"Believe so." I stood straight and proud.

"Huh." He closed his eyes and exhaled slowly, like a man finding air after a long swim. When he opened them, his eyes had turned to chips of glass. "My turn to say thank you."

He stuck out a wristless right hand. I shook it and tried not to wince when he squeezed too hard.

"Where is he?" Chambers asked. "I'd like to see him."

"Oh." It was like I'd removed some great millstone from around Chambers' neck. He wasn't looking at me with contempt, or even irritation. Something had changed between us. I'd done something he couldn't, that he hadn't. He respected me now. Which made telling him that his friend's bones were already en route to Baghdad even harder.

I reached down and put my hand on his shoulder, where armor met cloth. His shoulder was tense, but he didn't shrug me away.

"We good?" Chambers asked. He wasn't looking directly at me, but he wasn't looking away from me, either. His right arm had gone slack, and he was balling his hand into a fist.

"Yeah," I said. "We good."

With that, he was gone into the Ashuriyah night. I stayed on those stairs for a long time, chewing over his words and the miracle we'd just stumbled across.

26

The hell of July passed in a seared haze. Hours and days melted into one another under a sun so tyrannical the soldiers began calling it the Sultan. Siestas weren't sometimes anymore, but most of the time. On the barren stretches of no-man's-land and in the alleyways of town, we asked the Sultan for compassion. There was no response.

We patrolled during the mornings. For our efforts, the locals called us *majnuns*, madmen. They weren't wrong. "Don't you understand?" they asked. "The insurgents work at night." In between, I smoked a lot of cigarettes and drank a lot of Rip Its and watched DVDs about 1960s-era Madison Avenue and Prohibition-era gangsters. They made me miss home without reminding me of it.

We'd made national news for finding Rios. NO MAN LEFT BEHIND was the headline blasted out by the army to every news service that still gave a shit. I spoke to an Associated Press reporter over the phone, reading a statement prepared by a public affairs officer. "We acted on a tip provided by a local, evidence that Iraqis are ready and willing to take control of their nation," I said. "As important as this moment is for Americans and the U.S. military, it's just as important for the Iraqi people."

"You believe that?" the reporter asked. "The violence numbers are increasing all over the country."

"Sure," I said. "Why wouldn't I?"

My mom found my quote in ten different American newspapers and cut out and framed each one, even though they were all from the same AP article. "You'll want these someday," she assured me.

Even Will was impressed. "This is a big deal," he said. "And good leverage for you when you make your move against Chambers. What's the deal with that, anyways?"

"Nothing new," I said. I still hadn't told my family about the firefight or the medal for valor. I didn't want to worry my parents. I didn't tell Will for other reasons.

A two-star general called from the Pentagon, asking to speak to me about finding the remains. "You Porter brothers sure are something," he said. "I want you on my staff. Could use some hard-chargers back here, whip some bureaucrats into shape."

"Think I just want to stay here, sir," I said. "But thank you."

He laughed and explained that he'd meant after we redeployed. I took down his contact info.

Other than a long afternoon spent patching the security hole in the outpost Haitham had found before the firefight, the war went back to normal. The headaches lingered, something Doc Cork attributed to too many Rip Its and too little sleep. Each evening around dusk, our company's leadership gathered, the only time I saw Captain Vrettos anymore. And every morning around dawn, I met my platoon's night patrol as they filed into the outpost, scorpions on their shoulders, fatigue on their faces.

"Everything good?" I always asked Chambers.

Everything always was.

We settled into a strange sort of routine, the kind that demanded our time yet nothing of our attention. I began thinking that maybe we could really ride out the rest of the deployment and make it home all right. A few days later, I began believing it.

Then Snoop said the cleaning woman needed to speak with us.

Lying in bed, hands wrapped behind my head, I sighed and paused the DVD player on my lap. Among other things, my patience for counterinsurgency and its endless meetings had wilted in the summer heat.

"Fuck that noise," I said. It was late morning and we were alone in my room. "I don't care about Shaba anymore. Or sheiks, or their daughters. It's all bullshit, a myth for stupid people."

When I tried to go back to my show, Snoop shook the bed frame. "Yo!" he said. "She say she has information on Haitham."

Higher's need to capture Haitham had become a parody of itself. It's all they asked about, all they cared about. Captain Vrettos did his best to shield us from the Big Man's furies, though he'd taken to calling their meetings "Death by Colonel."

"Haitham," I said, pressing pause again.

"Haitham," Snoop repeated. He still didn't believe the town drunk was capable of being a terrorist mastermind. I put on my uniform top and boots, and we walked downstairs into a council office. Alia waited in the dark, already seated, the room smelling of honeysuckle and kerosene.

I flipped the light switch and we took a seat across from her in white plastic chairs. She had her hands crossed in her lap and her eyes on the ground.

"Sing me a song," I said. "And make it good."

Alia looked up at Snoop, confused.

"Damn it," I said, this time in English. None of the locals could ever wade through my Arabic, despite my being able to understand them.

"You found Shaba?" she asked. She'd varied her usual outfit with a gray head scarf and eye shadow the color of dirty ice. I nodded, proud of what we'd accomplished, no longer bothered by how it'd come about. She asked where his bones were.

"Texas," Snoop said. "With his family."

She bowed her head and mumbled something I didn't understand.

"Iraqi curse," Snoop said. "She's upset the body went to America."

I asked why. She raised her head and explained she'd hoped he'd be buried in Ashuriyah so she could pay her respects. I considered asking Snoop why she thought that would've happened, but remembered we'd ended our last meeting suspecting her of understanding English.

"Haitham," I said, trying not to sound irritated. I reached into a cargo pocket, pulled out a twenty-dollar bill, and set it on the table. "Where is he?"

She pulled the money to her. "He walks around the far southeast of town," she said. "Where the tribal leaders used to live, before the Collapse. I saw him there two days ago, standing at the gates of Sheik Ahmed's abandoned estate."

"Hmm." I pictured the map imagery of southeast Ashuriyah, then its wide, dusty streets, its sandstone mansions with balconies. It wouldn't have been where I'd hide out.

"Bullshit," Snoop said. I turned toward him. He was rubbing the top of his head with both hands. "Think about this, LT. Would a terror men leader walk around the middle of the day? He's not the Cleric. Someone wants us to think he is."

I turned back toward Alia, her face dropping again to the floor. She's being forthright, I thought. Nothing like the last meeting. Old questions forged within.

"*Sig-ue mi ej-emp-lo*," I said to Snoop slowly, telling him to follow my lead. I recalled Dominguez teaching our terp conversational Spanish at some point, though my own was worse than my Arabic. "*Comprende?*"

"*Sí*," he whispered.

"Tell her we know Haitham is the Cleric," I said. "And that we appreciate this information."

Snoop translated.

"But my friend here, Snoop. He's more skeptical. He thinks it's stupid to believe someone who's lied to us. He thinks you must be telling more lies."

"I'm no liar!" Alia waited for Snoop's translation, but barely. "Haitham's a bad man. You must find him."

"Alia." I shook my head. "Maybe that's true, maybe not. But why should I believe someone who forgot to mention she'd worked for Sheik Ahmed?"

Her lips pursed tight.

"A lie, which is half a truth, is ever the blackest of lies." Tennyson might've been too much, but I didn't care. "You worked for Ahmed, and guess what? So did Haitham! And now you're here, telling us he's hanging around the dead man's house. What a coincidence."

"Haitham never lied to us," Snoop added, first in English, then in Arabic.

She rolled in her chair like an angry ball. Long, hot seconds passed.

"You must get him," she finally said. I could barely hear her. "He's there. I swear by the shrine."

I reached into my cargo pocket and threw down five ten-dollar bills. "All yours. But the truth. All of it. If not, you'll never work in this outpost again."

She pushed the money away and tipped her head, eyeing me and Snoop with open disdain. "The people are wrong," she said, her Arabic like darts. "You're nothing like Shaba."

"I know," I said, biting my bottom lip. "I'm not dead."

"Though Allah will never forgive me," she said, "I'm no traitor like Haitham."

Behind fierce chestnut eyes, her long, elegant fingers gripping the table, this was the story she told us:

"It was the winter of the Baghdad snow. Sheik Ahmed invited the Horse soldiers to visit, like he always did with new Americans. It was always the same talk about power, about electricity, about peace. Just talk.

"The Horse soldiers came at dusk. There were three of them, and a translator. A captain, a lieutenant, and a sergeant.

"Yes, the first two were named Tisdale and Grant. They were like every other American officer, white with pink faces. But the sergeant was different. Even before he became Shaba, we knew that.

"He was small. And brown. And quiet.

"I watched the meeting from the hallway, behind a curtain. The sheik's daughter was with me. Yes, Rana.

"The first hour, the meeting was normal. Lots of promises, lots of jokes about women. Then Shaba looked at the sheik and asked about the rumors of his al-Qaeda son, in Arabic. Everyone became quiet. None of us had ever met an American who spoke our language so well.

"The sheik asked how he knew about Karim.

"'By listening,' Shaba said, pointing to Ashuriyah. 'They say the father wants peace. Then they say the son wants war.'

"The sheik said the rumors were true. We hadn't seen Karim for months, though, not since his father ordered him to leave his house for dishonoring the tribe.

"What was Karim like? Like his father. Prideful. He'd grown up believing he would be an important man. Before the Invasion, he studied engineering in Baghdad, which brought honor to the tribe. But after their mother died of chest cancer, Karim became angry with everyone, and with the world.

"Rana wasn't allowed at meetings. The sheik made her stay away from Americans. He believed they would go crazy from her beauty and rape her. But after I brought out the apricots and hummus, Rana asked if the new sergeant was handsome. I knew then she was up to something.

"She was always a brave child, but on the third visit of the Horse soldiers, it became something else. She walked through the curtain and into the sitting room, defying her father's law, wearing a blouse and American-style jeans. With no face cover! She sat between her father and the sergeant, put her hand out and said, 'Hah-loe,' like she'd seen in movies.

"How old? She was—sixteen that winter. Beautiful, like only a girl that age can be. Had the same circle mark on her cheek that her mother did. She wasn't angry like her brother, but had his temper when things didn't go her way. She thought the young men here were beneath her. Long before Shaba, she wanted to marry a man from Baghdad, maybe Basra, to get away.

"Shaba nodded at Rana, but didn't take her hand. He knew not to violate the sheik's law. But when the sheik asked her to leave, she didn't move. Her father was enraged but didn't know what to do in front of the guests. So she stayed and listened.

"The eyes of Shaba remained on Rana the rest of the meeting, and she looked back, smiling and twisting her hair. Neither spoke. The lieutenant, Grant, reminded me of a sad cow, he didn't know what to do. Eventually, even the sheik became silent. The translator talked about the weather until the meeting ended.

"That night, the servants and guards gathered in the courtyard to listen to Rana fight with her father. She said she believed in love at first sight. That she knew she would marry Shaba. He said no; he forbade it. She said she would have many babies with her beautiful soldier. He said she would have many babies with the son of a Ramadi sheik, as he'd planned. She said she would run away to America with Shaba and leave Iraq and the al-Badris forever. He said nothing to that.

"What did the sheik think? Probably that it was just the foolish wishes of a girl. But Shaba felt the same. He came to the gate the next night, no armor or helmet. Only a *dishdasha* that hid a small pistol. He and Sheik Ahmed talked for many hours.

"I listened at the curtain as much as I could. They spoke of Babylon and caliphs and the empire of the Turks. They spoke of al-Qaeda and Jaish al-Mahdi, of tribes from Anbar to Diyala. Sheik Ahmed said most of the Iraqis who shot guns and planted bombs didn't hate Americans, but that they'd been hired for that by men from other towns.

"'They need jobs,' he told Shaba. 'The key to peace is jobs. Idle hands find the trigger.'

"Shaba agreed. Then he explained to the sheik that he would seek the hand of Rana, but only if he was permitted to. He promised not to dishonor the sheik or his daughter. He said the most important thing was to bring peace to Ashuriyah. The sheik asked many questions—of Shaba's family, of his life in America. Shaba said he hated where he came from, that he'd never had a home. That was why he wanted peace in Ashuriyah. To make a home here.

"When I heard what he said about Rana, I went to her. She'd been locked away in her room, under guard. Her eyes shone brighter than anything when I told her. 'Go back,' she said. 'Learn more.'

"When I returned to the curtain, the sheik and Shaba had come up with a plan for the Sons of Iraq—the Sahwa. There needed to be checkpoints, they agreed, many checkpoints that gave Iraqi men purpose and means to provide for their families.

"They saved Iraq from chaos while the rest of us slept.

"We learned the next day Sheik Ahmed had given Shaba permission to visit Rana. She wept with happiness and kissed her father's feet. He seemed happy, too, the happiest he'd been since his wife lived, the older servants said.

"It became a love like you hear in stories. They met in the sitting room twice a week. Sometimes he came with other Horse soldiers for meetings. At first they pretended the other meetings weren't happening, but that stopped when the sad cow lieutenant made a joke. If other soldiers knew what Shaba knew, the lieutenant said, they would come to the sheik's home at night, too.

"He was just a sergeant? That's a stupid thing to say. Everyone listened to Shaba, especially his officers. He knew better than them. Once the Sahwa formed, peace followed. Slowly at first, but after the Americans paid the first time, more men wanted to join. The sheik started having meetings with sheiks from other parts of Iraq. They agreed to bring the idea to their American soldiers.

"One cold night in the sitting room, they told the sheik they wished to marry in the spring. The sheik clapped his hands and praised Allah for their love. He said he'd be proud to call Shaba his son. Shaba smiled like I'd never seen before, and Rana glowed like only a beautiful girl in love can.

"Yes, this was possible. That's another stupid thing to say. Because our culture is so different than yours? Muslims are like people anywhere, Lieutenant Porter. They fall in love. They get married. They build families. All of that is what Shaba and Rana wanted. All of that is what they would have had. What they should have had.

"The sheik hosted a feast for them. The old mayor came. The old sheiks, the old police chief, the old doctor and his wife. Even the *mukhtar* from the far villages. The sad cow lieutenant came with Shaba. The sheik's cousin drove from Karrada to play the cello. There was food and dancing, and Rana and Shaba kissed in the courtyard under stars. After he left, she said it'd been the happiest night of her life.

"Then Haitham ruined everything.

"Days later, when the sheik was away, Karim came home. He said he'd bombed the golden mosque in Samarra, and needed someplace to hide.

"We said his father hadn't forgiven him, which surprised him. But Rana was so happy to see him, kept holding his face and telling him how skinny he looked.

"I could tell something was wrong, though. He was so quiet. He took her hands off him. 'Is it true?' he asked his sister. 'You're to marry a dog of the occupiers?'

"She said she was in love and that he'd love Shaba, too. Karim wasn't listening, though. The battles had changed him. He started cursing and punching the walls, swearing revenge on his father and Shaba for destroying his family's honor. Then he threw Rana to the ground and said he'd rather have a Shi'a peasant rape and murder her than have her marry an American.

"The guards pulled him off and pushed him out of the house. He was screaming the entire time. We knew then a *shaytan* had taken him. Haitham was one of those guards, that stupid, stupid man. He said to Karim, 'Ashuriyah is a peaceful place now. People walk freely. Even American soldiers walk by themselves.' Karim spat on him and called him a liar. So Haitham told him how Shaba visited at night, by himself, with no armor. That is how Karim knew to set the ambush.

"After—after Shaba was killed, Rana cried and pleaded to Allah to bring him back. She turned crazy, madder than even her brother, and wandered the desert at night, alone. The sheik had his guards lock her inside her room and tie her up, so she could not kill herself with a knife or gun.

"What happened then? Everything fell apart. The peace ended, the war returned. Karim was killed. The sheik sent his daughter away and stopped working with Americans. Most of the servants stayed until he died, but then we had nothing. He gave all his money to the other sheiks, to pay their Sahwa. They were all he had left."

27

There were holes in Alia's story. Little things that lingered at the bottom of my consciousness like coins in a well. Shaba couldn't have invented the Sahwa. That started in Ramadi with the Sunni Awakening—there were books about it. And a quick Google search showed that snow had turned Baghdad white in 2008, a full two years after First Cav was stationed in Ashuriyah. Little holes that made me think there were bigger holes.

And yet.

"That's too crazy to make up," Snoop said.

He had a point. I kept thinking about our grandpa telling Will and me that the truest war stories made the least sense. He'd been talking about World War II, but maybe this was something our little brushfire war had in common with his.

I ate a turkey sandwich and drank coffee for lunch and thought about star-crossed love. I could see an American soldier making a play for a good-looking Iraqi girl. Even a sixteen-year-old. But I couldn't see it as the kind of grand romance Alia told. I wondered what the real story was.

Even though my hands were already shaking from too much caffeine, I chugged a Rip It and walked downstairs, following the sound of a low roar.

It was Sahwa payday. Dozens upon dozens of Iraqi men twisted around the foyer in a coiling line that extended out the front door. The Sahwa were separated by clothing and grouped accordingly: some wore khaki-brown shirts with matching baseball caps; others navy-blue armbands with Iraqi flags; while still others bore black vests and jeans. Glossy orange dust pervaded the air like dirt beaten from a rug, and sweat and moisture clung to my skin. I swung my rifle to my front and waded in.

"*Molazim* Porter!"

I heard Fat Mukhtar's deep voice to my right, remembering that I'd promised to push his group to the front of the line. Whoops, I thought.

The large man bumped into me, leading with his stomach. The sneer on his face suggested it wasn't a conversation I could avoid, so I waved up Snoop from the payment table and faced the angry tribal leader.

I feigned understanding as Snoop asked why he was upset, nodding through the accusation that I'd lied about payment order. Spit danced around my head. After a minute, I tapped my watch and spoke over him.

"First, you ever touch me with that flab again, we'll take you up to the canal and see if you can float." I didn't think Snoop's English was good enough to effectively convey the threat, so I poked the *mukhtar's* stomach rolls with my index and middle fingers. He took a small step back. Every Sahwa guard in Ashuriyah was watching—I needed to be the scorpion. "Second, why honor a man who knew about Shaba's grave? Third—there is no third. Just don't ever fucking touch me like that again."

That seemed to bury Fat Mukhtar's wrath. "It was him?" he asked.

"Yes," I said. "Dental records and DNA samples confirmed it last week."

He bowed his head and mumbled a short prayer. He looked up with earnestness. "He swears he didn't know," Snoop translated.

"What's done is done," I said, grinning at my own little lie. "They'll be first next time." It was unofficially official: that next time would be the last time we'd pay the Sahwa. Then it'd be the Iraqi military's responsibility. "A hallmark of progress," the PowerPoint presentation had called it. Even Captain Vrettos hadn't been able to keep a straight face.

Fat Mukhtar rubbed his hands together. I expected an Arabic idiom that resembled "Fool me once, shame on you; fool me twice, shame on me." He didn't say that, though. Instead he said something I didn't understand. Snoop made him repeat it. When he did, the terp blinked and blinked before turning to me, aghast.

"The *mukhtar* say a fatwa has been put on your Muslim soldier. For disturbing a wake. A death sentence fatwa."

I knew what a fatwa was, though I'd believed only Iranian ayatollahs could issue them. The Cleric, whoever he was, had declared it on Ibrahim, Saif, and any of the *jundi*s who'd unearthed the bones at Abu Mohammed's. The bounty for their deaths was "large." Why just them? Because the rest of us were infidels, Fat Mukhtar explained. "You don't know any better. They do."

"Don't worry, Lieutenant." Fat Mukhtar's face rose into a fleshy grin. "There are thirty thousand, maybe forty thousand people in Ashuriyah. How many will listen to the fatwa? Very few. Your man has nothing to fear. You know what happened the last time an American soldier tried to be one of us. You will keep him safe."

I thanked him for the information and staggered away, not sure whom I needed to alert first. Names cycled through my mind, though only one kept reappearing: Saif. I elbowed my way to the front table, a rickety white foldout. Saif sat in a chair behind it, counting out dollars and crossing names off a list. The fatwa filled my mouth like poison, but I couldn't spit it out until the Sahwa guard being paid walked away. Behind Saif stood a ring of *jundi*s and soldiers from my platoon, all armed. Dominguez, on the far right of the upside-down horseshoe formation, waved to me. I cut through a gaggle of midtown Shi'as in blue armbands and asked how things were going, trying to act normal.

"This? Bullshit, but standard bullshit," Dominguez said. "Just another day in the green machine. I need to talk to you about something else, sir."

"Send it."

He looked to his left and right and dropped his voice. "This split-platoon shit is bad juju. Us in the day, we're doing one thing. The guys at night? Totally different Iraq. I'm hearing things from the young-bloods."

That goddamn word again, I thought. Even Dominguez is using it now. But it wasn't Chambers' word, I reminded myself, it was the army's. So I just asked Dominguez to explain himself.

He shook his head. "You know, sir. Rumors."

"You want to check things out? It'd be too easy to get you on a night mission, if you want."

He furrowed his brow, chipmunk cheeks sagging. "No, sir," he said. "That's not what I'm asking."

I said I'd check things out, more out of fear of Dominguez's judgment than anything else.

"You're the platoon leader. The head motherfucker in charge. Don't let him push you around."

In his own way, Dominguez was pushing me around, too. I walked away, exchanged knuckles with a few *jundi*s, and took a seat next to Saif, now between payments.

"I'm thankful for your men," Saif said. "They brought order. Arabs, we hate lines."

"Fatwa?" I hissed. "A fucking fatwa?"

He rolled his eyes and called up the next Sahwa. "It's nothing," he said. "A scare tactic."

"Easy for you to say. You're used to this. What am I supposed to tell Ibrahim?"

He arched a bushy eyebrow soaked in sweat. "Whatever you think is wise, Loo-tenant. Things like this are why you're here. You're the officer. He's just—what do you all call them? A young blood?"

I snorted and began plucking my eyebrows the way Captain Vrettos did when he became overwhelmed. I was losing control of things again. Meanwhile, Alia's story kept tugging at me. And what was going on in Ashuriyah at night?

Saif counted out dollars for the last of the midtown Shi'as, a skinny teen in desperate need of braces. Fat Mukhtar and his khaki browns were next, a long, grim face with a flattop among them. Dead Tooth's older brother stared at me, hard.

The skinny guard slinked away. I put up my palm, signaling the escorting *jundi* to hold the line. "Saif, I need a favor." I'd made a decision. A couple, really. "Between us."

He bobbed his head slightly.

"I need to know where Rana lives," I said. "If she's still alive. But it's important no one else know."

"I see." Saif tapped his chin and considered. "My men need laser sights for their rifles."

"And?"

"And Americans keep extras in storage, but only Iraqi officers get them. To find the sheik's daughter, ten laser sights would be most helpful."

"You serious?" Something like a wrecking ball crashed through my gut. "Those things are crazy expensive. What happened to being partners, not allies?"

He shrugged. "Even partners make trades, Loo-tenant Porter."

"Three."

"Five."

"Done. But it'll take me a week or so, my supply connection is at Camp Independence. You know I'm good for it."

After a moment, he nodded. I patted him on the back and walked away from the table, fleeing the bitter, red-cheeked stare of Dead Tooth's brother, now pushing to the front of the line. Saif motioned the next Sahwa forward. The Son of Iraq walked up with a reckless smirk, a need in his step that could never be replicated by someone who'd known a full stomach and a warm bed his entire life.

Once through the crowd, I moved up the stairs, tottering a bit. Rather than face the Mother Hajj and Pedo bin Laden, I studied the ten smiling children in front of them holding the tricolored Iraqi flag. All of them had two dots for noses, not unlike the disfigured girl on the Sunni Strip who worked at the falafel shack. Halfway up, the low roar in the foyer rose sharply. I turned around and watched a pair of mid-town Shi'as in armbands push and shove with Sunnis in khaki brown; it looked like some of the Shi'as had arrived late and attempted to cut the line. There was shouting and fist shaking, and more Sahwas on both sides packed in close to join. I smelled the loose flesh of violence, all hot sweat and young rage, and fingered the ammo magazines in my pocket. Dominguez and two tall *jundis* stepped into the center of the throng and charged their rifles, restoring temporary order. Saif stood on the table brandishing a fistful of dollars to try to maintain it. From the center of it all, Fat Mukhtar laughed and laughed.

This is the legacy of Shaba and the sheik, I thought, in all its twisted, messy ambiguity. None of the Sahwa had been allowed to take a weapon inside the outpost, be they Sunni or Shi'a, sheik or guard, old or young. Allies or partners, I figured, would still have their guns.

At least we had meant well. Or something.

I continued upstairs and moved into our boxy, windowless room. Chambers was asleep in bed, resting for another night mission. I poked his shoulder and avoided looking at the black skulls on his arms.

"I'm coming tonight," I said.

He smacked his lips. "Sure thing."

"Awesome." I breathed out. "Any idea what we'll be doing?"

"Yeah." He sat up and cracked his neck. "While you were talking to the cleaning lady, battalion got a tip from the Rangers. Passed along the location of one of Dead Tooth's sleep spots. It's raid time."

My chest seized up and my mind turned to cream. He knows, I thought. How? Don't ask. Don't blink. He's probing. Acting like he knows more than he does. Be cool, Jack, I told myself. Be cool. A raid? I don't want to go on a raid. This is all Dominguez's fault. How. Does. He. Know?

"Looking forward to it," I said.

I turned away, hell-bent on getting to a Porta John to think things through. I was halfway out of the room before getting called back.

"One more thing, Lieutenant."

I stayed in the doorframe, like we'd been taught to do in elementary school in case of earthquake.

"Drug tests came back today. Few guys pissed hot for Valium. Washington. Tool. Some others. Must be getting it from the *jundi*s. Your buddy needs to rein in his boys. Busting them all down a rank, which means Washington loses his fireteam. You cool with Hog taking his spot? Kid's fucking ready."

"Hog? He's great, but what about that negligent discharge a while back? During the sandstorm patrol?"

"He's been counseled," Chambers said. He balled his fist twice, flexing his forearm, then stopped. "Onetime mistake."

"I'm fine with it, then. See you tonight."

"Looking forward to it," he said.

28

H ey, Will. It's me."

"Little bro! Good to hear from you. Everything okay?"

"I guess."

"What's up? No offense, but make it quick. Lady friend stayed the night. We're headed out to all-you-can-drink brunch."

"Oh. Sounds fun. It's just that, well, shit's hitting the fan and I was hoping to—I don't know."

"You get that local to write a sworn statement about your platoon sergeant yet?"

"No. And. Well. Things are different now. He—he saved my life."

"What?"

"It's a long story." I smacked my lips. "He pulled me to the ground in a firefight."

"Why were you were in that position to begin with?"

"Because I wanted to get shot. For fuck's sake. You think I did it on purpose?"

"Sorry, sorry. Old habits die hard. Once a combat leader, always a combat leader. But you're okay?"

"Yeah. They gave us a medal for the firefight. Well, some of us. It's fucking stupid."

"Oh yeah? Which one?"

"Army Commendation Medal with Valor."

"Nice. Still no Silver Star, though."

"Yeah. Okay. You got me on that. They're all shit, anyways."

"What's all shit?"

"Any stupid piece of tin given out by old men to trick young men into perpetuating bullshit myths."

"Slow your roll." He clucked his tongue. "Know you're stressed-out, and probably operating on zero sleep, but soldiers died for those pieces of tin. It's not the awards. It's what they represent."

"Whatever."

"You talk to Marissa recently? I don't think you want to hear anything I'm saying right now. A woman's voice would do you some good."

"About that." I laughed. "She told me not to call or write anymore."

"The hell?"

"It's my fault. Probably. I don't know."

"She's a good girl. Smart. Honest. You guys have had all sorts of ups and downs, and always manage to find your way back to each other. It'll happen again."

"Fuck her. She wouldn't know what it's like over here." I left out the part about not telling her what it was like when I'd had the chance. "She probably wouldn't even care if she did."

"What what's like?"

"All of it. Like another platoon accidentally shooting up a car because they thought it was a bomb but it wasn't, it wasn't anything but people."

He sighed. "Man, listen. I'm sorry you all had to deal with that. I really am. But, well. It's war. Shit happens."

"War? Weren't you listening? It was an accident."

"I'm trying to be patient, Jack, but you're making it really hard. Pull yourself together. Look within and ask yourself if you're doing everything you can for your men. For your mission."

"Shit. It's good enough for government work."

"Come on. Don't get snarky. Is this about the firefight? I'm sure you did fine. Besides, physical courage doesn't matter the way moral courage does. You know that."

"Here we go again. Spare me, please. If you were actually God's gift to the army, you'd have stayed in."

"You know what? Fuck you. You know how difficult it was for me to leave."

"Fuck me? Fuck you. I called you thinking you'd know what to do, not just lecture me."

"Do about what? Your kill-team sergeant? Sounds like you don't even want to get rid of him anymore, which makes me question just how much you looked into things at all. Or did you just want to get rid of him because he tested your leadership and you didn't know how to respond? Man up, make a decision, and live with it. That's the job."

I didn't say anything.

"And call Mom and Dad. But only after you get some sleep and chill. They'll freak out if they hear you like this. I'm going to brunch. I love you. Be safe. Be strong."

"Be safe? Be strong? What does that even mean?"

"It means what it means."

I hung up before I could tell him it meant nothing.

29

Why is the sky blue?

As first squad kicked in the door, I thought of the old, pointless joke from ROTC, the one the Vein liked to drill into us when we got lost in land navigation or fouled up a tactics quiz.

Because God loves the infantry. That's why.

No blue sky on a night raid, though.

Stacked against the side of the one-room hut, backs against a speckled wall of adobe, we communicated through hand-and-arm signals. We'd smeared war paint across our faces in swirls of black and brown and green. Night vision goggles hung from the front of our helmets over our eyes, just bulky enough to give our heads a slight tilt to the side of the dominant eye. Mine tipped left because I was a creative at heart. Shades of green ebbed and flowed before us, a hallucination of formless shapes and sizes that distorted the warm summer night.

The patrol there had been simple enough. The target house given to us by the Rangers was at the southeastern edge of town, in a quiet Sunni enclave. I gave a short brief and we moved out on foot, telling the soldiers that if—if—we came across armed insurgents, we'd turn their lives Jurassic.

Night patrols always sent my body into sensory overload, like all the turbo buttons of my brain were being mashed at once. Everything was more. I smelled the smoke from burning tires around town, rubber and sulfur blending together. I heard the insurgency of wild dogs and their damn starlight barks revealing our location. I tasted cool, bracing water from my CamelBak and chewed the mouthpiece with sand bits in it. I felt the terrorist hole rise up from below and seize my ankle, bringing my top-heavy armored body to the ground. I saw the night vision lasers crawl across any shadow that dared move, little green hieroglyphs that always spelled *k-i-l-l*.

We moved through Sahwa checkpoints without a word. Only some were in the right locations, and none had the required number of guards. Even in the mad heat of August, they huddled around their fires and idled. Snoop whispered to them that we'd slit their throats if they gave away our position. We took silence as acquiescence.

We arrived from the west and stacked against the building's side in stunted grunts. I took a breath of hot, honeyed air and checked the map one last time.

A hand motion made its way back, one shape at a time. First squad was ready. I turned around. So was second squad. Batule stood behind me, panting like an asthmatic. Behind him, another soldier chewed a wad of bubblegum. Stealthy we were. Delta Force we weren't.

I pointed forward, index finger extended.

First squad swooped in, the only noise a swinging door and the soft steps of boots on packed dirt. A flash of light washed out my night vision, then two shots rang out. I moved forward into the numb.

As I pushed aside the thick wool blanket hanging from the inside of the doorway, the smell of cordite filled the room. American bodies piled into the three corners away from the doorway, while another body lay splayed out in the center of the room on top of a mat.

"Clear!"

"Room clear."

"Sir, the hut's clear! One enemy target down!"

I could see all this my fucking self, since only eight of us could fit into the hut, and the flashlights on our rifles had lit the room like a flare. I called for Doc Cork to check the body, told a fireteam to stay inside to search for intel, and pushed the others outside to do the same.

Doc Cork turned over the body. "Gone, baby, gone," he said.

The man looked too old to be Dead Tooth, his skin sallow and lined. Too old and too small. Two scarlet pennies swelled through his shirt. The shooter had put the rounds through the chest three inches apart—a shitty target group, considering, but it had done its job, tearing through flesh and muscle and bone in spinning, raging angles to minimize the marginal effects and maximize the lethal one.

"Only thing we found is a bottle of cheap Iraqi whiskey." It was one of the soldiers. "Still looking for a weapon."

I nodded, the faintest pangs of what no weapon meant tapping at my soul. I looked back to the body. It wore an oversized soccer jersey, green, like the Iraqi national team's. A cherry fluid trickled out of the mouth, a ribbon of blood with nothing left to circulate. Its jaw hung open, loosing a thin purple tongue and a set of jagged teeth the color of rot.

"Oh God," I said. "Haitham."

I took off my helmet in the now-swaying heat and rubbed my hands through my short hair. I took a knee and asked very calmly and very particularly who'd shot and why.

"It was me, sir," Hog said. "I—I got stuck in the blanket, and when I pushed it away, I thought the bottle was a gun. He had it up like he was gonna shoot or something." Hog fell against the far wall, sliding down in a heap. His rifle lay flat on the ground, and he covered his head with his forearms, grabbing the top of his helmet with his hands. When he spoke again, it sounded like a small candy was lodged in his windpipe. "Oh fuck. Oh fuck, this is bad, huh? Fuck me. Sir? I didn't mean to, I swear to God, I fucking swear to God, sir. How bad is this? Talk to me. What now? What now, sir?"

"Everyone out." Chambers stood in the doorway. "Everyone out but Hog and Lieutenant Porter."

I felt seasick. I stayed on one knee as Doc Cork grasped Haitham's little dead fingers with his own and then left with the others. I knew what was going to happen before it did, but I just stayed there in the middle of the room, looking at Haitham's face forever etched in dirty sweat.

"Corporal. Calm down. Every Iraqi household has an AK-47. It's allowed by law." Ever certain. Ever clear. I couldn't bring myself to turn around and look at the doorway, so I focused on a speckle shaped like a leaf on the far wall. "That AK's got to be around here somewhere. I bet one of the other guys already grabbed it, and it's outside waiting for us. These things happen all the time. To good soldiers and good men. Isn't that right, Lieutenant?"

Isn't that right. Such a funny phrase, when I thought about it.

"Haitham was a wanted man." I stood up. "A good kill. Stand up, Hog. Let's get some air."

Hog looked up and laughed, full-throated. His amber eyes were fixed on something far away, and his mouth kept drooping as he tried to speak. He stood up and pulled out a cigarette. I lit it for him. As he followed me through the door, Chambers whistled in the back corner, low and without melody.

"All right." I gathered the soldiers together, near the entrance. The swinging door had fallen from its hinges and now lay in the dirt. A ring of cigarette cherries surrounded me, their orange eyes seeing through the blackness of my words. I found a crate and stood above them. "So we got the Cleric," I announced. "A good kill. No question. But you need to always remember the rules of engagement—don't shoot unless they're armed. You can't shoot unless they're armed. We're American soldiers. We're the good guys." My voice was shaking. "You fucking hear me?"

They all said Yes, sir, we hear you.

By the time I walked back into the hut, someone had found an AK-47. They took a photo of Haitham's body next to it. I stood in the back corner and radioed the outpost while the men pulled a body bag out of a backpack. As they unfolded the bundle, an olive-green sack designed to hold leaking carcasses, a camel spider jumped from one of its inner flaps. It was a hairy, ugly thing, the size of a baseball, primed up on its legs like they were ladders. It crawled across the ground and onto the dead man's face.

The soldiers assigned to body bag duty jumped back. I told the outpost to wait one. The spider burst under the heel of my boot, leaving guts, fur, and green juice splattered across Haitham's forehead.

"Clean that off before you zip him up," I said. When they didn't move quickly enough, I did it myself.

"Be easy, *habibi*," I said, closing his jaw and eyelids. Then I got back on the radio while the soldiers bagged him.

30

Saif came the next morning to the patio, where I was watching the pink-and-purple light of the seven o'clock hour blink out. The Sultan was rising again, a new day. I hadn't slept, and held a cigarette that wouldn't stop quivering.

"She's here," he said, handing me a photocopied map with a red circle on it. "Can you hear me, Loo-tenant Porter? This is where she is."

We went to her. I needed to do something with the day.

She lived in a hamlet west of the Villages, just across the Anbar border. I coordinated with the marines, since they were the landowners there, which suddenly sounded like such a ridiculous term.

Captain Vrettos commended me for my initiative when I said I needed to talk to a source outside our area. He looked almost healthy for once, even had color in his face. The news of the Cleric's death had already ricocheted up the command—we'd received congratulatory messages from the Big Man and brigade commander, and were expecting one from the division commander. Captain Vrettos thanked me again for what we'd done the night before.

I didn't say anything, because I couldn't. He asked if I was okay. I said I was. He said he was always there if I needed to talk about the rigors of war and leadership. I said that was cool to know.

"One more thing," he said.

"Oh?" I said.

"It's the first day of Ramadan," he said. "Just so you know."

• • •

We left Ashuriyah. I saw the Barbie Kid on the roadside, alone near the northern fringe of the market. He leaned against a crooked utility pole and his pink sweats shined in the morning like a fallen star. He still didn't have any shoes on his feet. I waved, but he just watched us and texted on a cell phone. We passed under the stone arch. Though I didn't turn around to face the dead cleric and his beard of snow, I felt his glasses on my back. Somehow, I thought, he knows I'm off to find his daughter.

We drove west, the countryside melting into shades of dun. Berms rose and fell like ocean swells. This is the desert, I thought, free and true. I took a gulp of Rip It from the back hatch and breathed in baked air and laughed because it didn't feel so strange anymore. None of it did. The soldiers asked what was wrong, and I brought up Ramadan.

"The Muslim fasting month," I said. "We should do it with them."

We hit an IED. One of the tire-popping kind that rattle the brain cage but fail to actually pop tires. A few months before, it would've caused an uproar, stirring the bantam energy of men yet untested. The vehicle's emergency system was the only one who spoke. "Exit the vehicle immediately," she said. We got out, checked our ears for blood, and made sure the Stryker still worked. Then we kept going.

At a dried-out reservoir bed, we turned south onto a thin road made of silt. Everyone seemed nervous, the radios clear of chatter, limbs taut and stiff. No one liked unfamiliar areas this late into a deployment, and before the mission I'd overheard some of the joes bitching about me "glory hunting."

I was surprised by how little I cared what they thought.

A herd of one-humped camels wandered onto the road, and we stopped. The men asked if we could drive through them, because it could be a delay tactic for ambushers, and who cared if we ran over a camel or two? I told them to shut up and wait, because they were just camels. The shepherd, a teenage boy wearing a Guns N' Roses concert tee, frowned as we passed, even though we'd waited for him and his herd.

About a mile down the dirt road, we spotted a half moon of five small mud huts. We parked there. I dismounted, tapping Snoop and Batule to follow. There was a small, square garden of green shrubs and dandelions in the middle of the houses, marked by two strands of barb-wire and four wooden poles at each corner. The air was windless and smelled of wildflowers.

The three of us walked by the huts. Nothing stirred, and the only sound I could make out was our own strained breathing. I searched the windows for peeking eyes or fingertips holding back curtains. Thoughts of an ambush flitted through my mind. I took off my helmet, grabbed the hand mic on Batule's back, closed my eyes, and waited for the sniper's shot I'd never hear, let alone see.

I counted to ten and thought of a train ride with Will when we were boys, all infinite hopes and forever dreams, play-fighting with our hands around each other's shoulders. We were pretending to be antiheroes like good postmodern American boys, he Batman, me Wolverine, watching the sleepy coastal towns of California blur by, slowly at first, then quicker and quicker until we couldn't even make out the names of the towns being passed, let alone the streets or mailboxes.

I'd worshipped my brother my entire life, though it sometimes came out wrong, like as resentment. Five and a half years' difference in age could do that. He'd been a tough act to follow, and I figured the last thing he needed was more people telling him how smart and capable he was. I knew everyone thought I'd joined up because he had, even our parents. Maybe he felt that way, too. But that hadn't been it, not exactly. It wasn't to be him, or to be like him. It'd been to believe in something the way he had. To know idealism as something more than a word. That had been what I wanted.

He'd lost that belief somewhere along the line, somehow. I doubted I'd ever had it.

Now he was learning to be a goddamn businessman. And me? I didn't even know anymore.

I opened my eyes, took in a deep breath of dust, and cursed. Ignoring Snoop and Batule, I walked to the center garden and studied the dandelions.

The sound of kicked pebbles brought my eyes up from the garden.

•

A small woman in an ankle-length gray dress walked across the half moon spinning an umbrella above her. She wore a shawl but no veil, and hair fell from her head in black waves. Her complexion was fair for an Iraqi. A coffee stain of a mark splashed across her left cheek, and an arrow nose pierced out at us. I lapped her up like water, lingering at the curves of her hips and again at the small dip in her neckline. It wasn't until I made it to her eyes, though, two jade ovals shining defiantly, that I knew we'd found her.

"Well-come," she said. Behind her, two boys wearing matching striped shirts clutched her dress. Neither stood taller than her knees. A small pink scar the width of Silly String ran down the elder's left earlobe to the top of his neck. He scowled at us while his little brother stared.

"Hi," I said. "My name's Jack Porter."

"Hello."

I pointed to the black umbrella and switched to Arabic. "What's with that?"

She smiled, revealing a set of blocky teeth stained light brown. A dimple sank into her cheek, under the birthmark.

"It seldom rains here," she said. Her English was awkward and slow, but clear. "But we need many umbrellas."

She kept spinning the umbrella in circles, clockwise twice, counter-clockwise once, again and again. I watched with my mouth agape until Snoop coughed.

"Would you and your men like any water?" she asked.

"No, thanks," I said. "It's Ramadan, you know."

31

August 18, 10:17 PM

LIEUTENANT PORTER—

I WAS INTERESTED TO RECEIVE YOUR EMAIL. IT'S GOOD TO HEAR THE EFFORTS OF MY COMPANY IN ASHURIYAH ARE STILL HAVING A POSITIVE IMPACT ON THE ESTABISHMENT OF A FREE AND DEMOCROTIC IRAQ.

THERE WAS AN OFFICIAL INVESTIGATION INTO THE DISAP-PEARANCE OF STAFF SERGEANT RIOS. IF IT'S OF INTEREST TO YOU AND YOU BELIEVE IT CAN HELP YOUR UNIT'S EFFORTS, I RECOMMEND CONTACTING YOUR BRIGADE'S JAG OFFICE. THEY CAN LOCATE THE OFFICIAL REPORT. THOUGH I HAVENT READ IT FOR SOME YEARS, IT WAS FOUND THAT STAFF SERGEANT RIOS VIOLATED OUR UNIT'S PROCEDURES BY WALKING AWAY FROM THE OUTPOST UNAUTHORIZED.

THERE WAS ALSO AN OFFICIAL INVESTIGATION INTO THE SHOOTING OF THE INSURGENT ENGAGED BY LIEUTENANT GRANT IN CLOSE QUARTERS. IT WAS FOUND THAT MY COMPANY ACTED IN ACCORDANCE WITH ALL RULES OF ENGAGEMENT.

THANK YOU FOR YOUR WORDS ABOUT LIEUTENANT GRANT. HIS DEATH WAS A TERRIBLE LOSS FOR ALL OF US WHO SERVED

WITH HIM. WE TRIED TO GET HIM THE HELP HE NEEDED. HE'S WITH GOD NOW.

PLEASE UNDERSTAND THAT GIVEN THE SENSITIVE NATURE OF YOUR INQUIRY, AND THE IMPLICATIONS SUGGESTED IN YOUR EMAIL, I'VE ALERTED YOUR CHAIN-OF-COMMAND TO THIS EXCHANGE, SPECIFICALLY YOUR EXECUTIVE OFFICER, A FORMER WEST POINT CLASSMATE OF MINE. HE'S A GOOD OFFICER. ANY FUTURE QUESTIONS SHOULD BE DIRECTED TO HIM.

YOURS IN SERVICE,

KENNETH TISDALE

MAJOR, INFANTRY

U.S. ARMY

32

Lieutenant Porter:

Your name was mentioned in our hometown's article as the officer who found Elijah so I am especially glad you contacted me. I had been wanting to say thank you for bringing closure to my family, especially my mom. We had another service for Elijah a couple weeks ago, this time with a proper burial.

It's strange to hear that my brother is still known in Iraq, but also good. To be honest, I don't really know how to answer your questions. We weren't close. When he joined the army, he stopped contacting us. He was very bitter—our father left when we were children, and he never stopped being angry about it. Hated school, hated Texas, hated us, hated himself. I didn't even know he knew Arabic until your message. We didn't know he'd been sent to Iraq until the army chaplain showed up on our porch to say he'd gone missing there.

As for good stories, there's this one, which is how I like to remember him. It was his junior year of high school, and he was working at the adventure park, saving up to buy a used car. Some friends and I went to the park after school, and a group of older boys started messing with us. They got on the log ride right after us, and kept taunting us from their log the entire time. They wouldn't leave us alone. Elijah saw the whole thing. So he waited for our log to go down the big drop, and when their log was at the very top, he shut down the ride and walked away. They were up there for hours, screaming for help. It was funny. Elijah lost his job, but he didn't care.

Maybe not the greatest story, but it was a nice, older brother thing to do. Don't have many memories like that.

Hope this helps some and Thank You For Your Service.

Sarah Rios

33

Night Flower—

    I'm sorry I didn't visit tonight. There was a mission on the other side of town and the Lieutenant insisted I go. I promise to make it up to you. We got some care packages today—would you prefer a Connect Four board game or a stuffed koala?

    Just kidding. I'll bring you both.

    Have you calmed down? You dream of America, but staying here is best. We can have the life you see in the movies, here in Iraq, in Ashuriyah. The America you imagine no longer exists, if it ever did. You need to know that your father lives in more luxury than anyone from my hometown. Until I came to Iraq, until I met your father, I had never been in a house as large as yours. Or known a man who owned five Mercedes. Or seen a marble fountain, like the eagle in your driveway. Be careful what you ask for, Night Flower, that's all I'm saying.

    We will visit, of course. I will show you the monuments in New York and Washington, and take you to the California beaches. But Ashuriyah will be home. Our children will know the meaning of family, and be part of the new Iraq.

    I know you're laughing now. Yes, a new Iraq. They call me the "money man" for a reason. I can—and will—make your father the most important sheik in the province, much more important than just being in charge of Sahwa. We will build roads. We will build schools. We will build power stations and plants. We're already planning the largest hospital in the country, bigger than anything in Baghdad,

212 · Matt Gallagher

something that will make Ashuriyah one of the most important places in the Middle East.

If you still don't understand, talk to your father. He knows. He believes.

Forty soldiers sleep around me now in the outpost, their minds far away, on everything that is typical. They are here to survive and endure, not to change. All they care about is getting home alive. I used to blame them for this, but that was unfair. I will get them home alive. But I won't be going with them. I'm staying here. For you. For us.

I met your brother yesterday. I'll tell you about it next time I visit.

Give your father my best. Good night, Night Flower, tomorrow awaits. Allah is One, the heart is one, and the heart only belongs to the One,

E.

BOOK III

34

None of the locals could remember a Ramadan like it, not even the elders. The summer heat was supposed to blow away in the wind, they said, not wash away in rain. If they thought it meant anything, though, they kept it to themselves.

I fasted through the holy month, alone among the occupiers. I didn't quite feel cleansed by it, but it gave me something to talk about with Rana. She was a source now. Our source. We came on the days she said to, when her husband was away in Baghdad managing his concrete business. Her information wasn't great, but it wasn't bad, either. She knew of some cache spots along the canal.

She didn't speak much of the ghost who haunted her, though during our third meeting she let me read one of his love letters. When I handed it back, I searched her face for signs of sadness or reminiscence. I found neither. Instead, she was studying me behind her arrow nose, probing, considering. I swallowed away a blush. She folded up the letter, placing it in a hidden pocket of the gray cotton dress she always seemed to wear.

Snoop came to the hut with me at first, but eventually he stayed with the men in the vehicles outside. "To play cards," he said. We were short-timers now. For the soldiers, home wasn't just a thing we'd left anymore. It was a thing that awaited.

Out there, the war endured. A land of bullets and fatwas, out there assured only death. I understood that now. The desert had always meant death for strange infidels far from home, from Alexander the Great to Elijah Rios. There were no dust storms in the sheika's hut, though, no scorpions or holy wars. It smelled of lush wildflowers, not hot trash. With her, I felt no headaches. We listened to the playful shouts of her boys, not the shrieks of mortar shells. The war existed beyond the hamlet. In the hut—in the hut was something else.

She spoke of the past with small, soft hands flitting toward the sky. I spoke of the present with anxious proclamations. I told her to smile more. She told me to find her reasons to.

One dreary afternoon, she asked how we'd come to find Shaba's remains. I didn't want to say, but she insisted.

I talked about the wake, about Haitham's call, about the fatwa that relegated Ibrahim to Camp Independence, about all the tribal leaders who knew the bones were there but had pled ignorance. "Don't worry," I said. "We'll get them. We'll get them all."

She stayed silent for many seconds.

"What?" I asked.

"Ashuriyah is hell," she said, her face setting like flint. "How do you defeat the devil in his own home?"

35

The summer before I joined ROTC was California bright and filled with crystal skies. Will came home for a few weeks and kept talking about the time he'd called in an airstrike on the Taliban. Marissa and I decided to give it another try, at least until we went back to our respective campuses in the fall, spending our mornings at the lake and our evenings in friends' basements.

Her sister Julie was to be married in August. Will, Mom, and I received invitations. Our dad didn't live in our subdivision anymore, so he didn't get one. There were rules in Granite Bay.

Julie and Will had never really gotten along, even though they'd gone to school together. Marissa and I liked to joke that the reason for the mutual distaste was their red-blooded lust for each other. "Our kids could be double cousins!" we said. Neither sibling ever laughed with us, but we didn't care. We had each other.

Despite their history of antipathy, neither Will nor Julie considered themselves unreasonable, something that proved helpful when the groom, Richie Gomez, asked my brother to be a replacement groomsman—something about a Venezuelan cousin having visa issues. Richie and Will had played high school baseball together, so it made some sense, though I harbored cynical thoughts about the groom's need to prove to the bride's family that he wasn't a Chavez-loving socialist, which meant trotting out Will's dress uniform and shiny medals.

"You're a fool," my mom said when I brought that up.

"You're an idiot," Marissa said when I brought that up.

The week of the wedding, I stumbled into our kitchen, seeking out the pantry. Will was pacing the linoleum tile floor.

"Scumbag," he said. "Creep. Coward."

I asked who he was ranting about.

"Tomas Butkus," he said. "He's coming to the wedding."

It was well-known in Millennial Granite Bay that Julie and Tomas had hooked up on a camping trip, months after she began dating Richie Gomez. Well-known to everyone but Richie. Gossip peddling being gossip peddling, and gossip peddlers being gossip peddlers, the story had swirled around Richie without reaching his ears.

"That was, like, a couple years ago," I said. "And Julie and Tomas are friends. That's who weddings are for."

"No, Jack. You're wrong." My potato chip munching rose with his voice, and I took a seat behind the counter. "Weddings are for people who will love and support your marriage. Not just a collection of friends."

"Then why are you going?"

"That's not the point. The point—this Lithuanian prick has no honor. He should have respect for her and for Richie, and stay the fuck away."

"Hmm." He was speaking so fast that I had a hard time keeping up. I was hungry. And stoned.

He went on to wax eloquent about HONOR. And INTEGRITY. And that lesser-known army value of NOT BEING BALTIC EUROTRASH. It all sounded quite significant and convincing, even to my pond-water mind, but one question lingered. When he finally stopped, it came off my tongue in a deluge of potato chip crumbs.

"Will. Like, why do you care so much?"

He looked at me, wild-eyed. "I don't. I'm just saying."

After the weed wore off, I figured out why he cared. The night after he'd graduated West Point, he had proposed to the daughter of a Connecticut senator he met at a Boston bar. She said yes. Some months later my family received a terse, slightly fanatical e-mail saying the engagement was off, the wedding was off, it was all off, that Will had sworn to himself that he'd never compromise and this was proof. He was going to be a man of principle, even if it meant sacrificing his own temporary happiness, because what was happiness in the long run but a silly, stupid emotion that was just a particular pattern of synaptic connections?

We never talked about the e-mail or mentioned it to Will. There wasn't much to say, other than we were there for him when he needed us.

The wedding ceremony went well. Will was sharp and polished in his dress blues, and though the old, rich white relatives picked at him like vultures, he didn't seem to mind. My mom patted my arm and told me perhaps I'd had a point earlier.

"Those are the type of men who will keep your brother at war," she said, her voice both proud and furious. "Not a grunt among them."

"How do you know that word?" I asked.

"Army moms know lots of words," she said. Then, after a pause, she smiled. "Navy daughters do, too."

The minister pronounced them man and wife. Bells clanged and spirits flowed. The world had never seen such joy, we all thought, and we all meant it. The stars were out, the night was calm, and the lakeside breeze blew with peace and joy and all sorts of particular patterns of synaptic connections.

Near the end of the reception, I slow-danced with Marissa. She wasn't a girl who got done up often, which made her loveliness all the more palpable. In her uniform of a floral, ruffled bridesmaid dress, half drunk on wine, she clung to me, describing our future house, naming our future babies, planning a life together as idyllic as it was ordinary. I beamed, belly full of beer, knowing that sloppy, irresponsible sex awaited. Shouts and screeching chairs suddenly came from behind us, near the bar. We turned that way, same as everyone else. Will was standing over a dazed Tomas, fist clenched.

"Who am I? Who the fuck am *I*?" Will said. In that moment, his words almost sounded natural. "I'm an infantry officer. I'm a man with purpose. I'm a man who knows what's right, what's wrong, and what you are."

Tomas had trouble finding his feet, but his friends surrounded my brother and started crowing, chests out, drunken mania gliding through their eyes. I told Marissa that I'd be right back. Then I grabbed a metal chair, pushed into the circle, and told them if they wanted a fair fight, the Brothers Porter could certainly oblige.

Mom polished off her glass of Irish cream and told us to get in the car—she was driving us home just as soon as she thanked Julie and Marissa's parents for the evening.

We didn't say anything to one another on the drive home. As I stared out the car window at the streetlights and cul-de-sacs, I decided I wasn't going to be a man of nothing. I wasn't going to be a man of the idyll and ordinary. I was going to be the type of man who punched out Baltic Eurotrash at weddings for principle's sake.

I was going to be a soldier. I was going to be an officer. I was going to be a leader of men.

Then I smiled at Will and patted him on the back. He needed that.

36

We waited out the afternoon fall storm, the insistent *pat-pat-pat* of water meeting packed slabs of earth. I stood at a window watching my men teach Rana's boys poker. They'd gathered in a Stryker to keep dry, but had lowered the ramp to let in air.

"You brought this," she said from across the hut. "We haven't had so much rain for years."

She was teasing. At least I thought she was. I smiled shyly.

Her home was neat and tidy, everything from winter blankets to tableware organized into wood baskets stacked like bricks in corners. I'd thought the baskets a sign of a transient lifestyle, but Rana explained she fashioned herself a "minimalist," preferring an open space.

"How'd you learn that word?" I asked.

"There is a show—*The Real Housewives of Cairo*. My cousin in Karrada has a television. We watched it for hours when we visited last year. It was very . . ." She knocked on her forehead as she searched for the English word. "Educational."

I ran a hand through my sweaty hair. I'd been growing it out some, pushing the regulation length. My helmet and rifle lay near the front door. A pair of Persian carpets covered much of the main room with red diamonds and purple snowflakes. I returned to my plastic chair on the carpets, facing her. Every Iraqi man I'd met with had insisted on sitting on the ground for tradition. Rana said they just enjoyed messing with foreigners. She rose, gliding like a specter to the window, her dress concealing her feet and long black hair falling behind her.

"It's kind of your soldiers to play with Ahmed and Karim," she said. Her English was no longer clipped by breaks between syllables, improving with every conversation. "They get lonely."

222 • Matt Gallagher

The other homes in the hamlet were abandoned and had been since the sectarian wars of 2006. Rana's husband, an older cousin so infatuated with her that he hadn't minded marrying the disgraced ex-lover of an American, maintained the other buildings in case any displaced al-Badris returned to the area. His name was Malek. I hadn't met him, nor did I wish to.

Rana moved to the kitchen counter, a thin piece of granite on the other side of the room. My eyes followed, and my nostrils filled with her perfume, a curiously muggy scent that reminded me of swamp blossoms.

"Still no chai?" she asked. "Or food? Most Arabs don't follow the rules of Ramadan, you know. Just the crazy ones."

My stomach growled from days of inattention, but I shook my head. Another meal of cold leftovers awaited after sundown.

She brewed her tea differently from Saif, with more familiarity and less care. She scoffed when I'd said not to use distilled water, and had been more interested in the cost of his electric kettle than dismissive of it. She began boiling water and looked up, catching my eyes before they could dart away.

"Tell me again," she said. "About finding him."

"Nothing more to tell." I'd grown weary of the topic. "Haitham told us where to dig. We dug. We found the skeleton and sent it home."

"To Texas," she corrected.

"To Texas."

"But how do you know it was him?" I marveled at the control in her voice, as if we were still discussing the weather. "Because of tests in a lab?"

"Yeah," I said. Then I tapped at a bottom tooth. "And this was missing."

A whimper escaped her throat, and she bent against the countertop like a broken vane. I stood, ready to do something, anything, but clueless as to what. Then the kettle whistled. I blinked and Rana was upright, pouring water into a pot. She let the green mint leaves soak and resumed her seat. At her gesturing, I did the same.

Had I imagined her moment of anguish? I wasn't sure.

"I remember the day he did that," she said. It took me a moment to realize she was talking about Shaba's tooth. "Some of our guards were playing tetherball and asked Elijah to join. He was so bad, but tried so hard. There was a lot of blood. It took many towels to clean his face."

"You must miss him a lot," I said.

She shook her head. "It was a long time ago."

Rana went to swirl the teapot. When she returned, she asked about California. I told her I hadn't appreciated it growing up, but missed it now: the sand, the ocean. Impressing her mattered more than the truth. Her eyes seemed to light up at the mention of the beach. I started to tell her I'd take her someday, if she wanted, but coughed instead. That wasn't possible. I turned toward the window, where the rain was being replaced by drips of sunlight. There were shouts and the sound of a soccer ball being kicked around. I didn't need to look out to know that Washington and the *jundi*s were playing with the kids.

"You sure they won't say anything?" I asked. "We don't want to get anyone in trouble. I know you're taking a huge risk talking to us. To me."

"Who is there to tell?" A caustic sound slipped out of her, something between a groan and a laugh. She had a point. We hadn't come across anyone else living in the area. "And they have fun playing with the soldiers," she continued. "They understand for that to continue, their father doesn't need to know."

"At least let me pay for information," I said. "It's been good. Found ten rockets at the canal yesterday."

She waved away my offer. "Just talk I hear. Glad it helps."

She moved to the kitchen counter again to pour herself a glass of chai. Impulsively, she started running in place, bouncing on her toes and lightly punching at the air, her sandals slapping against the floor. She stopped midstride and laughed at herself. "I can't believe I did that with you here," she said. "You must think I'm strange."

"Not at all," I said, though I did, a bit. "A workout?"

"Tae Bo? My cousin had videos of a black man who did this." It took everything in the world right then for me not to laugh; apparently the nineties weren't yet dead. "When you're alone too much, these things happen. And exercise is important, I want to stay—*petit*?"

"*Pe-tite*."

"*Pe-tite*." She returned to her chair and smiled, her blocky, stained teeth reminding me of where we were.

Her chai was lighter than Saif's, more beige than wheat gold, and watered down. While the drink cooled, she nibbled on a plate of goat cheese and crackers. I asked about her family.

"My family," she said.

I nodded. "I've told you about mine."

"It's boring," she said. "But all right." Before I could tell her that I knew that wasn't true, she began talking, her raspy voice leaving little space for interjection.

"My parents married when my mother was fourteen. He was much older. They were cousins. Most women would've been happy to marry the future sheik of the al-Badri tribe. He promised a good life. But she wanted more than that. She wanted someone to make her laugh, someone to recite poetry to make her cry. My father was a good sheik. But good sheiks don't do things like that.

"She gave birth to six children, but Karim and I were the only ones to survive the first year. So we were close. The three of us, at least. My father was always away, working. We rarely saw him. He was a figure, a shadow we feared."

"What was he like on the arch?" I asked. "Stern? Omniscient?"

She knocked at her forehead again. "Om-niss-ent?"

"Someone who knows everything."

"No, not at all! They only called him the Cleric after he died. Here, people become perfect after death. Especially old men. Especially old men like my father."

I laughed while she sipped her chai, a coy shine on her face. I asked about her brother.

"Karim was four years older. My protector, he thought. Especially after our mother died. I think that's the reason . . ." She trailed off. "He never stopped thinking of himself that way."

"What else?" I said.

"He cared too much. Like Elijah."

She continued about her childhood, about how her mother had been a religious woman but had kept her and Karim away from the mosque, because children of a sheik weren't supposed to mingle with towns-people. Geography had been her favorite subject as a girl, because of the maps. And though it was embarrassing to admit now, she'd had a crush on one of Saddam's sons for the longest time. It was all fine background, but not why I was there. I wanted her to get to the point. There's the past we wish defined us, I thought, and there's the past that actually does.

She was talking about her mother insisting she learn the oud. "What about Rios?" I interrupted. "Elijah, I mean."

She looked up from the carpet and tilted her head. "Almost there, Lieutenant Porter. It was at those music lessons that we met."

"Oh." I forced another cough. "My bad. Go ahead."

"I'd seen him from a window, coming to meet my father. He was already famous by then. And when the American trucks went through town, calling out a number for the people to call and tell them where al-Qaeda was, I thought, 'I could call and speak to an American.' That was exciting to me then. So I called the number and said I'd only speak to him."

"I thought you two met in your father's sitting room."

She laughed curtly. "No Iraqi would allow that. Especially not my father. We talked on cell phones. First about information. Later about other things. Then he started coming to my music lessons, paying the instructor for his silence."

Goddamn Alia, I thought, and her bullshit story. She'd made me look stupid.

"And Rios, I mean Elijah, he taught you English?"

She nodded. "I'd studied some before. But it's because of him that I'm good at it. He spoke Arabic, though his dialect was bad. So we learned from each other."

The air in the room felt humid, and I felt clumsy and jealous all at once. I pointed outside, changing the topic.

"Your boy, how was he . . ." I pointed to my own earlobe and drew an imaginary line down my neck. "Hurt."

She bit into a cracker and shrugged. "Sky bomb," she said. "We were lucky."

I stared at a carpet stain between my feet. The soldiers called her eldest Scowls, which only made him scowl more. Now I knew why. Ahmed also had sharper features and paler skin than his clever-faced younger brother, something I thought about a lot. Too much, probably.

I'd spent a lot of time fantasizing about how Rana and Shaba had fallen in love, using Alia's version of events as a template. I knew every scene, every line of that desert ballad by heart. Sometimes I was there, observing silently in a corner. Other times I became a participant, toasting to their eternal love with the dead sheik. Sometimes I even replaced Rios, and it was Jack Porter who held hands with a moony young woman in her father's courtyard. Still other times, I didn't replace Rios so much as I became him, speaking fluent Arabic and darkly brooding over the future of my new country. But it hadn't happened that way. None of it had. It'd happened on the phone.

"What's your dream?" Rana asked suddenly, bringing me back to her hut.

"Huh." It wasn't that I'd never chewed over the question. It was that where I came from, a person wasn't supposed to have just one answer. "Seek greatness, I guess." Then I smirked, hoping that got me out of the question.

"What does that mean?" Her response wasn't implicating, just confused. "I meant what do you want? From life?"

"Depends on the day, really." I didn't want to talk about myself anymore, mostly because her question had caught me off guard. "What about you?"

"It's better if I show you," she said. She moved to the bedroom, where the family shared a large cotton mattress. She returned a minute later, a faint reverence in her steps. She held something to her chest and pressed it into my hands. The smell of swamp blossoms filled my nostrils, and goose bumps shot up my arms, beneath my sleeves.

It was a postcard. An old one, with worn edges and deep creases. A drawing of a city on the beach covered the front, a coral-blue sky and palm trees nestled up against a long row of Gothic buildings. Flipping it, I saw that the back was covered in faded Arabic script.

"Naples?" I asked, looking back up. I'd no idea where the postcard was from. "Havana?"

"Beirut," she said, the last syllable a feather off her tongue. It was only then, listening to her talk about a trip her parents had taken to Lebanon years before, that I realized she was younger than I was. Despite everything she'd been through, despite everything she'd seen, she was still younger.

In America, I thought, she'd be in college.

A furious knocking filled the stillness. I looked at Rana in a panic. An army officer alone with an Arab woman, let alone a married one living in seclusion, couldn't be explained away.

I hadn't even done anything wrong.

"It's for you," she said.

The walls of my throat closed up as I rose and took three steps to the front door. It wasn't anyone important, though. Just Batule, in all his oafish, mouth-breathing charm.

"Sir!" he said. "It's Captain Vrettos. Just radioed and said we got to roll to the big mosque!" Loose words dribbled from him like saliva. "Dead Tooth, at the top. Firefight with the IAs. And we need to get over there. Like, now."

He ran back to the vehicles before I could respond. I grabbed my helmet and rifle and went to follow.

A soft, determined hand stopped me as I stepped into gray mist. I turned around.

"You remind me of him," she said, squeezing my palm. "Be careful."

Rifle in one hand, helmet in the other, I ran on air to the waiting Stryker.

37

The minaret seemed so far away. A little cream-colored dome crested the spiraling stone tower, a dark-age Ottoman relic. The afternoon had turned dim and chilly. I rubbed my arms. An oval of American soldiers and Iraqi *jundi*s ringed the base of the tower, watching the black flag of al-Qaeda flap rowdily from the small walkway near the top.

Dead Tooth was somewhere up there. The squad of *jundi*s that'd chased him here said three other insurgents were with him, as well as the mosque's mullah and a long black tube that maybe was a rocket-propelled grenade launcher. Or maybe not. It was hard to tell.

Baritone Arabic blared from a megaphone on the other side of the oval. It was Saif, demanding the insurgents let the mullah go. He'd arrived before us, and shortly after Chambers and his half of the platoon. Captain Vrettos and a group of headquarters soldiers arrived last, bringing the sum of Coalition forces attempting to wait out a petulant, cornered teenager to fifty-five.

I leaned against the front of our Stryker and sucked down warm water from my CamelBak, watching the sun fall. The adrenaline jolt I'd gotten from Rana's words—and hand squeeze—had waned. I wondered if I could find a warm can of Rip It in the back of the vehicle. During the onslaught of puberty, I'd stay in my room for hours after a fight with my parents or Will. This was sort of the same thing, albeit with a kidnapped holy man and the potential for geopolitical disaster.

"Sir!" Dominguez shouted from the gunner's turret. "Commander wants you at his vehicle. Leaders' powwow."

I flashed him a thumbs-up and then walked counterclockwise

around the ring of armored vehicles, helmet cocked back, thumbs tucked under the chest plate, and rifle dangling from its sling, thinking about Rana and her kids. They seemed so alone. And sad.

"Hey, gaucho, pick up the goddamn pace. Waiting on you."

"Sorry, sir." Captain Vrettos sat on the edge of a lowered Stryker ramp. His eyes were red and cheeks wan. "Didn't realize."

The commander sighed and shook his head, voice slurring past the tobacco nestled deep in his cheeks. He resembled a pufferfish whenever he chewed, the effect heightened because of his build, a Pez dispenser head on a pull-string body. I kept my head low and stood between Chambers and Saif.

"Ideas?" Captain Vrettos began. "If we don't solve this in the next thirty minutes, the division commander's coming from Camp Independence to personally fire us all."

"Can't blow up a mosque," First Sergeant said.

"Need to blow up the terrorists," Chambers followed.

"Blow up?" Saif asked, a lot of shock and a little awe in his question. "How?"

"I've done this before," Chambers said. "In oh-four, Sadr pulled the same shit in Najaf. He stayed in a shrine for three fucking weeks, surrounded, and still got away. Learned that lesson. We need to get them now, before the generals show. Then it'll be too late."

"Too late?" Saif asked. "For what?"

Chambers ignored him. "Sir," he said to the commander, "this is what I recommend. I'll take a small team of guys. Four-man stack, Room Clearing one-oh-one. The staircase spirals up like that. If we move quick, they won't get an RPG out the window fast enough for a clean shot. The fuckers are iced, and the mosque stands. Win-win."

"Americans aren't allowed to enter mosques," Saif said, pushing his way back into the conversation. His voice was brittle. "My men and I must do this."

"No offense, big man, but this isn't training. My soldiers are better. We go, the only blood spilled is terrorist blood." Chambers didn't look away from the commander as he spoke to Saif, his eyes pale as slate. "Trust me. I've been here before."

Captain Vrettos began plucking at his eyebrows, trying to think.

I said, "I'm going, too."

"No way, sir," First Sergeant said. "Can't have both members of a platoon's leadership getting wiped out in one move."

"I hear you, First Sergeant. But these are my men. I'm going."

Captain Vrettos groaned and let go of his eyebrow. "Okay, you three all go. Grab a *jundi* for point. Lieutenant Porter, take a radio, you're my command and control up there. *Molazim* Saif, you're the de facto terp, but with a rifle. Do not kill the mullah. Understood?"

None of us were happy, but we all nodded.

As Chambers stalked off grumbling about having to do this with "two fucking officers," Saif pulled me behind the adjacent Stryker.

"You must stop this," he said. "This is a terrible decision. There must be another way."

I found his voice too authoritative. Dark Irish fury tore through me like cinder.

"Fuck off," I said. "Orders are orders. We could be dropping a drone bomb. Get your gear on."

"So that's how it's going to be?"

"Yeah."

"I mistook you, Loo-tenant Porter. I mistook you for someone different."

"Grab your *jundi*. We'll meet at the base of the tower."

I went to walk away, but turned around to see Saif half grinning at my backside.

"I'll be there," he said. The smile he was wearing hadn't reached his eyes. "But only me. None of my men will go up there for this."

I rolled my eyes and played him the world's smallest violin, rubbing my right thumb and forefinger together. Then I found Batule and said he was walking point up the minaret. He started prepping his gear. Hog was there, too, sitting on the back of a lowered ramp with a bored look on his face.

"This is crazy, sir," he said.

"Sure is," I said. I'd been avoiding him since the Haitham incident. He'd probably been avoiding me, too. "How you doing?"

Hog looked down at his feet. "I don't know," he said. "I think about him a lot."

"Yeah." I chewed my bottom lip.

He looked back up, his eyes turning to gin. Before he could tear up, I tapped him on the helmet and said to keep doing a good job. Then I walked away.

We gathered in strained silence. No one in our four-man stack wanted to speak; nor did anyone who was staying behind. The plan was far from tactically sound, but that'd never stopped a military operation. Saif unholstered his pistol, metal glinting in the dusk. Pushing away three or four bad jokes, I cracked my neck, tightened my bootlaces, and crossed myself with great papist flourish. Then I followed Batule, Saif, and Chambers up the yellow stones at a quick trot.

To my ears, our boots on the path sounded like falling trees, each step a fatal alarm for the enemy above that possessed everything—high ground, larger weapons, the fervor of zealotry. As we rounded two, then three loops of the spiral ramp, the sand winds howled. We faced the dead of north on the third rotation, and it struck with an open palm; I had to stagger to my left to catch my balance. Only Chambers remained upright. Saif pushed past Batule, and we kept moving.

With two more rungs of tower to go, the dirty sky burst into patriotic staples of red, white, and purple. A green star cluster followed. Illumination rounds, I realized, meant to distract the insurgents in the tower. It's Independence Day in Babylon, I thought, turning back to the climb as the lead man tripped over a clear, ankle-high wire spread across the path, landing on his palms and knees.

There was a long, yo-yoing pause during which no one moved. All I could do was bite my lip and tuck my chin before the world exploded into stone. I thought of all the little things that make up life and the ancient howl returned, pushing me into the tower wall. I saw and heard nothing until I did again.

• • •

It was the falling debris that brought me back, earth raining back down on earth. I felt my face like a blind man reading braille. One lip, two lips. A nose. The eyes were still there, and they opened and saw dirty sky again, though my lenses had been blown off. I blinked and blinked, pushing away the thousand hammers pounding in my head, and stood up.

Everything was brown ash. As I leaned against the tower wall, trying to remember who and why, a shape came out of the cloud like a monster.

"Sir!" It was talking to me loudly. "Sir!"

"Batule!" I grabbed him by the chest plate and pulled him toward me. His face looked like meatloaf, and his hands were pressed against one of his eyes, his palms lapping up pools of dark blood. Pieces of his uniform on his arms and upper torso had been shredded, but he seemed able to walk. I said to keep his hands pressed against that socket and asked if he could make it down the tower path by himself. He said yes.

"Go," I said.

"No way, they need help."

"That's a fucking order!" I was yelling too loud but wasn't sure he could hear me, either. "You're combat ineffective. Go the fuck down!"

He went one way and I went the other, using the curving tower wall as my guide, toward belt lashes of rifle fire.

I floated through steps of exaggerated movement, uncertain where my feet would land, a spaceman sifting through the powder of the moon. Four, five, six steps in, I heard laughter, then the whistles of steady gunfire, then saw the hazy silhouette of a man on one knee firing a rifle up the path. I found my own still on me, dangling from its strap at my hip. I raised it to my shoulder pocket and flipped it to burst, firing into the fangs of the unknown, not bothering to aim, not caring to. A bright lodestar of a tracer lit the way every fifth round. Breathing in the hot cordite of spent rounds, breathing out the cold sulfur of rounds spent, I kept squeezing until the magazine ran dry. When I dropped it and reached into my vest for a replacement, I found Chambers to my left, on one knee, searching the brown cloud, squeezing off rounds one or two at a time.

"Welcome to the party," he said. He laughed again, low and loud, breathing in the slag around us. "Get some, hajj," he said. "Come get some. The infidels are at the fucking gate!"

I asked where Saif was, and he nodded to his far side. A body lay there, leaning up, firing a pistol up the path.

"He's in a bad way," Chambers said. "Gonna take both of us to get him down."

"Let's do it." I hadn't heard any counterfire since I'd sent away Batule. "While we can."

We each grabbed one of Saif's armpits and lifted, draping his arms around our shoulders. Saif's head sagged to the side. He mumbled something with glazed eyes and splashes of runny, hot drool. I tried not to look down but realized as we started that there was space where Saif's legs were supposed to be, two long holes filled with nothing. Something was dripping, like water from a broken tap. I clutched his body closer and kept moving.

We spoke to one another through labored breaths and grunts, Chambers and I shifting Saif's body to alter the weight placement, slow, waddling steps of minutes that felt like days. The fog of earth was thinning, but not quickly enough; we couldn't see farther than a few steps. Only sharp whimpers of pain now came from Saif's mouth. Just as my shoulder threatened to pop out and my chest and legs churned, Chambers leaned over to set his half of Saif down.

"Quick break here. Should answer that. It's been buzzing this whole fucking time."

"Huh?"

He pointed to the forgotten radio on my back. I set Saif down and reached across my back for the hand receiver. I hadn't heard anything.

"This—this is me," I said. "This is Hotspur Six."

"Hotspur Six!" It was Captain Vrettos, his words like hot silver to my ear. "Did you copy? Are all friendly forces clear of the top?"

"Yes." I panted through the words. "I mean, yes. All clear."

Almost instantly a deep rumble swallowed the sky. Then came crashing rock and glass above us, an upside-down earthquake bearing down. We grabbed Saif again and kept moving, an angry god's breath on our heels.

As we turned the last rounded corner of the path, a group of medics met us, relieving us of our burden and placing Saif on a stretcher. Doc Cork tied a tourniquet onto one of the stumps and began twisting. Saif screamed out with chants that sounded like prayers, every revolution of the baton bringing more. Slobber covered his chin and mustache. He grabbed my arm, pulling me to his face, close enough to see black quills of hair in his nose.

I bowed my head and closed my eyes, grabbing his clasped hands with one of my own. In a frail whisper he asked, "My legs. Like fire. How is—how is legs?"

I opened my eyes and told him as calmly as I could that they were fine, he'd be walking before he knew it, he'd be playing with his daughter soon.

His mouth fell open, and he pressed his pistol into my palms. Then he was gone, carried off on a stretcher to the awaiting medevac. I remained by myself for some minutes, tugging at my ears, staring up at the minaret that had tried to kill us, now just a dark splinter. It was evening by the time I walked down the remainder of the tower path, finding my platoon waiting. Everyone else had already gone home.

I don't even know his daughter's name, I thought.

The rumble we'd heard had been a main gun round shot from a 105-millimeter cannon on an outfitted Stryker. It caused much of the top of the tower to collapse in on itself, killing everyone in the rooms and on the walkway, including Dead Tooth, two other military-age males, an old man presumed to be the mullah, two unidentified women, and a child the official report described as "likely younger than ten years old." The dome had shattered into a thousand ceramic dishes. Iraqis contracted for disaster cleanups spent days sorting through the ruins, and a State Department official later estimated it'd cost the American taxpayer a cool million dollars to repair the mosque. "If the Iraqi parliament determines it worthy," he then clarified. "No guarantee. This is the middle of nowhere."

Both Batule and Saif were sent to Baghdad for emergency surgeries—Batule for a lost eye and a ruptured eardrum, Saif for his lost legs. Their war was over.

I spent the rest of the night smoking cigarettes and watching movies on my laptop, away from our room, where Chambers was. Something he'd said wouldn't go away. We'd been on the tower path, the medics working to stabilize Saif. "Mission accomplished," he'd said. Then he'd laughed.

38

We didn't go on patrol the day after the mosque got blown up. No one did. "A tactical pause," Captain Vrettos called it. For him, that meant explaining to higher what had happened. For the soldiers, it meant gym workouts and video games. For me, it meant going through my e-mail. There was a note from my brother, an apology. I didn't know how to respond, and even though I tried to write back, I didn't know what to say. He'd been right about moral courage mattering more than physical courage. I deleted the message.

I spent the day on the smoking patio, watching the walls of camo nets sway with the wind, breathing in wet cigarette. A light rain spat on the ground outside, steady through the afternoon. It would have been cold but for an electric space heater. I sat there reading a magazine article about the commanding general in Afghanistan getting fired for insubordination. It seemed like a stupid thing to get fired for, but things were going to hell everywhere.

Snoop found me there, alone.

"Yo," he said.

"Yo," I said.

"Crazy shit yesterday." He shook his head. "Fucking Arabs."

"Fucking Americans," I said. "Stupid. All of it."

He took a seat in the lawn chair next to me, his long legs sticking out like fishing rods. "Batule? *Molazim* Saif? They okay?"

"They'll live." I stared ahead.

Snoop pulled out a bag of sunflower seeds. He was a dark shadow in the pale light. We were close, maybe even friends, and I knew barely anything about him. I was about to try to rectify that when he said he needed some advice.

"I'll help if I can," I offered. It was such a first-world thing to say.

Snoop's special visa to America had been delayed, along with hundreds of others. The embassy hadn't given a reason or a time line. But he couldn't go home to Little Sudan anymore. Jaish al-Mahdi wanted his head on a spike. He was spending his occasional weekend passes at Camp Independence, an option that wouldn't be there once we left.

"What about the letter I wrote? I thought there was a big push to get terps stateside."

"Too slow. And only goes to terps who give moneys. I gave them a whole file of letters from American officers I've worked for. It didn't matter." He paused to spit out a few shells. His words were boring deep into my conscience, and I thought of Rana, the way she looked at her boys when she sent them out to play with soldiers.

"The right way doesn't work," he continued. "I want to go to America, but getting out of Iraq is first. The war won't end when your army leaves next year. You know this."

"Where would you go?"

"Anywhere."

I said I'd help, somehow, reminding him we still had a couple of months to figure something out. "Maybe my brother knows someone in Homeland Security," I said, though he probably didn't.

"Thanks, LT," Snoop said, standing. He seemed embarrassed and started moving to the doorway before turning around. "We never talked about Haitham."

Excuses darted through my mind like manic bats, but I didn't need them. "What you did was right," Snoop continued. "He was the Cleric, yes? It was the only thing a good lieutenant could do."

He was wrong, of course, but I still appreciated his saying it.

• • •

I found a few hours of rest sitting up on my mattress and against the wall, poncho liner draped over my head. I didn't bother to loosen my boots, like I was trying to trick myself into sleep. An arm shaking my own woke me at midnight.

My eyes felt like stomped grapes. I smacked my lips and concentrated on the foggy shape in front of me. It was the runner for the night shift. He could tell I was considering going back to sleep, so he shook me again.

"Battalion intel's on the line. And—well, we don't want to get the commander."

I smacked my lips again and cracked my neck. "He in the sack?"

"Yes, sir. And. You know how it is. He needs to stay down, while he can."

I slapped my face lightly and hopped off the bunk. "Glad you got me." The runner thought I was being sarcastic, but I wasn't, not totally.

I picked up the phone expecting the intel captain from Duke, but instead heard the voice of Sergeant Griffin. She sounded tired but solemn.

"Lieutenant Porter? I need to speak to Captain Vrettos. It's urgent."

"I'm the ranking officer on duty. What's up?"

"Just heard from a green-level source." She was annoyed to be talking with me, I could tell. "Al-Qaeda's planning payback for what happened to the mosque. Something big and soon. Supposedly in the next day."

I had no idea what "green-level" meant, but figured it meant "good" and "believable." I pantomimed punching myself in the face, which made the night shift laugh.

"You'll let your commander know ASAP?" Sergeant Griffin continued. "Green-level. This is real."

"No doubt," I said. I didn't question her intent, but I'd been through too many false alarms to take seriously vague threats. Something big? Something soon? Welcome to our everyday, I thought. I was setting the phone down when I heard Sergeant Griffin say, "One more thing," through the receiver.

I waited.

"Talk to Dan today?" she asked. She meant Chambers, though I'd never thought of him having a first name.

"Haven't really seen him," I said.

She said they'd talked earlier, online. He'd told her what had happened at the mosque, how it bothered him. That he wasn't a young fire breather anymore. That on this, his fourth combat tour, he'd finally had his fill. That he'd survived a lot of close calls, but that yesterday had been the most searing, the bridge too far. That he had his kids to get back to. That maybe he'd take up a friend's offer and work construction in Dallas. Or switch over to an admin job so he could reach retirement from behind a desk. That he had better things to be doing than running up ancient mosques to kill teenagers who'd had nothing to do with 9/11.

"Just venting, I think," Sergeant Griffin said. "But I'd never heard him like that. Maybe you can talk with him. Since you were up that tower, too."

It was his goddamn idea to go up there, I thought. And he didn't want his kids to grow up fatherless? This was the same guy who'd bragged about not knowing where two of his offspring had moved with their mother.

Then I thought about how I wasn't really the person I presented to the soldiers, either. There were parts I hid, parts I exaggerated. Maybe Chambers was the same.

Maybe.

I hung up the phone knowing there was no way I'd get back to sleep.

"Where's the last place you'd expect to find a lieutenant?" I asked the night shift. "Like, right now."

They told me.

• • •

Through night vision binos, Ashuriyah was a phosphorous green pillow. The joe in the north guard station of the roof wasn't asleep, but he wasn't quite awake, either. His body jerked when I came up behind him and put a hand on his shoulder.

"Go sleep, youngblood," I said. Among other things, I'd surrendered to the term. The private knew officers didn't pull roof duty, but was too drowsy to articulate it. He stumbled off with an "LT, thanks, LT," and I was alone.

That private, I thought. He'd shown up with Chambers, all those lost months ago. He couldn't have been more than twenty. He was from North Dakota? New Hampshire? South Carolina? He talked a lot about how smart his Doberman was. He also claimed to have only three chest hairs, and had named them Huey, Dewey, and Louie, something the rest of the platoon found hilarious. It was sort of funny, now that I thought about it.

I rotated the machine gun and scanned, the mechanized velvet of the turret rolling smooth. A hunter's moon gored the sky. Below, beyond the blast walls and mazes of razor wire, lights were scattered like lost candles.

We'd been here almost a year and couldn't even keep the goddamn power on. I thought about that while my index finger stroked the trigger well and I kept scanning, slowly. Nothing but quiet September black. An autumn chill nipped at my cheeks and at the slits of skin where sleeve met glove. We weren't supposed to smoke up here. It gave away our position. Revolutions were nocturnal beasts, though, and I figured the large camo nets and an occupation nearing a decade had also given away our position. I lit up a cigarette, cupping the cherry with a palm just in case.

My brother's message hadn't been the only one in my in-box. My old ROTC pal Chiu had finally e-mailed back. He was home in Irvine, armed with a medical marijuana prescription, trying to figure out where to go back to school. For what, he didn't know yet, but he knew school would at least get him away from his parents, who told him every day that having one leg was no excuse for being a derelict. REMEMBER, he wrote, ALL REAL VETS DIE BITTER AND ALCOHOLIC! (LOL).

He'd be okay. The world needed people like Chiu.

A gunshot echoed through Ashuriyah, a tongue popping off the roof of a mouth. When only dogs answered, I grabbed the walkie-talkie and reported in.

"One round fired to the north, approximately three thousand meters away."

"Roger that, logged," came the response.

One round could mean anything. Kids messing around. A negligent discharge at a Sahwa checkpoint. An execution in a barn. A sniper's tidy shot through a car window. Just another prayer bead on the death string of tribal warfare, no different from any other.

It wasn't that I hadn't known their names. The people in the mosque. I'd already gotten over that. I didn't even know what they looked like, though. They were complete ciphers, anyone and everyone all at once. "Locals," I'd call them in my war stories someday, to sympathize with the faceless people I'd unintentionally helped kill. "Iraqi citizens who wanted peace."

I finished my cigarette, stomping it out with the heel of my boot.

Some time passed. I thought about the mosque some more, then about what was left of it. Some more time passed. The metal door that led downstairs popped open, loosing a sliver of light. I gripped the stock and asked who was there, flipping up my night vision binos and squinting.

"Why you here?" It was Chambers, his voice flexing, always flexing, but strained, too. I couldn't see his face, but pictured it drawn and ashen.

"You look how I feel," I said, waiting for him to laugh. He didn't. "Still no patrols?"

"On standby." He grunted. "Spec ops are on a raid somewhere nearby. Might need to clean up their mess."

"Seems to be a lot of that recently." I chewed on my bottom lip and waited. I really needed to learn his trick of making people nervous by not responding. "Battalion says al-Qaeda is coming after us soon."

He rolled his shoulders and cracked his neck. Then he started balling his hands into fists, flexing his forearms. He stopped when he saw me staring.

"Why do you do that?" My question came out more strident than intended.

He did it again, just once, as if to prove something. "My dad was an addict. Habit I started in high school, to remind myself to not be like him. Guess it stuck."

"Huh." That seemed plausible, and made more sense than the bogeyman reasons I'd ascribed it. Still, I thought. Weird. We seemed so far from the time he'd joined the platoon and called me Jackie, so far from the weeks I'd spent trying to get rid of him because everything had changed with his arrival. Another gunshot echoed through the night, this one from the other side of town. More dogs barked. My report was logged.

Chambers leaned against the sandbags, stepping under the dim moonlight. He reached into a pocket and pulled out a wad of dip, sticking it in his mouth. I wanted him to leave so I could be alone again, but we needed to talk, and not just because his intel girlfriend was worried.

"Been smoking, Lieutenant?" He was looking at the butt on the ground. It was a bad example for the men, we both knew. It also didn't need to be said. I leaned down and stuck the butt into a cargo pocket.

"You okay, Sergeant?" I asked. "Yesterday was—well. Fucked-up, you know?"

He answered quickly, as if he'd been rehearsing.

"All good. I mean it. Yesterday was the result of a half-assed strategy set by old men in suits who don't have a fucking clue. They hear 'counterinsurgency' and think it's War Lite—a smarter, cleaner way. But it's not. War is always dirty. War is always about force. Yesterday's on a lot of people. But not us. We just happened to be the grunts sent there to do what no one else would. What no one else could."

I wanted to agree with him. I wanted us to absolve ourselves of blame, deflect the accountability elsewhere. I wanted to chalk up the ruin we'd wrought to something unknowable, like providence, or chance, or bureaucracy. But something inside implored me not to. That's too easy, it said. Be stubborn. Fight for understanding.

It had my grandma's voice.

"It wasn't anyone, though," I said. "It was us."

Chambers laughed, spitting out a wad of dip, the spartan creases in his face glinting. He pushed aside the droopy camo netting and looked over the roof wall at the pool of elephant grass below. A breeze stirred through the meadow, playing thistles, banging flowerheads.

" 'God, grant us men to see in a small thing principles which are common things, both small and great.' " He turned his hard gray eyes my way. I must've looked perplexed. "Still haven't read Augustine," he said.

"Oh." His quote had gone over my head. "Not yet."

"Doing right by soldiers can get messy," he continued. The smell of hot tobacco in his mouth filled my ears. "We have less than three months left. Three months until they're home with their wives, their parents. Fucking kids. Just get them home. Nothing else matters. Didn't always feel that way, but I do now."

"Yeah." Some other things mattered, I knew, or at least some other people, but I couldn't control any of that. Still, though—I'd decided that I wanted to leave Iraq having done one good thing. One good thing free of complication and ambiguity, one good thing that proved I wasn't the type of man who used drop weapons or destroyed mosques or couldn't remember his dead soldiers' faces. A good thing rather than a lucky thing, like being told where a man's bones were. I wanted to tell Chambers all this, even though he'd probably scoff. Before I could, he spat out another wad of dip and cleared his throat.

"Soldiers been talking, Lieutenant. What happens during the day? They say you got a slam piece out there. Not that I care, but be careful. A woman got Elijah killed. You already know that, I think."

I looked out at the dark and counted slowly in my mind. "Shit," I said, forcing a laugh too late. "I wish. Just a bored housewife with good intel." I almost said it was Rana, as if I needed his permission, but held back.

"Good." He whistled, low and without melody. "Keep lying so I have plausible deniability. Gives new meaning to 'Be the scorpion,' I guess."

I laughed again, but was bothered he didn't believe me, and even more bothered that he'd called Rana a "slam piece." She was many things, but not that. Never that. Something else lingered, too.

"What happens during the day is boring," I said. There was an edge to my voice I tried to dull but couldn't. I pointed out to the town, to the scattered lights. "What happens at night? On your patrols. Soldiers been talking about that, too. Like, where would you guys be right now if you didn't have to be here?"

He squeezed his eyes shut and shook his head. "Combat is a hard place for hard decisions. For hard men," he said, opening his eyes again. My question had disappointed him. "Leave the moralizing for the bystanders. You want to be one of us—be the type of officer soldiers will follow—you need to kill that part of you. Easy solutions don't exist. Not out here in Indian country. You should know that by now."

Maybe I agreed with him, maybe I didn't. I hadn't really been listening, because he'd been tapping his right forearm, where the five skull tattoos were, each one a moment, a memory, a life taken in the desert by a gun. His gun.

"What?" he asked. He'd found my eyes.

My mouth was dry, so I ran my tongue through it before asking my question. "You gonna get another skull when we get home?"

The night air pushed between us like waves. I tried to keep my breathing steady and fought off an itch in my armpit. I wished I could take back my question, but it was too late. He spat out the last of his dip over the ledge and into the meadow.

"Never ask me that again," he whispered, rubbing snuff bits from his teeth, unslinging his rifle so he held it from its vertical grip in front of him, barrel pointed straight down. "Sir." Then he was gone, away from the guard station and into the blackness. I didn't breathe until I heard the roof door close.

I was angry as I looked back out at Ashuriyah. Angry at Chambers. Angry at Iraq. Angry at myself. He's a goddamn mess of contradictions, I thought, and fuck it, so am I. But I understood myself, even when my thoughts or actions didn't make sense. Why couldn't I understand him? I wanted to, I really did, even though I'd been on only one tour and he'd been on four. He'd saved my life, and I'd found his friend. We were fucking even.

And Rana and Rios had been in love, I reminded myself. She was no one's slam piece.

I bowed my head over the machine gun and prayed for a long time, about a lot of different things.

The light patter of feet from behind broke my solitude and broke it too late. I tried to swing around the machine gun, but the tripod and sandbags held in place. I went to the ground on one knee, and my left hand dove for my pistol.

"Easy, sir. Just your guard relief."

"Hog." I took a deep breath and tried to push back the pulses threatening to puncture my skin. "Sorry about that."

"It's cool. Gets creepy up here."

Holstering the pistol, I looked down at the two chevrons on his chest he'd worked so hard to earn. Some months before, before Rana and before Chambers, before a lot of things, I'd taught him that "terp" wasn't short for "interpolator." In turn, he'd taught me that I wouldn't want to hunt birds with a military-style assault rifle.

I thought he was going to bring up Haitham again, but he didn't. He replaced me behind the machine gun, and I stayed up there with him during his shift, talking about home. Later he asked if Ramadan was over yet. I told him almost. We shared his bag of sour gummy worms. When neither of us could think of anything to say, we listened to the wind in the meadow.

After a particularly long silence, Hog asked if I'd learned about Adam and Eve in Sunday school.

"Of course," I said. "The first story for everything. Took place right around here, I think. To the south a bit." I chewed through a mouthful of gummy worms. "Been thinking those holy thoughts, my man?"

"Yep." Hog shook his head. "God's gonna have a lot to answer for when I die, that's for sure. He better have some answers ready."

I couldn't help but laugh at that, smiling into the void of night.

39

The next morning found my half of the platoon prepping the Strykers for a quick mission to Camp Independence. There was some state-of-the-art satellite dish that battalion needed us to put on our roof, because brigade said so, because division said so, because the Pentagon said so, because the satellite dish was a defense contracting job from 2005 that'd finally been completed.

I finished the brief by telling the soldiers we didn't have time for showers and food runs this time. Captain Vrettos wanted us back in Ashuriyah ASAP, due to the report of al-Qaeda's pending attack.

"Any questions?" I asked.

"Yeah," Washington said. "What's this dish do?"

"Need-to-know basis," I said. I figured the dish had something to do with surveillance drones, but it was just a guess. "And we don't need to know."

The soldiers groaned and walked to the armored vehicles. As I went to follow, Snoop jogged out of the outpost. His eyes were wide, and he held his cell away from him like a stinky piece of fruit. I grabbed it from him, but the line was dead.

"What is it?" I asked.

"Not sure," he said. "Surf's up, maybe."

Rana had just called. She was worried about us. A coworker of her husband's had said to avoid the paved road by the big American base for the next couple of days. Malek hadn't needed to ask why; he knew this coworker had family in the Sunni insurgency. Her husband had called in sick and was planning on doing so until he knew the road was clear again.

"She risked a lot calling," Snoop said. "Her husband would be angry if he knew."

"Right." It didn't take much to connect this with what Sergeant Griffin had called with the night before. I told the patrol to stand by. Historically, IEDs were a retaliatory tactic for local al-Qaeda. It made sense.

I radioed battalion and asked when the engineers had last cleared Route Madison.

"One week" was the reply.

"Roger. Got intel that"—this would need to be phrased delicately—"an attack is forthcoming along Route Madison. Recommend the road is shut down until cleared."

Battalion wasn't happy—they really wanted us to get that damn satellite dish—but after explaining to two majors and the Big Man that our source was credible, they agreed. Our patrol dropped the Strykers' ramps and hung out under low gray clouds, playing cards and talking about the best clubs in Hawaii to meet slutty tourists.

I was only half listening when Dominguez asked how my girlfriend was doing.

"Who?" I asked. He had a strange look on his face. I wasn't sure if he meant Marissa, or if this was his way of asking about the local "slam piece" rumors. Denial would get me nowhere, I knew. But neither would the truth. "Oh. Her," I said, turning it into a joke. "Honestly, I'm not sure."

He seemed to consider what that meant before turning back to the debate over clubs.

I walked away from the group to the back of my Stryker. It was open and empty. I lay across a cushioned bench and tucked my helmet under my head so it served as a hard, round pillow. I didn't know when it'd happened exactly, but I'd become the type of person who preferred resting in the day to resting at night. I was somewhere between sleep and consciousness when the explosion happened.

The soldiers thought a jet had crashed, because of the noise and because of the black fireball to the east. We thought we'd be sent out the gate immediately, but Captain Vrettos radioed and told us to remain on standby until higher figured out what'd happened.

We already knew, though. Two of us did, at least.

"That was the bomb in the road," Snoop said, crawling into the back of the Stryker to sit next to me. "That was meant for us."

"Maybe." I grabbed an orange from a food bin and started peeling the skin into small jagged pieces. When that was done, I split the orange into lumpy slices and swished one around in my mouth. Snoop just watched.

"She saved us," he finally said.

"Yeah," I said.

It was true. She had. Information about what had happened drifted down to us, slowly at first, like ticker tape, then faster and faster. The tip had spooked the engineers, too, so they'd sent their best mine-resistant vehicles to patrol Route Madison. They crept along the road at five miles per hour, scanning for piled trash and potholes.

Along the western edge of Checkpoint 38—Sayonara Station—a bomb exploded under the lead vehicle's front right tire. Forensics later estimated that the IED contained two hundred fifty pounds of home-made explosive, primarily fertilizer and acetone, designed to trigger under the pressure of an armored vehicle. The insurgents had taken advantage of our absence the day prior and had dug, dropped, and repaved without anyone noticing, or caring to.

The twenty-ton vehicle rolled forward like a shot elephant, its outer hull spraying the roadside with large metal chunks. All but one of the ballistic glass windows shattered upon impact. Inside, all five soldiers were hurt, two of them knocked unconscious. The final tally counted four concussions, six broken bones, and a fire extinguisher–induced gash along a neck.

Strykers weren't built to withstand massive IED attacks. Had it been us on that patrol, like we could have been—like we should have been—it would have been a matter of body parts and pink mist, not casts and splints.

"She saved us," Snoop kept saying to me, long after he left me alone to tear apart more oranges. "She saved us, she saved us, she saved us."

40

The room smelled of rot. I couldn't determine the source, couldn't parse it from the other odors—the rain outside, the bouquet of wildflowers in the corner, the foul stink of angry men in sweat-starched uniforms and man-dresses. Still, after another breath, there was no mistaking it. There was rot somewhere.

Twelve of us had gathered in Fat Mukhtar's sliver of a meeting room. The attendance of the Big Man, Captain Vrettos, and an Iraqi Army major meant I didn't have to speak; the presence of the *mukhtar* and a host of other tribal leaders meant I still needed to listen.

"The sheiks demand *fasil* for all the dead but Azhar," Snoop said. His voice cracked with angst. "They will not budge from this. They say all the others in the mosque were innocents."

There'd been drama even before we'd arrived. At the outpost, the Big Man took one look at Snoop's ski mask and plastic rifle and said our entire company lacked discipline. Captain Vrettos had tried to explain the complexities involved, to no avail. Snoop had saved his job by taking off the mask and setting down the plastic rifle. Time would tell if he'd traded it for his life.

Pallid Arabic brought me back to the meeting. Fat Mukhtar rose from the rug like a false idol, joints cracking, knees popping, the cement wall behind him bracing his back. Once he finished unfurling, he pointed to the far wall. The watercolors of American rivers and forests still hung there, but the *mukhtar*'s index finger wagged above them, at three portraits. His finger moved from frame to frame, tracing invisible lines.

"He wants the American officers to look," Snoop translated. "Those are the men who ruled here before. The one on the left was his great-grandfather, who worked with the Ottomans." The size of a paperback cover, the hot wax painting displayed a young man with a long, broad nose and a little chin. Soft curls bounced across his head, and his eyes were like two brown suns. "The man in the middle, with the beard? He was the *mukhtar's* grandfather. He worked with the British to overthrow the Ottomans." This man was middle-aged, the black-and-white photograph capturing an august face and rigid body, clenched fists dangling from arms tucked neatly into a *dishdasha*. Had he met T. E. Lawrence, I wondered, perhaps on the famous march to Damascus? "The third man? His father, who worked to bring down the last king of Iraq." Larger than the others, and slightly crooked, this color photograph presented a man more like the heir, round and mustached, dressed in olive fatigues and holding a large-caliber revolver. He possessed a physical poetry his son lacked, a sort of grace fixed in the photograph.

Have those always been there? I thought. Or did Fat Mukhtar bring them out for today? That felt likely, though I couldn't be sure. Perhaps I hadn't noticed them before.

"The *mukhtar* says he works with Americans now," Snoop continued. "Americans who will leave, as the Ottomans and British left."

Captain Vrettos loosed a soft whistle. The Big Man made a feeble attempt to explain why we were different. He mentioned clearing, holding, and building. My eyes moved from dead face to dead face to dead face. I tended to think that those who came before were worthier, more distinguished. At first glance, the same held true for these Iraqi tribal leaders. But Fat Mukhtar's great-grandfather, he of the biblical eyes, also had pouty lips. And his grandfather's mouth hung open, like a fool's. And his father—he must've posed with the gun for show, as tightly as he gripped it. I remembered Lawrence had been stationed in the outpost of Cairo only because his superiors had deemed him a goof and a nuisance. I belong here as much as anyone, I thought. Because at least I have the goddamn dignity to question being here to begin with.

"Lieutenant Porter." It was the Big Man. "Update us on your Muslim soldier."

The fatwas were old news, so none of the Iraqis acted surprised. The Big Man seemed to want them to be. Every time I bumped into Ibrahim at Camp Independence he looked more despondent than the last, but he never whined or complained. He just said "One day closer" over and over again, until I left him alone.

"We have nothing to do with that," Fat Mukhtar said, slumping against the wall and sliding down it, resuming his seat. "That's the Cleric."

"Not possible," the Big Man said, his fingers stubby rocks aimed at the *mukhtar*'s head. "Lieutenant Porter's platoon got him last month. What was his name again?"

"Haitham," I said, staring at a triangle of light from the window's reflection that'd gathered between my legs. His black-and-white mug shot was wedged into my Lawrence book along with every other document I didn't know what to do with. "His name was Haitham."

"And it was you who led us to him." Captain Vrettos spoke now, his voice charged with a voltage I didn't recognize. Recent events had amplified the pressure on him from higher, though the Big Man had supposedly refused to fire him when pushed to by the generals. I looked at Captain Vrettos and clucked my tongue to try to calm him, but his red-faced exhaustion had eyes only for the *mukhtar*. "You fed the Rangers that information. So, with Haitham dead, just who the hell is dictating the fatwas?" The volts surged. "Someone here knows the fucking answer to that."

The room turned helter-skelter. Tribal leaders shouted at one another and at us, fingers wagging, fists shaking; the Big Man yelled at Captain Vrettos, who yelled right back, saying he was sick of ignoring the obvious. I pulled my knees tight to my chest and watched the triangle of light dance between my legs. I wondered what Rana was doing. Probably hanging laundry to dry, or demanding Karim lie down for his afternoon nap. She'd said her husband would be home all week. She'd have called otherwise.

I looked up at the portraits of the dead men and sighed. We said we wanted peace. What we really wanted was calm, something else altogether. They said they wanted peace, too. What they really wanted was power, which maybe wasn't something else altogether. After we'd destroyed their mosque, it was tough to argue otherwise.

One of the tribal leaders, a younger guy I'd met at Abu Mohammed's wake, started shouting, "Nina leven, *fasil!* Nina leven, *fasil!* Boosh! Boosh! Boosh!" I winced. Captain Vrettos flipped him off with both hands, which made the Iraqi yell louder.

Through all the noise, I smelled decay again. I watched a man with a large lip sore and a salt-and-pepper beard emerge from the corner to shush the other Iraqis. The stench seemed to be coming from his sandaled feet, his toenails little gnarled knives poking out at the world. Wearing a gray *dishdasha* and a red-and-white checkered turban, thick wrinkles splayed across his forehead, sagging in the middle. Yousef's eyes studied the spaces between the men in the room, one a deep hazel, the other the cloudy brown of cataracts. I realized where I'd seen him before, even before the patrol through the sandstorm. He'd been the man demanding *fasil* at the car accident in the spring. I wanted to ask why a falafel man had been invited to this meeting, but stayed quiet.

"This isn't the time for blame." Snoop translated for Yousef with taut exactitude, as if he were afraid to neglect even a syllable. "We've all lost friends, American and Iraqi. While it seems wise to keep the American Muslim away, we must remember the death sentence was also placed on brave Iraqi soldiers." The IA major nodded vigorously. "And we must remember the neighborhoods of Ashuriyah are being covered with lists of targets stuck to telephone poles. Sunni and Shi'a. Not all are just threats."

While Yousef continued, I watched the faces of the other men in the room. *Wasta* isn't a thing to pursue, I thought, or even possess. It's not just power. Yousef knows this, and that's why he has it. Despite the Sahwa contract, despite the luxury sedans, despite all the bombast and circumstance, the *mukhtar* didn't. One glance his way showed he knew it, too.

Yousef was still speaking when Fat Mukhtar interrupted. At first the older man tried to speak over him, but when the *mukhtar* continued, he stopped and turned his head toward the ceiling, exasperated. Fat Mukhtar then stood up again to shout down his opponent. An argument ensued, one voice restrained and firm, the other wild as a roller coaster. The rest of us sat in awkward silence, watching while pretending not to.

"They argue about who's in charge," Snoop said slowly. "Fat Mukhtar say this is his house. The falafel man tells him to calm down, this is not the time."

Fat Mukhtar spat on the ground toward Yousef's feet and wiped his palms together like he was cleaning his hands. He said something to all the room with his arms spread wide and turned to Snoop and me, jerking his head to the door. Then he stormed out, slamming the door behind him.

Snoop's voice returned to a robotic pitch. "The *mukhtar* say he's the only one who can stop the terror men," he said. "Then he tell LT Jack and me to go outside with him, since everyone else here just wastes time."

"Go," the Big Man said. "Settle him down, we need him here." I stood, and Snoop began to do the same. "We need the terp." Anticipating a protest, the Big Man waved me outside. "Be creative, Lieutenant. Put that liberal arts degree to use."

I scooped up my helmet, slung my rifle, and walked out into a chalky sun.

• • •

The *mukhtar* stood in his driveway rubbing the hood of a black Mercedes. He watched me approach through the reflection of the tinted windshield.

"No Snoop," I said. "Bosses. *Mudirs.*"

After sneering at the house, he burped and pointed at the fleet of Land Rovers and Mercedeses in his flagstone driveway. Then he pointed back to himself with his thumb, the digit disappearing into a pit of white cloth.

"*Bayti*. Mine," he said, the English word like a pepper shaker in his mouth.

He gestured to follow him down the driveway. We walked under a canopy of palm trees, most of them sagging from overwatering. Some of the rolls of carpet that covered his lawns had bunches in them, little green tufts that belonged on a miniature golf course. The estate overlooked the Villages from a ridge wedged between hills. Below us, irrigation ditches zigzagged through hamlets with gridded care, a network of blue forcing structure upon dusty bedlam. In the far north, the sluggish waters of the canal gleamed, partially cloaked by the fruit groves. To the south was nothing but desert and dried-out ravines, and to the west—to the west Rana lay in wait, an exile in her own land.

"Mine," Fat Mukhtar said, spreading his arms wide to encompass everything from the canal to the villas behind us. "Mine."

We approached a group of Sahwa and *jundis* gathered near a woodshed the *mukhtar* used as an arms room. Across the gravel road, four Strykers sat like sleepy ogres, the tops of headquarters soldiers poking out from the hatches. I considered forcing some of them to interact with their Iraqi counterparts, but decided not to. How had Shaba put it in his love letter to Rana? "They are here to survive and endure, not to change."

I exchanged *shaku makus* and knuckles with the Iraqis on duty. One of the khaki browns shied away, turning his back. It didn't take me long to figure out why: Azhar's brother wanted nothing to do with an accord. He kept his thin shoulders straight and cocked and tossed the shiny rifle in his hands from palm to palm.

"Salaam," I said to him. There was no reply. He remained facing away, northward. I looked at Fat Mukhtar and arched an eyebrow. He shrugged.

"Mine," Fat Mukhtar said, referring to the Sahwa guards. Then he patted the laser sights attached to the *jundis*' rifles. It'd taken some wrangling, but the supply guys at Camp Independence had come through. I'd honored the deal with Saif, though he would never know it.

"Mine," he said again, pointing to my chest.

"Yours," I corrected.

He shook his head and grabbed a laser sight with one meaty hand and my shoulder with the other. "Mine," he said.

I closed my eyes and sighed.

As I opened my eyes, ready to convince Fat Mukhtar to go back to the meeting, I saw a familiar shape peek from behind the corner of the squatty woodshed. I pushed past the *mukhtar*'s arm and stepped over a strand of razor wire. Around the corner huddled a sullen teenager, more stick figure than man.

"The fuck?" The Barbie Kid lifted his good eye to me, his unibrow a dark question mark of its own. He still wore pink sweatpants, but his shirt was an oversized khaki top, like the Sahwa wore. New sneakers covered his feet, white socks rising up his calves like garden snakes. He remained huddled, even when Fat Mukhtar waddled up and clapped at him.

"Sahwa," Fat Mukhtar said. "Jadid."

Through broken Arabic and broken-er English, Fat Mukhtar conveyed that he'd hired the youth after the death of Haitham. They'd been family, he reminded me. It was the right thing to do.

I hadn't seen the Barbie Kid since we'd hit the small roadside bomb west of Ashuriyah. I'd wondered many times if he'd been a lookout for that attack. Now I knew whom he'd have called—not that it could be proven. I asked where his weapon was.

"Hah!" A dam of laughter broke in Fat Mukhtar's throat. He acted out shots hitting all around a target and then said, *"No bueno!"* since the last thing we needed was a third language. Under the dim of the shed, the Barbie Kid watched on in fury.

Fat Mukhtar clapped again, barking instructions. This time the Barbie Kid stood, walked into the shed, and picked up a broom and dustpan from the ground. The *mukhtar* nodded toward his house and

I followed, certain I'd just found another piece to the puzzle that was Iraq, but bemused as to where to place it.

The *mukhtar* moved quickly for a man his size, his steps sturdy and pronounced. I matched his strides, figuring him ready to return to the meeting. But we walked past the rusty door to the front room, instead heading into a courtyard that bisected his four eggshell villas. More artificial grass greened the lawn, a small red gazebo marking the center. Three women sat in the gazebo, their colorful *abaya*s a rainbow against the dull sky. They were laughing and folding laundry, watching a group of children jump on a trampoline in the yard. The toucan Sinbad croaked nearby, its heavy keel bill scrounging the bottom of its cage for seeds. I found no sign of the *mukhtar*'s imaginary Syrian bear. The thin wife, dressed in purple, noticed us first, hushing her companions and pointing to their husband and me. They all donned face veils and bowed their heads. Meanwhile, the children had lost all interest in their jumping and ran to us.

There were six of them, the eldest a girl of about ten, the youngest a little *mukhtar* clone I guessed to be Karim's age, my mind drifting westward once more.

"Mine," I said, slapping Fat Mukhtar on the shoulder, ruffling the closest boy's hair. I put my hands out and let them play with the hard plastic that lined the knuckles of my gloves, though the eldest rolled her eyes at this.

Fat Mukhtar beamed proud and stroked his goatee. "Mine," he said. He started quizzing his children on their studies; I picked out words like "math" and "spelling" from the conversation, but the rest blurred by. Then he clapped his hands, the children scattered, and he waved me on. I pointed back to the front house, but he shook his head. The wives remained motionless and silent in the gazebo, one of them still midfold with her husband's tracksuit. As we passed, Sinbad hopped across the birdcage and stuck out its bill. The *mukhtar* stroked it, but when I tried to do the same, it snapped at my finger and flapped its wings. I cursed and said I was glad its wings were clipped. Fat Mukhtar just laughed.

We continued to one of the rear villas. He opened a large metal door and held it open, gesturing for me to walk in first. The inside of the room was drab and dank. I felt Fat Mukhtar's grin more than I saw it, the left side of his mouth curving higher than his left. Images of beheaded soldiers and journalists came over me like a hood, bodies without heads, heads without bodies.

I couldn't even remember the list of things that American soldiers were supposed to recite under torture. Name. Rank. Social Security number? Why the hell would al-Qaeda care about my Social Security number? I walked into the room.

I held my breath and remained in the near corner while Fat Mukhtar followed, my ears hunting the shadows. He closed the door, a slice of gray light under the frame the only illumination in the room. He shuffled along a wall searching for something, bent over at the waist. I heard the pop of a prong entering a socket. Arcade neon blinked to life, revealing a blocky game meant for a mall.

"Big Buck Hunter?" I tried to embrace the moment as I took in the toy shotguns and virtual deer running across the arcade screen, but couldn't. "Why do you have this?"

Fat Mukhtar answered with another "Mine." I was familiar with the game from drunken bar nights in college, but how a machine had ended up in rural Iraq seemed too absurd even to try to comprehend. Fat Mukhtar grabbed the green shotgun and tapped its barrel against the screen.

"Ali babas," he said, calling attention to the antlered bucks. Then he tapped at a group of does. "No ali babas."

I flashed a thumbs-up to signal my understanding. The room smelled of sour mildew; the worn couch in the back and mini fridge filled with wine coolers suggested the *mukhtar* spent a lot of time here. I turned back to the machine, where Fat Mukhtar was setting up a match for two players. The level read ALASKA. He nodded to the orange shotgun, and I replaced my real gun with a fake one. High-definition cartoon Kodiak wilderness washed over our faces.

The sight was off, shooting half an inch high, but I adjusted during the first round, killing two bucks. Fat Mukhtar doed-out right away, which eliminated him from the round. He leaned into the screen with his gun, holding it under an armpit rather than squaring it into his shoulder. He watched me finish the round. I was up two hundred points.

"Surf's up," I said with a wink. Fat Mukhtar grunted, but I saw the mischievous curve of his mouth return.

The second round regressed to the mean. I hit a doe early when it dashed in front of a buck drinking from a snowy stream. Fat Mukhtar proceeded to hit all six bucks in the round, culminating with a head shot in the far distance. He seized the lead, laughing deeply, jowl wobbling.

The fucker had rope-a-doped me, I thought, something the third round confirmed when he killed five bucks to my one. He knew the board like it was kin, displaying foreknowledge of open shots and an accuracy he'd concealed at first. He'd wanted to watch me shoot to learn my strengths and weaknesses. Whereas I was reacting to the game, he anticipated it. There was a counterinsurgency lesson in this somewhere, but I had neither the time nor the patience to figure it out. The war didn't matter anymore. Wiping the grin off the *mukhtar*'s fat face did.

Down a breezy 1,100 points, I had two rounds to redeem myself. I knew I couldn't win fairly, he was too good, too aware of what was to come. While the game loaded the next board, I asked myself what would vex him the most.

I smirked at my own genius.

The screen instructed us to GET READY. I turned to Fat Mukhtar and smacked him on the ass, shouting incoherently and cupping a saggy cheek a beat longer than necessary.

He cursed and dropped his gun. I had free rein of the board, a frost-ridden forest where I had to contend with trees and does alike. By the time the *mukhtar* had regained his weapon, I was pumping the kill shot into my sixth hide. I was now 120 points away from the lead.

Fat Mukhtar's face quivered with anger, and he started to walk into me, belly first, until I raised a peace sign and pointed to the screen. He rearranged the green shotgun under his armpit in a salvo of Arabic vulgarities. As we waited for the sixth round, blocky letters of GET READY formed on the screen. We crouched in the wait, his feet parallel like he was at the O.K. Corral, mine staggered and clenched as I'd been taught in training.

The board began. A doe stood alone in a field, eating grass.

"Sheika," Fat Mukhtar said. Then he chanted. "Ra-na. Sheik-a. Ra-na."

He knew. Somehow, some way, he knew. It didn't bother me, though, or rattle me. It infuriated me, and as soon as the first antler pierced the edge of the screen, I started pumping out shots with abandon. "*Mukhtar*, ali baba!" I yelled as the first buck went down in a glow of orange, awarding me the kill. "*Mukhtar!*" In the back, under a large pine: a twinkle of dark brown. I deemed it worth the risk, and got bonus points for the distance. "Azhar!" A buck bounded down a hillside in the center of the screen, and we saw it in chorus. He shot it in the neck, and it didn't go down. I shot it in the chest, and it did. "Motherfucking Cleric!"

A quick glance to the top of the screen showed that I'd pulled ahead by 350 points. One last buck zigzagged across the screen, a muscular devil that dodged bullets and does with aplomb. He needed to kill it to regain the lead. I needed to kill it to keep that from happening. Our toy shotguns crossed as the buck reached the center of the screen. It wouldn't go down, as if our bullets were passing through a phantom. Fat Mukhtar howled murder, so I did, too. The screen turned red.

The ghost buck had slipped away, or so it appeared. We'd never know, because we'd each shot a doe, ending the round and ending the game. No one received points for the last buck.

I'd won.

He threw down his gun and then pointed to the screen, asking for a rematch. I shook my head. It was time for a victorious retreat.

I picked up my real rifle. "You say Rana," I said, jolted blood still pumping. "I say Haitham. I say Fat Mukhtar is ali baba. I say Fat Mukhtar kill—Fat Mukhtar *keel* Haitham."

He inhaled sharply, then bent over to pick up the toy gun he'd tossed. Standing back up, he ran a hand through his black thatch of curls and narrowed his eyes. "No," he said, pointing at me. "Haitham mine."

We'd been through a lot together, the *mukhtar* and me. And kept even more from each other. I was thinking about how easy it would be to shoot him in his own den when someone banged on the door twice. There was a blast of raw light.

"There you are." It was Captain Vrettos. "Meeting's over. Time to roll."

I followed my commander outside without a word.

After the war found him and turned him into a martyr, I often wondered what thoughts flitted through Fat Mukhtar's mind as we walked out of his courtyard that day. There must've been many.

In the Stryker, Captain Vrettos said that we'd relented and agreed to pay *fasil* for all the mosque dead but Azhar. Lose a battle to win the war, he said.

"That Yousef guy is something else," he continued. "Wish he was more active in the community. It would have been good to work with a man like that."

41

The outpost was a zoo the next morning. Another platoon was driving out the front gate to deliver the *fasil* payments as the logisticians arrived with a delivery—the last shipment of foam mattresses from a contractor leaving Kuwait. First Sergeant said we didn't need them, but could hand them out to locals. They also had the infamous satellite dish. Meanwhile, a group of Rangers arrived unannounced, a captain built like a viking needing to talk to someone about "high-value targets." The rest of the Rangers remained in their Humvees, eyeballing our soldiers with carefully cultivated disdain.

On the outpost stairs, Captain Vrettos admired the pistol holstered on my chest plate—Saif's olive Glock—and asked what I had planned for the day.

"I could meet with the Rangers if you want," I said. "But I have a meeting slated with that source from out west. Going to take us to a graveyard in town. Something about the real Cleric."

"No, I'll handle the Rangers." The commander's mind seemed elsewhere, perhaps at Camp Independence, where the Big Man had said he had no second chances left—it was peace or bust. "Stick with your patrol. Just get some good intel, please. We've got to figure this out."

If I felt any guilt about misleading my commander, the thought of spending time with Rana quickly displaced it. I'd called the previous night to thank her for saving lives—our lives. She again refused the offer of cash, but said there was another way I could repay her.

"Anything," I said.

"My family is buried together, in south Ashuriyah," she said. "I haven't visited them in years. Perhaps you could take us."

"Of course," I said. "But this is a small thing. We're still not even."

I didn't let her hang up until she agreed with that.

A daisy chain of sweaty, grunting soldiers led down to the foyer, with a variety of items being passed up the stairs from large cargo trucks outside, crates of Rip It and jugs of bleach and Memory Foam pillows that'd come with the mattresses. In a corner of the first floor stood Alia, mopping the red-and-white tiles with indifference. She wore a gray *abaya* and leopard-pattern head scarf, and her attention was focused across the octagonal foyer. She was watching Chambers, still in his body armor, yelling at soldiers to daisy-chain faster. I watched her watch him while the same section of tiles got mopped again and again. Then, as if her Spidey sense had tingled, she turned with her mop into the corner.

I walked over to Chambers and placed a hand on his shoulder. We hadn't spoken since the roof.

He looked up with a jerk. "Lieutenant," he said. "What's the patrol today?"

I tried to visualize him the way Rana remembered him from 2006: eager, brash, more peacock-like than Machiavellian. It didn't quite fit what I saw in front of me.

"Source meeting out west, again. About the real Cleric. Think we're getting closer."

"Really." He crossed his arms and looked at me out of the corner of his eye, as if he were testing a new angle to see me for what I really was. "Think I'll come along. Be good to get out in the day again."

No way, I thought. You'll ruin everything.

"Be great to have you," I said. "For any patrol. But honestly, man, this is the source that saved us the other day. You're the hammer. These people remember you."

"'The hammer'?" I thought he'd be pleased at being described this way, but it seemed to bother him. "Hajjis call me that?"

"Yeah. You do your thing, we do ours. Seems to be working." I swallowed. "Seems like it'll get the guys home. Nothing else matters."

"Nothing else."

His eyes crinkled with doubt, but when he unbuckled his helmet strap, I knew I was safe—that *we* were safe. I turned to walk outside to the Strykers, but Chambers called me back.

"Lieutenant," he said. "You still a believer?"

I'd tried to read the opening of *The Confessions of Saint Augustine* but found it tedious. "I don't always get God, but, yeah, I guess I am."

Cloudy green met pale slate again. I stood up a bit straighter and stood out a bit wider, mentally counting to ten in Arabic.

"Not that," he said, pushing past and smelling of ugly sweat. He walked upstairs, not bothering to glance at the mural above. Pedo bin Laden and the smiling children looked surprised at this for some reason. The Mother Hajj didn't.

On the patrol to Rana's, I considered what Chambers had meant. I wasn't sure. Then I considered the rumors about Rana and me. Today wouldn't help, I knew. But she'd earned it.

She's a good source, I told myself. She saved us. I'm not overvaluing her info because I like her. Though I do. As a person, I like her. She's interesting. The ramp dropped just then, and I saw Rana and her boys in the daylight.

They'd dressed for the occasion. Ahmed and Karim wore matching white collar shirts tucked into navy trousers. The eldest wore a brown belt and his ubiquitous scowl, while Karim stared at the declining Stryker ramp with mouth agape, his bug eyes wider than usual. Both boys had slicked down their hair with water so it clung to their scalps like hay. Their mother wore a black burqa made of silk with a translucent veil that didn't entirely conceal the greenness of her eyes.

I took off my headset and smiled.

"You're the best, Jack," she said. "This means so much."

"No problem," I said with a too-casual shrug. "Rana."

She asked if we would take a picture of them dressed up. Snoop hopped out and played photographer, using her cell phone. None of the Iraqis smiled for it. Then they took a seat on the cushioned bench in the rear of the vehicle, Rana in the middle, holding her boys' hands.

Karim nuzzled into his mother while Ahmed whispered into her ear. Across from them, Snoop laughed.

"They think they're in a robot," he said. He leaned forward and spoke to the boys, offering them sunflower seeds. Ahmed didn't respond, but Karim gave the terp a shy smile and accepted a handful. The ramp closed slowly, like a drawbridge, the ochre glow of electronics filling the space between. It *is* kind of like a robot, I thought.

The crunching of tires on silt turned to the quiet of smooth pavement. As we pushed east back to Ashuriyah, Ahmed asked Snoop where his mask was. Snoop groaned and said something about losing it. Since the Big Man's edict, he'd also given up carrying around his plastic rifle, becoming more remote and moody in the process. I needed to talk to him again about his plans for after the withdrawal. As soon as I had the chance, I would.

I switched the Stryker's internal screen from the digital map to the camera of the driver's view, so the boys could watch the passing landscape. Even Ahmed's face brightened with interest, and he tugged at his mother's sleeve to make sure she was watching, too.

"How long?" I asked Rana. "Since you've been to the cemetery."

"We came for my father's burial." She patted Karim on the head, ruffling his hair. "This one had just been born."

Compared to Snoop, the Iraqis looked like baby birds on their bench. Rana's legs barely reached the floorboard. As we swung south into Ashuriyah and under the Cleric's arch, Ahmed fell back into the legs of the joe standing out of the rear hatch. If the soldier even noticed, he didn't show it, remaining upright and rigid. In the meantime, Snoop helped the boy back to his seat, and I put on my headset to yell at the drivers to slow down.

"Are you eating?" Rana asked as I removed the headset again. She tilted her head toward me. "Your face looks thin."

"Back to three meals a day," I said. My appetite hadn't returned with the end of Ramadan, though I ate enough to keep functional. I flexed a bicep. "Can't you tell?"

"I don't like being lied to," she said, her dimple flashing in amusement. "I already have two boys. I don't need a third."

I smiled back, though it felt like the corners of my mouth were glowing warm from embarrassment. I changed the subject.

The four Strykers halted at the graveyard's entrance. Over the radio, I told Washington to join us on the ground as security and everyone else to remain with the vehicles. Valium addict or no, the two children loved him.

I stepped into the late morning. The graveyard lay at the end of a road of packed dirt on the outskirts of town. There was nothing south of it, only dusty badlands cleaved by the occasional ravine, but a convenience store sat across the road in a cement bunker. A wrought-iron fence the color of milk enclosed the graveyard itself, a swing gate the entrance. A small bronze plaque hung from the gate, pink and green graffiti covering the engraved Arabic script.

"Message from Jaish al-Mahdi," Snoop said. "It say, 'Home for Sunni donkeys.'"

"What up, Scowls!" Washington joined us at the entrance, greeting Ahmed with an exaggerated hand slap. A learned smirk and jutted chin I recognized as my soldier's own crossed Ahmed's face. Karim, still holding his mother's hand, tugged her down and said something in a soft voice, pointing at Washington and Snoop, and then at me. The terp laughed heartily.

"He wishes to know," Rana said, "why some Americans are painted and some are not. I've tried before." She turned my way. "Perhaps you have an answer?"

I racked my brain for a simple way of explaining to a child the racial history of humanity. I pointed to the gray sky and then to the skin on my arm. "The sun," I said. "My ancestors lived far to the north, where there's less sun. Your ancestors lived here, where there's more sun. Their ancestors lived in the south, where there's even more sun. We're all the same underneath. It's just the skin that changed, depending on where people lived." I turned to Snoop. "Think you can translate that?"

"Nice work, LT," Washington said. "Not even that racist."

Karim nodded, rubbing the back of his head, which produced a spiky cowlick. His mother thanked me. I blushed again.

Rana opened a black umbrella to keep the sun off, and we followed her through the entrance, one at a time, Washington conducting a radio check with the Strykers in a brittle cotton drawl. We walked in pairs: Rana; Karim at her heels, holding on to her dress; me and Snoop; and then Ahmed and Washington in the rear.

The dirt path soon turned to disordered mounds of earth and sandstone markers, graves upon graves jumbled together. There was no grid, no discernible system whatsoever, just sun-blasted rocks and calcified yellow dirt. As we eased down a knoll, the graves became more spread out and distinctive: some had stucco tombstones; others were marked by small religious flags hung over them. A group of tabbies with fur like sunbursts had gathered between two tombs for shade. Most watched us pass indolently, though a tomcat draped in dead flowers hissed.

Umbrella in front of her like a pike, Rana pointed to a crypt made of sun-dried brick with a porcelain-green dome, but my eyes drifted left, down the hill. In a depression lay lines and lines of markers, uniform and ordered. Plastic flowers rested next to the markers, the nearest adorned with portraits of young men holding rifles and wearing bandoliers of ammo across their chests.

"For Sunni insurgents," Snoop said. "The sign calls it the 'Garden of Martyrs.'"

A pair of gravediggers were planting shovels into the ground on the far end of the depression. I waved at them. One waved back. I squinted my eyes hard until the markers fell out of focus and I tried to see the soft green hills and marble heads of the garden of martyrs back home.

It didn't work.

As we neared the al-Badri crypt, the mounds thinned into a pathway. A square of brown grass surrounded the crypt. Rana leaned down and pulled a few blades from the ground, shaking her head in frustration. A splintered wood door about my height led into the crypt itself. Rana produced a key and pushed it open. I instructed Snoop and

Washington to stay back, pushing Ahmed forward to join his mother and brother, but Rana waved us to the fore.

"My father thought well of Americans."

The crypt smelled of sour earth and incense. Removing my helmet and gloves, I ducked down into it, finding a wide, circular room that could've fit twice our number. A shuttered window at the top of the circle allowed for gashes of air. The floor of mosaic tiles fell into a pit in the center of the room, round cinder tombstones marking the graves. I looked up at the underside of the dome. It'd been painted with the golden-black eagle of Iraq, wings tucked, talons clutching a scroll.

Rana asked Snoop something in Arabic.

"Gene-a-ration," he said to her, sounding out the syllables. "Gene-a-ration."

"No," I corrected. It's gen-a-ration."

"Yeah, that's what I say."

Rana's voice slipped back into rutted English. "My father's grandfather is buried here, too. Three gen-a-rations of al-Badri sheiks rest beneath us. Or gene-a-rations."

Walking along the pit's edge, she indicated which marker belonged to each dead sheik. Then, grabbing both her boys' shoulders, she leaned down and told them of the powerful, wise men whose blood flowed in their veins. Karim looked into the pit with the clean smile of a child, feeling the gaps between his teeth with his fingers, but his older brother nodded darkly, as if he'd felt the ghosts guiding him through the world all along. Now he knew their names.

Leaving Snoop and Washington in the back of the crypt, I walked to the far right of the pit, where Rana had indicated her father had been buried. I did my best to make the moment feel surreal. Here lay Sheik Ahmed. I fought off a seditious yawn and asked about the marker next to Sheik Ahmed's.

"For my brother," Rana said. "He wanted to be buried in the garden outside, with the others, but our father wouldn't allow it."

"Oh." I stared at the small rise in the ground and wondered how it fit a prince of al-Qaeda. "I shouldn't have asked in front of your children."

She moved to my side like wind wrapped in black, touching my arm. I turned to look at her through the veil. "They will have his mind. They will have his kindness, his caring for other people. They will not have his anger." She folded her arms and looked down at the remains of her family. "So they must learn about him."

Rana let go of my arm and moved to the floor, tucking her legs under her and facing the pit, telling Ahmed and Karim to do the same. Snoop followed suit. I turned around and shrugged at Washington, who shrugged back. We joined the others in Muslim prayer, something Karim found humorous, as he kept sneaking furtive smiles at Snoop. His brother ended that with a quick smack of the head.

Rana muttered in impenetrable Arabic for a full minute, Snoop and Ahmed joining her for bits and pieces. She bowed quickly, producing a small bottle of rosewater from an unseen pocket and sprinkling it down upon the ground beneath us. Once the bottle was empty, she returned to her knees.

"How do the Irish bury their dead?" she asked me.

"It's similar," I said. Closing my eyes, I probed my mind until I found something suitably nondenominational. "May the road rise to meet you. May the wind be always at your back. May the sun shine warm upon your face. And rains fall soft upon your fields. And until we meet again, may God, may Allah, hold you in the hollow of His hand."

When I opened my eyes, they again fell upon the graves of the legendary sheik and his defiant son, two smeared moons of cinder in the dirt. I thought of Shaba's burned carcass and grinning skull. I've found you all, I thought. Now what?

I joined the others on my feet.

A solemn quiet filled the crypt, a draft of wind whistling through the room from the window. Karim started puckering his lips. Ahmed told his brother to stop, which only made him do it more. Ahmed then put him in a headlock and punched him in the ribs. Rana was still staring into the pit. She asked her boys to go play outside. Washington and Snoop followed of their own volition.

"Elijah was supposed to come here," she said, once we were alone. "But al-Qaeda would not give us his body."

"Why not?" I asked, even though I knew why.

She sighed, the swamp blossom scent of her perfume coming with it. "Life was impossible back then. First came the Collapse. Then the Shi'a death squads and the civil war. It didn't matter to them that Elijah had become Muslim. It didn't matter that this was his home. It didn't matter that we were to be married." Her voice turned to chrome. "Only the war mattered."

I waited for tears that didn't come. She patted my hand with her left one, sending quivers like light up my arm. "Wish I'd met him," I said. "Like his tattoo about liberating the oppressed."

She let go of my hand. "He only had one tattoo. It didn't say that."

"*De Oppresso Liber*?" I said, sounding out the syllables. "Latin. On his chest."

Even through the veil, I could see her eyes turning to splinters. "He had a tattoo on his chest. It said"—she knocked her forehead as she searched for the pronunciation—"'In-fi-del.' He said it was a joke for Americans."

"Oh." Fucking Chambers, I thought. What a goddamn fraud. "I see."

"He was a man, like any other." She sighed again. "And I loved him very much."

We looked into the pit for another minute or so. Then we left.

The noon sky had grayed out, hinting at rain. Snoop and Washington sat nearby, leaning against a pile of rocks they had to know was a grave. Rana asked where her children were.

"That way," Washington said, pointing over a ridge that led deeper into the graveyard. "Was playing tag."

I wanted to chew them out for letting the boys wander, but Rana didn't seem bothered. She walked up the ridgeline, calling their names. After a few moments, Karim's head poked up from the other side of the ridge.

"What?" Rana's voice flexed in worry. "Where's your brother?"

She began running before the words were even out of her youngest's mouth.

We followed, moving up and through rolling knolls, dodging headstones and crevices of dirt, unable to catch her. By the time I got to the knoll she'd stopped at, gasping for breath, she had sat Ahmed up against a dark boulder shaped like a dinosaur egg. The young boy's face was as faint as the land, and he seemed disoriented.

Rana grabbed his arms, running her hands down them like a tailor. "No," she said. "No."

A pair of matching bite marks glowed like juice stains on Ahmed's wrist. His mother began slapping his cheeks, which caused him to smile vaguely.

The others ran up, Karim pointing to a small batch of camelthorn and shouting. Snoop pulled out a long Bowie knife I'd never seen before and started hacking into the brush. The brush rasped in anger, causing Snoop to push Karim back and stomp into it between hacks. Washington directed his rifle at the camelthorn, but Snoop shook him off, reaching into the bush and pulling out a thick beige rope two feet long with a bloody anvil for a head.

"Viper," Snoop said, throwing it down, then following it to the ground. He began to saw off the snake's mashed-in head with his knife. "These have powerful poison."

Rana lifted her son's hand to her mouth and began trying to suck the poison out, then spitting, then sucking from the bite again. "I don't think that actually helps," Washington offered, but his words were ignored.

I walked over to the camelthorn and watched Snoop work. The viper had two horns that crested a broad, flat head, and a set of scales that alternated among yellow, brown, and gray rectangles. Snoop held up the snake head when he was done.

"Doctors will want this," he said.

"Washington, radio the vehicles and tell them we're en route," I said. "They need to be ready to move."

Rana had tipped Ahmed's head back against the boulder, slowly pouring the contents of another rosewater bottle into his throat. Karim stood nearby, tugging at his black bangs, his eyes filling with long tears. Still conscious, Ahmed kept spitting up the water and saying something about bad smells. He started running his fingers over the pink scar on his neck until his mother said to stop.

I looked down at the now shaking boy. His wrist was beginning to swell. Too scared to scowl now, he suddenly looked like his father had in the *mukhtar*'s photo, plain-faced and grim. He's Shaba's blood, I thought. He's Shaba's son. And it's up to us to save him.

I put my hand on Rana's shoulder as she forced water down her son. "We're taking him to the hospital," I said. "Now."

I tried to scoop Ahmed into my arms. Rana wouldn't let me. "I'm carrying him," she said. "I'm his mother." Washington and Snoop jogged ahead to let the patrol know we were following. Her face veil removed, with her son draped across her arms and the hem of her dress bunched together in one hand, Rana moved through the hills like a hero of old. She shook off my attempts to share the burden and told Karim he needed to keep up. I didn't know what else to do, so I had the younger boy hop onto my back. He was heavier than expected. The air tasted hot and angry, and sweat ran all over my face and into my eyes.

Doc Cork met us at the entrance with a fleece blanket and medical kit. He stuck an IV in Ahmed's arm and checked his vitals, telling the boy to keep his arm below his heart. Ahmed nodded feebly, raising his hand to touch the scar on his neck again before remembering not to. The boy's wrist had continued to swell like a balloon, and the skin around the bite marks had morphed to a dark yellow.

I looked around at the coolers and folding tables spread between the vehicles. The men had been playing cards.

Snoop pulled out the viper's head and showed it to Doc Cork, jiggling it like it was a voodoo skull. Doc Cork stared at it, transfixed.

"I don't know what the fuck that is," the medic said. "This is way beyond my training. We need to get him to a hospital that has antivenoms. I don't . . ." he trailed off, but I pressed him. "We'd have to go to Baghdad to get what he needs. That's too far, though. His heartbeat is through the roof."

"What about Independence?" I asked.

Doc Cork's shoulders slumped. "We're not allowed to bring locals to base for medical treatment, not anymore. Not even for emergencies."

"That's insane."

"I know—but remember the car accident? On Route Madison? First platoon wanted to do the same thing. Battalion told them it's a no-go. They're supposed to use their own hospitals."

"Please." Rana grabbed my shoulders and pulled me close. Swamp blossoms and hard breath filled my nostrils. "We must go to your base. It's the only way."

I kept my eyes on Rana as I spoke. "Don't doctors have a code of ethics? Like, they have to treat a patient if one's brought to them?"

"I—I think so," Doc Cork said.

"So we'll bring him straight to the aid station."

"Okay." Doc Cork tugged on my sleeve to get me to face him. "But, Lieutenant." I turned to him. He was whispering now. "We'll get crushed for this. You especially."

Doc Cork kept turning from me to Ahmed to the ground, from me to Ahmed to the ground. My mind was thrashing. It'd been trained to equivocate, molded from birth for clever escapes and third options. It kept grasping for something beyond the either-or, anything but the either-or, except there was nothing, nothing but the either-or.

For the first time all deployment, maybe the first time all war, there was only one decision to make. Clarity imbued my chest, then my words.

"Hotspur," I said. "Mount up. Camp Independence, time fucking now."

42

Jack—

I'm sorry we argued like that on the phone. Not sure if you've read my emails apologizing—doesn't matter. I'll say it again and I'll say it better: I'm incredibly proud of you. Always have been, but especially now. I've no idea what you're dealing with, because I don't stop and consider people the way you do. I just bulldoze through life, and that's not right. Your empathy makes you a good leader and a better man. Like the accidental shooting you talked about—caring like that makes you special. Don't let this war take that from you, no matter what.

You should know that I'm not the hard-ass I probably try to come across as. During every one of my deployments, I was scared out of my mind. Every time I said good-bye to you and Mom and Dad, I thought for sure I'd never see you all again. And over there—over there, as you know, it's worse. It gets so bad you stop caring. At least I did, especially the last time.

You should know why I got out. It wasn't just business school. That last deployment to Baqubah, man . . . it was bad. And I mean that in the most non-melodramatic, non-bullshit war story way possible. Before then, it'd kind of been a game. But command broke me, it really did. It's taken me a while to realize that.

The battle wasn't like the articles or books. It was . . . I don't know. I don't even trust my memory of it. We were tasked with seizing twin bridges and setting up a blocking position. We did that. Then came the IEDs, then the ambush, then it was night and it was all over. Everything in between is a total blur.

I'm not sure if you ever saw it, but when I received my Silver Star, I got interviewed by the news. The quote they used was terrible, made me sound like a sociopath. Something like, "I was just spraying guys and they kept falling. They would just drop—no blood, no nothing." Crazy thing, I don't even remember saying that, but there's the footage, for all the world to watch.

My kids are going to watch that someday.

The things the award citation and the articles don't say: that I didn't get the third guy out of the Humvee before it blew up. That my planning fucked up the blocking position, leaving a ridgeline open, which is why we had no idea about the ambush. That the reason some of us survived that clusterfuck was because of 20-year-old joes who received no award, did zero interviews, and now might be lucky enough to work as Walmart greeters.

What does any of that mean for you? I don't know. Wish I did. Obviously, I'm still sorting through things myself, and I've been back awhile. We're always learning the wrong lessons from history, I know that much. And I know that compartmentalizing things like I said to do isn't always best. It got me home, but maybe it made things worse in the long run. So if that doesn't work for you . . . it doesn't work. That's okay. I just want you to get home. Just get back here, damn it.

I got drunk with Dad after my last deployment and told him everything. Something he quoted has stuck ever since: "He, too, has resigned his part In the casual comedy; He, too, has been changed in his turn, Transformed utterly: A terrible beauty is born."

It's from a Yeats poem about the Irish revolution, which I'm sure you already know. (I'll admit to having to look that up. No poetry classes in B-school.) But—those words. Those fucking words. This isn't very profound or anything, but they've helped me. Maybe they'll help you too.

I fear I'm lecturing again. Or rambling. Both are nasty habits. Maybe finding a local willing to write a sworn statement is the solution. Maybe reporting everything you know is. Maybe doing nothing is. Point is, you'll figure out what to do, as a leader, as a man.

Pray. Think. And act. Just do what you feel is right. Everything else will fall into place.

Since most of this letter has been all about kissing your scrawny ass, I'll point out that you were wrong about one thing. "Be safe and be strong" is not bullshit. It's all I have to offer from over here, but that doesn't make it disingenuous. So. Be safe. Be strong. And get the fuck home, you crazy goon. We need you.

With love and respect,

Will

There'd been a lot of questions about what had happened in the graveyard. The Big Man had found my lack of understanding of Coalition protocol "alarming," though he blamed Captain Vrettos for that more than me. After I'd stood at attention in his office for thirty minutes, silently counting his analogies to football, the Big Man dismissed me with one last piece of counsel: "We can't save them all. I know your heart's in the right place. But as an officer, your head's got to be in the right place. Remove it from your asshole. Now."

If nothing else, I appreciated the vividness of the order.

The intelligence officer proved more skeptical and probing than the Big Man. "I don't understand," he kept repeating. "The Cleric is dead. Both of them. So why were you out there?"

It was the look of betrayal on Captain Vrettos' face when we returned to the outpost, though, that left spots on the soul.

As for Rana, we'd entered into an unspoken understanding that day at Camp Independence—she was a source, nothing more, who'd begged us to save her child. She'd played her role well, better than I'd played mine. I wasn't sure we'd speak again. I wasn't sure that was such a bad thing, either.

Then, a week later, Snoop woke me from a nightmare. He pressed his cell phone into my hands.

"It's her," he said.

I stumbled into the lit hallway, not bothering to find my fleece top or boots. My watch said it was almost dawn.

"Sorry if I woke you." Her voice sounded hoarse through the grainy connection.

"How is he?" I tried not to interrupt but couldn't help it. "Is Ahmed okay?"

"He is." I was overwhelmed with relief. "I've kept him inside, though he says he's going out today no matter what."

"What happened? The last—the last I saw, the medics had to strap him down, he was shaking so much."

She clucked her tongue at the memory, and I could practically see her pacing the carpets, looking out a front window to watch the sun rise over her garden. "They gave him a shot to make him sleep, then medicine for the poison. We stayed until the night, when he woke up and could walk. Then they called a taxi. The doctors were very good."

"I would've stayed," I said. "I just couldn't."

"Jack, you did so much. You did your duties, the doctors did theirs."

Something about the way she enunciated the word "duties" made me consider just what those duties were. There'd been a time before when I'd thought those duties meant "The Mission." Then I'd thought it meant protecting the soldiers in my platoon, from the war, from battalion, from themselves. I'd neglected those duties recently. After Ahmed's emergency ride, I was certain they'd mutiny, but the exact opposite happened: they revered me now, nicknaming me Iceberg Slim and telling other soldiers I was the only lieutenant in the entire army worth a fuck. One night, late, I'd asked Dominguez about it.

"If you're enlisted over here, you get used to doing stupid shit that doesn't make sense," he'd said. "That was stupid, sure, but it made sense. And you did it cool, relaxed. Makes you different than most officers."

It was nice, being admired for once.

"I wanted to stay with you all," I said to Rana again. "But I couldn't." The conversation felt strangely vacant, and I couldn't blame it entirely on the connection. I was about to ask when I could come visit again when she said she needed to talk to me about something else. Something complicated.

She was right about that. Her husband had returned home the previous night demanding to know about the new American she met with, the new American who'd gotten Ahmed bitten by a viper. She'd denied everything, blaming it on gossip from jealous townspeople. Even her sons had lied, saying they wished the Americans would come and play, they'd be happier if they did. He hadn't believed them.

"I don't think we're safe with him, not anymore," she said.

He'd left for work just before she called. She hadn't known whom else to turn to. All her close friends and family were either dead or had fled the country.

"To where?" I asked.

"Beirut," she said. Most Iraqi refugees ended up in Jordan or Syria, but Beirut is where they all wanted to be, where she now planned to go, no matter what. She needed to get her boys away from the war that'd taken so much, away from a husband who'd taken so much, away from a home that'd taken everything. I asked how I could help.

"There's a smuggler in Ashuriyah," she said. "A people smuggler. They say he's the best."

His name was Yousef. He owned a falafel shop in town. "Yes," I said. "I know who he is."

She asked if I could ask him what it would cost to get a woman and two children to Beirut as soon as possible. We still owe her for saving us, I told myself. That's why I'll do this.

She thanked me for helping and said she needed to make her boys breakfast. Her voice scratched out with a simple good-bye. I sat there on the sandbags shivering in the early morning chill, body tingling with a thrill I couldn't define but recognized from another time and place.

I walked across the outpost to return the phone to Snoop. Our proud citadel was empty and quiet, smelling of mop water. I checked my watch. It was fifteen minutes past six. The other half of the platoon was due back soon from their night mission. It was just a counter-IED patrol, I reminded myself, just driving roads to prove there were no roadside bombs there.

Unless they'd been doing something else.

Snoop sat in a metal folding chair outside the terps' room, a headlamp strapped to his forehead, reading a translation of C. S. Lewis' *The Screwtape Letters*.

He took his phone back. "LT, I didn't want to wake you, so I made her tell me why she was calling."

"Uh-huh," I said.

"I—I hope to go, too. I need to go."

My eyebrows arched in surprise. I'd need him to speak with Yousef.

"You don't think there's a better way for you?" I asked.

He shook his head, the beam from his head moving like an agitated lantern. "It's the only way," he said.

I didn't think that was true, but hadn't found an alternative, either. I said we'd see what the smuggler thought. He nodded. The heavy shroud of conspiracy draped us both. I owe him, too, I thought. Maybe even more than I owe Rana.

Stomping boots echoed through the outpost, gear jangling downstairs. I went to the command post and found Captain Vrettos hunched over the radio, poncho liner wrapped around his shoulders. His eyes were even more bloodshot than usual.

I asked what was wrong.

"The *mukhtar*," he said, choking out the words. "Dead and gone."

43

By the time we got to the Sunni Strip, most of Fat Mukhtar had been scooped into pots and pans for burial. Belly guts hung from a palm tree like red banana clusters. An old woman was trying to dislodge them with a broomstick that didn't reach. Across the road a pair of wild dogs fought over a tibia bone wrapped in calf muscle.

While Snoop questioned the old woman, I walked around the remnants of the black Mercedes. Both the windshield and the driver's-side door had been blown apart. What remained looked like a hollowed-out clock, burnt black. The frame of the passenger seat had survived, as had the car's rear tires, perching its back in the air at an angle.

"This ain't no part-time job." It was Dominguez, coming around the other side of the vehicle. "Whoever did this knows the craft. My guess: rocket under the driver seat. Remote-detonated."

I followed his index finger to the void where the seat and steering wheel were supposed to be. In his own Mercedes, I thought. Which means someone who had access to the *mukhtar* had put it there. Which means an inside job. Which means . . . what?

Bowing my head, I forced myself into a moment of reflection for the dead *mukhtar*. I told myself I hoped he hadn't suffered, and probably meant it.

I turned to look down the road. The wedged dirt seemed to run straight into the sun. Somewhere down there, at the other end of the Strip, lay Yousef's falafel shack and, potentially, an answer to Rana's problems. That'd have to wait, though.

Snoop joined us at the car, the old woman heading to her house to fetch crates for a tall soldier to stand on.

"Happened about forty minutes ago," Snoop said. "Big boom, woke the whole neighborhood. She say if we got here twenty minutes ago, we could've helped get the bigger parts."

Dominguez laughed, then apologized for laughing.

"Any idea who might've done it?" I asked.

"No," Snoop continued. "But she say the Sahwa guards disappeared during the night. They should be right there, at the intersection."

So it had been an inside job. Which narrowed it down to . . . eighty, ninety people? The real question was who'd paid the emplacer, and why. I walked down the dusty yellow Strip and channeled my inner Irish beat cop. If not who or why, I thought, how about where? Ten feet in front of the Mercedes, I took a knee and looked over the area. Remote-detonated meant close, but not too close—no one would be stupid enough to blow up a *mukhtar* right in front of their own house.

Nothing made sense. I rubbed my eyes, and my nostrils flared. Then I stopped looking in front of me and started looking sideways at things, studying a small constellation of huts north of the Strip, on a crooked hill.

"There." I pointed. "That's where I'd do it. Whatcha think, Sergeant?"

Dominguez walked up beside me and squinted his eyes. "Hmm," he said. Then, "Not bad, Iceberg Slim. Not bad at all."

I snorted and looked behind us. The victorious dog gnawed on its trophy, having already torn through the meat. Doc Cork was steadying Washington, who was on his tiptoes on stacked crates to knock down the flesh slop from the palm, the old Iraqi woman shouting instructions in Arabic.

This is it, I thought. The Suck.

I left Washington in charge of the bomb site and walked up and around the hillside. A scratchy wind pushed against us. We moved in a diamond, Dominguez in the lead, then Snoop and me, then Doc Cork. Doc Cork was whining about getting stomach bits on him. I asked him to stop.

"Sorry, LT," he said. "It's just weird. We were at his place last week, eating falafels with his guards."

I nodded, wondering where my horror for things like disintegrated men had gone. There was just a nothingness, an acknowledgment of fact. Then Dominguez brought up the possibility of a house-borne IED in one of the huts.

We searched the huts with jaded efficiency. The first two were the same act from the same tired play: no one knew anything, no one had seen anything. They'd learned long ago to stay inside when explosions happened. At the third hut, though, after we'd flipped up mattresses and turned over hampers, the mother pulled aside Snoop. She had a long, narrow mouth and eyes that kept darting to the kitchen window.

"She say to look in the side of her yard," Snoop said. "She saw the little girl next door throw something this morning. She say her family has nothing to do with it."

We moved outside to the side yard. In a mound of dry tumbleweed, I glimpsed a black box with a bright white button that ran up it like a skunk stripe. I reached in and pulled out a garage door opener.

"Bingo," Dominguez said. "The detonator. Think she's lying?"

I shook my head and pointed to the last hut, a small mud house with red bars on the windows and a flat roof. The five of us surrounded it in a horseshoe, and I knocked on the door.

The door opened in a low groan and Alia stood there, fierce chestnut eyes tucked under a black head scarf, her stout frame blocking the entrance. Snoop's mouth fell wide open. I said hello.

On the inside, the three-room hut was nicer than those around it; all the furniture, from the kitchen cabinets to the dining table to the dressers, was a matching beech wood. A large flat-screen had been mounted in the main room. Dust sat in corners and under furniture, and clothes and pillows sat in cluttered piles, a far cry from Rana's pristine home. I smelled old food in the kitchen, spotting withered dishrags. Through it all, an old man in a wheelchair watched from the corner with a glassy stare.

"How'd you afford the television?" I asked.

"My nephew's," Alia said. "Bought it for his grandfather with Sahwa pay."

My soldiers roused the nephew from bed and pushed him into the main room. Sleepy and tense, he shared his aunt's dumpy build, and a bald patch marked the crown of his head. I tapped at a framed photograph that showed the teenager standing back-to-back with a young girl, their hands formed into finger guns, each striking a James Bond pose. I asked where the little one was.

"School," Alia said. "Of course."

I questioned Alia and her nephew separately. She had the day off from work. He'd left his Sahwa post the day prior, and wasn't due back until the afternoon. Of course she'd heard the explosion. He'd slept through it, but his aunt had woken him up about it. She said the Sahwa guards should've been at the Sunni Strip intersection. He said the same. She didn't know the names of the men on the Sahwa night shift. He said the same. She didn't know anything about Fat Mukhtar, she was just a cleaning woman. The *mukhtar* had been his boss' boss. Though he didn't know anyone who wanted the man dead, maybe he'd been driving drunk again and that was what had caused the accident?

I told him that seemed unlikely.

"Lots of things happening at night," Dominguez said. He was looking directly at me, puffing out his cheeks one at a time. "Still."

I tried to keep my response flat. "Not for long." Somewhere between the mosque and the cemetery, I'd finally decided to do something about the other part of the platoon. Something.

"What about him?" Dominguez tapped the wheelchair of the old man. He hadn't moved, nor had the distant look on his face changed. Alia moved to wipe away a pool of spit that'd gathered in the corner of his mouth.

I held the old man's hand and looked down at him sadly, thinking of my grandma, who'd passed through her own desert so many years before, on the way to California. "Alzheimer's," I said. "Or something like it."

The old man squeezed back, lightly. A large wart covered the bottom of his thumb. Alia glared at me. Doc Cork said they hadn't found anything unusual in the house. I let go of the old man's hand and turned to his grandson, holding up the garage door opener.

He stuttered out excuses, first saying he'd no idea what it was, then saying he could guess, then asking if it'd helped kill Fat Mukhtar. Alia interrupted, but Snoop forced her to be quiet.

"They told us to go home early," the nephew finally said, his eyes filling with tears. "I didn't ask why."

Dominguez suggested we swab his hands for explosive residue.

"He's Sahwa. Handles weapons every day," I said. "Won't he test positive, whether he's making bombs or not?"

Dominguez shrugged. "Old rule from Afghanistan: bring in anyone questionable, let the interrogators sort out guilt."

A better lieutenant would've come up with a fairer, more innovative solution, but I wasn't going to make things harder to protect people lying to us. So I had the soldiers zip-cuff the nephew and keep Alia away from me. I didn't want to deal with her.

He tested positive for both PETN and nitroglycerin. "Could be anything," Doc Cork said as he held the cotton swabs up against the sun. "These tests are pretty bush league."

As the Stryker ramp closed shut, the nephew said something in Arabic.

"He asks if he'll be home by tonight," Snoop said. "He needs to tutor his sister before Sahwa duty."

I told him that seemed unlikely.

44

I spent the night on patrol with the other half of the platoon. It was an uneventful counter-IED mission on the highways near Camp Independence. Chambers just shrugged when I'd said I'd be joining, saying there was no time at night for "slam piece stops."

"Good," I'd said. "'Cause I don't have one."

He responded by making another joke about plausible deniability. I didn't laugh this time.

The night guys rolled with black scorpion flags attached to the Stryker antennas, but other than that, I couldn't sniff out many differences. Some wore the scorpion patch on their shoulders, some didn't—same as the day soldiers. And they seemed as interested in our habits as I was in theirs. Though none called me Iceberg Slim directly, I heard it floating around, and I had to tell the cemetery story four different times.

"It always this quiet?" I asked, to different soldiers at different hours over the course of the long night. We left the vehicles twice, once to stretch our legs, the other to find that a reported IED was actually an unspooled cassette tape of Bon Jovi's *Slippery When Wet*.

"Pretty much," they always said.

We returned to the outpost a little after sunrise. I went straight to bed. Three hours and two Rip Its later, I was back out of the wire for an electricity recon on foot. I asked Captain Vrettos if we could make a stop on the Sunni Strip. "Potential new source," I said.

"Of course," he said. "You're getting good at this counterinsurgency thing, you know?"

Four old men playing dominoes on top of an ice chest marked the entrance to Yousef's. Across the street, a young man with slicked-back

286 · *Matt Gallagher*

hair feigned gangster, kneading prayer beads and watching us with forced disinterest. Snoop, Dominguez, and I stepped over the domi-noes game while the others stayed outside. I knocked on the BEST FALAFEL IN ALL IRAK placard, and we filed into the tin shack, Snoop trying to enter first but Dominguez muscling him out of the way.

The pasty scent of dough greeted our entry. As I took off my lenses and rubbed my eyes, other smells became identifiable: olives, figs, cin-namon, goat meat. The pit in my stomach panged; I'd skipped breakfast again. The shop was tiny and crammed with round tables and chairs. A low roof added to the hobbit hole feel.

I turned to the counter on my right, where the falafel man himself stood, wearing a gray *dishdasha* and a red-and-white checkered tur-ban. His beard was full and salt and pepper, and a large lip sore cratered a gaunt face. He spoke to Snoop, then clapped his hands at the two boys on the other side of the shop. They hurried outside.

"He say, 'The Curious Lieutenant finally comes,'" Snoop said.

"Dominguez. All looks clear in here, yeah?"

Dominguez looked at me bemusedly, and walked the length of the store, leaning over the counter to see what was behind it. Then he fol-lowed the two kids out and into the day, leaving the door open a crack.

The old man pointed to the far side of the counter. We followed him there, separated by a clear glass case that contained a variety of ostensibly fresh ingredients.

"Good to see you again, Yousef. My condolences about the *mukhtar*."

He dipped his head down and raised his hand to his heart, cupping it. A pair of fruit flies danced in front of my eyes, and I swiped them away.

"He's glad that you come, he's watched you for many months," Snoop said.

I took off my helmet, swiping away fruit flies again.

"Watched me? I . . ." I let the other question drift away into seared air, unsure how best to broach the topic of human smuggling.

I watched Yousef as he and Snoop spoke. His gaze didn't move from the space over my left shoulder, burrowing a hole through the back wall. The little hairs on my arms rose.

"He's passed through your road stops before. Talked to you about the weather."

I tilted my head and tried to catch a germ of emotion in Yousef's face. "Ask him if he knows who would want to kill Fat Mukhtar."

I couldn't keep up with either's Arabic. As I waited, the fruit flies returned, one landing on the tip of my nose. I smacked at it, but it disappeared like steam. A small one landed on Yousef's turban, but he either didn't notice or didn't care.

"He's surprised you ask," Snoop eventually said. "He believes the Americans killed him."

"What?"

"For revenge," he said. "Because the *mukhtar*'s men shot at Haitham the night the American soldier died." Snoop's voice rose in distress. "LT, does he mean Alphabet?"

My nails dug into my palms. Of course, I thought. The sheik's old vendetta. We'd been pawns in a game of side war and hadn't even realized it.

"Forget Fat Mukhtar," I said, breathing out slowly, smacking a fruit fly that'd landed on the glass case. "Just ask if he's the man to talk to if I want to get some people out of Iraq."

Yousef smiled as Snoop spoke, revealing a mouthful of small sharp teeth, like an eel's. His gaze didn't move, but his good eye shined, now on the Iraqi Army pistol holstered on my chest.

"He knew you'd come for this," Snoop said in a low voice. "He's heard the Curious Lieutenant helps the sheika and her children."

So people know about the cemetery, I thought. No wonder Rana and the boys need to leave.

"He say you're a good man for this, though you should be careful," Snoop continued. "Yousef hasn't seen her since she was a girl, but the people call her *majnooni*—the crazy woman."

"How much?" I growled. "One woman. Two children. Beirut." Did

I possess any secrets that the people of Ashuriyah weren't privy to? It seemed like they were following me everywhere, watching and whispering.

"Fifty million dinars, total. For Beirut. Thirty million for Syria. Syria's much easier." Snoop tapped his helmet with his index finger. "So, fifty thousand dollars, about? A lot, even for this."

"Way too much." I leaned over the glass and stared at Yousef, our noses inches away. He smelled like dirt and falafel. Even now, his eyes didn't even flicker, aside from the soap bubble of a cataract. He spoke again, a mist of halitosis forcing me back.

"He say it's a long journey to go where the sheika wishes. Long and dangerous. Especially for children. He promises to take care of all the papers, though, and send his best driver. He say it could be worse. It'd cost more if she were Shi'a."

"And if we take our business elsewhere?"

"He's the only smuggler left here. I know this," Snoop said. I looked over at him; his face sank to the ground. "I looked into it," he said. "The *mukhtar* was the other. Don't be angry, LT Jack. I just want a good life."

It wasn't anger I felt, but something else, something less easy.

"O-nly one." Yousef's voice cracked the air. "Me."

I leaned over the glass yet again. "Nice English."

"*Shukran, Molazim* Por-tur," he said, thanking me. "Surf is up."

We stayed in the falafel shop a few more minutes. Snoop asked how much it would cost to get him to Syria or Jordan. The slump in his shoulders said he couldn't afford it. I said to Yousef I'd be back in a couple of days to let him know about the other three people. He nodded and asked if we wanted a falafel, free of charge.

Neither of us answered, letting the screen door bang closed behind us.

I wanted to go straight to Rana's, or at least call her, but Captain Vrettos had radioed while we'd been in the falafel shop. He needed me at the outpost; the Rangers had requested another meeting. I gave the sun a jerking-off hand motion to signify how much I cared about all that, much to the soldiers' delight.

It was funny, the things they thought made a good officer.

We returned on foot. The afternoon had remained dry, though the clouds were thinning out into sheer. My men, proud infantrymen that they were, spent most of the patrol talking shit about the Rangers, how they thought they were better than other soldiers even though they had it easier, because anyone could raid a fixed location once a week, but it took true badasses to live in Iraqi villages for months on end like us. That lasted all the way to the outpost's front gate, where the Rangers stood around their Humvees, probably talking shit about regular infantry units and their contributions to the war effort. The men sized each other up, chests out, faces fierce. I turned my left shoulder their way so my own Ranger tab showed. They might've been bigger than my guys, but they didn't look tougher or meaner. And they were definitely less dirty.

The viking captain was waiting in the foyer. He followed me into a council office, the same one in which I'd met with Alia so many months before. Two of the electric lamps had burned out, leaving the room in a soft murk.

"It true? The *mukhtar*'s dead?" I hadn't even finished taking off my gear before the Ranger captain began. "How?"

"Car bomb." I rubbed a layer of sweat from my forehead and pointed to a coffeemaker on a corner table. "Cup?"

"Black." He had a wide, thick face and a snowy nose that looked to have been broken before. I was envious of his long hair and sideburns. "Fuck. We'd just turned him. Was going to give us a big insurgent commander in the area. Who killed him?"

"Not sure yet." The coffeemaker hissed to life, and I replaced the filter before realizing the packaged coffee was all upstairs.

"Don't worry about it. We won't be here that long." I smirked at his understatement and took a seat across from him.

"So yeah, not sure yet," I said. "Found the detonator nearby. Picked up a Sahwa a couple hours after. Interrogators have him now."

"His Mercedes?" I nodded. "Someone he knew, then." I nodded again. "Maybe the commander got him. What do you know about the Cleric?"

I tried not to laugh but couldn't help myself. "Sorry," I said. "Just that the Cleric isn't a real guy. It's just a name locals say to scare people. It's a ghost story."

I stood to turn on the industrial fan in the corner. It coughed like a sick man but wouldn't spin. "Huh," I said, resuming my seat. "Worked fine last week."

"The Cleric is real." The captain looked so heartfelt with his broad shoulders and flossed teeth, such a testament to clean American living, that I almost believed him. "Weapons smuggler for al-Qaeda for many years. Now he's been moving people out of the country for profit. We tracked the *mukhtar* to him." He closed his eyes and cursed again. "Don't have a photo, but we know he's old. Blind in one eye. Owns a business of some kind. Ring any bells?"

"No," I said, perhaps too carefully. I didn't like lying to another American officer, but Rana and her boys needed to get out of Iraq.

I continued. "It's not like Fat Mukhtar was a good guy. He gave us a fake tip a couple months back to settle a personal score." I paused for effect and tried to remember what Haitham looked like, failing to come up with more than flitting eyes and rotting teeth. "An innocent man got killed. A good man."

"They all do that shit." The captain shrugged. "Part of the game."

I decided I didn't like the viking captain very much. He pointed at my chest. "Porter? Any relation to Will?"

"My brother."

A wide smile crossed his face. "Served with him in the 'Stan."

When I told him Will had left the army, he looked surprised. "A damn shame," he said. "Will was a fine officer."

"A shame?" It'd been a while since I felt defensive about my brother. It was reflexive. "How much can one man give before it's enough?"

"Easy, little brother." The viking smiled again, and I considered punching him in the throat. "You got his temper, for sure. I'm there myself. Not sure I want anything to do with a peacetime army, especially not a peacetime officer corps. Just have no idea what I'd do. I'm not the business school type, you know?"

I did know about not being the business school type.

The last remaining electric lamp started flickering. We both looked up.

"Someone should change the bulbs," he said.

"Yeah," I said. "Someone should."

The Ranger captain pulled out a notepad and wrote down a string of digits. "Give me a ring if you hear anything." I gulped, nodded, then gulped again.

He was five steps to the door when he turned around and pointed to the blinking light. "I really respect what you guys do out here," he said. "Out in the wilderness."

"Thanks." I stammered a bit. "We respect what you guys do, too, of course. I hate night raids, honestly."

He laughed. "Like anything else, little Porter, the more you do something, the more normal it becomes."

45

Snoop called Rana's cell four times before someone picked up. It was a man's voice, and it was angry.

"Who is this?"

Snoop hung up and turned to me in alarm. "Her husband must've taken her phone."

We couldn't call her, nor could we chance visiting. For two days I pretended everything was normal again, even though all I could think about was her and her boys and fifty million dinars for Beirut. Or thirty million for Syria.

"Syria is much easier," Yousef had said.

I went on two more night patrols, another counter-IED mission, and a dismounted patrol through a field of elephant grass, looking for a crashed drone. Nothing close to nefarious happened on either one, though Chambers kept asking what I expected to find.

We returned from the drone expedition later than usual, half past eight. Pulling double duty on patrols had taken its toll, and I had a long nap in mind as I trudged into the outpost, my boots caked in red mud and my face covered in night sweat. October had proven brisk; I could still taste the wind on my chapped lips. Snoop was waiting in the foyer and pulled me to the side as the soldiers passed.

"She's here," he mumbled, trying to act casual. "In the council office."

"Who?" I yawned. The center of my back was throbbing. I started unstrapping my body armor and took off my helmet. My scalp gasped.

"Her," Snoop said, drawing out the word and darting his eyes to the hallway that led to the council office. "Alia got her in. To see you."

I was halfway to the office before I wished I'd had a little time to clean up—I felt grungy and knew I looked it, too.

Alia was leaving the room as I approached it. Her nephew had been released after forty-eight hours for lack of evidence, and was back on the Sahwa beat. She brushed past me and ignored my hello, not that I blamed her.

I walked into the room and locked the door. Rana was jogging in place on the taupe carpet, another impromptu burst of Tae Bo. She'd taken off her sandals, holding them in her far hand, and I saw her feet for the first time, bare and small as a child's. Her toenails shone with powder-blue polish. Under the flickering electric lamp, the black of her hair seemed to pulse. She'd been snuck into the outpost as cleaning help, wearing a black *abaya* and head scarf like Alia's.

"This carpet feels nice," she said, ending her session. "Hope that's okay."

She must have no idea how serious shit is now, I thought. Tae Bo? Now?

After piling my body armor and rifle into a corner, I sat down at the table, across from her. I tried not to stare but couldn't help myself; it'd been only a couple of weeks since I'd last seen her, but it felt much longer. I like her as a person and it's okay to like her as a person, I said to myself. So chill out.

"I talked to Yousef," I began. I'd never seen Rana with makeup before. But under the lamp, I made out a large dab of concealer around her left eye. Hints of swelling lay under it.

"He hit you," I said.

She looked right through me, her green eyes firm. I blinked and blinked, waiting. The portrait of the dead mayor and his mustache smiled down at us from the wall.

"He thinks al-Qaeda will come for us now that the town knows I've helped Americans."

"He can't hit you."

"This isn't America, Jack."

A quiet like air pressure rushed the room. She was right, but that didn't make me wrong. I looked down at the table and told her Yousef's prices for Syria and Beirut.

"I don't have that kind of money. What—what am I going to do? We must leave soon. We must."

I was struggling to raise my head, so I didn't.

"How much do you have? Yousef seemed pretty firm, but maybe if you're close?"

"No, Jack. You don't understand. Even if I borrowed, even if I sold my mother's jewelry, I'd have no more than ten million dinars."

"Fuck him," I said. "If Saif were still around, he'd know what to do."

She closed her eyes and slid down her chair. I forced myself to look up toward her, then at her. "Perhaps," she said. "But don't blame Yousef. He's the only one who can help."

She put her face into her hands and started rubbing her temples. I expected tears, but none came. She had the face of a seer, distant and purposeful. I wondered where Ahmed and Karim were. Probably kicking around the soccer ball, hoping for soldiers to show up and play, which was ridiculous, even in a war zone.

I kept watching Rana rub her temples. Something about it reminded me of my mom, and my mom with Will and me, dressing us for church on Sunday mornings, back when she would always lay out matching khakis and polo shirts for us. I'd usually protest like a punk, until Will would grab me and say if I didn't quit, he'd beat the hell out of me, that Mom needed this, so we were going to go to church in matching clothes and we'd be happy about it. I'd tell him fine, I was going to do it, but not because he was telling me to.

I want to leave Iraq having done a good thing, I remembered. I need to. A good thing free of qualifiers, of ambiguity. A thing that actually matters.

Helping a mother and her two boys matters, I thought. It matters a lot. It probably matters more than the entire war ever will.

"I'll do it," I said. "I'll get the money."

I didn't know how yet, not at all. But I would.

"No," she said, her dimple sinking into a small smile. She thought I wasn't serious. "That's very nice. But it's too much for anyone."

"I insist." My voice sounded like a stranger's. "I can't leave the three of you here, alone. Let me do this."

That was when they began. Only two or three drops slipped down her face, but still, there were tears and there were tears because of what I'd said I'd do.

"I hate crying," she said. "Mostly I hate people who cry."

I thought about reaching across the table and taking her hand in mine, but unseen irons held me fast. We sat there for many minutes, her thanking me, me reassuring the both of us that things would be okay. I was a sentimentalist playing stoic, but she didn't seem to mind.

"It's gotta be Beirut," I said. "Syria seems like it's about to implode. We can't send you there."

She nodded. The tears had faded by now, replaced by cold pragmatics. She'd heard that some smugglers had plenty of room for personal effects, whereas others said to bring only what you could carry. She'd tell her boys they were going on a trip. And what of Malek? She didn't hate him, he'd tried so hard, but there was no way he'd let them go if he knew. She'd write him a letter.

"Easy," I said, pushing my hands downward against the air, which I hoped was a universal gesture for slowing down. "We've still got some time. I've got to pay Yousef, for one. Remember to breathe."

She grinned shyly, as if to hide her stained teeth. "I know. It's just—if I don't think like this, I'll think about how scared I am. I've never lived anywhere else. I've never even traveled outside Iraq. We must leave, but. This is home."

"Of course." I breathed in her muggy perfume and could feel my heart pounding against its cage. I coughed and pushed away the many less-than-noble thoughts that were raging within. "Yousef has done this for others? They've arrived safely?"

"Many," she said. "Some from my tribe." She was putting her sandals back on, and color was returning to her face. "Do you think it's like on the postcard?"

I remembered the drawing of the beach and the blue sky and the palm trees. "Beirut's not heaven," I said. "Been a lot of strife there for many years." She nodded like she knew, but her frown gave her away. "But it'll be a nice place to raise Ahmed and Karim. You'll be safe."

Cold pragmatics were seeping into my mind as well. They'd be vulnerable on the road, easy targets. But Snoop can go with them, I realized. He'll keep an eye on them and get them there. I smiled wide at this thought, something Rana took to be for her. Standing to go, she pulled out her cell phone and snapped a photo of me sitting there, arms draped across the table.

"Handsome," she said. Then she walked around the table and squeezed my hand. I squeezed back and looked up and into her, determined to show that I wasn't the type of man who made promises he couldn't keep, that I was different.

"Thank you," she said. "You're no Shaba. And that's a wonderful thing."

She bent down and kissed my cheek with dry lips. Then she was gone, the office door closing after her, and I was alone under a flickering light.

I pushed away from the table and stood. "Don't look at me like that," I said to the mayor's portrait. "I'll figure it out."

I walked into the hallway and saw Chambers at the end of it. Rana had to have walked past him to leave the outpost. He'd removed his uniform top, and his arms were crossed, his face drawn like he'd just seen a ghost. In a way, for him, he had.

He'd regained his composure by the time he made it down the hall, following me into the office. He started whistling, low and without melody.

"So she's the one you're fucking," he said.

"No. She's a source," I said slowly, in that way of sounding calm while conveying the opposite. "She saved us from the IED at Sayonara Station."

"And you never bothered to tell me it was Rana al-Badri?" He spat out her name, voice cracking. Then he slammed his fist into his palm.

The skulls on his right forearm shook from the impact. "I'm your fucking platoon sergeant. I deserve to know these things."

"Whatever, man." He couldn't talk to me like that. I was the head motherfucker in charge. "I'm not going to get lectured by a guy who lies about fallen comrades. *De Oppresso Liber*? Try 'Infidel.'"

His gray eyes narrowed, followed by an ugly sneer. I braced for a punch that never came; instead, he sat down on the table and gripped its underside with his wristless hands.

"And you think we've been hiding shit at night," he said, shaking his head. He started rummaging around his cargo pockets for something, probably dip, but couldn't find any. "Unreal." I thought we were about to have a heart-to-heart, or something near it, when his head snapped up, the creases in his face cutting through the shadows of the room.

"If I'm a hammer, you're a snake, sneaking around like this," he said.

"Fuck off." I didn't like being called a snake, no one would, so I turned sarcastic. "And let's stop with the incongruent animal metaphors. Scorpions. Snakes. Spiders. Beasts in the hearts of fighting men. We get it, okay?"

It felt good to be standing up to him, even though it'd taken the embarrassment of being caught talking with Rana to bring it out. He was surprised by it, too. He took a deep breath and searched his pockets again, to no avail. Finally, he hooted, just once, like he'd done in the spring after shooting the goat.

"'*In-con-gruent.*' Hell of a college word."

I felt my shoulders relax. "Pretty sure I used it correctly, but I'd have to check."

He leaned back and crossed his ankles, tapping one boot against the carpet. He wanted an explanation, I realized. Maybe he deserved one.

"I haven't done anything wrong, I swear," I said. "Just knew you'd freak if you knew it was her." The half lies were coming out so easily, little drops in a bucket that had room for more. "Her intel is good. Let me do my thing, Sergeant. This isn't my first rodeo."

From outside, I heard wind rambling across the desert. The forecast called for more rain in the coming week. Chambers seemed most interested in a sore that had developed below one of his earlobes, he kept picking at it. It took a lot to not tell him that was how things got infected. He eventually stopped.

"She got him killed," he said. "Maybe not on purpose, but that doesn't matter. He turned into a goddamn maniac because of her. Started going off post by himself. Started talking about staying here." His voice sounded remote, wistful even, until it wasn't anymore. "Some men can't act rationally when there's poon involved. Elijah was one. What do you think, Lieutenant—you able to keep your head around females?"

"I already said I haven't touched her." My teeth were clenched. "I'm not going to say it again." That wasn't exactly a counter to Chambers' statement, but it needed to be said again. When he didn't respond, I walked to the door, saying I needed some sleep. I felt his eyes on my back, hard and doubting, but he said nothing.

46

I called Will and asked for five grand. He didn't inquire why, just when and how. "I trust this matters" was all he said.

The Bank of America branch at Camp Independence proved more inquisitive when I pulled my savings account, twenty thousand dollars in all. I said it was to help pay for a new pickup truck from the base dealership.

"Tax-free over here," I said. "Couldn't resist."

That still left me—left us—twenty-five thousand dollars short of Yousef's price. Something the unit's Sahwa payment could cover.

It seemed easy, in theory. Purchase a black backpack at the base exchange. Sign out the Sahwa money and the second black backpack. Return to the outpost, leave the backpack with the money in the Stryker while taking the empty backpack to the outpost's arms room. No one would notice it was empty for a couple of weeks, not until Captain Vrettos got around to scheduling the payday. By then, Rana and Ahmed and Karim would be safe in Beirut.

It had to be now. After this payment, we were done paying the Sahwa. It was the Iraqi government's turn.

It had to be now.

The soldiers won't notice the pack switch, I thought. They leave Iceberg Slim business to Iceberg Slim.

Four days after Rana came to the outpost, we returned to the falafel shop.

I told the soldiers to remain with the vehicles as Snoop and I went to meet with Yousef. "Won't be long," I said.

I couldn't tell if the soldiers in the back of my vehicle were interested in the black canvas backpack I held or if I was imagining it. "An old friend, by the telephone pole," Dominguez said through his headset as the ramp dropped. "Might want to say hi."

Sure enough, as I stepped into the afternoon, I spotted the Barbie Kid across the street, sitting on his cooler. He was dressed the same as when I'd last seen him at Fat Mukhtar's: pink sweatpants caked with mud, oversized khaki top, sneakers on his feet. He flipped us off with both hands, his unibrow bending into a frown.

"Arab fuck," Snoop said, balling his hands into fists. "Must want trouble."

"No need, man," I said. "Leave him be."

The tin shack smelled of hot goat and dough. The shop boys left. I placed the backpack on the glass case.

"Hope you accept dollars," I said.

Yousef reached for the pack, but I pulled it away. "One thing. You take him, too." I nodded at Snoop. "A young man to help the driver will make the journey easier."

He agreed without much fanfare. Snoop couldn't contain his grin; he hadn't believed me when I'd shared the plan. I handed over the backpack, and the Iraqi started counting. When he finished, Yousef looked up, hazel and cataract brown finally finding its mark.

"Half now." The Sahwa money. "Half later." The Porter brothers' money, currently in a mandated seventy-two-hour withdrawal hold. "When they arrive safely." I'd seen gangster movies. I knew this was how it worked.

Rather than agree or demand full payment, Yousef pointed to my chest, where Saif's pistol was secured.

"He wants the Glock," Snoop said. "A weapon of power for Iraqis, especially that color. He will give a better deal for it."

"This was a gift," I said. "From a friend."

At that, Yousef laughed and coughed in tandem, an ugly sort of throat swirl. Then he asked how I felt about the concept of truth. Snoop translated, confused by the old man's words. The money sat on the glass case between the three of us like roadkill, no one wanting to touch it, no one able to look away, either.

I shrugged and said that while I didn't believe in truth anymore, I'd listen, as long as he made it quick. Rana needed to know things were going to be all right.

"You ask people about Karim and Shaba?"

"*Sí.*"

"They were arrogant. Dogs," he said, waiting for Snoop to translate. "They thought this was a game. It wasn't about Rana. It was about power."

The sticky air soaked up Yousef's words. Beneath the body armor, my sweat-soaked undershirt clung to my body. The accounts of these dead men were always so disparate from one another that it felt that with each thread I found and pulled at, the entire past was unraveling into a meaningless pile of knots. Yousef waited behind the glass case, slowly putting away the backpack, his eyes back to the wall behind us.

"Okay," I said. Snoop figured out the details of when and where they were to meet Yousef's driver. I'd already cracked open the screen door when I turned around.

"Snoop?" My voice rose like a weapon. "Ask him what he knows about Chambers. What he knows about the kill team."

I waited out Snoop's query and follow-ups, seconds that turned into a half minute. Even after the many months in Iraq, even after getting decent at understanding some words and phrases, I still had no idea how so many words in Arabic translated into so few words of English.

"He asks, 'What do you want to know?' Now that you're businessmen together, he will say anything."

I walked back to the glass case.

Yes, he'd heard the rumors about Chambers killing civilians. Yes, those rumors had been around during the time of Shaba, even before the death of Karim. No, he didn't believe Shaba was involved, but then again, maybe so. They'd been friends.

Yes, he believed the rumors were true. Didn't all Americans do that?

But, well. There'd been the news reports of the murders of civilians in Haditha and Mahmudiyah around the same time. And people panic when they get scared.

Who else had been killed? Oh. People. There'd been a butcher named Mohammed. Other people. Friends of friends. He couldn't remember their names.

"It's been many years, *molazim*," he said. "Many years."

Would he be willing to write a sworn statement about all this? Sure. He'd do it to honor our mutual friend, the *mukhtar*. Had he himself seen Chambers shoot a civilian? It depended.

"On what?" I asked.

"On what you wish me to write, *molazim*."

We left and returned to the outpost. The soldiers didn't want to be on patrol anymore, and neither did I. I couldn't call Rana, either. We had to wait for her to reach out to us.

Chambers was in our room, so I went to the smoking patio. I tried reading a magazine, but couldn't concentrate. I tried smoking, but my hands were shaking too much to light the damn cigarette. I tried thinking about what life would be like once we got back to Hawaii, but I couldn't get past next couple of weeks.

I'd just robbed the U.S. military to pay off a smuggler connected to al-Qaeda. That had to be a felony.

Maybe even treason.

I'd never had a panic attack, so I didn't know what the symptoms were, but suddenly I found it difficult to breathe, and my mind found it difficult to focus on anything. I got cold, so I plugged in the space heater, but then I was hot and started sweating a lot, especially my neck. My leg wouldn't stop twitching. My thoughts were many and varied, but eventually they landed on Rana as I forced myself to inhale and then exhale and then again and then again.

I imagined how our conversation would go when she reached out. A phone call seemed easiest.

"Hey," I'd say. "It's me. It's Jack."

"Jack! Any news?"

"Yes. Though I'd prefer to tell you in person."

"Oh." A clumsy hush would fall across the conversation. I'd chide myself for being so goddamn direct. This isn't California, I'd remind myself, and Rana isn't a California type of girl.

"I don't know," she'd finally say. "Malek doesn't share his schedule anymore."

"Well, it's taken care of. All of it."

"And your man, Snoop?" she'd ask. "Were you able to pay for him, too?"

"Something like that," I'd say. "He'll be with you. Going to take care of you and your boys. Whatever you need."

It'd been many years since I'd been unnerved like this, even in pretend—composing wishes, anticipating and destroying those chewy seconds that awaited on the other side of the phone. It was a nice feeling. Even in pretend.

"I think I'm falling in love with you," I'd say. "I'm sorry if that's too abrupt or too American or too whatever. But it's how I feel. I want—I want you to know I did what I did because it was the right thing to do. But also because of how I feel about you and your children." I'd stop, just for a second, to show how earnest and well-intentioned I was. "Thought you should know."

The rest of the conversation would pass like smoke. I'd tell her to wrap her mother's jewelry in clothing. Then I'd remind her to bring potable water and snacks for the trip. I didn't trust Yousef or his people for any of that. "And layer," I'd say. "Make sure you layer." She'd chide me for being a nag.

"I'm the mother," she'd say. "Not you."

Then we'd laugh, together, a laugh rich with both possibilities and implications.

"What are you smiling at, LT?" It was Snoop, and we were on the smoking patio. It was raining lightly outside. "You okay?"

I groaned and checked the corners of my mouth for drool. The terp carried news on his face.

"Yousef just called. Change of plan. He say to be on the road at the reservoir bed at sunrise tomorrow, near Rana's home. His driver will meet us there."

"Tomorrow?"

He nodded.

I asked if he was ready. He said as ready as he'd ever be. He was worried about what the platoon would think. I said I'd handle them. I asked about his family in Little Sudan. He said they'd understand. I asked what he knew about Beirut. He said he knew there was a beach and a mountain with snow on it. I said that was probably enough. He said thank you, he'd never know how to repay me, that a lot of Americans talked about helping terps, but I'd been the only one who actually did. I said no problem, that he could buy the beers when I came to visit.

"Only thing left, then, is Rana and her boys," I said.

"Yousef already took care of it." Snoop cleared his throat. "She already knows to be there."

"Oh." Pangs of disappointment fell through me. I'd wanted to be the one to deliver the news. I turned and spat on the ground. "That's great."

47

The next morning, we waited at the reservoir bed in the elastic pause before dawn. And through it. And after it.

Eventually Snoop looked over at me from the other rear hatch of the Stryker. It'd been two hours. "I don't think they're coming, LT."

He braved a smile. I ignored it.

"Call her again." No one had picked up the previous ten calls, but maybe someone would this time.

No one did.

"Something must've gone wrong." I shouted through the headset to wake the driver. "We're heading back into town."

The patrol moved east, into a hard yellow sun, and I told the driver to go faster, faster, until he said he wasn't sure a twenty-ton armored vehicle should be going so fast, especially with the glare in his eyes.

I said to go goddamn faster.

We sped under the stone arch of Ashuriyah and the eyes of its watcher. Yousef wasn't at Yousef's. The shop boys didn't know where he was, they hadn't seen him since the day before. He was usually at work by now. Did we want any breakfast falafels?

We returned to the Stryker. "Where to now, sir?" Dominguez asked.

"I don't know," I said. "Give me a minute."

I sat with Snoop and Doc Cork on the benches inside the vehicle. I took off my helmet and loosened my body armor. I made the driver turn off both the iPod and the external radio so I could think in silence.

"Sir?" Doc Cork asked gently. "What the hell's going on?"

"It's complicated."

"Does it have to do with the Iraqi woman?"

I nodded.

"We got your back," he said with a sincerity I found patronizing.

I ordered the patrol west again, back through the stone arch, to the hamlet with five small mud huts.

We dodged an IED on the way there. The driver saw a milk crate over what had been a pothole an hour earlier and swerved around it. The vehicles behind stopped short. We'd been half a second from potentially blowing into meat ornaments, and all I could think about was the delay this would cause.

"We gonna call the bomb squad?" Dominguez asked.

And sit here for three hours waiting for them? I thought. But I said, "No. Pull up parallel to that bitch, recon by fire, and we'll keep going."

They didn't like it, but did as ordered. They were good soldiers.

Dominguez's machine gun ripped into the milk crate. The heat of the red blast washed over me as I watched from the hatch, understanding that at this moment, for this person, I'd be willing to do anything.

We kept driving west. The outpost radioed to ask if we'd heard an explosion in our area. I ignored it. They stopped trying to reach us after the third call. The song of passing desert replaced the crackle of their faraway voices, chapped earth always, chapped earth forever, a hymn of holy yellow poison.

We turned onto the thin silt road. A blue Bongo truck sat in front of the nearest house with a drip pan underneath it. I'd never seen the Bongo truck before and looked at it as if it were a lumpy testicle. It didn't belong. There was a stiff wind that smelled of oil and animal shit. A man was standing alone at the square garden. Doc Cork, Snoop, and I dismounted. Washington and some others joined from another vehicle. Everyone looked ready for a fight, up on the balls of their feet, shoulders cocked, rifles at the low-ready. I locked and loaded, too, the bolt chambering a round with an anvil's grace.

The man didn't turn as we approached, keeping his head bowed at the garden. He wore a button-down stained with paint and harem pants that danced in the wind like flags.

"Stay back, sir," Washington said. "He could have a suicide vest." We stopped ten feet short of the man, fanning out. Snoop shouted through the wind. The man turned around, keeping his hands deep in his pockets.

Stupid tears streaked Malek's face. His beard was patchy, with gaps along the jawbone. He put his hands in the air.

Doc Cork patted him down while Washington kept his rifle casually situated on Malek's gut.

"He's clear," Washington said.

Snoop waved the Iraqi man up to us. He moved slow and without care. He was no taller than Rana and had the short, trunky arms of someone who worked with his hands. He wiped his face and nose with his shirtsleeve and spoke to Snoop.

"He asks why we interrupt him on his day of grieving," Snoop translated. "His wife has taken his children and left him forever."

"Get him to explain, Snoop. Make it seem like we don't know anything."

As Snoop and Malek spoke, I studied Rana's husband. He had thin lips and a forehead much too long for his face. There was a moony quality to him that I couldn't place, an uncertainty in his speech. In a different time and place, I'd have commiserated with him. I reminded myself that he'd hit her, and hit her because of me. No, I thought. This man is your enemy.

Snoop's voice bit with a cold neutrality. He said that Malek didn't know much, just that he'd returned home this morning to find his wife and sons gone, and their belongings, too. She hadn't even left a note.

"He's fucking lying." I grabbed Malek by the collar, twisting my knuckles into the pressure points under his chin. "What did you do to them? The fuck did you do?"

His black, stupid eyes were welling up again. I tossed him to the dirt and had the soldiers follow me into their hut. Malek remained on the ground.

The home was abandoned. The structure still stood, but everything that made it Rana's—the blankets, the wood baskets, the coloring books we'd brought the boys—had all been gutted from it, leaving a fish skeleton of two rooms. Even the Persian carpets were gone. We checked the bedroom. The family's mattress and the two plastic chairs sat undisturbed, as well as a basket filled with Malek's clothes.

As the soldiers searched the other huts, Snoop and I walked back to the garden, where Malek had found his feet. Snoop asked if I had any questions for him, and when I shook my head because everything seemed fuzzy and distant, he asked his own.

After a minute of dark thoughts, I interrupted. "The hell are you guys talking about?"

"Gardening," Snoop said. "These are his plants. He made it for Rana to try to make her happy."

I laughed, loud and brittle, and started moving away. I heard more Arabic behind me, and then Snoop called out. Malek wanted to know my name. I turned around.

"Me?" I smiled big, one of all-American-boy charm and fluoride shine. "My name is Elijah Rios."

Snoop didn't need to translate. Malek's face started trembling, not side to side like a person would from anger, but up and down, like a guillotined doll. Then he began barking, at first low and hoarse, then higher and shriller, removing a shoe and flinging it at me, missing widely. I kept my cocky smile plastered across my face and patted my rifle. Snoop took a few steps away from Malek, but the Iraqi made no move to follow. He just kept barking, and then threw his other shoe at the garden. We returned to the Strykers.

The other huts were as empty as ever. We boomeranged back east to Ashuriyah. As I looked back from my hatch through the kicked-up brown dust, Malek was still standing there, woofing, a wounded animal bleeding to death in its garden.

The stone arch hadn't moved. Things moved through it and around it, but it remained firm. It was now the meridian hour, and Yousef was at Yousef's. I didn't wait for the shop boys to leave before I reached across the glass case and grabbed the old man and asked very calmly and very politely just where the fuck Rana and her boys were.

Halitosis blew all across my face, but I held fast. One hazel eye and one cloudy brown eye avoided my stare.

Snoop gasped. "LT? He say he has no idea. He pretends he doesn't know Rana. He pretends he doesn't know us."

The barrel of my Glock found the inside of the old man's mouth. *Tink, tink, tink*, I probed like a fisherman with a tackle, counting one eel molar, two eel molar, three eel molar. I kept going in a symmetrical pattern and flipped the safety trigger to semiauto when Yousef raised his index finger. I removed the pistol from his mouth.

He spoke in short, clipped sentences. Before he finished, Snoop leaned across the glass case to grab Yousef himself. He started choking him, and Yousef gagged. I pulled the two men apart.

"He's a lying coward!" Snoop was indignant. "He say that he has no idea about any sheika or any smuggling, he's just an old blind man who sells falafels. He doesn't care if you put a gun in his mouth again and pull the trigger, because death means nothing to him. I'm going to murder him, LT. I must. For honor."

I raised my pistol again and put it under Yousef's nose. In my palm, the steel felt like jelly. "I got this." One of the shop boys started whimpering. I thought it appropriate that Saif's weapon would kill Yousef, considering this was their country and all. "Any last words, my man?"

Yousef flashed his mouthful of small teeth. "The *majnooni* was wrong about you," he said, his English smooth as sky.

I concentrated on an ache in my feet until most of the anger waned.

"You're the Cleric," I said. "Always have been. And you ordered the hit on the *mukhtar.*"

"Maybe," Yousef said, his good eye still watching my finger on the trigger of the pistol. "Or maybe there isn't a Cleric. Maybe there never was. Tough to say."

That was as close to a confession as I'd get, I knew. I also knew that whatever chance she had left, whatever chance they had left, might depend on me still. If they weren't already headless in a ditch somewhere.

I lowered the Glock.

"Dead," Yousef said. He knew I wouldn't shoot him now. "You both."

I smirked, thinking of the viking captain and the Rangers. I made the sign of the cross on Yousef with the pistol. "A fatwa for you as well." Then I cleared the Glock and removed its clip, placing the pistol on the glass case, near the spot I'd dropped the backpack the day before. It was all I had left to offer. In stunted Arabic, I found my words carefully.

"Hate us. Fine. But save them. Rana is good. Ahmed is good. Karim is good. Save them. I will still bring the second payment. Take them where you promised. For them."

He didn't nod or agree, but he didn't deny me, either. Slowly, he slid the pistol to his body. Then I walked out of the shop, pulling Snoop after me, who wanted to know if we could beat the old man senseless if we couldn't kill him.

I was no killer. I'd long suspected it, but now I knew it. There was shame in that, certainly, for a man in combat, for a leader at war. But there was also relief.

My body was shaking. The Barbie Kid watched us from his cooler across the street. He sat under the sun in a thin gully; everyone else had already retreated indoors for the late-morning siesta. I moved his way, stopping a few feet short.

"We took everything from you," I said. His lazy eye stayed fixed to the ground, but his good one cut through me like black shale. "I can't bring back your uncle, or your goat, or your job. I'm sorry." He blinked and flexed his unibrow. "For what it's worth."

He must've grasped enough of what I said, because his middle fingers rose like tiny brown towers. I bowed my head and said in Arabic that he deserved peace and prosperity, and walked to the Strykers.

He remained sitting on his cooler, staring at my footprints in the dirt like they were a Martian's.

Numb—so very numb—and suddenly exhausted, I ordered the patrol back to the outpost. There I called Rana's cell myself. It didn't ring through this time. It went straight to the dial tone of a disconnected number.

48

The next few hours ate away what remained of my soul. There was Rana's disappearance to consider. And Ahmed's and Karim's. And the missing Sahwa money. And Captain Vrettos' sad, broken eyes. And lying to the Rangers. And the death sentence placed on Snoop and me. And Chambers, dirty Machiavellian Chambers, the most dangerous threat of all, because even after everything we'd been through, even after he'd saved my life and I'd listened to him and embraced the beast within, he'd remained an enigma, a man beholden to laws and codes he alone understood.

With Rana gone, the headaches returned. I spent much of the day with Augustine's *Confessions* in a rancid Porta John, trying desperately to find a way out. The few sentences I was able to grasp suggested that looking for a way out was the wrong thing, but there weren't too many practical alternatives offered. The half Presbyterian in me talked to God, but He wasn't answering, so the half Catholic in me thought I needed to find a proxy. And there was only one priest of war in Ashuriyah. I decided to confess my sins, to ask forgiveness, to seek repentance.

I found him in bed, a DVD player on his lap, alone in our room. He seemed to be sleeping, his chest rising and falling in slow breaths like hills. Our boxy, windowless confessional smelled of wet tobacco. I approached the bunk and knocked on the beam. He looked up with eyes pale as slate, black skulls on his forearm throbbing, and pressed pause.

"I need help," I said. The deep lines slitting his face tightened. "Your help."

That was when the world wobbled.

"Earthquake?" Then came another crash, and then another, and I realized it wasn't movement but sound, like drunken continents tossing around tectonic plates.

"A Spectre dropping some pain on hajj," Chambers said. He hopped up and threw on his uniform top. "Maybe a Spooky. You know they got howitzer cannons in those gunships?"

I didn't, but nodded anyhow. We jogged to the command post, where Captain Vrettos said to prep the vehicles. He was going to need our patrol to search whatever it was that the air force had bombed back to the stone age, as soon as higher gave the okay to do so.

"The *mukhtar*'s funeral is tonight," he said. "I'll be there. But keep me updated."

Six more gunship defecations later, we sped into a blue autumn night. I had a lot of misgivings about leaving the wire—I'd become paranoid enough to wonder if it was all a trap set by Yousef—but I knew I couldn't stay in the outpost anymore. The mere act of motion meant I didn't have to think about the consequences of my decisions, and that superseded everything else.

The coordinates we'd been given were in the Sunni southeast. The strike had been ordered by a spec ops unit—they believed the targeted house had been wired to blow up. Black plumes sucked at the horizon, darkening the night sky. Traces of ember turned into gulps of smoke as we pushed south.

We stopped a hundred meters away. A small blaze had engulfed the house. I radioed the outpost and let them know that one of the gunship's artillery rounds had enkindled its target, and asked them to contact . . . the fire department? Our Strykers formed a defensive position.

Craters the size of bowling balls ringed what had been a front yard. Much of the adobe roof had collapsed, and what remained looked as if it were held together by toothpicks. The warm blast of the flames functioned as an outsized furnace as I waited for Snoop to finish talking to a group of men and women who'd come out of the neighboring houses. Most shouted angrily at us.

"They say that house has been abandoned for years, ever since the

Invasion," Snoop said. "They say there's no wires or bombs in there. Their kids use it to play hide-and-seek."

Maybe, I thought. Everyone made targeting mistakes, but spec ops were the best. The fire was moving south, into a field of poppies and purple hyacinths. I left Snoop to handle the crowd of a dozen and waded into the ruins myself, pulling up the top of my undershirt to cover my nose and mouth, putting on a pair of clear lenses to protect my eyes. Hellish heat came from every angle.

I walked through the entryway, and a heavy middle-aged woman emerged from the smoke, coughing, and pushed past me. Hers was a face I'd not forgotten: the mother who'd lost her son at Sayonara Station all those months ago. I smelled overdone meat. I turned a corner and saw why. Three dog carcasses were splayed across the parallel room, orange and blue flames dancing on their far side.

The locals are using the fire to cook, I realized. I checked to ensure each dog was already dead, then got out.

"Gnarly in there." Doc Cork stood outside as I came back into clean air, breathing deep, his thick silhouette a stain against the night. "There's poor. Then there's this."

The crowd around Snoop had doubled, growing louder and more agitated. Chambers stood nearby, keeping an eye on the terp, pushing back a group of angry, shouting women. "These bitches are getting truculent," he said as I passed. "Might need an exit strategy." I ignored him.

Young men ran past carrying buckets of water. As I approached the crowd, Snoop's eyes widened in relief. "LT! They say the fire is spreading fast. They need help or they will lose their homes."

They were right, cinder trails were pushing east and west now, little tentacles of fire shooting out. I said not to worry, that I'd already radioed for help, and that I'd go check to see how much longer it'd be.

I called the outpost. Captain Vrettos answered.

"Hotspur Six, you need to proceed to Camp Independence, time now," he said. "We've been tasked with escorting a supply convoy to the north gate of Baghdad."

"Roger, sir," I said. "Quick update: house was clear, totally abandoned. But it's getting bad down here. There's a fire, and it's spreading fast."

"I understand that." Even through the radio static, his irritation punched through like jabs. "We've notified the Iraqis, they're on it. Remember, this is their country."

"Sir, this one is on us. We need to stay."

"Negative. Proceed to Camp Independence, time now."

"But, sir—"

"Did I stutter?" The uppercut stunned from miles away, using my own sardonic language. "This is a direct order. Gather your men and report to Camp Independence for your mission. Now."

I chucked the hand mic into the bowels of the Stryker, ripping it off the radio body. I walked back to Snoop and the locals, giving any soldiers I met along the way the mount-up motion, a halfhearted twirl of my left index finger. The blaze had savaged the house, dragon snorts engulfing it room by room. More young men were moving buckets from the other houses, having established an assembly line that passed full buckets down and empty ones back. A strong wind stirred from the west and pushed east, bringing sparks with it.

"Tell them we're leaving, Snoop," I said.

He did. The Iraqis yelled even louder, and Snoop backed into me, and I raised my rifle to keep them away. Somewhere behind us, Chambers laughed.

Once we got inside the Strykers, all four surrounded by clamoring Iraqis, I ordered the men to throw down all the jugs and bottles of water they could find. There were some objections about what we'd drink if we got thirsty, but I repeated Captain Vrettos' direct order to me and dared them to challenge it.

"Do what he says," Chambers said across the platoon net, from his Stryker. "So we can get the fuck out of here."

I opened my hatch and climbed out to unstrap a plastic jug we'd been keeping for emergencies. I handed it down to the short Iraqi mother with wide shoulders. Under a dark red head scarf, she shouted at me, the hard eyes of poverty never blinking. Beneath the guilt and the shame, I felt a curious sort of release. Then we left.

As we pulled onto Route Madison and pushed east, I turned around and looked back at what we'd wrought. Under sad yellow stars, billows of smoke swirled in the wind, and a sheet of wildfire tore through what had been the field of poppies. Flakes of ash drifted through the air. I stuck out my tongue and caught one.

We met the supply convoy at Camp Independence and escorted them south. We dispersed the herd of fobbit vehicles between us: one Stryker, then the fuel tanker; another Stryker, then the cargo truck and a water trailer; then our last two Strykers. The irony of the full, lumbering water trailer only miles away from a burning Ashuriyah proved too much. Not even the joes mentioned it.

I remembered how back in the early days of our tour we'd pretend to see IEDs and RPG launchers just to scare supply soldiers making a rare trip out of the wire. I didn't feel like doing that anymore. Neither did anyone else. The hour-long drive passed in silence. Black dogs barked and barked in my mind, but I ignored them, or tried to.

A vast gold dome marked the north gate of Baghdad. We passed under a sandstone tower with wooden scaffolding and parked on the side of the highway; now we waited for the landowning unit's escort to show up and take the supply convoy to the airport. Wanting to get some air and stretch my legs, I stepped onto the ink-black pavement. The supply soldiers' leader, a sergeant first class with short, braided cornrows and an eye patch, did the same.

"Going home?" I asked. "Good for you all."

"We've done our time," she said. I hadn't thought my question hostile, but she'd taken it as such.

"Sorry," I said. "Didn't mean to call you out."

"Uh-huh. Tough-guy infantry. All we hear is fobbit this, fobbit that." She pointed to her left eye. "I didn't get this raking leaves."

Maybe there had been undertones laced into my words after all. I didn't know how to interact with people anymore, just infantrymen. I asked whom she was going home to. She just shook her head.

Their escort didn't arrive for another hour. With the joes getting tired from the tedium, I had them switch up the vehicle crews for the return trip. Hog climbed into the back of our Stryker and slapped Doc Cork on the back. "Hey, sir," he said, all canted-eyed affection. "Like old times."

On the way back, we passed Route Pluto, a thin artery that pushed southeast past the Tigris and through the insurgency's heartbeat of Sadr City. So many soldiers had died on that three-mile stretch of blacktop, I thought. Too many crevices and curves to hide away small boxes wired to blow. I wasn't sure wars like ours got monuments, but if it did, it belonged on that road.

The sky had darkened into black knots of clouds. Our iPod played tangy hipster music. There were still no signs of the fire, which meant they'd put it out, somehow. Near Checkpoint 38, the radio squawked. It was the outpost.

"This is the CP. Be advised of a large gathering of locals at the entrance to Ashuriyah. Orders are to disperse it, by any means necessary."

"Roger," I said. "Any more info? Like why they're gathering?"

"Negative. Captain Vrettos is still at the *mukhtar*'s funeral. His patrol radioed us saying that the gathering started there before moving east to Ashuriyah. Our guards on the roof report they've started a bonfire near the arch."

"So be ready for anything, pretty much."

"Roger that."

My head was throbbing again. Doc Cork and Hog laughed bitterly. I couldn't help but join them.

"Go there and figure it out when you arrive," Doc Cork said. "Improvise. If it goes well, higher gets credit for planning it. If it goes poorly, we morons on the ground fucked it up."

No different than any mission we've done over here, I thought. Probably no different than any mission anyone's done.

A tall orange flame marked the entrance to Ashuriyah, perpendicular to the stone arch. The bonfire had been built on a dry meadow, a halo of rocks controlling the burn. Dozens of Iraqis lined the road, with another group circling a crooked utility pole to the side. Judging from the loud chants and large banners, it seemed we'd been ordered to disperse a protest, not a gathering. We pulled over to the shoulder of the highway.

"This is retarded." Chambers' voice cut across the platoon net like a saw. "This has ambush written all over it. We need to drive through and come back with more men. Like a battalion of fucking SEALs."

"Hear that," I said. "Wait one."

I pushed back against the CP, calmly explaining just how crazy their order was. They referred me to the operations center at Camp Independence. I repeated my request to push through and wait for the protest to fizzle out from a distance.

"Hotspur Six." It was one of the majors. "Do you sleep with a night-light?"

"No, sir," I said. "But even if I did, I still wouldn't send us out into this."

"Sir, this is Hotspur Seven," Chambers interrupted, and I was glad for it. "My platoon leader ain't exaggerating. It's chaos out here. In my experience, waiting this one out is the only option."

"You all are a platoon of infantrymen, correct?" The major's question sounded rhetorical, so no one answered it. "I've been wondering why Ashuriyah is the only place in Iraq that's still a disaster. Now I know why."

"Sir—" I said.

"Do your fucking job," the major said. "Disperse the gathering. Report back when mission complete. Out."

"You heard the man," I said over the platoon net. I was scared but knew I needed to hide it. "*De Oppresso Liber.*"

I said I'd check things out quickly, asking for volunteers to join. Snoop and Doc Cork followed without a word, while Hog sighed heavily before doing the same. Four more emerged from the other Strykers, all joes on their first deployment. Iceberg Slim didn't have the same *wasta* with the night soldiers, but he still had some.

I drew everyone in tight and pointed across the knife of a road, reminding them to stay close and that no one was to cross the median. We were discussing fallback options when Chambers emerged from the shadows. He shook his head in disgust, but said he was coming, too.

"Two minutes," Chambers said. "We're in, we're out, we go home."

"Agreed," I said.

We sank across the highway like stones, forming a wedge. The night lashed at our bare faces and wrists. I realized why there was a bonfire: the electricity in this area of town had gone off again. We stopped at the edge of our headlights' reach.

A small group had gathered in front of the crowd, under the eyes of the arch. They kept pointing to us and gesturing. After a minute or so, five of the men walked our way, carrying small torches and flashlights and assault rifles. The many locals behind them gathered around the bonfire and faced out, chanting with raised fists. I guessed them to be about four hundred meters or so away—definitely within distance of a decent shooter with a scope.

"What they saying?" Doc Cork asked.

"Not sure," I said. I could make out "America" but nothing else. "Probably better that way." Snoop stayed silent.

I didn't recognize any of the approaching men, though three wore the familiar khaki brown shirts of Fat Mukhtar's Sahwa. A wiry middle-aged man took the lead. Looking beyond them, near the base of the fire, I caught a glimpse of a small woman with long black hair holding the hands of two small shapes. Or I thought I did. Why would she be here? I thought. Of all places, why here?

"Go!" the lead Sahwa said, wiping his palms together. "America keel *mukhtar!*"

"No," I said, trying to keep my voice low and putting my hand on the Iraqi's shoulder. He shrugged it off. "America no kill *mukhtar*. Yousef kill *mukhtar*." I wiped my palms together, then drifted my fingers through the air like little kites. "Go home. *Bayt*."

He repeated his own words and pointed to the crowd at the arch. Banners displaying a jowly, grinning Fat Mukhtar were shaken at us by the larger group. I searched again for the shadow Rana and shadow boys, but couldn't find them.

Someone at the bonfire trumpeted with their voice. The larger group then started marching toward us, to the envoys' dismay. Two ran that way in an attempt to stop them. Mob rule had taken the night.

"Time to go, Lieutenant," Chambers said through clenched teeth. "I see crowbars." Some of the other soldiers began shuffling their feet and playing with the safety triggers of their rifles.

I grabbed the wiry Sahwa by the collar and pulled him to me, smelling fire on his clothes. "Rana," I said. I searched for the right Arabic words, then for any Arabic word. They fell through my mind like water through a fist. "Rana al-Badri. Where is she?"

Wide black eyes brimming with incredulity looked back at me. "*Majnun*," he called me. "No Rana Ashuriyah, *majnun*. No Rana Ashuriyah. Go!"

Arms, the muscular, taut arms of soldiers, pried me from the Iraqi. Then he was gone, and I saw the advance of the mob clearly, some hundred meters away now, and closing fast. Some cable in my being snapped tight, and I shuddered, telling the men that I was good, they could let go, it was time to leave.

That was when the Strykers on the highway shoulder began honking their horns.

Another angry crowd of shadows and torches was approaching from our rear, moving along the highway, east to west. It was as if they'd materialized out of the sand berms, dozens and dozens of them, almost as large as the first group. They weren't carrying the banners of the *mukhtar* but the beige water jugs of the U.S. Army. Our empty jugs, I realized, as a young man in blue jeans and a checkered turban began beating one against the side of a Stryker.

The jaws of the mob closed on the highway shoulder, with us stuck in between. The vehicles' machine gunners swiveled their turrets like spintops, unsure if they should shoot to save those of us on the ground, unsure where they'd even start shooting if so. I said, "Stop," and raised my rifle, but no one listened. The soldiers who'd remained with the vehicles now prowled the top of the Strykers, pointing their rifles down at the crowd, shouting in English. I smelled the loose flesh of violence again, all hot sweat and young rage. The lead Stryker tried to drop its ramp for us, but Chambers made them stop for fear of the mob getting inside. The nine of us backed up against the side of that Stryker, shoulder to shoulder, surrounded by a hundred revolting locals.

I couldn't see Yousef, but he was out there, somewhere, directing this horror show. I raised my rifle to my chest, barrel flat, and flipped the safety trigger to burst.

"Sir, what are we doing?"

"Lieutenant Porter, we need to move. Now."

"Sir!"

As hands started reaching for us, trying to pull us into the mass of the riot, three simple words hung on my tongue like a scythe: light them up. To my right, I saw Chambers raise his rifle to do just that. Above me, I heard the soldiers on top of the Stryker doing the same. To my left, I saw Hog drop to a knee, head bowed. He wasn't praying or renouncing himself, though. His eyes stayed open as he cupped his heart with his trigger hand, furiously, over and over again, while pointing to a banner deep in the crowd with his left hand. I looked that way. It showed the dead *mukhtar* with his arms around his Sahwa, smiling, fat fingers raised into peace signs.

I heard a voice to the far left yelling, "Fire!" It was Chambers. "Fucking fire!"

I shouted, "Hold! Hold!" as loud as I could and dropped to a knee, too, rifle draping my lap. A hand pawed at my shoulder. I took off my helmet and looked up at the bodies through the black of night, trying desperately to show neither fear nor aggression. Another hand yanked at my chest plate, but I remained firm. Some arms still reached for us, and one scratched at my ear, drawing a streak of blood across my face, but then, slowly, surely, the arms receded, and I wasn't being grabbed at anymore. Through the yellow glare of the headlights, I saw human beings, mostly young, as confused and mad and foolish as we were.

I heard Doc Cork curse at me, then at himself. Then he took a knee, too.

Chambers yelled for us to hold our ground while voices in the mob answered, imploring the others forward. But the possibility of rampage had collapsed. One by one, American soldiers took off their helmets, some cupping their hearts, others saying "Salaam Aleichem" on repeat, still others flashing the peace sign as if to answer the banner of Fat Mukhtar. No one else took a knee, but they didn't need to. I looked around to find soldiers still on top of the Stryker, the barrels of their rifles no longer pointing out.

"Fucking cowards, stand up!" Chambers stood alone, facing us. "You're soldiers! Soldiers don't kneel."

"We're not kneeling," I said. "We're taking a knee."

I looked to the black knots of clouds to thank Allah and Jesus and Yahweh. The gray silhouette of a keel-billed bird streaked across the sky. I blinked, and it was gone.

As the Iraqis turned back, most walking to the bonfire, others moving down the highway, a thick man with a mangy beard in a black-and-white tracksuit pushed his way to the front, fists shaking, loud words spraying. As I stood to intervene, a narrow-shouldered Iraqi in a tight dress shirt and khakis appeared, whispering into the ear of his larger friend. He'd grown his flattop out some, but I still recognized the tidy mustache and flat berm of a face. Azhar's brother led away the man in the tracksuit, before I could thank him for keeping the most fragile of peaces.

No one said anything as the Stryker ramp dropped. We just got in and drove to the outpost, under the arch and through town, the desert falling into a clean sleep no one deserved.

49

We met on the back patio as the night sounded its rale. I'd been sitting on a wooden picnic table in a long-sleeve shirt, trousers, and unlaced boots, smoking cigarettes. There'd been a steady rain through the early morning, and Ashuriyah smelled of wet dust. The burn pit had kept me warm in billows of thick smoke and soot; I'd fed it lithium batteries and Styrofoam and plastic bags through the hours, drenching it all in lighter fluid. Once the flame had reached my height and swollen out twice as wide, I tossed in the contents of our history. First the three sworn statements from 2006. Then the photograph of Shaba's bloody vest. Then Haitham's mug shot. Finally I burned the book itself, Lawrence's tome folding in half and crumpling like a lost kingdom.

It wasn't my past to dredge up anymore, if it'd ever been. The smoke made me cough, but I stayed until I had nothing left to burn and the fire turned to ash.

They're probably dead, I realized. A mother and her boys. And it was all my fault, because I'd tried to help.

I was lost in those lonely stirs of nothingness when Chambers found me.

"You almost got us killed."

Serenity cloaked his words, his movements neat and trim. He still had his body armor on, rifle at the ready. I couldn't see his skulls but felt them through the black, pulsing. I took one last drag and tossed the butt to the ground.

"You're toxic," I said. He stood perpendicular to my line of vision, and I refused to turn, instead watching his piano frame out of the corner of my eye. "You won't infect my platoon any longer. You're going home, tomorrow. For our sake and yours."

"Me?" His voice crashed through the night. "You're the one chasing ghosts. You're the one who's turned patrols into fuck dates." He was so angry he was stammering. "You're the one who—that was fucking insane. I gave the order to shoot."

"And I gave the order not to." I shrugged. "Wouldn't do it again, but it worked."

Another fire had been stoked. "I'm not going anywhere," he said. "You, though—you got a lot to answer for with that empty backpack in the arms room. I think you gave it to the hajj bitch. That's what I think."

"Prove it." I forced a yawn, silently thanking the soldiers for staying true to Iceberg Slim. "Junior officers don't get fired for negligence. Not ones with war heroes for brothers." I didn't believe any of that, but convincing him was what mattered. "You, though, drop weapons galore. Anyone who'd defend you is already dead."

"Prove it."

"What do you think I've been doing this whole fucking time?" I wanted to push him past the controlled anger, past the fury, to find what lay on the other side. "People like you win battles. People like me win wars. Get over your bitch boy Elijah and you'll see that."

It wasn't the threats that did it, but the "bitch boy." A sound beyond rage burst from Chambers, a niagara of mania and broken nobility. The shadows blurred and then softened into a hard shape. His fist landed under my left eye, and I heard something pop. My head went astral and snapped back, but I managed to hold on to the top of his collar as I fell back onto the picnic table. Long seconds passed into blankness as I fought for consciousness.

I blinked and blinked until I could focus on the moon above. The world seemed fuzzy, especially at the edges. Something hot and wet ran down the side of my face and into my cracked lips. I'd held on, though. By clutching his collar with my right hand, I'd managed to sneak the M9 pistol I'd been hiding up under his chin, where his helmet couldn't protect him. Sour breath blew down on me, and for the first time I recognized that the pouches on his face were too heavy for a grown man, like a baby's cheeks were. Chambers had baby cheeks.

"You tricky fuck" was all he could offer.

"You know, Sergeant," I said, concentrating on the thin vine of muscle wrapped around the pistol trigger, keeping my breaths shallow. "Punching an officer used to be a death sentence." I smiled like a clown. "Firing squad, usually."

His eyes were like gray flares, and his nose folded into the bottom of his forehead. Then he managed a hollow laugh.

"Quite the Mexican standoff." His breathing was slowing, and the killer shine in his eyes was fading. I counted to thirty in my mind. The hand holding the pistol became damp, but I held it fast. He closed his eyes and tucked his overbite behind his lower teeth. For the second time in one night, the possibility of rampage collapsed.

He opened his eyes. "What happened to nothing else mattering but the youngbloods?" he asked.

I considered his question, then his pet phrase. "Means different things to us, I think."

"He really was my friend." He wasn't speaking to me so much, not anymore. "He really was the best man I ever knew. That's not bullshit. Every year, though, it's like . . . sometimes I can't even remember what he looked like."

The first trace of sun touched the horizon. He asked if he could remove his helmet. I asked why.

"To show you a picture. It's in the crown, under the padding. He's been with us the whole time."

I said I didn't want to see it. Sliding off the far side of the table, I kept the pistol leveled at him. Runny blood fell off my face; I felt my cheekbone with my free hand and figured he'd broken it.

He sat down on a bench and took off his helmet anyhow. He looked into it like it was a kaleidoscope, acne scar pockets marking his temples, his high-and-tight cut a strip of order in the midst of chaos. It's not that he lacks a conscience, I decided. It's that the one he has is broken in the center, because that's what going to war over and over again does to people. I walked around the patio backward, lowering my pistol. I'd already opened the door and propped it open with a foot when I remembered something.

"You need three for a Mexican standoff," I said.

"I know." He patted the top of his helmet. "That's why I said it."

I thought about that for a few seconds. "For what it's worth," I said, "I never would've pulled the trigger." He didn't say anything. "Why didn't you shoot? Last night, I mean. You just gave the order. They would've shot if you had. You know that."

"Still figuring that one out," he said. His voice was so low, I could barely hear him. "Let you know when I land on something." He looked up, so tired and so old.

"Let's get them home," he said.

"Let's."

"I'm sorry I punched you."

"Sorry I pulled my pistol on you."

"We good?"

"Yeah." I was still going to get rid of him. "We are."

As the metal door rang behind me like a cymbal, I cleared my pistol with shaking hands. The inside of the outpost felt very cold. I didn't think I had much in my stomach, but the urge to defecate was sudden and strong. Climbing the stairs, using the banister to keep my balance, I noticed someone had smeared a crude veil over the Mother Hajj's face, an eclipse of paint. Probably a *jundi*, I reasoned, or maybe someone from the town council. A soldier wouldn't have put in the effort.

My legs had turned to juice, so I took a seat halfway up the stairs. The foyer was empty, and yellow light was spilling into it. I took in a breath of mop water and floaty, orange air and listened to a finch call from outside. I stayed there for a while. Then I walked to the command post.

The night shift sat around the radios in a semicircle of lawn chairs, all morning breath and jaded stares. I asked where the commander was.

"Camp Independence," a sergeant said. "Helping plan for an expedited withdrawal. Sounds like we're going home early. Sounds like everyone is."

"Just marking time, aren't we?" I said.

"Haven't we always been?" A beat later, the sergeant said, "Sir, you know your face is bleeding?"

I said I'd fallen down the stairs and that it hurt like a motherfucker, because it did. Then I radioed battalion and told them to relay to Captain Vrettos that I needed to speak with him, as soon as possible. One way or another, I needed Chambers out of the platoon.

"Roger that," came the reply, distant and sleepy. "He left word to conduct a show-of-force mission. Exact location is up to you."

"Show-of-force?" I asked. It was a term from the pre-counterinsurgency era that roughly translated to *Show the Iraqis who's boss.*

"Yes."

Options, I thought, too many options. I was standing in the hallway, alone, when Snoop came by, walking off sleep in his loose basketball shorts and do-rag.

"Yo, LT," he said. "You look— Bad night?"

I laughed, massaging my broken face. "Patrol leaves in an hour," I said before walking across the outpost to wash my face and wake the guys.

The brief took place in the foyer. No *jundis* showed up, and none of us bothered to go find any. All the soldiers wanted to talk about was the riot. Other than Doc Cork, none had been there, but that didn't stop the stories.

"I heard it was like a thousand Iraqis."

"Not that many. But their leaders were carrying machine guns, like Rambo."

"Yo, sir, it true you said you'd kill everyone if they didn't go home?"

I shook my head and exchanged a knowing glance with Doc Cork. I looked out at the twenty gaunt faces in the open, sunny octagon of a room, and saw them in all their boyish grace, all their earnest bravery. I hated myself for the times I'd been reckless with them, for the times I'd been less than worthy of them. Maybe getting them home wasn't the only thing that mattered, but it still mattered, and mattered a lot.

"Hotspur!" they yelled, the last syllable reverberating through the outpost.

"Hotspur," I repeated, more to myself than to them, noticing that they still wore the scorpion patch on their uniforms, though it meant something different to them now. At least I'd done something right.

• • •

We drove directly to the Sunni Strip, then walked to the small mud house with red bars on the windows on the crooked hill. Alia stood outside her open door, waiting, holding a long lead pipe like a club. She spoke menacingly as we neared.

"She say we can't take her family again," Snoop said.

We finished the climb, and I looked past Alia into her house. Her niece stood in the small kitchen, putting on her shoes and backpack for school. She wore a purple head scarf and had black gemstones for eyes and a gaping red void for a nose, burns covering much of her upper body. I flinched, remembering the young girl from Yousef's some months before delivering falafels and asking for a tip. Snoop remembered, too, pointing. Another jigsaw piece snapped into place.

"It's not what you think," Alia began, but I interrupted her.

"I don't care about that," I said. "The *mukhtar*'s dead. Where's Rana?"

Alia swore she didn't know. She was waving the lead pipe around so much that Snoop asked her to set it down so she wouldn't accidentally strike one of us.

"If she wanted to run away, she may have gone to her father's old house," she said. "Where she grew up."

She gave us directions to the abandoned estate, then asked us to leave.

"But we want to help," I said. "Your family needs help. What can we do?"

"Leave now," she said, like it was the most obvious thing in the world. "I have neighbors."

Perhaps for the first time, I listened to Alia clearly, and took our patrol away.

We pushed east and then south, to the far edge of Ashuriyah—not so far from Haitham's final hiding spot, I realized, or the Sunni graveyard. "You'll know it from the big moon gates," Alia had said, and she'd been right.

We gently rammed the gate with a bumper to get in. It was a thin ribbon of a building, shaped like an upside-down *T*, much smaller than I'd imagined. Weeds of brown overgrowth covered the house's roof and sandstone walls, and a small marble fountain lay in the center of the circular driveway, dry as a salt flat. There'd once been a statue in the core of the fountain, but scavengers had long ago broken off the eagle's head and body. All that remained were the base and a pair of long, wide talons.

I went in alone. Dominguez insisted I bring a portable radio.

The house smelled of dust and hot air. There were no doors or windows anymore, just frames. Anything of worth had long ago been looted, though I found a rotted-out cabinet in one of the bedrooms. I opened it, and the door fell off its hinge.

I moved to the back of the house and into the courtyard. It was a wide rectangle and, save for a hunched brown cypress in the rear, there was only chapped yellow earth.

The great sheik's courtyard, I thought. Not so great.

"I don't know where you are," I said, to her, to myself, to the barren land in front of me. "But I hope you're safe. I hope you find whatever it is you're looking for." I paused, swallowing to wet my throat. "I hope you're not in a ditch somewhere."

The portable radio on my hip buzzed. "Hotspur Six," it said. "You're needed at Camp Independence ASAP. Commander's orders."

I smirked. It was reckoning time. I kissed my fingers and placed them on the sandstone wall of the house. It seemed the thing to do. Then I left.

We drove straight to Camp Independence, and I tried to appreciate the baked air and dust slapping at our faces in the breeze. Battalion had been trying to get ahold of our patrol all morning. They refused to say why I was needed, so I prepared myself for the worst. At least I'd gotten to say good-bye.

I met them in the Big Man's office. The battalion flag hung over the room like a big baggy clock, its infantry blue and crossed rifles symbols from a forgotten life. The Big Man looked up from his desk, all bald gravity. In front of the desk sat Captain Vrettos, hunched over. Between them was the intelligence officer, teeming with short-man energy. The Big Man motioned with his fist for me to enter. I took a deep breath and walked in, posting to the position of attention.

"Lieutenant Porter," the Big Man began, "we are aware that a fatwa has been placed on you by insurgents and have reason to believe you've known this for some time." I opened my mouth. "Don't answer. I don't want you to implicate yourself. I admire your dedication to the mission." The intel officer sneered but kept quiet. "The Rangers brought this to our intel team, and we confirmed it this morning."

My confusion betrayed me. "Sergeant Chambers," Captain Vrettos said. "Talked to him an hour ago on the phone. He spoke very highly of your loyalty to the platoon. But that riot last night, Jack—that was all staged to get you, the Rangers say."

"Anything can be a fatwa," I said. "They're not just death sentences. And I'm pretty sure you have to be Muslim to get a fatwa. And really, no one in Ashuriyah takes them seriously. It's coming from a crazy person."

"I take them seriously." The inflexion in the Big Man's words suggested he'd already issued his own fatwa on the matter. "Your war's over, Lieutenant. You'll spend our remaining month here as part of my staff. We can't risk you being out of the wire anymore. You've served your country honorably. You've cleared. You've held. And you've built. Be proud."

It surprised me how quickly I was willing to drop the world. I wanted to avoid getting into trouble. I wanted to go home. I wanted to live.

I thought of my men. "What about . . . Hotspur?"

"It's one month. Sergeant Chambers can get them home."

I nodded meekly, knowing that, despite everything else, he could do that, and that he would.

"Your war's over," the Big Man repeated. This time, I couldn't help but relent.

50

I waited on the patio of Pizza Hut, stirring my soda water with a straw and poking at an untouched slice. A raw December wind pushed through the gulch, spraying sand pebbles into the faces of passing soldiers and contractors. A few hats blew off heads and onto the ground. No one was bothered. We'd all be in America in a week's time. I readjusted my fleece cap and went back to playing with my food, right leg twitching and twitching.

Where is Ibrahim? I thought. He's fucking late.

I'd become a witness to my own war. Since higher wouldn't let me go on patrols anymore, I'd embraced my inner fobbit. Hot showers. Steady meals. Steadier sleep. Sure, I made PowerPoint slides and charts. But mostly I counted off calendar days, killing time.

There'd been guilt, of course, a little about the missing Sahwa money, mostly about other things. But I'd learned something about myself during the blanched, neutral weeks at Camp Independence: I was no martyr. The truth mattered less to me than survival did. If that made me a coward, then at least I was a coward who'd been shot at.

Then they'd found the empty backpack.

Fingers were pointed and words were yelled, and through it all I stayed silent as a monk. "This isn't going to show up in your bank account, right? That's the first place they'll look," my JAG lawyer kept repeating. He claimed that a defense of negligence, even the gross negligence of losing twenty-five thousand dollars, would keep me out of jail. "I wouldn't count on get getting promoted, though." I'd just shrug, say I was planning on leaving the army anyhow, and repeat the half truth that I'd dropped off a backpack in the arms room.

My leg was twitching so furiously that it bumped the underside of the table, loosing a ricochet of sound into the late afternoon. A few nearby soldiers turned to look. Needing something to do to get away from their eyes, I stood to throw out my drink and pizza. When I sat down again the watchers had gone back to their meals, and it was my turn to observe as a familiar face strode the length of the gulch to the base exchange.

Sergeant Griffin walked through the automatic doors of the exchange. She's going home to take her son to first grade, I thought. And that matters. It matters a lot. Then I pushed away images of Rana doing the same with Ahmed and Karim. I tried not to think about them anymore, though that hadn't stopped the nightmares. Nightmare, really, since it was always the same one. Three heads in a ditch, lined up like nesting dolls, their jaws hanging open in everlong shock, smelling of smoke and maggots.

A hand slapped my shoulder from behind.

"Easy, sir." It was Ibrahim. He took a seat and pushed his plastic-rimmed glasses up the bridge of his nose. The table creaked under his weight. "Got the thing."

As he pulled a file thick as a fossil from his bag, it took great restraint not to snatch it from him. He set it on the table. I touched it with a thumb just to make sure it was real.

"Awesome, man," I said. "Know this wasn't easy."

"All good," he said. "My buddy's an interrogator. Once he heard this was the guy who put the fatwa on us, he was happy to help. Muslim brotherhood, you know?"

"Thank him for me," I said, finding the folder label with the name YOUSEF AL-NASIR on it. The falafel man's interrogation transcripts, weeks' worth, ever since the Rangers found him hiding under a pile of blankets on a roof. "No one else will see it, of course."

We sat together for a few minutes, listening to the cadence of empire. Cargo planes rumbled through the winter sky while helos sliced at it. Soldiers made jokes about small dicks and big dicks. With the sun falling into the west, someone in the gulch trilled the Zulu chant from the beginning of *The Lion King*.

I smiled in spite of myself.

Ibrahim seemed to be doing well. Less depressed, at least.

"Lot better," he said. "Almost went crazy out there. Now it all just seems like a bad dream, you know?"

We shook hands, and he saluted. I watched the large man walk into the sludge of dusk.

"Be the scorpion!" he called over his back. I didn't answer.

I placed the transcripts in my own pack. I wanted to read them more than anything, but knew if I started I wouldn't be able to stop. I'd save them for my housing trailer later, where no one could see me.

First, though, I had to go back to battalion. There was a graph about local business grants I needed to finish. The major had been quite clear about that.

Even though I was late, I took the long way there, walking up the gulch toward the tank graveyard. The yard was a laser show, dozens of Iraqi contractors wearing fireproof suits and wielding blowtorches. According to base gossip, it took ten hours to destroy one Stryker, cutting each vehicle into pieces small enough to feed industrial metal shredders.

General Dynamics had no need for their war machines, and neither did the U.S. Army—Strykers didn't work well in Afghanistan, the terrain was too rocky. Turning them over to the Iraqi military seemed out of the question, since every vehicle was filled with state-of-the-art technology. So there was only this, hiring locals to destroy them, shredding Strykers by the thousands.

I walked to the fence of the yard, sticking my fingers through the chain links. The heat from the blowtorches blew across my face.

A shadow approached the fence through the near night. "Twenty dollars."

It was one of the Iraqi contractors, his fireproof suit dark yellow and covered in soot and burn marks. I asked what for. He held up a tiny green cube. The remnants of one Stryker, ground into a square to sell locally. I pulled out my wallet and handed over a twenty for the armored cube. It felt smooth and flat in my palm, like glass.

"Thanks," I said to the contractor.

"No," he said. "Thank you."

I walked up the asphalt road that led to headquarters and crossed the yellow-grassed quad. I opened the door into the operations center slowly, hoping to get to my workstation unnoticed. It wasn't dim laptop green illuminating the room, though, but the bright yellow of electric lights. Soldiers weren't sitting and typing, quietly going about the business of war bureaucracy. They were standing around, prattling. They spoke at once, as if they'd rehearsed it, so I couldn't associate the message with anyone particular.

"Sergeant Chambers," they said. "Sergeant Chambers is no longer with us."

Bodies reached for me, drawing me to their circle of grief. Ostensibly they wanted to console, but they really wanted something else, something they could break from me and take home for themselves. I wouldn't let them, though. I stood there casual as a stone, arms down and body rigid, until they let go.

"It hasn't hit him yet," I heard them say, and I let them think that, because it meant being left alone.

Later I'd learn that he found a scorpion in his boot that morning. That was what some soldiers said, at least. Others said that was bullshit, just a stupid story. After all, the cynics argued, who ever found a scorpion in their boot in Ashuriyah?

They all agreed on how it happened, though. It was the Day of Ashura, a Shi'a festival. They'd gone on a foot patrol through the market blocks and found a large crowd watching a young man whip himself with chains. The soldiers said that while some Iraqi kids were laughing at the man whipping himself, none of the adults were.

"He was bleeding a lot," Doc Cork said.

"So much," Snoop said.

"Like a stuck pig," Hog said.

Some of them remembered the Barbie Kid being there, across the street in a ditch, just watching the festival like everyone else. Others swore he materialized out of nowhere, that they would've remembered him walking across the street, dragging his cooler like a gypsy wagon.

We're soldiers, they said. We were trained to notice things like that.

No one would admit to remembering what came next, not clearly at least. No one would talk about it, either. No one but Hog.

"He started looking through his cooler," he said. "I thought he was looking for porn mags to sell us, or maybe Boom Booms. I was walking over to Snoop to ask about the whipping guy, when I heard two shots real quick—like BANG BANG. Then a different shot, which was Sergeant Dominguez shooting the Barbie Kid.

"Doc Cork ran to them both right away. But he'd shot Chambers straight through the brain. And Sergeant Dominguez had shot the Barbie Kid in the chest. They were already dead. It all happened so fast."

"The shots were different?" I asked.

"Different sounds," Hog said. "The first two were pistol pops. Glock, I think. The last one was a whistle, Sergeant Dominguez's rifle."

I thought about the strings I'd pulled to get the Barbie Kid out of jail. It had seemed the right thing to do then.

Then I wondered where the Barbie Kid had found a Glock. No way, I thought. No way.

I asked how Dominguez was. "He killed a kid. That's not something you just get over."

I didn't know any of that in the operations center, though. I just knew an Iraqi kid had shot Sergeant Chambers, and I was supposed to be surprised about it but I wasn't, not at all. The major said I didn't have to finish my PowerPoint graph. So I left.

· · ·

Roaming the gravel paths of Camp Independence, I ended up alongside the eastern gate, as far from Ashuriyah as I could get. To the south lay the dulled lights of the airfield, the mire of Halliburton trailers, the club I'd never made it to. Through the muddy night to the north was the aid station we'd taken little Ahmed to. And to the west were softball fields, the bank, the detention center housing Yousef.

I checked my pack to make sure the file was still there.

I retraced my steps, passing the tank graveyard again. The contractors had set down their blowtorches for the night. The housing trailers rose into sight. I again thought of Chambers.

I'd never know why he'd kept quiet about the Sahwa money. If anyone could've sealed my fate, it'd been him. But he'd spared me, for reasons I'd always wonder about. Maybe he thought he'd won. Maybe he thought I'd gotten what I deserved.

In my trailer, I poured myself a glass of Rip It over ice. Two packed duffel bags stood in the corner, ready to leave at a moment's notice. The pressed, pure uniform of a fobbit hung in the closet, ready to fly home and greet my family at the welcome-home ceremony. I sat down and opened the file. One hundred forty pages of interrogation transcripts awaited.

Most of the pages had to do with Yousef's weapons smuggling and al-Qaeda contacts. His denials and nonresponses became names and connections around page 39, after loud Metallica songs became part of his daily regimen. What a weird thing to break someone, I thought. It wasn't until page 92, though, and a second glass of Rip It that I found what I sought.

Q: *You said earlier that you smuggled things other than weapons.*

Detainee 2496: Yes.

Q: *What?*

Detainee 2496: Not what. Who.

Q: *People.*

Detainee 2496: People who wanted to get out of the country.

Q: *Where did you take them?*

Detainee 2496: Depends. Syria, usually. Jordan, sometimes. Lebanon.

Q: *And you did?*

Detainee 2496: Of course. It was a business. I'm a businessman.

Q: *Who would you do this for?*

Detainee 2496: Whoever paid. Rich, poor, Sunni, Shi'a. Police, imams. Even worked with an American once.

Q: *An American?*

Detainee 2496: Yes. An officer.

Q: *Why would an American officer work with you?*

Detainee 2496: Business.

Remarkably, the interrogator didn't follow up, steering the questioning back to weapons smuggling along the Syrian border. The whole transcript carried an air of disbelief—someone had scrawled "Broke too easy, probs not believable" on the top of page 48. I didn't care about any of that, though, even the part about me. I read Yousef's "Of course. It was a business. I'm a businessman" response a hundred times, trying to glean meaning from it.

There's nothing here, I finally thought. No secret, no veil, no encryption. Which meant they'd made it. Or at least maybe they'd made it, which was something. And having something instead of nothing felt like everything.

EPILOGUE

We alter the past for the sake of the future, memories bending like light.

I came to Beirut fleeing and seeking. Fleeing home, where I'd started drinking too much and had crashed my dad's car into a neighborhood birch tree. I left the army under a cloud of scrutiny for the missing Sahwa money, though they never could figure out where it went. I chalked that up as a victory for personal initiative over bureaucracy, took a piss one night on the commanding general's lawn, and left Hawaii eager to sleep in and grow my hair out, honorable discharge in hand.

After six months of falling into all the normal veteran traps—not just the booze but also believing my own bullshit stories, believing in my own invincibility—a fresh start seemed necessary. So when a Middle Eastern studies scholarship to the American University of Beirut presented itself, I didn't hesitate. The desert awaited, again.

Snoop moved here soon after I arrived, though I don't call him that anymore. He's Qasim. He got across the Syrian border just as the last American Stryker moved into Kuwait. He doesn't say how, and I don't ask. We share a flat above a tattoo parlor on Hamra Street. The GI Bill pays for most of our rent, and the money he earns from selling pirated DVDs covers the rest.

We both like smoking hookah with pretty young women, so it's working out. I wish he'd do the dishes more, and he leaves sunflower seed shells everywhere. I remember him being more responsive during the war. If I've gotten soft, he's gotten lazy.

My mom and Will visited for a couple of weeks in the winter. I took her antiques shopping, and to lunch with one of my professors. I think she wanted proof that I was attending classes. She liked Beirut, though;

said it had dignity. Will couldn't stand being back over here, though. Creeped him out. He wouldn't eat at any of the local spots, and kept ordering takeout from an Italian restaurant. When I made fun of him, he accused me of going native. He's proud, though, I can tell.

We don't spend all our time looking for Rana and her boys, not anymore. This is a big city. More than two million. They're here, somewhere. Sometimes I walk the refugee ghettoes and ask around. Qasim tells me not to go alone, but I've led men in combat—I'm not afraid of the slums. Though fingering a cube of hard green metal in my pocket is a far cry from carrying an assault rifle.

I just want an answer for why. That's all.

Last month on TV, we watched al-Qaeda plant black flags on top of government buildings in Ramadi. Only thirty miles southwest of Ashuriyah; I looked it up. It wasn't quite the Fall of Saigon, but it felt close enough.

Every day brings more refugees, more from Syria now than Iraq. I was worried it'd make the searching more difficult, but the Iraqis and Syrians keep clear of each other. "Like scorpions and camel spiders," Qasim likes to say. I hate that joke.

I thought I'd found her last week. I was walking the ghettoes and spotted a young woman wearing a gray cotton dress. I pushed past people, then took off after her at a trot. She wore no face cover and her hair fell across her back in black waves. She turned a corner, and for a moment I saw a coffee stain of a birthmark and an arrow nose piercing out.

I ran around the corner shouting her name. But there was nothing there, just the faint echo of my own steps.

Acknowledgments

My gratitude to:

Parents Deborah and Dennis, brother Luke, and the Gallagher, Boisselle, Scott, and Steinle families;

Friends and colleagues Ted Janis and Phil Klay;

Friends and readers Elliot Ackerman, Nick Allen, Lea Carpenter, Eric Fair, Will Gehlen, Brian Hagen, Fahad Khan, Sanaë Lemoine, and Nick McDonell;

Friends and chiefs Brandon Willitts and Words After War and Paul Rieckhoff and Iraq and Afghanistan Veterans of America;

Educators Loni Byloff and Mary Chrystal at Brookfield; Shelly Brewster and Hardy McNew at Bishop Manogue; Simone Caron and John McNally at Wake Forest; and David Ebershoff, Richard Ford, Lauren Grodstein, and Victor LaValle at Columbia;

The soldiers and interpreters of 2-14 Cavalry and 1-27 Infantry who served in Iraq from 2007–9;

Agent extraordinaire Amelia "Molly" Atlas and ICM Partners;

Atria editors Daniella Wexler and Peter Borland and Atria publisher Judith Curr, who believed in this book;

And, of course, fierce and lovely Anne.

To those I mentioned, and to the many others I didn't—*Sláinte*.